ALL THE STOLEN VOICES

Scarlett Rosewood

Trigger Warnings

Please read responsibly.

Violence Against Women
Missing & Murdered Indigenous Women
Open-Door/ Explicit Romance
Implied Sexual Assault
Mentions Of Drug Addiction
Death Of Pregnant Woman (non-explicit description)
Graphic Depictions of Torture
Stalking
Anxiety
System Injustice

I dedicate this to the little girls who've become women that never felt like their dreams were worth shooting for. Who were told that they were 'too much', yet somehow never enough.

You are enough.

And to my husband for believing in me and making Christmas's special again.

To my friends and so many in the book community.

Especially my Alpha readers, you all were the real MVPs—keeping up with those late-night, unhinged chapter-by-chapter emails and allowing me to bounce my ideas off of you while seeing the forest for the trees, as they say.

Contents

CHAPTER 1
Loriah

If a hungover detective didn't scream professionalism, I didn't know what would.

I winced at the white, unfamiliar, and too-bright ceiling, blinking hard to clear my eyes. My head throbbed with remnants of the previous night's ill-advised tequila adventure that still lingered like a bad decision, made worse by the melodic screeching of the phone's alarm. Pulling myself free of the tangled sheets, I groped along the edge of the bed till my hand wrapped around the source of the noise. Silencing it, I checked the screen to see that no calls or texts awaited. Relief seeped in, and I lay back against my pillow.

It was supposed to be my fresh start. Not *just* a new life in New York City's homicide division, but the day I'd been waiting for ever since that phone interview— the one that had me pacing my Texas apartment at the same time that nerves ate at me and the anxiety of being *good enough* chewed holes in my self-esteem. Until someone said, *you've got the job if you want it.*

I swung my legs over the edge of the bed, planted my feet on the cold wood floor, and dragged myself out of the room to fumble my way through the cramped kitchen in search of electrolytes.

"*Big city style*," I mockingly told the inside of my glass around a mouthful of liquid. Allie's words taunted me from the recesses of my clouded brain. I couldn't remember what the hell we were toasting—just that by the end of the night, tequila was her love language, and the word "no" was very clearly *not* a part of her vocabulary.

After showering so briefly the water didn't have time to warm up, I dressed in my favorite thrifted professional find—a cream number with pinstripes—fought my unruly auburn curls, and bolted out the door, forgetting my coffee and running late.

The city noise hammered into my head like a case of tinnitus. From commuters' impatient shouts to the crunch of yellow and red leaves that mixed with the occasional garbage underfoot, I barely made it onto the train after dodging a shoulder check from someone who barked, "Watch out!"

Welcome to New York, indeed.

Two weeks, and I still felt like an outsider.

The lobby hummed with an undercurrent of energy. Officers strode purposefully across its polished floors, badges gleaming under harsh fluorescent lights while a mix of muted conversation, radio static, and the distant ring of a phone floated through the air. Amid the sea of blue uniforms and no-nonsense stares, my gaze snagged on something unexpected.

Behind the long reception desk, a woman perched on her chair like a queen on a throne.

And... she's looking right at me.

I'd been reciting my introduction over and over in my head when her eyes met mine, and she grinned, bright and unabashed.

"Visitor?" she chirped, pulling a lanyard from a drawer with theatrical flair, matching the same vibe as her watermelon-hued hair.

"Detective Loriah Fairsbane," I replied, offering a polite smile. "I'm meeting, Detective Perez?" I'd hoped I'd remembered his name correctly.

"Good luck with that, babe," she said with a wink, sliding the pass across the counter. Her tone was light, but the words left me puzzled.

OK...

I adjusted my blazer with a half-hearted *thanks* before moving through to the waiting area. It was a comforting reflex as much as an attempt to steady myself. Fidgeting of any sort calmed me, and soon I found the pass's plastic edges bit into my thumb as I absentmindedly traced it, a mantra I'd been practicing earlier still running on repeat through my head.

You are Loriah Fairsbane; you are a good detective; you earned this. You are Loriah Fairsbane, you are a good—

The words were untangling themselves; slowly I could see the threads moving through my mind.

Until *he* arrived.

Detective Agustin Perez cut through the lobby like a thunderstorm rolling into a calm sky. And I don't just mean that in the cheesy romantic way, but damn. He was taller than I'd expected, and even more striking. A tailored black suit wrapped his broad frame, resembling something made for Forbes's CEO rather than a simple city cop. A fresh, white bandage was wrapped around one hand, its stark contrast drawing my attention as he flexed his fingers. His face, though, that was the most startling of all. If you looked up the definition of *'unapproachable,'* his picture would be proudly framed next to it, I was sure.

He stopped in front of me, large and imposing, eyes appraising with the detached scrutiny of someone assessing a suspect *or* a potential liability.

"Detective Fairsbane?" he asked, voice low and rough with a subtle Spanish accent that softened the consonants but retained all its authority.

"Detective Perez?" I questioned, equally as formal, before extending my hand and fighting the urge to waver under his piercing green gaze.

For a beat, he didn't move, and the air seemed to close in around me. Then, when he finally clasped my hand, he let go—as if the contact had been a chore.

"Follow me," he said, turning away. No small talk, no pleasantries. No, how do you fuckin' do, or welcome to the force.

I exhaled and rolled my eyes, my grip tightening around the visitor's pass.

This will be fun.

Perez led us through the maze of desks and offices, his long strides forcing me to double my pace when we exited the elevator. At once, the familiar patina of controlled chaos hit me—an orchestra of phones ringing, papers rustling, and the stench of overcooked coffee that seemed to seep into the carpet itself. Oddly, it comforted me, like seeing an old friend.

By the time we reached Chief Daniels's office, I was a mix of nervousness and determination. I hadn't spoken to him since he had offered me the job over a month prior. Daniels was warm, though, greeting me with a firm handshake and a booming laugh that put me instantly at ease—until he said, "Now that you'll be partners, there will be plenty of time to get to know each other."

The word *partners*' came out in slow motion. The kind you hear on kids' Saturday cartoon shows.

Perfect.

The man who looked like he'd rather be actively walking into traffic with a blindfold was now stuck with me, and my stomach flipped. But I'd survived worse, like 12-hour watches with a partner who never learned the importance of not eating cabbage before a stakeout.

In all his infinite pleasantness, Perez barely tolerated my presence as he showed me the ropes and led me around to make introductions, making me feel more like a resented stepsister he was forced to take to meet his friends than a fellow paid employee.

His version of a "tour" only allowed a fleeting moment to snap a picture of my new badge and send it to my dad—letting him know Allie had left me alive, if not a little unwell—before Perez unceremoniously dropped me off at the rec room. I started to protest when my belly's grumbling told me Tylenol and water weren't going to cut it for the rest of the day.

Tearing into my hoagie, a voice sounded from behind.

"Fairsbane, right?" His voice had a twang of familiarity.

My stomach somersaulted, and until that moment, I hadn't realized how homesick I was. Charisma rolled off him in waves: a dimple marked one cheek, and his baby blue eyes glinted with amusement. He mock-tipped a hat to me with one hand and bent over, grabbing a chair to scoot in closer. "I'm Jackson."

I glanced down at my clothes, suddenly aware of the marinara I'd piled onto my sandwich, and waved limply. "Sorry, I'd shake your hand, but—"

"Don't worry about it. We're cubicle neighbors, but I haven't had a chance to say hi."

"Oh, yeah, it's no problem. I've been slowly making the rounds."

"I've seen that. Perez really is all work and no play, isn't he?"

"Maybe? I'm trying not to make assumptions just yet, you know how this first-day stuff goes."

"I gotcha. Hey, I know this is totally out of left field, but do you like country music?" he asked, raising his eyebrows in hopeful anticipation.

"I do..." I said cautiously, giving him a side eye and setting down my food, not understanding where the line of questioning would lead.

"A few friends and I are going to a concert this weekend. I thought—well, I just thought, maybe you could use some friends, too? If I'm wrong, please tell me to back off, and I'll stop embarrassing myself. I know it's your first day and all."

The self-conscious stammering was endearing, causing my defenses drop and my shoulders relax. After the weight of the day—and my new partner making it clear he didn't want me around—I really did *want* to say yes. If I were honest with myself about how unfortunately desperate I'd become, then 'need' might be a better description.

"I promise I'm *not* a weirdo, and this wouldn't be a date. If that helps."

"Thanks for clearing that up. Although that's *exactly* what a weirdo *would* say."

He dramatically exhaled and sat back, a grin spreading across his face once more.

"Well, Jackson, who is definitely *not* a weirdo—"

"Can we *stop* saying weirdo?"

"No, sir, it's sticking for now."

"I'll blame myself for that one. Proceed, what were you going to ask?"

"Can I bring a friend?"

"Definitely; the more the merrier. I scored some extra tickets, so it's no big deal. Just let me know how many you'll need."

The rest of the break continued in companionable chatter. I learned of Jackson's two brothers, who helped run the family business, and a sister who had died tragically. I wasn't willing to push for an explanation that wasn't owed and, instead, decided to focus on swapping stories of old hangouts and warm summer nights spent camping on the Red River.

"Well," he said, standing to push the chair back in place. "We'd better get back to work before the *warden* notices you've been gone too long."

"He's hardly a warden. More of an unwilling sidekick?" I allowed myself a small laugh while walking from the room, Jackson in tow.

But the feeling of ease didn't last. When we returned, Perez was waiting at my makeshift desk, arms crossed and appearing to scowl at no one in particular. When he saw me, his expression relaxed a fraction before tightening again when his eyes landed on the man behind me.

"Officer Jackson," came the acknowledgement, all cold and judgmental rolled into one.

"Ah, good to see you too, Perez, pleasant and chipper as ever."

"And you, already scenting out fresh blood, I see."

"Oh, come on, we Texans gotta stick together."

Perez's stance made it clear—he thought I shouldn't be sticking myself to anything but my desk. As the tension thickened between the two men who refused to back away, I cleared my throat and shifted uncomfortably away from Jackson to address my partner.

"Is there something I can help you with, Detective?"

"There is, actually, follow me."

Before I could think, he strode away. I glanced back and gave Jackson a shrug, to which he winked and shook his head.

I stood at the edge of Perez's desk, feeling his gaze cut through me with a piercing assessment as he took a seat and stared back. It was expected, though, the inevitable interrogation that came with being the new Detective in town—especially one with my history of stirring the local political pot to get what I needed.

"So," Perez began, leaning back in his chair with arms crossed, tone carefully neutral, but his eyes shrewdly assessed me in the most disquieting way. "Why'd you really come to New York? Was Texas too slow for you?"

Are we really doing this?

I squared my shoulders, cut my eyes at him in return, and walked around to take a seat facing him in a worn leather chair—annoyance prickling beneath my skin.

OK. We are doing this.

"Texas wasn't *slow*," I said, leveling my stare at him. "If anything, it was too... I don't know." I trailed off, my voice thickening. I cleared my throat, feeling all at once foolish for the flood of emotion washing over me. "Girls turned up missing too frequently. As I'm sure you know, young girls are trafficked from all over: Mexico, Honduras, Florida, up as far as Canada, even here. The communities cried out. And yet, no one listened. At least not until it was too late. But I cared. I *tried* to help them."

Perez's brows furrowed, but he stayed silent.

"I'd go home every night and feel it, this pressure. Like, no matter how many cases I closed, something was still missing. The ones we discovered alive were shattered, and the ones we didn't—" My voice caught for a moment, and I shook my head. "Well, it's not that I *wanted* to walk away from it—I'm not a coward. I think I just needed a change. Space to breathe again."

Perez watched me for a long moment, appraising, but not unkind, making me feel too exposed, too raw, for sharing so much. Finally, he nodded, which felt more like an acknowledgment than a dismissal. Thankfully, there wasn't pity. I hated pity, and I didn't know if I could stop myself from tearing up if he tried to make excuses for me by citing all the cases I *had* solved. Just like everyone else had tried when I told them I needed to search for something else, *somewhere* else.

"Sorry to say, Fairsbane, I don't think New York is the place to come for any break. There's a reason you got this job," he said. The regret lacing his words was more telling than anything else when he set a file down in front of me.

I hesitated before picking it up. When I finally did, the manila folder felt heavy and ominous in my hands despite its thin appearance, sending a wave of unease through me. I flipped it open, scanning the contents: a grainy photo of a teenage girl, a few sparse details about the scene where her body had been found, and a harrowingly small note of the individual being pregnant at the time of death.

An odd sense that the room was tilting came over me. The outer rim of my vision blurred. My chest tightened. Back home, I'd seen too many faces like hers—too many young girls the system ignored, never worth saving in its eyes. But this one, it felt personal in a way I couldn't quite put into words. Perhaps it was the faint resemblance to my own mother and cousins, with their almond-shaped eyes that carried generations of resilience and pain.

"You good?" Perez's voice broke through my thoughts, grounding me back in the present. "I know it isn't what you expected on your first day, but..."

I shook my head quickly. "No," I said, though my voice came out tighter than I'd intended. "I'm good, though, this is it?" I asked almost accusingly, flipping through the pages with their paltry details. It felt like I'd fallen into an alternate dimension and awoken on a bad 2000s-era prank show.

The problems I'd left sixteen hundred miles and eight states behind had followed me.

"Look, Woods, my old partner, wasn't exactly *thorough*. I haven't had time with everything piling up since he's been... gone," Perez replied, though I caught the faintest flicker of discomfort at the mention of his partner's name.

"A pregnant sixteen-year-old was murdered, Perez," I said, forcing my voice steady. "Not exactly the kind of case you'd choose to let gather dust."

Perez's jaw tightened before running a hand through thick, dark hair.

I exhaled sharply, matching his unease. "We owe that girl better than this, don't you think? I can try to track down notebooks, computer notes, anything that might help."

"That won't be necessary," he snapped before regaining his stillness. "I have a handle on it."

"Fine," I said quietly, biting my tongue on a retort. "You said I got hired for a reason? Then *let* me help you."

I rose and started toward the door, unwilling to waste another second without chasing answers for our Jane Doe. At the threshold, I remembered the manila folder and doubled back to snatch it off the desk. Perez's head was tilted back, and his eyes closed. I studied him as his chest rose and fell in slow movements.

"What is it, Fairsbane?" he asked me, eyes still closed.

"Won't you need this, too?"

He turned then to look at the file before returning his attention to the aging ceiling tiles.

"Unfortunately, I already intimately know *every* detail of what's in there, Detective. Keep it."

There was no malice in his words, only a fact that he stated with the weariness of a man carrying too many burdens for *too* long.

Staying late that night, I combed through each minute detail of our Jane Doe's case till my eyes ached and I wondered what Perez had meant when he said his partner was "gone." I rubbed at my temples; something gnawing at me, pulling at a memory I couldn't place. It wasn't until I saw it for a second time—a note scribbled in the margins in an elegant script, that it clicked: *Possible Native or South American trafficking connection?* The words were underlined, along with small doodles and the faintest outline of a sketched face. *Jane Doe's* face. I traced the lines with my fingertips, imagining Perez sitting for hours, poring over this same small folder.

What were you thinking, Detective?

I quickly pulled open the tab on my computer to the MMIP site and began scrolling through name after name, accompanied by the last photos provided—faces frozen in time, unaged, and blending into a painting of tragedy. From infants to the elderly, there was no rhyme or reason, no clear pattern—only countless faces begging to be seen.

Kendra Longhorse.

Tiana Ramirez.

Cara Morales.

On. And on. They went.

When my eyes began to mist over, I stopped and sat back with a deep exhale, disappointment burrowing into my bones till we became one.

I didn't know who she was. *Yet.*

But I knew one thing: I wouldn't stop till I found out.

CHAPTER 2
Loriah

The next few days crawled by without a single hit, but I knew all it would take was patience.

Perez, *surprisingly*, had been coming to me to brainstorm, although red tape delayed us at every turn. Surveillance footage from nearby cameras was under review—an agonizingly slow process, even with the aid of AI technology.

Most days, my true enemy was an unseen and relentless adversary called *time*.

The more that we became stalled by bureaucracy, the more I'd find myself sitting in the quiet—pissed off—and left alone with my ever-intrusive thoughts. Over and over, they'd wander back to my mother and the way authorities had brushed aside *her* death. Nobody had cared enough to see her as anything more than a "disillusioned housewife with a penchant for narcotics."

She'd died alone.

The day had been sunny and warm when I found her sitting in a bathtub; the cheap mascara she'd always worn was still wet on her cheeks, and the world simply *moved on*. As easy as the pappus detaches from a dandelion to float on the breeze of summer, her life drifted away, while Dad and I were left to pick up the pieces.

Barely a handful of days had passed before we stood at her graveside. Two figures cutting a sad outline on an otherwise beautiful sunny day with no one to witness our tears, other than Father James and the groundskeeper.

Emptiness and questions were all that was left in her wake, much like with this girl and countless others before her.

I thought possibly I hadn't been at the job long enough to grow accustomed to the detachment that others blanketed themselves in. Maybe I never would. And *maybe*, that was a good thing. Our girl deserved better; she deserved justice. But if I had to tackle the case alone, I'd do it.

"Jackson, can you come to my desk?" I called out, rubbing the bone above my brow for relief.

His head popped around our divider.

"Why are you yelling?" he teased.

"Sorry, I didn't realize."

"No worries. Needing fashion advice?"

I laughed despite myself. "No, I think Allie's got that *more* than covered. I wanted to ask about the street cameras. Have we got any more footage of that alley's block or nearby streets?"

He shook his head, offering me an apologetic look.

"Nothing concrete, *yet*. I roped in a couple more people to help with the review, but it's a real slog. Monday, I'm planning to visit shop owners and see if they'll let us access their cameras without needing a subpoena."

"Smart. I might be able to help with some of that," I said, though the thought of shop owners refusing access made my teeth clench. The resistance from civilian and governing agencies alike could wear anyone down.

Jackson leaned casually against the partition, his tone shifting to something lighter. "Off topic, but are we still on for the concert? I held the tickets for you and Allie, although I can find someone else if you've got other plans."

"No, we're definitely on," I said quickly, pulling out my phone to text her.

> **Me -** *Hey! Are you still good for the concert tonight? Jackson wants to confirm.*

> **Allie -** *Yesss! Please get me out of this apartment.* I've been buried in reports all day, and now my head's ready to explode.

I chuckled and typed a quick response, letting her know I'd be home soon. No doubt she would be prepping drinks and waist-deep in clothing when I walked through the door. I looked up to Jackson, watching me, a bemused look on his face.

"Allie's good to go," I said, breaking the silence. "We'll meet you there, if that's okay?"

"Perfect," he said, happily slapping his hand on the top of the divider. "I have to go get some copies of this file."

"Going out tonight?"

I jumped at the deep voice that seemed to emerge from nowhere.

Oh, a real Sherlock.

"Are you eavesdropping on me, Detective?"

"I don't need to with as loud as you're talking. Pretty sure the whole office knows your plans."

Asshole

"Yes, Perez, I'm *going out*. You don't strike me as the type to have fun, but I do enjoy having a life outside of work and away from"—I gestured at my computer—"this." I tried to maintain a nonchalant tone, but the way he stood, staring at me with his arms crossed, had my defenses rising.

"*You*, don't know what I like," he said smoothly, his tone and accent curling around the words in a way that made me pause. A faint smile played at the corner of his mouth as he watched me for a reaction.

"Oh, I see" I narrowed my eyes on Perez's smug face. "That sounds like a challenge."

There was something about him—a calculated intensity underlying a brooding darkness—that both intrigued and frustrated me. But I wasn't about to let him get in my head.

Jackson cleared his throat, breaking the tension and looking between us.

"Alright, well, I'll text you the address," he said, brushing past Perez with a sideways grin and a stack of papers.

Three long hours later, I was climbing the stairs of my fourth-floor walk-up. The smell of butter chicken wafted from the second landing, and I paused to take it in, my quad's protesting the ascent with every step—the previous day's workout steadily wreaking havoc on my body. Allie's door stood ajar when I finally reached our own floor, and the sounds of a catchy tune blasted through the hallway. Pushing it open, I watched her twirl around her cramped living room, gripping onto a pair of boots as her partner and curlers bouncing in her golden hair. Clothes lay scattered across the floor and surrounding furniture.

"Allie!"

"What the *hell*?" she yelped. A roller fell from her head, and a lone pink boot thumped to the floor. She clutched at her chest. "Lor! You scared the shit out of me!"

I gave her an amused smile. "You're lucky I hung my serial killer hat up years ago, but you have to be more careful."

She waved me off with a grin. "Please. I've got you to inflict vengeance if anything happens. So, see? I'm doing *you* a favor, because then you can put your hat back on. What would your name be anyway?"

I rolled my eyes, but her words made me smile. That's how Allie was—lighthearted, carefree, and entirely too trusting. She was my opposite, yet also my kindred spirit, in so many ways. Maybe that's why we worked.

"Oh, I got it!" she continued, undeterred.

"Do I *want* to know?"

"The twangy tickler!"

"What the actual fuck, Allie?"

"What? It's good. Maybe you tickle people to death?"

"Eew. Pretty sure Dante should have made that one of his levels of hell," I said and threw a roller at her.

"You're going to turn every head in the place," Allie said an hour later as she handed me my drink once we finished getting ready.

"And step on *every* toe," I quipped before downing the liquid courage I had a feeling I'd need later.

We grabbed our bags and headed out the door, linked arm in arm, both checking each other's eyes for any stray mascara. Souvenirs of too much time spent laughing till tears came.

For one night, I didn't want to think about all the dead, unnamed girls that haunted my waking hours, the bureaucratic red tape, or Detective Perez and his little storm cloud of a personality following me. I just wanted to be a normal woman, in a sea of millions, who was going to dance with a man.

Just, normal.

CHAPTER 3
Loriah

When the Uber rolled up to an old beer hall, I immediately knew I was in for something special. The old brick building was a gem amid the urban sprawl of NYC—twinkling lights flashed intermittently from inside the doors, casting a golden hue on the small crowd gathered outside.

People milled around in outfits that ranged from classic western to what I could only describe as emo-cowboy chic, with black leather fringed vests and chunky Doc Martens. One woman sported a fitted jean button-up over a paisley skirt that swayed in the light breeze. It was truly a mosaic of personality and style, all drawn together by one shared love—the promise of good music and even better company. I couldn't help but grin with giddy excitement.

I pulled out my phone and fired off a quick text.

> **Me -** *Hey, we're here! I'm with the girl in the obnoxiously pink boots. You can't miss her.*

Sliding a cash tip to the driver, I thanked him for the ride.

"You ladies let me know if you need a ride home, too," the driver called after us. "These parts can get a bit rough after closing."

"Will do. Thanks again." I waved to him as Allie and I stepped onto the curb.

A sharp whistle split the air, drawing my attention to a group standing a few feet outside the entrance—Jackson stood at the center like the eye of a storm, flanked by two pairs of men and women. And, *wow*.

There wasn't another word for it. I'd always prided myself on keeping a professional distance from those I worked with, often to my own self-isolating detriment. But there were moments like that when it became so much harder to maintain the line drawn and not step back to appreciate what was right in front of me.

I walked closer, Allie still chatting animatedly at my side, before stopping a few feet away. Jackson's smile was slow and a little crooked as he let out the smallest huff of a laugh, making my insides flutter and my neck grow hot. The hum of music filtered through outdoor speakers, playing a gentle, happy melody, and the people around us faded into the background as he drew nearer. For a moment, time stopped.

The man was a walking vision of rugged charm, the type that you read about but rarely saw; his pearl-snap plaid shirt fit perfectly across his broad chest and sat half-unbuttoned, revealing a teasing glimpse of sun-kissed muscle and chest hair. Jackson's hat sat canted to just the right angle—the kind that told a girl he was planning on getting up to no good.

His gaze swept over me, unhurried, as if intent on memorizing the tiniest details. I slipped into a mock curtsy and bit my lip, trying to suppress a grin that threatened to spread across my face like a child on Christmas morning. My body felt off kilter, and I gladly blamed it on whatever thrall held me.

So much for those solid boundaries huh, Loriah.

It wasn't until a smaller woman with a wild tumble of brown curls stepped forward and spoke that I realized other people were milling around.

"*This* is your new detective?" she teased, incredulous, with an open smile that made it impossible not to like her immediately.

"She is," Jackson replied, his grin widening, mirroring my own feelings.

He removed his hat and brushed his fingers through mussed hair before placing it back on and pulling two folded tickets from his pocket. "Here you go, m'lady. And for you. Allie, right?"

"That's me," Allie sing-songed with an easy laugh, used to the attention. She handed her ticket to the doorman, then yelled over her shoulder, "Now, where are the drinks?"

As soon as I handed over my ticket and stepped inside, she took my hand, pulling me toward the bar and leaving Jackson to manage the rest of his group.

"What the hell, Loriah?" she whispered conspiratorially into my ear, her eyes flicking toward Jackson's crew once we'd gained some distance between us and them.

I laughed, shaking my head. "It's nothing. *We* are nothing. Only work friends. I told you."

Allie rolled her eyes, clearly not believing my half-assed attempt at an explanation, and leaned in closer, her hair tickling my cheek. "Ok, Lor, have your secrets."

"I swear," I told her, crossing my heart.

A rough hand grazed the bare skin at my back, and I turned to find Jackson leaning in close, his smooth Texas drawl brushing my ear. "What are you drinking?"

The heat of his fingers sent a shiver down my spine, one he didn't miss by the way he pressed them against me, fingers splaying.

"Want me to remove it?" he whispered.

I glanced back, meeting those ocean-blue eyes. "N-no," I said. "I don't mind."

"Really?" His smirk stretched into a grin. "Because it's kind of obvious."

Confused, I peeked down and spotted the tag dangling from my top. My face burned. "Oh my God," I mumbled, fumbling to yank it off and place it on the bar. I'd never been the coolest girl in a group. And if that moment didn't reinforce that fact, nothing else would.

Jackson chuckled and leaned in again. "Now, about my hand..." His words tickled the shell of my ear, minty and warm. "Do you want *that* removed, too?"

This time, the shiver *wasn't* from embarrassment.

I tilted my head, meeting his gaze with as much composure as I could muster. "I think I'll get a drink and hit the dance floor with Allie first," I said, forcing a teasing smile. "Priorities. You understand."

His chest rumbled with laughter, low and rich. "Oh, so that's how it is? Alright, Detective lady. I'll see you out there."

The band kicked off their set with an upbeat number, and people eagerly paired off, spilling onto the parquet dance floor. Allie linked her arm with mine and swept us into the rhythm of the crowd.

"Sorry!" I laughed, spinning a little too far to one side again after kicking her foot.

"You're doing alright!" she called over the music, her eyes sparkling with amusement.

"I think that is a polite way to say I suck?"

"Not my words!"

We danced through two more songs, the steps coming easier, and the laughter flowing until we both appeared to be a little paler than when we arrived.

"I need air," I told her when the perimeter of the room blurred into a haze of faces and lights. Excusing myself, I headed to the bar for a glass of cold water—and hopefully a glimpse of Jackson. It didn't take long to spot him, swaying to the music with a stunning woman in his arms, a smile plastered across her face.

The cool night air brushed the hair from my damp forehead as I pushed through the heavy door, a welcome relief from the heat and the press of bodies. I took a deep inhale and scanned the area. To my left, a group of smokers chatted and laughed. One man, dressed in a patchwork Canadian tuxedo, caught my eye.

"Mind if I bum one?" I asked, sidling over.

"Sure thing," he said in a slightly slurred voice and held out his pack. As soon as my fingers brushed the edge of a filter, he snatched the pack out of reach. "But what do I get in return?"

I sighed in exasperation.

"If it comes with strings, keep it."

He laughed, sliding an arm around my waist. "Aw, don't be like that, sweetheart—"

"Look, mister, you're going to take your hand *off* of me."

"Or what?"

"Or I'll break a finger. Wouldn't want that now would you?"

"Come onnn"

The man started to grab for me again as a fist connected with his jaw. The audible crunch sent him sprawling to the pavement.

CHAPTER 4
Loriah

"P*erez*!" I snapped, whipping around and closing the distance between us, fury tightening in my chest. I glared up at him, heat burning behind my eyes.

"Fairsbane."

"What the fuck do you think you're doing? I had it under control."

"Clearly. Is that why his hand is still attached even after you warned him?" His tone dripped with sarcasm. Without hesitation, Perez hoisted the offending man off his feet and tossed him into the street like a rag doll. A mix of shock and rage was plastered on the guy's face as he scrambled along the concrete to collect himself *and* his scattered belongings.

Perez loomed over him with a commanding presence, cold and unyielding. When he spoke, his voice brokered no argument. "Get the fuck out of here. Now!"

"I'm gonna call the cops!" he shouted, wincing and stumbling to stand.

Perez was deadly calm as he stepped closer, pulling up his shirt to reveal the badge clipped to his jeans. "Please do."

The man's bravado faltered, and he staggered off into the night, grumbling to himself but not daring to turn back.

The whole exchange left me fuming *and* cigarette-less.

"What was *that?*" I demanded, gesturing behind me. "Where did you even come from?"

He didn't flinch, his nonchalant demeanor only fueling my irritation when he stared down at me. "My friend owns this place," he said. "I work security during events to help out. What are *you* doing here dressed like *that?*" His gaze flicked over my outfit, lingering on my exposed legs and too-short denim shorts. Judgment shone clear in his eyes, like he thought the whole thing simultaneously amusing *and* ridiculous.

I bristled, resisting the urge to cross my arms against the scrutiny. "I'm here with friends," I told him, taking a step closer. "It's none of your business, though, seein' as I'm off duty. But thanks for the help, champ." I gave his chest a tap before turning to walk back in.

"Loriah?"

My attention snapped from Perez to Jackson, who appeared confused and furious, a flush of anger creeping into his cheeks. "What's going on?" Jackson asked, gesturing to where Perez was standing.

Surveying me, as if Jackson hadn't spoken at all, Perez spoke. "Why is *he* here?"

"Excuse me?" Jackson took a step forward and I moved between the two men.

"I'm *fine*," I said, attempting to defuse the tension. "*Seriously*. It wasn't Perez. Just a poorly dressed freak who thought he could manhandle me when I asked for a smoke." My voice wavered with residual anger as I rolled my eyes and stepped away from Perez.

"Jesus, Loriah. Are you okay?" Jackson asked, his tone softening as he turned his attention back to me. He reached into his pocket and pulled out a pack of cigarettes, holding them out in offering. "Next time, ask me. I'd have come out with you."

Taking one, I said, "Are there contingencies for this kindness?"

"Yes, actually." He grinned. "You owe me a dance."

Before I could reply, Perez cut in, his presence was unwelcome as ever.

"Next time, be more aware of your surroundings, Fairsbane. *You*, of all people, should know better," he chastised.

I shot him a sweet, venom-filled smile as he came closer. "Thanks for the advice, *pardner*," I quipped in an exaggerated drawl, blowing out a stream of smoke from the cigarette Jackson lit for me, before handing it back to him. My defiance was juvenile, sure, but dammit if he didn't seem to bring out the crazy in me.

The way Perez got under my skin so quickly was a phenomenon that could have been studied and weaponized.

Tugging Jackson toward the entrance, he flicked the butt into the street, throwing a crooked grin at Perez when he passed. I didn't *have* to turn to feel the heat of Perez's glare on my back.

As the band struck up *Tennessee Whiskey*, Jackson wasted no time pulling me onto the dance floor. A soft, romantic glow bathed the hall as I relaxed into his embrace. His hand rested securely behind me, the other clasping mine and holding it close to his chest as we swayed to the music. He led effortlessly, spinning us through the crowd.

When his eyes met mine, he stopped, then started again to speak, "I don't think I could've asked for a better partner tonight."

"You flatter me, but this is all you." I chuckled. "I appreciate you inviting me out. I contemplated staying in, but I think this is what I needed. Time away from the case and the madness of trying to fit in. I've got to be myself tonight, and sometimes I forget how much I like *this* version of me."

"It's tough finding your place in a city this big. I get it," he said softly.

I nodded, turning away for a moment—the words finding and hitting their mark.

"Yeah, I imagine you do."

He smiled, eyes crinkling at the edges. "So, can I take you out sometime? Show you around? Just as friends, of course," he added quickly, his sincerity unmistakable. "But call me Christian. Everyone else does."

I hesitated, then nodded once. "Okay, Christian. Friends."

The song ended, and we wove our way back to the bar to regroup. But as my gaze drifted toward the door, I froze. Perez, his dark eyes shadowed, was watching me—not just looking, but *watching*. For the short time we'd worked to-gether, I knew most of his tells already. And this? Something sharp tinged that look, something close to jealousy, maybe. Possessiveness? Irritation? Whatever it was, the weight of it sent a slow heat crawling up my skin. One I was intent on ignoring.

I definitely have had too much to drink if I think that man is looking at me as anything more than an inconvenience.

Before I could figure out what to make of it, he turned away, laughing at something the other bouncer said. Real laughter. Even from where I was, I could make out its deep, rich sound, and it caught me off guard. It took the harsh edge off his typically severe demeanor, transforming his stoic face into one that was captivating. Beautiful. A sight that I *couldn't* turn away from.

It felt like not realizing I'd been living in darkness until a thread of light captured all the prismatic colors, making them dance—and knowing in that moment that I could have seen them all along, if only I'd been looking hard enough.

The rest of the night flowed with dancing, drinking, and enjoying the company of my new acquaintances.

A glance at my phone showed it was approaching mid-night, along with a missed call from Dad. It had been our weekly ritual for as long as I'd lived on my own, and usually right after he got home from church. I could already picture him, grinning, and asking if his "favorite daughter" was left alive and well.

"Alright, we're gonna play one more and wrap up; we've gotta hit the road to Boston tomorrow." Stapleton's warm rasp filled the room as he addressed the crowd. "I love y'all, and thanks for coming out." Everyone cheered and hooted.

Couples paired off, pulling each other close for the final dance. Jackson had already partnered up with the beautiful girl from earlier, leaving me to sip my Shiner from my perch at the bar. I didn't mind watching the dancers swirl across the floor, their faces glowing with happiness under the light—it was its own kind of joy, and I was happy to soak it all in. The sticky warmth of the wood bar beneath my hand anchored me, and for a moment, I felt content.

When I turned to order one last drink, a hand appeared in front of me. I followed the line of a tattooed forearm to a face I *hadn't* expected to see again.

"Do you want to dance?" Perez asked, his voice low.

"Seriously?"

How can one man make such simple requests sound as if there's no other obvious answer than compliance?

"Yes. I've got a few minutes, perks of knowing the owner."

"How *positively* rebellious of you," I quipped, narrowing my eyes. "Are you sure you want to be seen dancing with *irresponsible* lil' ole me?"

"Are you going to keep complaining, or will you shut up and enjoy the last song?" he countered, his tone challenging in a teasing way.

I hesitated, our fingers barely touching, before I planted my hand in his. It was rough and inviting, his grip firm but gentle. My gaze lingered on the bandage wrapped around his knuckles, a reminder of the brawl that had taken place outside.

The opening chords of *You Should Probably Leave* floated through the room as Perez led me onto the dance floor, his hand shifting to the small of my exposed back, the other holding mine as he guided me into a spin. Laughter bubbled out before I could stop it, and the grin that split his face at my delight was undisputable.

Two rare sightings in one night? I am spoiled.

The world spun for a moment before I landed back in his arms, a surprised gasp leaving my chest with a whoosh when my body collided with his.

"Holy shit, Perez. Warn a girl next time."

I felt his chest vibrating with a throaty chuckle as my ear hovered near his shoulder.

"I told you," he murmured, leaning me back into a dip, my hair spilling down like a fountain of dark copper, "you don't know what I like." His eyes locked onto mine, a hint of amusement sparking in their depths.

"Well, I can say with certainty, dancing was *not* at the top of my list."

"Are you still complaining? You've stomped my foot *three* times, and I'm not making a big deal of it," he chided, his voice softer than usual.

"Really? Because it kinda feels like you're whining," I told him, which earned me another laugh. The rarity of the moment felt like a small secret between us.

There he was. What I thought was the real Perez, peeking through the cracks. Not the brooding, closed-off man from the office, but someone else entirely.

"What are you doing here with him, anyway?" His voice dipped so low I barely caught the words. I tried to ignore the question, but when the silence dragged on, and he refused to speak again, I decided an answer was the easiest route.

"He invited me," I said. "Plus—I needed to get out, clear my head. This case is... it's eating at me."

He nodded, spinning me again before pulling me back to him. The warmth from the closeness of our bodies was too much. His cologne—woodsy with a hint of sandalwood and smoke—wrapped around me like a memory I couldn't quite put my finger on.

"We'll find answers. I know you came here expecting it would be a fresh start away from Dallas, and now you're right back in the thick of it, but this isn't going away. We can figure things out, I need you to trust me."

The sincerity in his voice caught me off guard, slipping past my defenses. And for a moment, I wondered if I *could* trust him.

As the song ended, he stepped back with a slight bow but continued to hold my hand. A strange moment passed where neither of us felt ready to let go. I started to speak, but he released his grip, shaking his head to himself, and walked away—leaving me standing on the dance floor, trying to make sense of what had happened.

I wanted to tell him he was right—that it *was* hard. *Really*, fucking hard. That I felt alone, sometimes scared, and like no one truly understood. But he did. He'd seen me. His words had proved that. And trust wasn't something granted because we were partners, but it was something we could *build*.

"Alright, who knew that uptight asshole could dance?" Jackson said in my ear as he appeared beside me.

"Yeah, who knew?" I muttered, my eyes following Perez's retreating form as he disappeared through the door.

Allie, suddenly at my elbow, nudged me toward the exit while pulling up the ride app. We said our goodbyes and exchanged hugs with our new friends before slipping into the waiting vehicle.

I closed my eyes, letting the hum of the car soothe me as I wrestled with a quiet pull in opposite directions.

CHAPTER 5
Loriah

I sipped my coffee as the subway's A line car swayed and bumped, watching people shuffle on and off at each stop. Monday morning's commute gave me too much time to think. My thoughts rotated like a carousel between the evidence we had on file, the details we didn't yet have, and Perez's words.

I need you to trust me.

I turned that one real glimpse of my partner over in my mind. My rare, intimate interactions with Perez made me want to believe his sincerity—but he still hadn't earned it. The way he was always so quick to push me away didn't feel right. It felt deliberate—too much like *forcing* me out. We would take one step forward, then two steps back, constantly keeping me at an arm's length, stuck in a battling tango of wills that I couldn't escape.

"Canal Street," the train's automated recording called over the din of chatter.

I muttered a quick apology as I squeezed past a woman juggling her baby and a designer stroller far too wide for rush hour. Outside, the city's hum wrapped around me—a delivery truck idled in front of a small bistro where a man covered graffiti with broad strokes of black paint, music drifted through the open door of a coffee shop, and pigeons cooed, squabbling over the last scattered crumbs of an unidentifiable pastry. By a miracle, I was early and able to cut through the small park leading to work, stealing a few precious moments of greenery before reaching the office.

My head was swirling with conflicting emotions as I approached the station's steps—worn smooth by decades of foot traffic—when a familiar arm crossed my peripheral. The chilled air faded, replaced with the warmth of a voice to match.

"Let me get that," Jackson said, reaching for the large brass-handled door. His cologne, subtle but present, brought Friday night and the feel of his hands on my bare skin rushing back. My cheeks heated with the thought, and I peered down, trying to avoid his notice.

"Thanks," I said, stepping inside. "Ready for the week?"

"Kind of. I wish I could go back to bed, but Friday night was worth it. Now, I'll have to think hard about where to take you next to top that."

I smiled. "I'm sure you'll come up with something. I don't need much."

The elevator ride was a comfortable, quiet reprieve, filled only with the mechanical whirring of pulley wires and occasional thunks as we climbed higher to the third floor. We had just stepped into the bullpen when Chief Daniels intercepted me, a broad grin on his face and bushy eyebrows waggling in a playful gaiety.

"Good news, Fairsbane," he boomed. "Your office is ready. You can set it up however you'd like. If you're missing anything, go check the storage room and take whatever you want."

I followed him past desks and partitions, reaching a door with my name already on the placard. My throat tightened unexpectedly as I ran my fingers along the ridges etched into the black background: **Detective Loriah Fairsbane**.

Suddenly, the move, the job, giving up being near my dad, everything, all hit me at once. The name plaque only hammered it all home.

Snapping a quick picture, I made a mental note to send it to Dad later. I knew he'd be thrilled to hear about this little milestone—no doubt at the Elks Club by evening, telling anyone who'd listen that his daughter was an *official* NYPD detective.

"This is amazing," I said, taking one sure step inside my new office. Something about the moment branded it as the beginning.

"We had the nameplate made weeks ago when you accepted the job," Daniels explained. "Your cards are on the desk, too. Perez and a couple of the guys gave up part of their Sunday to get this ready for you."

I whipped my head around and quickly recovered my shock by adding, "Thank you. I appreciate it. *And* them."

"It's well-deserved. Perez is next door, so collaborating will be easier. I'll leave you to it then, Fairsbane."

I nodded, watching him go, and thought *easy* wasn't a word I'd associate with working alongside the closed-off wall of a man. My fingers drummed against the stack of business cards—*my cards*—before I caught myself and stopped. I moved to the open window, looking down at a passing bus and pedestrians going about their day. Then a cough sounded from the doorway. I turned, thinking Chief had forgotten to tell me something, but instead it was Perez who leaned casually against the door jam, his face betraying nothing of what he'd done to help make my office possible.

"I'm heading to Woods' place this morning to meet with his wife and get what I can."

"Want me to come with you?" I offered.

"No. I've got it."

"Alright, well, let me know if you find anything. I'll follow up with IT on the camera footage and then check out the businesses in the area. Hopefully someone saw something."

Don't let him know it bothers you, Fairsbane. One dance won't change everything.

He hesitated for a beat. "Wait for me. I don't want you going there alone."

"You sure?"

"Yes. Wait for me." The finality of what he said left no room for argument, but the imploring tone made me look at him more sharply. He left without another word, keys jingling as he strode off.

Our two-way street to Trust Town started beautifully: *he* didn't want me tagging along, and *I* got told what to do.

Again.

Around noon, I stole a moment to break from the never-ending stream of email correspondence and make my way to the workplace, where Al, the IT guru, called home. I peered through his tiny door window and spotted him sitting at his desk, face aglow, and three mugs of various liquids at his elbow. Slipping through the door without a word, I pulled up a chair and watched him work. Footage zipped by in a blur across his screen, his eyes glued to the monitor. Then, finally, he tapped his mouse and froze the image.

"Well, we've got a few hits." He began speaking to the monitor while addressing me. "This is from a camera near the alley. See here?" Al pointed to a shadowy figure moving in the frame. "She matches the description: same height, build, clothing. But after this, she's out of view. About thirty minutes later, a car leaves the alley."

"Any plates?"

"Partial. I'm running them now." He leaned back, cracking his neck. "The car showed up hours before she did, so I'm thinking it might belong to someone who works nearby."

"What about earlier footage? Which direction was she coming from?"

He clicked back a few frames. "South, heading North before turning into the alley. That area's mostly dumpsters and service doors—nothing good."

"Any other movement in those hours? Anyone coming or going?"

"Nothing." He sighed, scratching at his beard. "If I had to guess, the plates are stolen. That alley connects to *Harmonies*—a strip club catering to high-end clientele. Not exactly the type of place a sixteen-year-old should be hanging around on a Friday night, unless–" He trailed off, discreetly ending the line of thought and cutting me a look that said everything he didn't.

Icy tendrils of dread emerged to snake their way through my veins, making my head feel heavy.

Tick-tock, tick-tock, my internal watch taunted.

"Send me everything: the footage, car image, and whatever you have on the plate."

"Will do."

Leaving the office, I stuffed my notebook into my pocket while Al's discovery gnawed at me. I took a second to lean against the wall and take a fortifying breath.

High-end clientele? I'm sure they'll be excited to see uniforms darkening their doorstep again.

Walking back into my office, the smell of coffee hugged my senses as Jackson sat waiting with a to-go cup.

"What's this?" I asked with a smile.

"Monday fuel," he said, handing me the hot drink. "Best coffee in the city."

"Thank you, I could use this right about now. What's up?"

We both sat, and he drew forward in the seat. "Well, we got a lead from Oklahoma." At that, I set my coffee down and looked at him, and hope bloomed for the first time since taking the case. "Tribal Law Enforcement sent a report. They're trying to confirm if it's *her*. But, we should have a photo soon."

"Rez girl?" I asked him, somehow knowing the answer before he replied.

"Yeah. No one notices until it's too late, do they?"

"No. They don't. Have there been other cases like this recently?"

"At least one. Maybe more. I'll dig into it for you."

"Thanks," I said before sending up a silent prayer that there weren't others.

"No problem, Detective Lady." He grinned as he stood to leave. "Let me know if you need anything else."

I watched him walk away before turning to my computer and opening the tabs that held the NCIC and NamUs databases to search for missing women from the past year who met specific parameters. The list was long, though not as extensive as I'd expected. Each name was a poignant reminder of how invisible these women were to the world they inhabited.

A text pinged on my phone.

Perez - *Come down.*

Ok, pushy.

I snatched my badge off my desk and used the stairs, feeling the urge to get the hell out of the office and run headfirst down the following path toward answers. Once I pushed open the door, Perez was waiting, his eyes hidden behind dark sunglasses.

"Where to first?" I asked as he pulled onto the street, lights flashing to part traffic.

"*Harmonies*," he said. "But don't expect them to help. Strip clubs like that don't keep records unless they *have* to."

"They'll have them if we apply the right pressure."

"You really believe that?"

"I do. I'll even bet you lunch, right now, that I'm right."

His undignified snort of disbelief cut the tension, and I glanced at his bruised hand where it flexed on the steering wheel.

"Prepare to lose, Fairsbane."

"Hey. I wanted to tell you. The other night–"

He cut me off.

"We don't need to talk about it."

"I just want you to know, I wasn't drunk."

"It doesn't matter."

"I doubt you think that." I shot back.

He glanced over, his lips twitching. "Listen, Fairsbane. I don't need you to *like* me. I need you to trust me. *That's* all."

"Then why do you do things like get my new office up and ready for me? You knew when you danced with me, and you said nothing."

"Well," he started, and twisted his hands around the steering wheel, not glancing in my direction. "I see someone has been tattling on me. I thought it might make things feel a little less," He paused, choosing his words with unusual care, "*tenuous* for you." The word came out softer than his usual gruff inflection, clearly testing the unfamiliar ground of *partnership* between us.

The sincerity surprised me, stealing the retort I had planned and making me smile into the window as I turned my head away. Rather than try to find words that could shatter our small truce in the battle of wills, I connected my phone to Bluetooth and let R.E.M.'s *"Losing My Religion"* fill the car.

As I sang along, I caught the faintest hint of a smile dancing along his lips before he shifted in his seat and sang along under his breath, fingers tapping out a minor symphony against the wheel.

And just like that, things felt normal again.

CHAPTER 6
Loriah

I slid out of the car, observing everything around us, my hand on the car door's frame, imagining Jane Doe's last moments, and hoping that something about it would somehow *feel* different. The alley reeked of piss, garbage, and a thing I couldn't quite place. Wet brick and sadness?

I had turned back to shut the door and grab my phone when I gasped, suddenly extraordinarily aware of how close Perez was. He had approached with a feline stillness and stood by me, taking in the same scenery.

"For fuck's sake, Perez. Make a little noise next time."

"It'd take the fun out of it if I did."

"Good God, you're the worst."

"Eh, I doubt that. Even by your standards."

I ignored him, looking around and seeing that the rain from the night before had left behind puddles, and the morning's fog still blanketed the area, lending an eerie feel. A few dumpsters lined the narrow space, surrounded by garbage cans and piles of trash that spilled out like urban vomit. The scene was as unpleasant as it was ordinary.

"So, which one was it?" I asked, scanning the dumpsters. None screamed, *crime scene*. They all struck me as unremarkable—belonging to a universe where nothing extraordinary *ever* happened.

Perez gestured toward the second one on the left. "This one," he said, strolling over to it.

The dumpster was your standard WM type—green, tagged with graffiti, and smeared with garbage where lazy workers had missed their mark.

Seriously, how hard is it to toss a bag into the container with a five-foot opening?

I had no patience for inane laziness, even from strangers.

"The file says the body was found lying on top of everything else in the dumpster," Perez said, reciting the report from memory as much for me as for himself. "Some haphazard bag of trash had been thrown on top of her, probably by the poor bastard who called it in. She had ligature marks around her neck as well as obvious signs of a struggle. Her nails were clean, and forensics found nothing when they tested the scene. No sexual assault, either. No identification. No cell phone. So, whoever did this knew *exactly* what we'd be examining for."

I crouched to inspect it, not expecting much, but wanting a closer look at where she had last been.

"Why wasn't this taken into evidence? Usually, things like this would get a more thorough once-over."

Perez shrugged. "From what I heard, they combed through it and took the contents, but that's about it. We're short-staffed and overworked, so it's not unexpected if they got nothing."

"Doesn't *seem* to be combed through." I frowned, wiping a smudge of grime off my hand. "Did they dust it for prints?"

"They did," he confirmed. "They're running all the prints, but unless they're in the system, we've got nothing."

I stood and scanned the alley knowing what he said was true. Why had that girl been here? The grainy footage from the municipal camera showed her glancing around, as if she were waiting for someone.

Gotcha.

Spotting a small black camera mounted where the other one's range cut off, I walked closer and snapped a picture, just in case the owner decided to "misplace" it before we got a warrant.

"Want to take the honors with the door?" Perez asked, rounding the corner toward the building. "They're not expecting us, so I don't anticipate a warm welcome."

He was probably right.

"Yeah, I'll take the lead," I said, mentally bracing myself, then I pointed at him, a smile playing at my lips.

"I don't think I like it when you look at me like that, Fairsbane. What are you scheming?"

"I was thinking, not scheming, that you'll play the bad cop. *Naturally.*"

"*Naturally,*" he echoed with an exasperated sigh.

Unbuttoning the top two buttons of my blouse, I tousled my hair and hoped my appearance would disarm whoever opened the door. Perez shot me a glare so sharp it could've cut glass.

"And what exactly are you going for here?" he asked, crossing his arms.

"Oh, I think you know," I teased.

He groaned. "*Jesucristo*! You're playing librarian Barbie at a fucking crime scene? These guys see tits and ass all day; they're not going to give a shit about yours."

"Language! But, I bet they will," I said in a sing-song voice. "Remember our wager, when I win, won't you?"

Perez muttered something in a rapid-fire mix of Spanish and English about bad ideas and weaponizing a body, but he nodded. "Never mind. By all means, continue. You'll be the one buying lunch, and I'll be getting a free show."

I knocked twice on the heavy red doors. *Nothing*. Minutes passed and I was beginning to think I'd underestimated my confidence when the locks finally clicked, and the door opened to reveal a squat man in tailored trousers and a slicked-back hairdo. He gave us a once-over, unimpressed.

"We don't open for another five hours. Fuck off," the man barked in a thick Brooklyn accent.

"Actually," I said, letting my Texas drawl seep into my words as I slid my badge from my belt, "we're with the NYPD. We've got a few questions about the body in your dumpster a couple of weeks ago. I promise it won't take long."

"Oh well, why didn't you say so? Just come on in," he said, the disdain rolling off every word.

"I promise. It *really* will only take us a couple of minutes."

For a moment, the man's eyes lingered exactly where I wanted them, and when he looked back up to my face, I was using my best pageant-style smile. His scowl softened, but apprehension was still there. "Fine. Wait here," he said, shutting the door.

Perez exhaled sharply. "*This*, is your big plan?"

"Shut up," I said, knocking into his shoulder. "It'll work."

Ten minutes later, the door swung open. "Follow me," the same stout man said, gesturing us inside.

The music hit like a physical force; a deep bass reverberated off the walls. He led us through the club to a private elevator and swiped a key card, opening black metal doors that gleamed like mirrors. Perez and I exchanged a glance and stepped inside.

"Told yah."

"Alright," he grumbled.

The elevator opened into a luxurious office—floor-to-ceiling windows framed the city's skyline, and the air was thick with the smells of tobacco and leather. The pounding sounds from the club couldn't be heard, much like stepping into an audiologist's booth, though a slower, sensual tune was playing at a modest volume. A stunning, naked woman occupied one dance pole on a raised platform. She moved with fluid grace. The curve of her heavy breasts swaying and long legs fluidly wrapping around the metal was hypnotic. I'd never seen anything like it.

Behind the desk, a silver-haired man dismissed her with a single word: "Leave."

She obeyed without hesitation.

"Detectives," he said, gesturing to the chairs in front of his desk. "What can I do for you?"

I took a seat and pulled out my notebook. When Perez didn't sit, instead moving closer to stand behind me, the man leaned back, the leather groaning.

"Suit yourself. I'm Francesco Baldini. What's this about?"

"Mr. Baldini," I interjected, keeping my tone soft to ease the tension. "We're here about your camera. One that might be covering the back alley. Would you happen to have footage from a couple of weeks ago?"

Baldini appraised me with sharp, pale blue eyes. "I might. Are you asking *officially*?"

"Not yet," I said with a polite smile. "We could go that route, although I'd prefer we didn't."

He raised an eyebrow. "If I did have such a camera, what specific date would you need?"

"September 22nd," I replied. "And perhaps the days leading up to it."

Perez didn't wait. "You know the night, Baldini. The one where a girl wound up dead in your dumpster. Or is that just another day in the family business?"

Baldini's smirk widened. "I don't trouble myself with such details. My son handled all that. A detective had already spoken to him. Woods, I believe, was his name."

Perez stiffened, his features hardening at the mention of his late partner. Baldini's keen eyes didn't miss it, and an eyebrow raised slightly. He reached for a sleek black box on his desk and opened it, revealing a row of uniform cigars nestled in cedar and a pillow of green velvet. Removing a cigar, he clipped and lit it with practiced ease. His gaze slid back to me.

"Cigar fan?" he asked when he caught me staring.

"Not me," I said, smiling faintly while gesturing to the *easily* twenty-thousand-dollar humidor sitting on his desk. "But my dad is. I've only seen *those* in magazines."

"Ah, a shame. Winston Churchill had a quote along the lines of, 'Cigars are like falling in love,'" Baldini said, his voice dropping into something poetic. He took another drag. "First, you're drawn by their shape. Then, you savor their flavor. And above all, you never, ever let the flame go out."

He blew another ring of smoke, holding my gaze. There was a magnetic quality to him—powerful and dangerous. He was the kind of man who got what he wanted, and you couldn't mistake it for charm.

"Unfortunately for me, that'd be highly inappropriate," I replied coolly, shifting the conversation back to business. "But I would appreciate your generous cooperation with the footage. It's crucial to our case."

Baldini studied me. "If I *did* have such videos, they wouldn't be so simple to obtain."

I edged forward slightly, my arms pressing gently into my breasts, and gave Baldini a coy smile. When I spoke again, I kept my tone light. "Is there someone you could call to help? This investigation hinges on certain details, and you're in an excellent position to help me."

With a theatrical sigh, Baldini picked up his phone. He dialed while his eyes never left mine. "Rico," he said. "I need everything you've got from the week of September 22nd. Yes, the night of the girl. Consider it a favor. Good."

He hung up with a satisfying click in the phone cradle. "You'll have your footage tonight, Detective. *Unofficially*. Too bad for me, I'm a sucker for beautiful women in need."

"Thank you, Mr. Baldini," I said, sliding a card across the desk. "If you or your son recalls *anything* else, don't hesitate to reach out."

Baldini stood and moved around the desk. When I offered my hand, he took it—but instead of shaking it, he angled in close. The scent he exuded matched his office—tobacco, leather, and a hint of bergamot—it invaded my senses and wrapped around me like a second skin. The urge to scrub every inch of my body clean started to tingle up my spine.

"If *you* ever want a change of scenery, you can give *me* a call." He slid a card into my palm. I looked down to where his hand was still in mine and then back up to Baldini's face—a greedy grin creeping along his mouth.

I knew the shameless exploitation was costing me by the little huffs that Perez kept letting escape behind my back.

"I appreciate it, but I wouldn't go betting the family jewels on me changing careers just yet, Mr. Baldini. This should be the last time we bother you."

"That is a shame. I could personally deliver the footage to you, Detective."

Perez appeared at my side, his hand closing around my elbow.

"That's enough for today," he said, steering me toward the elevator.

A soft chuckle followed us as the doors closed. I let out a shaky sigh, Baldini's cologne clinging to my skin and leaving me wishing I hadn't let him so close.

I turned to Perez, his large hand still wrapped around my arm in a possessive grip. He looked down, realization dawning, and dropped his hold on my arm, leaving a tingling sensation of warmth in its wake.

"Was that truly necessary?"

When I didn't respond, the elevator's descent matched the drop in temperature between us. Perez didn't say anything for a few heartbeats, his jaw clenching once, twice, before he added, "You shouldn't get mixed up with that family. They're bad news. You're not from here, so maybe you don't know that. But I do."

I filed the moment away, wondering if his apparent dislike of Baldini had anything to do with his late partner, or on a personal level.

Perez was an enigma, but I was patient.

I couldn't resist a taunting smirk, trying to break the tension. "So, about that lunch *you* owe me?"

Perez groaned, dragging a hand down his face with, "Unbelievable."

CHAPTER 7
Loriah

Rain pelted the windshield as we drove. I'd smelled the earthy dampness of petrichor—promising a storm—when we left *Harmonies*. I wasn't, however, expecting the sudden torrent as the door shut with an audible thud behind me.

"Well, if the dumpster wasn't *cleaned* before, it will be now," I muttered to myself.

"Is that pessimism, you're showing, Fairsbane?"

"Huh? Oh–" I hadn't realized I'd spoken aloud. "Just making an observation."

The wipers beat furiously, causing the water to run in heavy rivulets down the windshield, creating a mesmerizing blur of headlights and streetlamps. Evening had begun its slow descent, painting the city in muted hues of light and shadow. Dallas was big, but it had nothing on this. I took out my phone and snapped a picture to send to my dad. Knowing he'd appreciate that I'd been thinking of him.

I sent up a silent prayer that we would get the footage, and Baldini wouldn't leave us high and dry. He was one of the only people who could provide more information than we had, and if that meant a little brazen cleavage display, it was worth everything. *I hope this is worth everything.*

Perez glanced over.

"I can hear your mind whirring," he said, his gravelly voice cutting through my internal chaos and fighting to be heard over the continuous pelting of rain. He shot me a sidelong glance, the corner of his mouth twitching like he was fighting back a smirk.

I hummed noncommittally.

"I hope you like falafel," he added, the sudden switch in gears disarming me.

A small stand was tucked against the side of a weathered brick building when we pulled up. Perez grabbed a black umbrella from the back seat, though the rain had eased into a gentle drizzle when we stepped out.

"Here. You'll get soaked," he said, making his way around the car to hold the umbrella over me before shutting my door.

"Come on, I won't melt."

"If you get sick, who else will I have to do the work I don't want to?"

I laughed at the teasing remark. The faint scent of his cologne, warm and woody, greeted me when his arm came around to give shelter. Where Baldini's fragrance had made me feel ill at ease, Perez's tugged out forgotten memories of campfires, music, and dancing under truck lights in a simpler time.

"Hey, Horus!" Perez called, pulling me back into the present.

The thickset man at the stand yelled over his shoulder as he handed change to a customer, "Yo, Agustin!" He turned around in his bright orange shirt that read *Horus* and grinned. "How yah been, pal? The usual?"

Perez nodded. "The usual, yeah."

Horus pointed at me with a ladle covered in tzatziki sauce.

"And who the hell is this?"

"*This* is Detective Fairsbane."

"Well, damn, Detective," Horus said, chuckling as he piled hummus into a takeout box. "You can arrest me anytime."

"I really don't think you'd want that," I replied, laughing at the gentle ragging. "You'd have to kill someone first."

"Whoa! Never mind, then. But hey, murder this falafel for me, alright? On the house. Anything for you, Agustin. And you, Detective."

Perez handed me the umbrella and took the boxes. I stretched my arm out, feeling the drizzle fading into a lingering mist. He slipped a twenty from his wallet and tucked it into a small jar that sat on the stall's tiny counter.

"One day, you'll let me buy lunch," Horus said, shaking his head.

"Not today. I lost a bet," Perez replied with a sly grin and a wink to me that hit straight through the chest.

Back in the car, Perez took us to a quiet alley to eat where I savored the break from the relentless office grind.

"So, do you think Baldini will actually send the videos?" I asked, trying to speak around a mouthful of food.

Perez's brow furrowed as he stabbed at his food with a fork. "I'm hoping he keeps his word. But if he *doesn't*"—he pierced me with a stare—"you can't go back there. Not alone. Not without solid proof *or* a good reason. They'll lawyer up to stall us, and if we find anything, you bet your ass it'll get buried."

His words were almost accusatory, and I averted my eyes down at a tomato.

"You have to promise me, Loriah."

Speaking my first name caught me off guard. It was so purposeful and hung in the air, waiting for me to grab it and give a reply.

"I don't want to promise something I might not be able to keep," I said quietly.

"At least try." He sighed, his voice softening. "For your sake. For your family. When you think no one is watching, I see you. I mean, I see you sending your dad messages and pictures." He looked down again to get more food on his fork before looking back at my face and meeting my eyes with intensity. "Don't put yourself in a position you can't come back from. These people—they operate by their own rules. They don't care that you have people you're important to."

I wanted to tell him he didn't need to shelter me from the nastiness that society offered. I had faced more than a few *Baldini's* in my career, and I wasn't afraid of them. It took more than some self-important peacocking man to make me turn my back on a case like this. But the sound of his phone ringing disrupted the moment. We both glanced at the screen and saw the name, *Chief Daniels*, before he answered.

"Yes, Chief? Understood. Send us the address."

"What is it?" I asked, my pulse picking up.

"Another body," he said grimly. "Same area, just a few blocks over. Looks like another girl around our Jane Doe's age, possibly native or Hispanic—that's all they know, so eat quick."

The siren blared, lights bounced, blue and red off the raindrop-covered surroundings as we wove precariously through New York's rush-hour traffic as fast as we could. The streets quickly packed with commuters doing their best to get home, only inching over the barest amount to allow us the ever-so-slight advantage of creeping along ahead of them.

When we arrived at the spot Chief had sent, yellow crime-scene tape had already been erected between barrier poles, keeping the growing crowd of rubberneckers at bay. A camera flashed repeatedly, and uniformed officers busied themselves redirecting foot traffic and shielding the perimeter.

Perez stepped out first, his movements brisk and purposeful.

"I'm Detective Perez, and this is Detective Fairsbane." He announced to one of the officers nearby, "Who's first on the scene?"

The officer, a young man with an air of unease, nodded. "That'd be me, Detective. The Examiner and Pathologist are suiting up now. Rendezvous tent is over there," he said, pointing toward a blue tent near a forensics van where personnel pulled on Tyvek suits and sterile blue gloves.

Perez gave a curt nod, and we headed to the tent.

Collecting statements, directing forensics, and examining the details of the scene made the hours pass in a blur. The body of a young woman bore strangulation marks, similar to those on our Jane Doe. She'd also been left in a dumpster. Seeing that a pattern was forming, my stomach twisted at the implications.

I had finished interviewing a bystander when I was handed a cup of coffee. Looking up, I was met with a smiling face. Jackson.

"Hey! I didn't expect to see you here." I wrapped my hands around the cup, letting the warmth seep into my frozen fingers. The caffeine was a welcome boost after hours of unyielding focus.

"Chief needed more people to keep the press at bay," Jackson said. A lanyard with ID bounced against his chest as he gestured. "I figured I'd also check for any cameras in the area. How are you holding up?"

"Well, I could be watching a chick flick and eating ice cream with Allie right now, but this coffee will take the edge off for now," I replied before taking a blissful sip.

He laughed, the moisture curling like smoke in the cool evening air. "Glad to help. Want to grab a bite after this?"

"Yeah, sure. You pick, though, please. My brain is fried!"

"Deal, I'll see you later." He gave a lazy half-wave and disappeared into the mass of people and cellphones, all fighting for a look at the scene.

A chill was settling in, the sun long hidden behind the jagged skyline. Across the tape, I spotted Perez, his countenance a mix of profound fatigue and grim determination, though he caught my eye and gave a single steady nod before turning back to the officers around him.

I'd been about to jot a note down when I noticed her—a girl standing apart from the group, arms wound tightly around herself, posture stiff and uncertain. Her eyes kept darting nervously toward the dumpster, like she was deciding whether to run or not. I approached her like I would with a baby deer—slowly—hoping not to spook her.

"Has anyone talked to you yet? Are you okay?" I asked, keeping my voice soft, hoping she would stay and confide in me.

"I was hoping to talk to you," she whispered, voice trembling and eyes flicking to a group of officers. "They make me nervous."

"The police?" I coaxed. "Or the men?"

Her eyes widened slightly, and she nodded. "The men."

"I can understand that, but don't worry about them, they're only here to help."

The poor girl was silent so long that I'd thought she'd gone into shock, but before I could check, she sniffed and dragged a hand across her nose.

"I– I know her. Fuck. Knew her?" Her timid, cracking voice and twitchy movements made me wonder if she was using, but I pushed the thought aside and ushered her toward the tent, away from the noise and chaos.

Please be reliable.

"What's your name?" I asked as soon as we stepped out into the damp night.

"Angel," she murmured.

"Angel...?"

"Navarro."

"Okay. Miss Navarro," I said, meeting her wary gaze. "Let's go ahead nice and simple: What's your friend's name?"

"Addie. But I don't know her last name."

"That's great, Angel. Can you tell me what you saw? Or how you knew her?"

Angel fidgeted, pulling her coat tighter around her thin frame. "I walk this same path every day to get to work. Sometimes I meet her along the way, but today–" Again her voice cracked, choking on a sob. "I was running late."

"What made you late?" I asked, trying to keep her talking.

"It sounds so stupid."

"Try me," I told her, and grabbed a box of tissues.

"One of the people I live with has a dog, and it hides shoes. He's still a puppy. Even though we're not supposed to have one," she said, her voice trembling with a fragile kind of embarrassment. "Anyway. I couldn't find one of mine, so I borrowed someone else's." She gestured to her feet, where the worn shoes sat loose around the ankles, though they were cinched as tight as possible.

"So, you're running late, and then what?"

Her eyes darted toward the dumpster. "I saw their car pull up. Two guys got out and then they had her pinned against the wall. She spat at the taller one, and I heard the other guy say she'd already been warned. And then–" Her voice broke, tears streaming down her cheeks. "I'm sorry. She didn't deserve this."

"No one does," I said as I pressed a tissue into her small hand. "What happened next, Angel?"

"One of them cut her shirt open with a knife and then called her a whore and punched her. Her nose was bleeding all over the place. He said she was *theirs*. Some people walked past, but they ran when they saw the knife I think."

I handed her another tissue and asked, "Who do you work for?"

Wariness and recognition flashed across her features. She froze, her whole body going rigid. "I—I don't want to say."

"Angel–" Leaning closer, I placed my hand on her forearm, "I can't help you *or* your friend if I don't know who's behind this."

She swallowed hard, the fight leaving her shoulders before the words came tumbling out like a rock slide of words. "I work at a nightclub. It's really nice. They brought us to work. I don't even know the guy's name! I think Addie might've found something, though. She had been more nervous lately. Withdrawn. That's why they–" Her words dissolved into quiet, wracking sobs.

I brought my voice to a near whisper. "Angel, I want you to come to the station tomorrow, okay? No appointment needed, just ask for me. If I'm not there, then my partner, Detective Perez, will help you. Lock your doors tonight. Say you're sick, avoid work, do whatever you need to. We'll go over everything tomorrow. But I need to get this all straight so we can find who did this."

"I *can't* miss work," she whispered.

"Angel," I said firmly, "you're friends with the victim, *and* you're late for work. If they see you here, it won't take much for them to connect the dots. Go home. Please."

She nodded slowly in understanding and stood.

"One more thing," I added. "Can you tell me about the car before you go?"

With brows furrowed in worry, she wrung the tissue in her hands till it was a soft, fraying mess.

"It was black. Tinted windows. There was a circle with three points on it, like a star or something. Mercedes? I don't know. I think the license plate started with KD and ended in an 8, but it could've been a B."

"Thank you, Angel. Get some rest, and I'll see you tomorrow."

I watched her leave, making note of the direction she went and what I thought was the direction of home. Then I turned, scanning the scene for Perez. I waved him over, frantically motioning until he came striding toward me, that same strange amusement, undercut with weariness staring back at me.

"Taking up interpretive dance since I last saw you?" he asked, raising an eyebrow.

"Shut up. Never mind that," I said quickly with barely suppressed excitement. "We've got a lead! Black Mercedes, license plate starting with KD and ending in 8. Maybe a B. Have someone run it."

"Please?" he teased.

"Please," I relented with an eye roll. "Are you teasing me, Mr. Perez?"

"Don't get used to it."

"Oh. Okay, fine. You'll be finding your own ride back with that attitude, mister."

I left him chuckling to himself, his deep, rumbling laughter oddly comforting against the backdrop of the somber evening.

CHAPTER 8

Loriah

Me - *Still up for keeping me company?*

Jackson - *Of course. Feeling Chinese?*

Me - *Sounds good!*

The walk-up to my apartment felt like an Olympic event in my exhausted state, but I made it in time to find Allie knocking on my door. She cupped her hands around her mouth and yelled, "I *know* you're home!" into the wood like a paranoid town crier.

"You're going to wake Mr. Brewer if you keep shouting like that," I said, startling her as I came up the last of the stairs.

"Lor! I've been trying to get a hold of you!" she exclaimed. "Remember Jackson's friend Tory?"

"Uh, yeah. I think so."

"Well, we're grabbing drinks, and you should totally come with us!"

"I love you, but I'm gonna have to go with a thanks but no thanks," I replied, fishing for my keys. "It's been a long day. I'm going to shower and wait for Jackson to bring me some fried-and-sauced sustenance."

"Suit yourself! I'll catch up with you later when you're free from Mr. Dimples. Be safe! Don't do anything I wouldn't do." She flipped her hair dramatically as she walked off, throwing in an exaggerated wink—though Allie couldn't wink properly, so it came off as an adorable, awkward blink and a crooked smile.

"Wait! Mr. Dimples?" I called after her, cringing at the nickname.

But she was already gone, her laugh bouncing off the walls as she went.

I leaned against my door frame, still chuckling to myself, listening to her boundless energy carry her down, wishing I could bottle even a fraction of it for myself. All I wanted, though, was the quiet comfort of my apartment and the promise of food.

The rain hammered and thunder cracked beyond the bathroom windows as I showered. My thoughts wandered while I scrubbed my skin raw and warmed my muscles under the searing spray, trying to melt it all into a swirling mass of suds to slide down the drain. Stepping from the tub and toweling off my hair, I heard heavy knocks echoing through the apartment.

"Coming!" I called, scrambling down the short hallway to my room.

I threw on an old George Strait sweater and green camo-print bike shorts, hair half-wet and curling in tendrils down my back. Cheeks flushed, I opened the door as Jackson raised his hand to knock again. He stood there in a simple black shirt that was soaked through and clinging to every inch of his body. His blue eyes caught mine, and he smiled, knowing I was staring. His expression was stuck somewhere between playful and guilty, like I'd interrupted him doing something he shouldn't.

I'd been ready to collapse on the couch and await food while in a sleepy haze, but seeing him standing there, rain-drenched and smiling, sent an unexpected current of energy through my worn-out body.

"Sorry," he said. "I wasn't sure if you'd heard me or maybe fallen asleep. I can leave the food if you're too tired."

"God no. Don't be sorry," I said, stepping aside. "I was just in the shower, but I'm starving—come in, come in!" I practically dragged him inside, taking one of the bags and heading to the living room only a few steps away. "I hope you don't mind eating here. I don't have much for any formal dining."

"I've eaten in worse places."

"Is that supposed to be reassuring?" I asked him, taking a glance around with a grimace.

"I didn't mean it like that!"

"I'm only messing with you. Do you want a dry shirt? I think I've got one that'll fit."

"Yeah. That'd be great," he said, running a hand through his damp hair. "Pretty sure someone propositioned me on the way up. Something about judging a wet T-shirt contest?"

"Oh no!" I covered my face, mortified. "Big hair, big glasses, loud TV in the background, floor two?"

"Yep," he said with a laugh. "You know her?"

"Unfortunately. Mrs. Lawrence would love that, though. I think she's lonely. So she might tip extra."

As he peeled off his shirt, I busied myself unpacking the food. But I couldn't help sneaking a glimpse. His muscles shifted as he moved, and the sheer physicality of him struck me. He pulled on a dry shirt—one I was pretty sure I'd stolen from my dad—and caught me staring.

"Should I slow down for you?" he teased, still holding the shirt in his hands, breaking the tension.

My face burned, and I spluttered, turning to dish food out instead. Jackson's hand brushed mine when I passed him the carton of sweet and sour chicken, and the fleeting contact felt charged.

"So," I echoed, grateful for the distraction from my racing pulse. "Thank you for taking care of me. *Again*. I owe you so many favors at this point, I've lost count."

He smiled. "Guess I'll have to cash them in," he suggested, his tone playful. "Let's start now—tell me something about yourself no one else knows."

"Seriously?" I asked, surprised.

"Yeah," he said, his voice softening. "I'll go first if you want."

"Sure, I. I don't know what to share. That the noise of a flushing toilet at night still scares me?" I studied my hands, suddenly too aware of all the messy bits of my life that lay hidden in the shadows of my own haunting memories, and knowing that I couldn't always hide behind humor.

He moved closer to me, the apartment suddenly feeling smaller. The warmth of dry clothes and fragrant food cocooned us in a bubble of comfort and intimacy.

"Not exactly. I told you I had a sister, right?"

"Yes, but Christian, you don't have to—"

"No, I want to share with someone; it's been so long since I've been able to talk about her." He scooted closer to me, the cushion dipping under his weight, his heat warming my chilled skin. He cleared his throat and continued, "She was so beautiful, Loriah. God, she was *perfect*. When we were little, she had gotten cancer, and after that, she was this... I don't know. Like an otherworldly being, we all orbited around. I didn't mind, though; she was the best of us. But she had been fine for so long that we never even thought she'd ever be anything *but* healthy. Against the odds, she was amazing. Until she wasn't."

I slowly slid my hand over to hold his, and he let me, his fingers caressing mine.

"She met this man. He was the son of my dad's business partner, and we thought everything would be okay. He treated her like a princess. However, when the stress of family and business began to mix, it became too much for her. Her cancer came back, and I had to watch her deteriorate from afar. Slowly. She would smile and laugh, and the fucked-up thing was she would comfort *us*." He paused then, for so long I didn't think he would pick up again.

His fingers paused their ministrations. His hand tensed, gaze going distant and rheumy. The rain held its breath, the whole world pausing to hear what would come next. The only sound was the beating of our hearts.

"Jackson, I—"

"Don't say you're sorry." His voice was soft but firm, eyes refocusing on me with unexpected clarity. "She was perfect and hilarious, and she loved this ridiculous city—soaking up everything about it like it was the oxygen she needed to survive. That was who she was: the embodiment of *living a life you're proud of.*"

I hesitated, but his sincerity was enchanting. Vulnerability was a gift. At least, that's what I remembered reading once. Maybe it was time to try it, if only to distract him.

"She sounds amazing."

"She was."

"I never had any siblings. But I always wondered what it would be like to have someone else to share life with other than my parents."

"I can't imagine not having mine."

"When I was eight, my mom went on a bender. A particularly nasty one. I sometimes don't think she could have handled more children," I began, my voice steady despite the emotion rising in my chest. "She was addicted to drugs. And alcohol when she was *clean*. But this one time, my dad and I drove around all night, searching for her and checking every place we knew she usually hid out when she was too embarrassed to come home. No one had seen her, though. I cried until I couldn't anymore, blaming myself."

"Loriah" he said quietly, reaching for me.

I shook my head. "Let me finish. I haven't voiced this in, well, I don't know. Ever? Maybe it's time. Consider this my *free* therapy appointment, Dr. Jackson."

He pulled me closer, his arms anchoring me as I spoke. "I told my dad we should pray to the saints, like we did when we lost other things. I mean, if it worked for a teddy bear, why wouldn't it work on a person, right? So, I prayed.

I prayed so hard my head hurt for two days, and then one day, just like a miracle, she came home. She was dirty and thinner, and didn't feel like herself, but I was so convinced that the saints had answered my prayers that I didn't care. For weeks, I'd lose things on purpose, to pray and find them on my bed later. It took me *years* to realize it was my dad all along: bringing back my toys, bringing her home, keeping me whole. *He's* the reason I became a cop. I wanted to help bring others home. Or give them answers."

A tear slid down my cheek, surprising me—I hadn't realized how deeply I'd let myself feel that moment. Jackson brushed it away with his thumb, the calluses on his fingers rough against my skin, but his grip was impossibly gentle. The kindness and understanding in his eyes undid me, dissolving the carefully constructed walls I'd maintained all day, all year, perhaps my *entire* adult life. The exhaustion from earlier vanished, shifting into something else—a willingness to surrender.

Before I could think, his lips touched mine—soft, tentative, unhurried, as if we could erase all the hurt with each press of our lips.

The kiss deepened, and before I knew it, Jackson's hands were on my waist, pulling me closer. He moved with a deliberateness that sent a wave of heat through me. His fingers skimmed up my back, tracing the hem of my shirt, hesitating only a heartbeat before pulling away to regard me. I knew that whatever he saw in my eyes was the same in his. Need.

Returning his lips to mine with a feather-light caress, he asked, "Is this what you want?"

"Yes," I whispered against his mouth with an urgency.

In one swift motion, he lifted my shirt over my head, our mouths parting for the briefest of moments.

He pulled back again, panting hard, and paused, his eyes taking in the tiny tattoos scattered across my body. Then he bent to kiss along each one, sending shivers down my skin.

"Do you know how incredible you are?" he asked, his voice barely above a whisper. He had wiped away another tear and placed a kiss on my cheek, then slowly, tenderly, trailed more down my face, my neck, and onto the sensitive parts of my collarbone till gooseflesh rose in their place.

"You're sure this is what you want, Loriah?" he murmured against my skin.

I nodded, my fingers running up his chest to frame his face. "It is," I whispered, leaning in to kiss him again. "I'm sure."

His hands moved to my hips, digging into the soft skin, pulling me up and onto his lap, but as the moment threatened to consume us, a buzzing sound shattered the quiet.

Buzz-buzz. Buzz-buzz. Buzz-buzz

My phone vibrated incessantly on the coffee table, intruding like a splash of cold water.

"Just ignore it," I said against his mouth, fumbling to silence the damned thing and trying to recapture the moment, desperately wanting to stay in the sanctuary we'd created, shielding us from the press of the outside world.

Buzz-buzz. Buzz-buzz. Buzz-buzz.

"Damn it!" I groaned, sitting up and snatching the phone. The rhythm of the evening disintegrated as I read the name on the screen. My stomach dropped, reality rushing back in—*DET. PEREZ.*

Of course, he would choose now.

"What is it?" I snapped into the phone, frustration thick in my voice.

"Busy?" Perez asked. The clink of ice in a glass echoed faintly on his end.

"It's late," I replied, glaring at the ceiling. "Is this a drunk dial? What do you need?"

"Ha! No, but I'm working towards it."

"Don't you have a life?"

"I have a life," he drawled. "But I also have news. IT pieced together that partial tag you asked for so nicely."

"And? What is it?" I asked, greedy for the knowledge.

Jackson bent closer, his lips brushing the shell of my ear. "He's desperate for you," he whispered, his tone low and teasing, his hands trailing down my neck to tease the fabric over my nipples.

I couldn't stop the hitch in my voice as I said, "Perez!"

The sound of my partner's quick inhale on the other end was unmistakable. "Are you alone?" he asked, his usual confidence faltering.

"I don't think that's any of your business." I was trying for self-control.

"It's *him*, isn't it?" His voice dropped, barely audible.

"It's *a* him," I replied, the tension crackling through the line. Somewhere, miles away in the city, he would be thinking about just who that *him*, was. And hating it.

Perez exhaled hard. "Listen, it was Chief Daniels's car."

The words hit me like a physical blow. I snapped upright, nearly toppling Jackson off the couch. "What did you say?" I asked, holding up a hand to quiet Jackson as I focused entirely on the call. Though my body was warm from his touch, I reached for my shirt, feeling the need to be clothed to absorb the significance of what he said.

"The car. The partial tag matched a vehicle impounded in a drug bust. But Daniels took it out. I don't know why or how, but it *was* him."

The implications hung heavy. I ran my fingers through my hair, trying to ground myself. "Are you sure? Could it just be a coincidence?"

"Positive," Perez said. "I'm hoping there's a reasonable explanation, but I'll ask him tomorrow. Cop to cop."

I swallowed hard, forcing my voice to remain steady. "Do you want to handle it formally or..."

"Informally—for now," he said. "I'm trusting your optimism here, Fairsbane. Don't make me regret it."

"Was that a partial compliment, Perez?" I goaded, trying to lighten the mood.

"I told you, don't get used to it," he replied dryly. Though if I had to bet money, I would say that I could hear him smiling around his words when he said, "See you tomorrow."

The line went dead, a couple of beeps signaling he'd hung up, and I lowered the phone—my mind racing. Jackson had stopped his light caresses to watch me, brows furrowed with concern.

"It was nothing," I said, trying to reassure him, though the words rang hollow even to my ears.

"Loriah," he began, his tone soft.

I reached out, placing a hand on his chest. "I know. We got carried away." I managed a small smile. "But you have nothing to apologize for."

His lips quirked up in a sad smile as he leaned forward, pressing a kiss to my forehead.

"We can take a step back," he said gently. "But I assure you, Loriah, I'm not the least bit sorry. We'll grab a smoke, some coffee maybe, and cool off. But that, that was... *needed*. In case you couldn't tell."

I nodded, standing up and pulling at the edges of my shirt. After the admissions of earlier, and Perez's phone call, I felt as raw and exposed as when I'd been scrubbing my skin earlier. Even if it was only for a short while, something had fundamentally shifted something between us. The discussion only paused, not discontinued. He wasn't wrong—it wasn't the night for unraveling *all* the parts of ourselves. Not yet. But I couldn't shake the weight of Perez's call, or the storm it was bound to unleash.

That same pull I'd felt before tugged at me once again. Like I was only *half* where I needed to be.

CHAPTER 9
Loriah

6 AM wake-up calls came faster than I thought possible. I rubbed my eyes to find them puffy, a combination of too much salt in last night's Chinese food, too little sleep, and the inescapable humidity hanging in the air after two days of driving rain. The intense kissing—and the few tears I'd shed—probably didn't help, but I wasn't about to admit that to anyone, let alone complain.

I chose a navy suit with a burnt orange silk button-up underneath, something that made me feel put together despite the exhaustion. My hair was left loose, and generously applied concealer hid the evidence of a rough night. My hands paused on my bag, a thought crossing my mind: *It was Daniels's car.*

I shook it off, attempting to save mental space till I could speak to Agustin and sort things out.

"Morning," Perez greeted as I walked into my office. He was perched on my desk, file in hand, appearing irritatingly well-rested.

"You could've at least bought me coffee before wanting to talk shop," I quipped, dropping my bag on the chair.

He smirked, pulling a coffee cup from behind his back.

"Already thought of that. I loaded it up with too much cream and sugar—just how you like it—for a child."

"Well, well. Maybe you're not as awful as I originally thought," I said, taking the cup gratefully.

"Aren't you a delight. Though, with that attitude, I'm thinking last night wasn't *as good* as you'd hoped?" He raised a brow over his coffee cup.

"Careful, Perez," I teased, "or you might end up sounding jealous."

He rolled his eyes. "Shut up, and drink your coffee while I fill you in."

I made a noncommittal sound and sank into my worn chair. The first sip of coffee was ecstasy, and I closed my eyes, listening to the Spanish lilt in his voice as he continued.

"There've been some developments while you were catching up on your beauty rest. It seems Baldini pulled through." Even with my eyes closed, I could hear the scowl on his lips as he mentioned Baldini's name. "IT received his video files. The night shift was briefing Al earlier, and we'll need to review it with him. They caught something, not perfect, but clear enough to make a difference. That's as far as I got."

"And Woods' hard drive?"

"Our team's close to cracking it."

"Okay," I said, grabbing my stuff in one arm, and coffee in the other, and making my way through the office with Perez by my side until we paused at the elevator. "I'll head down to Al and see what he's got. Are you going to talk to Daniels?"

Perez nodded and pressed the button down for me.

"I am. I have to handle this myself."

"I know."

Stepping inside, I turned to face him, his sad eyes never leaving mine as the doors closed. For a moment, he let me see that, despite the quips and side smiles, he was only deflecting the pain. Daniels wasn't just a boss to him; they had history. Confronting someone you respected, especially under those circumstances, wasn't straightforward. I hoped Perez would keep his cool, but the look we exchanged before the doors shut told me he wasn't sure he could.

Walking into Al's cold little glowing dungeon of a workplace, I immediately regretted leaving my jacket.

"Good God, Al, are you a polar bear?"

"Hey, Loriah," he acknowledged with a rare chuckle, glancing up from his monitors. "You get used to it."

"I will have to take your word for it."

"Pull up a seat. Where's Perez?"

"He'll be here later. He had something to take care of first," I said, grabbing a chair.

"No problem. I'll get started then if that's alright. Let me know if I'm going too fast; I can rewind or slow it down. I'm also making an encrypted copy for you to review later, just in case. "

"Thanks, Al," I said, leaning in and rubbing my arms for warmth. "Start from before they met."

The video played on the monitor: a dark, grainy, yet discernible street view, with Jane Doe pacing back and forth, silhouette sharp against the dark alley. Her hands kept returning to her lower belly—a protective gesture visible even through the surveillance camera's limited scope. Each step betrayed her anxiety—quick, then hesitant, as if rehearsing words she couldn't bring herself to say.

A black BMW rolled into frame, its headlights momentarily blinding the camera's feed before a man, in black sweats and a hoodie, stepped out. His ball cap shadowed his face, but his left hand caught the streetlight—a flash of something that had to be a ring. Jane Doe walked toward him, her steps hesitant, with a posture that spoke to her courage in wanting to confront the man.

Al sped forward through the video: mouths moved at lightning speed, the man's stance growing more defensive. Our girl began to cry as he gesticulated wildly, pointing to her belly, then shoving her chest hard enough to make her stumble. She was openly sobbing by then, swiping at her eyes as he kept moving toward her, stalking toward her, like an animal cornering its prey. When he was close, he placed her in the shadow cast on him by the streetlamps, her shoulders hunched, and her head dropped. He bent down slightly so his face was in front of hers, eye to eye, and cocked his head with a tilt that left his mouth visible, saying something that might have been, *get rid of it or I will*, before standing back up.

"Can you replay that part slowly for me?"

Al pressed rewind and took us frame by frame until I was almost positive of the words.

"Hmm, thank you."

We continued through the footage. When she shoved him, her push barely moved the large man, but his response came with no hesitation. Pulling a rope from his pocket, he got her in a chokehold. I gasped out as a reflex, and my hand flew to my mouth. Al sat back, but didn't turn away.

He wasn't planning on letting her go. He was toying with her.

I pressed closer to the screen, my nails bit into the palms of my hands, bringing me back to the present. The way my stomach knotted as she clawed at his hands—her legs kicked as he dragged her behind the dumpster—made me want to scream for her. His head darted in paranoia, unaware of the camera recording his every movement.

The door opened behind us, allowing a sliver of light from the hall to enter and illuminate the room before being plunged back into the eerie glow of screens and darkness. The familiar scent of a fireside warmth and cedar—Perez's cologne—cut through the heavy air and hugged my senses. He laid a hand on my shoulder and bent over me to peer into the monitor—his presence a balm to my nerves amid the horror playing out before us.

"Fairsbane." His deep voice broke the trance of the footage. "What've we got?"

"She's struggling with him," I said, barely above a whisper. "He's strangling her with some kind of cord, I think."

"Rewind it a little, please, Al," Perez said, leaning in closer. I couldn't tell if his meeting with Daniels had gone well or if it had completely fallen apart.

Perez's response was more contained than mine, though I could see the tensing of his jaw, betraying his emotion. Continuing from where I'd left off, Jane Doe's fight grew weaker. She grasped his hands as if it were her last small and desperate act for freedom before going limp. Tears pricked my eyes as I watched how he robotically cleaned her body before hauling her into the dumpster like a piece of garbage.

I stood and turned away, heading for the door.

"Thank you, Al. You're doing good work," I told him without looking back.

Perez was murmuring his thanks and asking for stills from the footage as the door clicked shut behind me. The oxygen in my lungs suddenly felt inadequate, and I fought through the panic, my heart pounding. I had been seeing a therapist before leaving Dallas, but the coping mechanisms I normally used were struggling to break through my runaway train of a brain.

I just needed three sounds.

The door shutting, the clicks of a fluorescent light going out above me, and Perez.

"Fairsbane?" Joining me in the hall, he kept his voice low.

"I'm fine. I'll be fine," I said, steadying myself on a deep inhale, not wanting Perez to think I was weak. "She was a kid, that's all."

I heard him rustling around in his suit jacket before a tissue was placed gently in my hand with a squeeze, my pulse thundering away into his grip.

"We *will* find out who did this."

I lifted my eyes to meet his gaze in the hallway's low light. Tears brimmed in the edges of my eyes, threatening to fall, and I dashed them away with the tissue. But there was no shame or disbelief at what I was letting him see.

"We will. I promise," Perez said with finality.

And I believed him.

A message pinged on my phone as we walked back down the long hall to the elevator after I'd composed myself.

Alice (reception) - *Detective, good morning. There's a girl here to see you. She refused to go to your office without you.*

Me - *Perfect. Keep her there. We're on our way.*

Perez headed to the interview rooms, and I went to collect Angel, hoping she'd yield more answers than we could come up with.

Angel was in the lobby, picking at her nonexistent nails, her dark brown eyes bloodshot and puffy. A disheveled black bob of hair rested at her shoulders, making the bright geometric earrings she wore stand out against the ebony backdrop. When she saw me, she stood abruptly, pulling her hoodie closer around her slight frame.

"I came," she said. Her voice—barely above a whisper—carried in the open lobby.

"Thank you," I said softly, and guided her toward a long hallway. "Let's go somewhere private."

"Will there be anyone else?"

"No, just us."

As we approached the open interview room, I paused and turned to face her. She seemed so small, so fragile, and it struck a deep chord in me. Memories flooded back—of being a young girl, not much younger than Angel, and standing in a similar room, giving my statement to officers after my mother had died.

"Angel, I need to record this for accuracy. I know this all seems scary. I have been in a similar situation with someone I cared deeply about, so I won't push you. All I ask is that you're honest with me. Can you do that?"

She nodded. "Yeah, I can."

We stepped into the room and took seats opposite each other. The atmosphere was sterile and uninviting.

I pulled the slim recording device from my pocket and set it on the table.

Angel fixed her eyes on one small gash in the metal table.

The ominous click of the **Record** button caused her head to snap up.

"We're going to begin. Today is October 10, 2022. I, Detective Loriah Fairsbane, am conducting an interview with—"

"Angel. Angel Navarro," she said quietly.

"Angel, can you tell me the deceased's name for the record?" I asked, keeping my tone calm and steady.

"Addie," she said, her voice trembling. "I don't know her last name. We loved how our names sounded together. Angel and Addie. The customers liked it too."

Of course they did.

A chill ran down my arms at the thought of some creeps calling their names and asking for them specifically. Asking for children. No respect for the natural boundaries—none of the protection adults were supposed to give. Just predators pretending it didn't exist because of *anonymity*.

"I'm sorry?" I said, stumbling from thought.

"I said, I think it was her real name."

Angel's sniffles brought me back, a tether back to reality before my thoughts could wander further.

"How did you meet Addie?"

"We shared a room together, where I live now. When you work there, they give you a place to stay. Sometimes, the girls get moved into better places if they're making enough. But, she was my best friend—my only friend."

"Thank you for sharing that, Angel," I said gently. "It's clear how much she meant to you. Can you tell me about the place you work or who your boss is?"

Angel hesitated, again picking at the skin around her nails.

"It's okay," I reassured her. "I will never judge you for what you *had* to do. I'm trying to understand and paint a picture of Addie's life so we can see the full sequence of events."

She nodded once before continuing. "We work at a club called *The Enchanted Sanctuary*. It's exclusive. Or so they tell us. You need a password and an invitation to access it, kind of like a speakeasy. All the girls want to work there because it's where the big spenders hang out. I only got the job because one of the girls went missing a couple of weeks ago." She looked down, her voice dropping lower.

"Does that happen often?"

"What?"

"Girls going missing?"

"Sometimes. Maybe a couple times a month."

"And no one keeps in touch?"

She looked uncomfortable at the question.

"We're not supposed to *make friends.*"

"Hmm. How did you all end up in New York?"

"Most of us came to New York the same way. A guy messaged us online—through social media. He offered us a way out of our small-town lives, usually off the rez. That's how I ended up here. Some girls, though, just show up."

"Did you fly out?"

"Yeah. They sent fake documents that said I was a New York resident with a different name and added a couple of years to my age. I only turned eighteen *after* moving here."

I made a mental note: forgeries getting past TSA meant serious resources.

"What kind of work do you do at *The Enchanted Sanctuary?*" I asked.

Angel fidgeted, tapping her finger in a rhythm against the side of her chair. "We wait tables. But if someone talks to our handler, this other woman, Daniella, we go to *a private* room. The girls who only strip don't have to, but I did. *We* did."

"Together?"

She nodded her head.

"Angel. Do they force you to have sex with clients?"

She nodded again more slowly.

"Anything they want. There's alcohol, drugs, whatever it takes to make us *compliant*." Her voice wavered, but she pressed on. "It *felt* like rape at first. I think, maybe, it was? They liked it that way, I know that. The crying. The begging. But after a while, it became my *job*. Now I don't feel much. It's just a show."

"Oh, Angel. What those men did to you? You don't deserve that. None of you do, no matter the money." I let her words sit for a moment longer before asking, "Who runs the operation?"

"I don't know his name," she said, her voice barely above a whisper. "But he reports to some Italian guy. I don't know how old you are, but he seems older than you, maybe? If we don't do what he asks, then we're punished."

Her words came out as vague, but I could see the fear in her eyes. "That's helpful information, Angel. You're doing so well," I said, my voice warm and encouraging. "Can you tell me where this club is?"

" I—I don't want to. I'm already in so much shit if they find out. Look what they did to Addie!" She got louder, the tension rocketing as she spoke.

"I'm sorry. Angel, I know you don't want to, and I know it's more than difficult to talk about, but I need to help her and those other girls. I can't do that without you."

The silence was a dull roar in my ears, but I remained motionless, only stealing a glance at the two-way mirror for unseen encouragement.

Angel buried her face in her hands, locked in an unseen battle. I silently hoped she could push past her anxiety and find the strength to help. But I couldn't force her—not when she was so clearly unraveling, scared out of her mind, and barely holding on. Who wouldn't be?

If experience had taught me anything, it was that patience often yielded more results than pressure ever could.

"It's *Harmonies*," she said. I had to lean in close, the smell of her floral perfume filling my nose. "*Harmonies*."

My blood ran cold, but I remained calm.

"And you say it was a younger man that you dealt with sometimes? Or is he older?"

"Definitely younger. This place, though, you can't just *get* in. You have to know someone."

"Don't worry about that. I only need information, that's it. You don't have to worry about anything beyond that."

Angel scanned the room, noticing the camera hanging on the wall, then the two-way mirror. "Are those on? Is someone watching?"

"No. It's you and me. You'd see a flashing light on the camera if it were."

"Sorry, I'm—freaked out."

"That's understandable, don't be sorry. I need to ask you a few more questions, and then we're done. Do you know where Addie was from?"

"Yeah, Stilwell. In Oklahoma."

I glanced toward the mirror, knowing Perez would already be working to follow up on the lead.

"Angel, is there any way to get a picture of the man or the others at the club?" I asked.

"No," she said quickly. "We're not allowed to have phones. But I have a picture of Addie from before. Before she died."

"Would you send it to me?"

"I can, yeah."

"That would be helpful. Thank you," I said, my heart heavy with the knowledge that her life would be in danger if anyone knew she was working with us. "If you need anything—anything at all—call me. Stay with someone you trust, and refrain from returning to work. Can you promise me that?"

"I have a place I can stay," she said hesitantly. "I'll figure it out."

"Angel, I have to ask one more thing, and I know it's uncomfortable. Do you want us to perform a rape assessment at the hospital? I can go with you."

The minutes on the interview room's old clock ticked by with the unusually slow speed that often accompanied hard questions.

"I—"

"Think about it."

"Do I have to go now? Like *right* now?"

"It would be a good idea to, but if you want to call me tomorrow, there is a small window of time."

"I'll... yeah, just let me think about it."

"OK. Good. Keep your phone with you, at *all* times," I said, clicking the **Stop** button on the recorder and pocketing it once more. I reached across and took her cold, clammy hand in mine. "We're going to take care of this. And again, I'll be here if you need me." I squeezed with as much reassurance as I could.

"Thank you," she whispered, clutching her bag close to her body.

I opened the door for Angel, who trudged out of the room when Jackson passed us in the hall, heading toward forensics. He nodded at me, flashing his friendly signature smile. Angel stopped short; her entire body stiffened, and she snapped her head away from his direction, letting her hair fall to cover her face. After what she'd been through, I couldn't blame her for being wary of men.

"Hey. Are you okay?" I asked softly, steering her down the hallway.

Angel kept glancing back over her shoulder, her face pale. "I know him," she said quietly. "Or, I *think* I do."

CHAPTER 11
Loriah

My mind reeled. The temperature in the hallway plummeted, and the noise of the station dulled in my ears. If an elevator were ever to suddenly drop beneath my feet, I imagine it couldn't have felt worse than that moment.

She had to be mistaken. It was a mistake, right? She's in shock.

"Where do you think you know him from?" I asked, forcing my face to remain indifferent despite the absolute fucking chaos waging war in my head.

Angel's gaze was steady. "From the club. I swear I've seen him before."

"Doing what? He's a cop, so maybe he was running security?"

Her slitted eyes said it all: Lady, you don't actually know how this city works, do you?

My cheeks burned with embarrassment, but I wasn't ready to accept what she was implying.

"I saw him talking to another man," she said. "Only once, *maybe* twice. He wasn't in uniform, though. No, I'm positive it was him. They were arguing. And the one guy had something in his hand he kept waving around." She seemed confused on that part, but continued, "I couldn't see what it was, though."

"What did the other man look like? Did you catch a name?"

Her brow furrowed. "No name. He wasn't as tall as him—older, maybe, like my dad's age—with brown hair, and he wore a suit." Angel shook her head. "That's all I remember, sorry."

"It's okay," I said gently, trying to mask my growing unease. "I'll look into it."

She nodded. "Okay, you'll call me if you hear anything, right?"

"Of course, I will. Try to lie low and stay safe. But think on what I asked. It might be important if we can get something."

Out of you. The thought came unbidden, and I shoved it aside, knowing that I was hoping on a wish and a dream that we could gather anything substantial enough to convict the well-to-do city elites frequented that place.

"I will." She shuffled away, exiting into the late morning light without a backward glance.

I drifted to the elevator on a cloud of confusion—my thoughts in a haze of doubt—and pulled out the card Baldini had handed me days earlier. I was running my fingers over the raised lettering as the doors slid open, interrupting me with a ding. Perez froze when he saw me.

"Hey," he said, his brows knitting. "You okay?"

"Yeah." I swallowed hard and quickly placed the small card in my pocket. "Perez, I need to talk to you later. Can we talk privately? Preferably with a stiff drink?"

His face relaxed, and he nodded. "Sure. I know a place around the corner. I've got something to share too—it's nothing bad, so don't look like that, okay?"

"Like what?"

"Like your sky is falling. It'll be fine there, Chicken Little."

The normality of his teasing me dulled my growing anxiety a little.

"I really dislike you."

A smile tugged at the corner of his mouth. "You're lucky you're not Pinocchio with all those lies you tell yourself."

By the time I'd reached my desk to kick off my shoes and pull open my computer, I knew what I had to do. I fired off an email to Baldini requesting a meeting at the station. The reply arrived almost instantly, surprising me. It was a polite but pointed refusal. A heavy sigh of disappointment escaped my lips at his words, but I was willing to push to get what I wanted.

To: Loriah.Fairsbane@ny.pd.gov
From: Francesco.Baldini@Harmoniesclub.net

Detective Fairsbane,

I would prefer to meet you in my office. I don't see a reason to come to the station without my lawyer—you understand, I'm sure. However, I'd be happy to invite you to my restaurant in Greenwich for a more cordial conversation. Let's say Friday at 6:30? Please, come alone. That partner of yours can be somewhat over-bearing.

Saluti,

Francesco

Staring at the screen, I debated my response. Should I insist on a formal summons, or should I go along with it? Baldini *had* given us the videos, after all. Would someone guilty cooperate like that? Still, why not report the crime as soon as possible? All the jumble of what-ifs and maybes had me ready to throw my keyboard.

Finally, I replied:

To: Francesco.Baldini@Harmoniesclub.net

From: Loriah.Fairsbane@ny.pd.gov

Mr. Baldini,

That would be great. I hope you'll manage to keep things professional and answer my questions like a gentleman. Otherwise, our friend the judge might have to get involved.

Regards,

Det. L. Fairsbane, shield #9217

The rest of the day passed uneventfully. When I called Perez's desk, he didn't answer. A few minutes later, though, my office phone rang, and I held the receiver to my ear. An all-too-familiar voice purred down the line.

"Why don't you come to my office? Save us both some trouble." Then he hung up.

Rude.

I grabbed my notebook and walked the short distance to his office, shutting the door behind me with a little more force than usual. "Tell me what you know," I said, skipping the pleasantries.

"Well, hello to you too," Perez replied, leaning back in his chair with a crooked grin. "Such a warm greeting."

"Get on with it, Perez. *Please?*"

That earned me a chuckle. "Fine. Pathology says they drew a blood sample the night our Jane Doe came in, but it went missing sometime last week."

I frowned. "And *no one* finds that strange?"

"Not really. Happens more often than you'd like to think."

"Great. So, can we get more samples? Is that a thing?"

"They're working on it. Should have new results in one to three weeks."

"One to *three* weeks? That's ridiculous!"

"That's how it goes, Fairsbane. You're lucky we could even *get* another sample. They'll try to expedite it for the case, but don't get your hopes up."

I pinched the bridge of my nose, frustration mounting. The whole day was threatening to consume any remaining patience I had. "What about Stilwell? Did you call?"

Perez nodded. "He's looking into it now. I'll forward you his info."

"Thanks. Maybe Addie knew our Jane Doe. Seems like these guys are preying on small-town girls. Especially since *adult* is a verry loose interpretation of her age."

Perez reclined in his seat, running his hand across his chin. "I agree. Do you think Baldini's club is connected?"

"Honestly?" I asked, observing his face, feeling like he had read my mind.

He hesitated, then shook his head. "No. Not Baldini Senior anyway. He's sleazy, sure, but he's always been upfront about his business. And trust me, we've tried to pin things on him for years."

"What about his son?"

Perez's jaw tightened. "Different story. He's a wildcard and enjoys rubbing shoulders with the higher-ups in the city. He's been here a few times for fighting or roughing up girls, but the charges never stick."

"Think we can get him in for questioning?"

"Who? Dante, the son?"

"Yeah."

"We can try, but he's slippery and confrontational." Perez jotted down Dante's contact on a slip of paper and passed it to me. "Maybe you'd have better luck."

"Noted. I'll get us prepped for briefing with what we have then," I said, tucking the information into my pocket. "Thanks."

I turned to leave, but his voice stopped me. "Fairsbane."

"Yeah?" I asked, glancing back.

"I should have told you sooner: Good work."

I only smiled and pushed a strand of hair behind my ear before walking back to my own office.

Dante Baldini's number burned a hole in my jeans, like money to an eleven-year-old. I'd have to meet with the elder

Baldini first to see what my next move would be. Friday loomed in the back of my mind, and I couldn't help the feeling it would be anything but pleasant.

CHAPTER 12
Loriah

Paperwork was the absolute bane of my existence, something those flashy cop shows never prepared you for. Investigations weren't all car chases and dramatic interrogations. No, they were mountains of repetitive, mind-numbing, itty-bitty details that never seemed to end. Strangers, whom you prayed not to let down, counted on you. Somehow, no matter how long I did it, I didn't think I'd ever become okay with it all. The passage of time would have to become my salve to ease the burn of life.

A knock on my door pulled me out of my thoughts. Perez leaned against the frame, arms crossed nonchalantly. One hand ran along the scruff on his face.

"Are you ready?" he asked.

I glanced past him and noticed the cubicles, nearly empty, and the lights had gone out due to the lack of office movement.

"Shit, sorry, I didn't realize how late it was. Let me grab my stuff."

We headed out together, Perez strolling with the kind of effortless stride only someone his height could pull off.

"Is this place close?" I asked. The last thing I wanted was an epic trek across the city. Because epic and daunting were what it felt like with the shoes I had chosen to wear.

"Not far," he said as we stepped into the elevator. "Don't complain, Fairsbane, it's a nice evening."

He wasn't wrong. The cool breeze was refreshing, though I regretted not having my coat for the second time that day. I shoved my hands into my pockets for warmth, trying not to shiver.

"Did you get anything else from Woods's computer?" I asked.

"Not yet. His wife's supposed to send me a picture of his password book tonight. If she does, I'll start working to crack it tomorrow."

"That's great," I said, feeling a flicker of hope. "I don't know. I have this feeling, like if we crack it, we might finally get somewhere."

"Maybe." He paused mid-stride and slid his coat off his shoulders.

"What are you doing?" I narrowed my eyes.

"Just take this." He offered it up with one hand. "I swear everyone can hear your teeth clacking like one of those children's wind-up toys."

"You're the worst," I bit out—though there was no real malice behind the words—I turned on my heel and walked at a faster pace. "I am not."

With his long steps, he caught up easily and wrapped his wool coat around me, stopping me in my tracks. The warmth immediately eased my shoulders that had crept up to my ears and blanketed me in the comforting scents of Agustin Perez.

"Stop being stubborn, and just say thank you," he told me, grasping the lapels and staring me in the eyes, mere inches from my face. "Say. It," he growled with more command.

I rolled my eyes. "*Thank you.*"

Suddenly, a burst of laughter at the situation's ridiculousness bubbled out of me, and soon he was laughing along, caught up in the moment. When he released me, we continued walking, a sly smile playing on his face when he shot a sideways look at me.

In those briefest of instances I had a view of the person he was when he wasn't trying to push me away, making me wonder. No, not just wonder, but beg to know what was going through his mind.

Take your chance, Fairsbane! Let the intrusive thoughts win.

"Why do you push me away?"

His steps faltered, and he looked at me, one eyebrow raised.

"I mean—why do you push me away when this is so much easier?"

"I don't push you away."

"Not all the time, maybe. But probably more than you realize. You know I'm not fragile, right? You don't *have* to protect me."

He paused then, running a hand through his hair and turning to pierce me with the full intent of his gaze.

"I want to believe you're not. I think I *know* you're not. But I—I can't lose another..."

"Partner?" I supplied.

"Yes."

"You won't. Lose me." We continued again, the chill air nipping at my face as we walked and dodged more pedestrians in awkward silence. "Can I ask you a question?"

"Do I have a choice?"

"Not really. How did Woods die?" I ventured, keeping my tone light. "No one's told me. You don't have to if you can't."

Perez hesitated, his jaw tightening. We stepped aside to let an older woman pushing a cart laden with bags shuffle past. I began to apologize—cutting myself off when he spoke.

"No. I will. I want to tell you. I've meant to tell you for a while now, I just haven't ever been able to find the right situation," he said, his voice quieter. "If I don't, someone else will, or you'll read it in his file, which, I'm surprised you haven't already, with as nosy as you are."

That earned him a smack to the arm.

"Anyway. The staff found him at the gym where he always swam before work. Sometimes he was late, but he'd always let me know to expect him. Except that morning. Not even a call. I figured he'd overslept or was following up on something for our case. Now, I only wish I had asked more questions or checked in on him more often. He—well, they wrote it off as a suicide."

"I'm so sorry, Perez."

"It's okay. Well, it's not okay. It's been hard to reconcile with. Woods wasn't that type of person. He was there for his family and friends. For me. He'd been having some problems toward the end, but he wouldn't share what it was. I didn't—don't, get it. All I know is that it doesn't make sense."

"Do you think he did it?"

"No. I don't. And you're the first person to ask me that."

"If your gut is telling you something isn't right, then we need to look into it."

"That's not how things work around here. You should know that by now."

"We can try."

"We?"

"I said what I said, Perez."

Coming to a stop, a pub with peeling black paint and a big green sign that read "O'Cannlon's" in bold white letters was visible from across the street. Warm lights and large, worn oak barrels flanked the door. Traditional Irish music spilled out onto the street. The place belonged in a quaint village, not in the middle of New York City's concrete jungle.

"Wow, Perez," I said, raising an eyebrow. "Didn't peg you for the Irish pub type."

"Let's just say, it grows on you," he replied, holding the door open and waiting for me to step inside first. His hand rested on the small of my back, coaxing me into the building. The gesture was so innocuous for the type of shiver it sent down the rest of my body, and the seriousness of the conversation from minutes ago was left to tumble away on the sidewalk.

The warmth inside hit me immediately, along with the scent of wood and whiskey. The pub embraced us with old-world charm: worn wooden beams that had been privy to many an intimate conversation, paneled walls, and cozy cushioned furniture that seemed to exhale stories as we settled in. Tiffany-style chandeliers cast a forgiving glow that softened the coldness I'd felt from the day's events, while a brick fireplace crackled in one corner near a small stage.

A four-person band played lively covers while patrons gathered near the bar and hearth, clinking glasses together in random toasts—amazing me at the humanity of it. How people could be joking and laughing, while for us, only a few hours had passed since we watched one of the worst parts of humanity snuff the life out of a young girl and her unborn child. It all seemed so... *strange*, the vicious circle of life unfolding all around us.

Perez led us to a quiet booth in the back, smiling at the bartender as we passed.

"I'll grab drinks. What'll you have?"

"A Magners cider, if they've got it."

"They'll have it." He reached across the table to grab a couple of coasters and throw them down in front of me. "Be right back. Don't get into trouble," he said with a smirk before disappearing toward the bar.

I rolled my eyes at his back, knowing that was highly unlikely.

No sooner had the thought passed than a man in a leather jacket slid into the seat across from me. Here we go. He wasn't bad-looking—scruffy, with a crooked, infectious grin, and kind brown eyes—but I wasn't exactly in the mood. My obsessive mind was busy moving through what I would say to Perez and the discussion I'd had with Angel.

"Wanna dance? You look like you could use a turn," he asserted, nodding toward the makeshift dance floor where a few couples swayed to the music.

"That's actually pretty far from what I *do* need right now," I replied, laughing a little at his forwardness. "But thank you. I'm waiting for—"

"Me," Perez interrupted, his voice sharp as he appeared, drinks in hand. The man glanced up, his posture stiffening under Perez's looming presence.

"Him," I finished, gesturing toward Perez with a thumb and a smile, hoping to defuse the already awkward tension between them. "Thanks for the offer, though."

Dejected, the man stood and wandered off. Perez watched him go, something predatory in his face before he slid into the seat across from me, setting the cider down with care.

"Look at us," I teased once he looked like he wasn't ready to leap over the booth and chase an innocent man down. "Just two normal people having a drink. It's like we like each other, though I use the word normal loosely," I raised my glass, and to my surprise, he clinked his against mine, eyes softening.

"I've never said I don't like you," he replied evenly before removing his tie and letting loose the top two buttons of his shirt to reveal the edges of tattoos that lined his chest and stopped right at the base of his neck.

The simplicity of his words caught me off guard as much as the casual bit of undress. I took a sip to hide my reaction, my lashes lowering to steal a— very unprofessional—peek at him over the rim of my glass. He wasn't looking at me any longer; instead he was studying the band with interest, giving me an unfettered break to drink him in. I let the pause stretch on till I felt comfortable saying, "Well, you know what they say, actions speak louder than words. Sometimes."

He assessed me, returning his attention to my face before speaking. "That's not always true."

Choosing not to press and feeling a little guilty after he had given me his coat, I shifted the conversation.

"So, how did the meeting with Daniels go?"

"It didn't go poorly, just uncomfortable," he said after a moment, turning his glass between his fingers. "It was a whole misunderstanding. The impound officer's report was accurate. Daniels took the car out to send it to auction. But, get this, police seized it in a drug bust a month earlier, and no one ever claimed it. He drove it to the lot, and from there, someone lifted it."

"So do you think someone targeted the lot, hoping for unclaimed cars to use in the crime?"

"That's exactly what I think. Chief had all the paperwork. Everything was clean. The cameras weren't working, though—a stupid, fucking coincidence."

I nodded, letting that sink in. "What else did he say?"

"Not much. We talked about the case, the lead with Angel. Just basic updates."

I hesitated, swirling my drink as the words that needed to be spoken soured on my tongue and caused my heart to quicken till I wasn't sure I could breathe.

Three things I feel.

The wood grain of the table under my elbows, sweat from my mug between my fingers, Perez's leg where my foot bumps it.

When the room felt like it had air for me to breathe again I continued.

"About Angel. She mentioned something after the interview. I didn't want to bring it up, but—"

"Out with it, Fairsbane," he said, his voice hardening. "You know you can't say that and then stall."

I took a long pull of my cider, summoning courage from a reserve tank that was bordering dangerously on empty.

"She said she saw Jackson at the club," I said in a tumble of words, forcing myself to meet his glowering face. "Before the girl turned up dead. She said he was meeting with someone, arguing with them."

A muscle feathered in his jaw, but he sat, silent as a mime. The only tell that he was agitated and barely keeping himself together was when he ran a hand through his hair before leaning back to pierce me with a look that could freeze lava.

"I'm going to talk to him," I added quickly, my hand betraying my body as it moved toward him, trying to close the gap he had created between us. I grazed my finger tips along his, hoping he would stay calm, so that I could do the same. "Maybe it's a misunderstanding."

"There seems to be a lot of those going around lately," he muttered, taking a long sip of his drink, nearly draining the amber liquid as his throat worked. He slowly pulled his hand away and flexed his fingers before placing his hand down on his thigh.

"Come on." I leaned back to match his frown.

The warmth of the moments we'd shared during our walk—the quiet conversation, the feeling that we were finally closing the distance between us—vanished as easily as mist in the morning sun.

"Come on?" he growled, leaning in closer across the table. He set his glass down with such force that the remaining liquid sloshed a tiny amount of beer over the rim. A patron at the bar glanced toward the commotion, but Perez was too locked in—too consumed—to notice. When he spoke again, his voice was low and threatening, setting me on edge. "We're in a murder investigation, and you think a witness telling you she thinks she saw Jackson at a club where girls get offed at, is what? A nasty little *misunderstanding*?"

"Yes, come on! For all intents and purposes, it appeared Daniels had been using the car that was at a murder scene to meet up with the victim, yet you're allowed to choose to believe his paperwork? Good for me, but not for thee. Is that how it is?"

I couldn't believe the double standard he was applying due to his own prejudices toward Jackson. The sweet taste of my cider was quickly becoming acidic in my mouth. I knew there was a history there, but this was too much; my palms itched with the need to release my own anger.

"What is your issue with him anyway?" I practically spat, the fire now burning through my chest.

Perez mirrored me and crossed his arms as well, refusing to back down. "I don't trust him. And you seem to be getting close to him pretty damn quickly."

"Not as close as you're thinking," I countered, the muscles in my neck tightening. "Plus, it's none of your business."

"Really?" He raised an eyebrow. "Because the night I called you, he was at your place, wasn't he?"

"Yes. He was. He brought me food!" My voice was rising and becoming shriller. The same man at the bar glanced over again, took a sip, and faced forward, probably only seeing a crazed woman with a few too many to drink. I willed my pulse to slow. In through my nose, out through my mouth. Perez didn't move or say anything. Just waited for me to continue. As soon as I thought we'd make headway in whatever little fucked up partnership truce we had, he came burrowing himself right back underneath my skin like a nasty rash. In a very low tone, I said, "You don't like him. I get that. But I've got a handle on it."

We locked eyes, the weight of the unspoken taking up too much space between us.

The band was beginning a lively tune, the crowd erupting into a sing-along, but all I could hear was the charged silence within the tense bubble we'd created.

"And you hear a distant calling, and you know it's meant for you.

Then you drop what you were doing and you join the merry mob.

And before you know, just where you are, you're in an Irish pub!"

The crowd was clapping, stomping, and swaying, their collective joy clashing against the invisible wall of tension between us. Perez leaned back, arms crossed, his light eyes locked on mine. His lips pressed into a hard line as he struggled to contain whatever was clearly running through his mind. He chose to bottle it, shutting me out like all the other times and expecting I'd move on happily.

"Are you going to keep staring at me then, or are we done here?" I asked, my voice sharper than I intended, cutting off the last thread of whatever connection we'd shared earlier.

"Loriah–"

"Don't," I cut him off. "Don't call me by my first name like we're friends unless you're going to tell me why you care so much."

Before he could reply, the man from earlier reappeared, his leather jacket gone and his grin even broader. The timing couldn't have been worse—or perhaps better, depending.

"How about that dance now?" he asked, holding out a hand.

I glanced at Perez, whose posture shifted instantly. He moved and draped his arm casually along the back of the booth, but the drumming of his fingers betrayed his irritation. "Look, pal," he said, his tone cutting, "she's not interested."

"Maybe she can speak for herself," the man shot back, unfazed and oblivious to the hornet's nest he was about to kick. "What do you say?" His outstretched hand hovered closer.

Perez stood then, uncoiling like a spring, shrugging off his suit jacket in one fluid motion. The sleeves of his shirt had been rolled up, revealing tattoos that snaked up his forearms, visible in the low light. He wasn't much taller than the man, but his presence filled the space, radiating a barely controlled threat.

"Would you like to dance with me?" Perez asked, voice like a low growl.

Oh, for God's sake.

The man faltered, his confidence flickering as he glanced between us. "Are you her keeper?" he asked.

"No," I said, standing abruptly, having had enough of Agustin's attempt to control me. "He just thinks he is."

I placed my hand in the stranger's, a decision fueled purely by defiance and cider. His warm fingers closed around mine. "I can decide who I want to dance with."

A hand shot out to catch me around the wrist, letting a thumb stroke over the soft inside of my arm, once, twice. "Don't be foolish," Perez warned, his voice tight with something that might've been concern, but I ignored him. My patience with his cryptic moods had run out.

I jerked my hand away from him and was led to the small dance floor, my hand clasped in the stranger's, to join the throng of swaying bodies—music enveloping us. Nick, as I learned he was named, spun me once, and despite my irritation, I laughed. His carefree confidence was a welcome distraction, even if it felt a bit forced on my part. I had turned in time to see Perez throwing daggers with his eyes when he downed the rest of his drink in one swallow, stood, and stalked out the door of the pub, leaving his jacket behind like a silent promise he'd return.

After a few songs and two quick shots of something intense and vaguely fruity, the warmth in my belly was undeniable. It didn't take much to dull the harshness of the last hour and relax my body.

"I want some air," I told him when my hair was starting to stick to my neck, and the band was winding down for a break. "Let me grab my friend's coat. I think he forgot it."

"Some *friend*," he commented. But I chose to ignore it.

Nick pulled a pack of cigarettes from his jacket and lit one, passing it to me. I accepted it, taking a slow drag and watching the smoke curl into the crisp night and float away on the breeze. The sharp bite of tobacco momentarily cleared my head, and my mind wandered to how I had left things with my *partner*.

That's when I saw him.

Perez leaned against the wall about ten feet away, half-hidden in shadow, his hands tucked into his trouser pockets. His eyes locked on mine—a brooding, immovable shadow in the night.

I sighed, handing the cigarette back to Nick. "Give me a minute."

Nick raised an eyebrow, but didn't object as I walked toward Perez, his gaze tracking every movement as I approached.

"Loriah," he said as I got closer to him, voice low and apologetic. I wrapped his coat tighter around my shoulders. "I'm sorry."

"Really?" I retorted, feeling my frustration bubble back to the surface as I faced him directly. "We're not friends, Perez. We're just two people hired to work together." My words were sharper than I intended, causing him to flinch before he regained his composure.

"I can care about what happens to you." His eyes cut behind me, catching on something.

"Everything okay here?" Nick placed his hand lightly on my back. The strain between the two men was so thick you could taste it.

"Of course it's okay," Perez said, his words laced with venom. "Why don't you get lost?"

Nick didn't move, though. Either from too many drinks or sheer stupidity, I couldn't tell. "She doesn't seem like she wants to leave with you tonight. Tough luck, huh?"

I groaned inwardly. *Stupidity it is.*

Perez straightened, thrusting his suit jacket into my arms, which I scrambled to grab onto. The streetlight caught the discolored knuckles, still bruised from the last time he got into a fight—over me, no less.

"Excuse me?" he challenged, stepping closer to Nick, who held his ground.

Nick smirked, flicking his cigarette butt toward Perez's feet. "I'll repeat it, she doesn't want you, buddy. Maybe take a *fuckin'* hint."

Shit.

He'd chosen the worst words a man in his position could have. And like an oracle, I knew what was coming before it ever came. Perez's fist connected with Nick's self-assured face in a blur of motion, sending him stumbling back, curses flying. Blood trickled from Nick's nose as he recovered, his expression twisting into one of confusion, then fury.

"Perez, stop!"

But he didn't seem to hear me.

Nick rushed forward like a linebacker, and Perez pulled his arm back, ready to swing again. But instead of hitting Nick, his elbow glanced off me as I attempted to step between them. The blow that caught my temple was sudden and forceful. Pain exploded in my head, bright lights pulsing behind my eyelids as I staggered back, barely catching myself.

Someone from the growing crowd announced frantically, "I'm calling the police!"

I turned, flashing my badge, and coughing out. "It's okay. We *are* the police," I managed. "Please, go back inside. Everything's alright."

The group hesitated before dispersing, their curiosity waning now that things had escalated too far, and the band had picked up again, catching more attention.

Perez froze, shifting his gaze from fury to horror, realizing what he'd done. "Loriah," he said, voice raw as he reached toward me, but he stopped short, hand suspended in the air between us.

Nick was picking himself up, his glare shifting between Perez and me. "Are you leaving with him?" he asked incredulously, wiping at the blood on his face.

"I'm going home," I snapped. "Alone!"

I turned on my heel and began walking, my head throbbing with each step, and my vision narrowing at the edges. I wasn't okay, but I refused to let either of them see that. I fumbled with my phone through the building nausea of pain.

Perez followed me, his footsteps echoing close behind.

"Go *home*, Perez!" I shouted at him.

"Absolutely not, Loriah Fairsbane." I could tell by his tone that not all the fight had left him yet.

When my Uber arrived, he climbed in after me without a word. I didn't have the strength to argue anymore. His long legs took up more space than necessary, his large body angled toward mine in silent defiance of my attempts to create distance.

"You didn't need to come," I muttered, leaning against the cool window, seeking relief for my throbbing head.

"I did," he said quietly. "Plus. You have my jacket."

He thinks now is the appropriate time for a joke?

"You're lucky I don't throw it out the fucking window!"

The rest of the ride passed in tense silence, broken only by the hum of the city outside and my occasional sharp gasp when the car hit a pothole. When we reached my building, he trailed behind me up the four flights after paying the taxi, occasionally placing a hand on my back when I'd stall on the steps in pain.

"Please, Agustin, you've done enough."

I paused in front of my door and tried to collect myself, though my hands shook and tears threatened to spill and give me away.

Ever so slowly, Perez took the key, his warm hand brushing against mine. He unlocked the door and held it open, expectant.

"Don't make me carry you in," he said in a gentle tone that was so at odds with his threat.

I hesitated but stepped inside, knowing he wouldn't leave until he was sure I was okay. The door shut behind us with a quiet click.

Loriah Fairsbane. What the hell are you doing?

CHAPTER 13
Perez

I knew I shouldn't be intruding on her space, knew I was only being reckless and desperate. That silly, perpetually optimistic, sassy woman had me rethinking all I knew to be true about myself and the world. She consumed every spare thought I had, like it was her personal fucking job.

But hell! Her beautiful, freckled face had the hint of a bump, a bruise taking form. One that *I*, of all people, had put there. I felt so worthless. She didn't look at me, she didn't even invite me in. I had coerced her in the only way I knew how, with a threat.

I stayed in the doorway, taking everything in for a moment, trying to calm my beating heart. Her apartment wrapped itself around me, small and cozy in a way that could only be hers. Still, half-packed boxes whispered she hadn't quite settled. Oriental rugs spread warmth across the floor. A well-loved leather couch faced a planked coffee table ringed with the memory of mugs, and stacks of book tethered precariously.

The shelves lining one wall sagged under the weight of novels. Warm Christmas lights hung loosely across the walls, their soft glow lending the room a dreamlike intimacy. It was too much, too personal. I didn't want to know this part of her—it made things so much harder.

Loriah walked toward her small open kitchen and stood at the counter, staring at the ground and clutching my coat to her face. She looked like anything I'd ever wanted, and knew I couldn't have even with a bruise blooming on her creamy skin.

I walked tentatively to her, not wanting to startle or anger her, but even if she did, I would drink it like a dying man and thank her for it, knowing that it was all that I deserved.

"Agustin," she said softly, her voice barely above a whisper.

She had never used my name before; instead, she always chose to call me by my last name, Perez. Hearing her say it like that, though, it sent a low, dangerous heat through me. Thoughts of me having her cry or moan it out in release flooded my senses. I fought the urge to let it show, but I couldn't stop myself from taking a step closer, absorbing the space between us like I'd been beckoned by one of Homer's sirens that called to Odysseus.

Tentatively, I reached out, brushing aside a stray strand of her auburn-red hair to assess the damage. She flinched but didn't pull away, shoulders relaxing slightly.

Her hand moved to her cheek and as she did so, her hand brushed mine.

"It's not that bad," she said, trying for lightness but falling short as she moved her face away from me.

Catching her chin between two fingers, I tilted her face toward me. "I *am* sorry." My thumb brushed along her jaw reflexively. The faint contact sent a jolt through me, so intense it felt like I might burn from it. "Do you have ice?"

She gestured to the fridge behind her, but didn't break our gaze. "Freezer," she murmured. "And you were a real dick head, you know that?"

"I do know," I said, stepping behind her to grab a dish towel and filling it with ice. By the time she turned to protest my help, I was already pressing the makeshift ice pack to her cheek, holding it carefully so as not to hurt her further.

"I've got it," she said, reaching up to take over, but her hand rested lightly atop mine. Her touch was searing, and I realized how close we'd moved—her scent, something fresh and citrusy, enveloping me.

She smelled like... *home*. My heart stuttered for the briefest of moments.

We stood there, frozen in that moment, big blue eyes locked on mine. It could have been seconds. Hours. I didn't care.

"Why?" she asked finally. One word, but it carried the weight of a thousand questions.

Why had I come? Why had I hurt her? Why was I standing in her apartment, unable to walk away like a God damned idiot?

I swallowed hard, unsure how to answer, and defaulted to what I did best. "Because I needed to make sure you were okay."

"You know that's not what I mean."

"What do you want, Fairsbane?" My voice was harsher than I intended, but I couldn't stop myself. "I can't take it back. If I could, I would."

"I want you to stop keeping me at arm's length with the only rules being the ones you make for us! We can be friends—we can be partners—you're the one saying we can't be both. You make it seem like neither of those things is possible. One second, we're fine, the next–" Her voice cracked, and the hurt in her eyes twisted something deep inside me. "I know you're afraid or maybe apprehensive to let me in. But what's the worst that comes from it?"

I stepped closer without thinking, and she instinctively backed into the fridge. "I told you—but, look what happens when we try to be friends. Tonight is a perfect fucking example. One asshole and I'm throwing punches, then hitting you. You have every reason to hate me and yet. Here you are..."

"I couldn't hate you. Agustin—"

I didn't let her finish.

The second time she'd used my name—*my* given name. Not "Perez," not "Detective," not the barricade of formality *I'd* imposed between us. My name in her mouth was a key turning in a lock I didn't think could anymore. I went still, then like a tide breaking through a seawall I allowed my fingers to find her and cup her face in my hands. Her eyes went wide before she relaxed into my palm

"If you tell me right now to leave, I promise you, Loriah." My voice dropped to a tone barely recognizable as human, each word deliberate and heavy with what I struggled to express. "I promise you, I will walk out of your home and never touch you again." I hesitated, overwhelmed by the pain of considering walking away without at least touching her one last time. The thought felt like it might drive me to the brink of madness, but I knew I had to do it. I owed her that respect. "If you can't say that one word–"

My eyes searched hers wildly from left to right, silently pleading for her to push me away for her own good. To save herself from me and all my bullshit.

No reply came, and her lips parted silently, expectantly. All rational thought dissolved like ice.

Before I could stop myself, my hand slid behind her neck, twining my fingers in the soft curls at her nape. She made a sound—half surprise, half something needier—and I pulled her toward me, my hand wrapped around her waist.

My lips crashed against hers with all the intensity I'd been holding back. There was nothing gentle about it—nothing restrained. It was fierce, raw, and consuming. Testing us both, pushing our boundaries to breaking points I couldn't see but could *feel* approaching.

And to my surprise—my goddamned shock—she kissed me back with as much strength. Her hands found their purchase in my hair, nails scraping my scalp as her body pressed firmly against mine. Her curves fit against me like she was made for it, like we'd done this a thousand times in another life.

I knew at that moment I was like a man truly lost at sea with no desire ever to plant my feet on solid ground again.

She let her hands roam over me, leaving trails of need in her wake. They skimmed down my arms before playing dangerously close to the buttons at the bottom of my shirt, then returning to undo them. Pushing the material back, she ran her delicate fingers over my bare chest, sending sparks of need through me as I felt her hands explore. My body melted into the press and sounds of her. Her lips tasted like the best thing I had experienced in years.

I had to stop. If I didn't pull away, I knew there'd be no going back. And this was going to hurt. As quickly as it began, I pulled away, breathing heavy and instantly filling every crevice of my empty heart with regret.

"I– I can't do this," I said, stepping back, though every fiber of me screamed not to. My hands lingered on her hips, digging into them before I forced them to drop, shaking from the will it took not to grab her again and pull her into me. "I'm sorry. I shouldn't have—"

Her features crumpled—hurt, and confusion washed over her. The sight of it was too much to bear. My pulse roared in my ears.

"And now you're a liar?" she asked, her voice small and uncertain.

She raised her walls again, pulling the drawbridge tight around her fortress. I caught it in her stance, arms folding into armor. I'd made things worse, thrusting us into something even *more* complicated. I played with her emotions. And for that, I was the monster she thought I was.

"But–"

"I need to know you'll be okay." As much as I wanted to, I couldn't keep the desperation from pouring its way into my words.

"You only need to, to ease your conscience, Perez. You're no better than anyone else."

I'm worse.

"I'm sorry," I told her once again as I moved toward the door to put my jacket back on and grab my coat. The thought of smelling her on it while I traveled home nearly brought me to my knees.

"You keep saying that." She walked to the couch, covered herself in a blanket, and took a sip of a beer she'd grabbed from the small fridge before holding it to her face. "You can go now, Perez."

When I didn't leave immediately, she shouted, "Just go!"

For the second time that night, she was shouting at me to leave her, and for the second time, I knew in my soul I would be making a massive mistake by doing what she asked. I moved to the door, stealing one last glimpse before stepping out.

As I closed the door behind me, one thought echoed in my mind: I wished like hell I could be the man she needed.

But if she knew the truth of who I was, she'd never want me anyway. And that might be the cruelest gift of all.

CHAPTER 14

Loriah

What. The. Fuck. Just happened?

The day's events crashed over me like a rogue wave, taking all the breath I had left in my lungs when he shut the door behind him. After a long, scalding shower, I dragged my emotionally wrecked body into bed, pulling the blankets tight against the sting of my own thoughts.

His scent lingered in the air, mixing with the phantom taste of him on my lips. Closing my eyes, I could feel the warmth of his rough hand on my neck, the unyielding press of his body against mine. His chest had been heaving, muscles taut, as if the effort to restrain himself was the greatest pain. I knew he had been equally as affected, but he was the only one willing to lie first to himself, then to me, about what happened.

We'd gone too far. The only explanation I could come up with was adrenaline and alcohol—a combined heady rush that had warped my judgment. But the spark of pleading in his eyes cut me. It confused me, and that made me angrier.

Thinking of him as anything other than my closed-off, infuriating partner wasn't going to be an option. He'd made that abundantly clear when he pulled away and left. I tried to shove it all out of my head, but it clung to every thread of thought.

When the early light of dawn finally seeped through my window, casting a soft blue haze over the room, I succumbed to a restless, heavy sleep.

And I dreamt of him.

Buzz-buzz. Buzz-buzz. Buzz-buzz.

The unrelenting noise pulled me into consciousness, and I groggily reached for my phone, confident I'd already silenced the alarm. Twice. It wasn't my alarm, though. It was the ringer.

"Hello? Fairsbane," I answered, my voice scratchy with sleep.

"Where are you?"

"Who is this?"

"It's Christian. Loriah, do you know what time it is?"

Shit. My pulse spiked as I sat up, fumbling for the clock—8:27 *AM*. I hadn't set an alarm after last night's whirlwind of emotions.

"I'm getting up now. I'll be there in thirty," I said in a rush, throwing the covers off. "Can you tell Perez I'll be there soon?"

"Perez isn't here either." He spoke in a clipped tone, and I could hear an edge that hinted he wanted to ask something. After a pause, he added, "I can call him if you'd like."

"Yes, please. And forward any calls to my cell in the meantime. We had some things we were waiting on, right?"

"Yeah, a few. But I got it. See you soon." The line went dead.

Why wasn't Perez at work?

A small, unwelcome thought crept in—maybe he'd spent the night with someone in a way that I couldn't. Not that it was any of my business. Still, the jealous idea pricked at me. Shaking it off, I pulled myself together.

Where the hell was my hairbrush?

In twenty minutes, I was out the door, the suit from my first day steamed and looking near perfect, my hair left loose, makeup doing its best to hide the nasty bruise near my cheek.

I locked my door and spun around, nearly colliding with Allie.

"Hey! Late night?" she asked, scrutinizing me.

"Oh, yeah. Work stuff."

"You sure about that?" She leered with a twinkle in her eye, and I braced myself for more questions.

"Yeah, nothing exciting. Just work." Reliving *that* kiss was the last thing I had time for. She'd keep me there for hours getting every detail out of me like she was bleeding a turnip.

"If you say so. But you're a terrible liar." She let it drop with a shrug before immediately brightening. "Hey, there's a ballet class this weekend. We've got a couple of spots left, and I remember you saying you wanted to get back into it."

She wasn't wrong. I missed moving my body for the sake of joy rather than running on sheer survival.

"That actually sounds like a lot of fun. I'll have to dig out some clothes, though."

"Wear anything; it's casual, Lor. You're not auditioning for Juilliard."

We both laughed, and the tension eased.

"Okay, Saturday morning, 9 AM, with coffee in hand," she said, clapping her hands like she'd won a prize.

"It's a deal."

We parted ways at the bottom of the stairs—she to the subway, me into a cab.

"Fairsbane!" Jackson called out as I stepped into the office, a steaming coffee in his hand. He walked toward me at a near jog, clearly trying not to spill it, and thrust it into my empty palm before ushering me into my office. "Here, take mine, you'll need it."

"Thanks," I told him, confused, and took a seat.

"I can't get a hold of Perez," he said, shutting the door. "His phone's off or out of range. IT cracked something on Woods's computer last night, and they need to brief him. I figured you'd want to know."

"Perfect. I'll handle it for now. Thanks." I set the coffee down but didn't sit. "Jackson, I need to talk to you about something. And I need you to be straight with me."

He blinked, surprised, and moved to sit across from me. "Sure. What is it?"

"The girl who came in yesterday? She said she recognized you. How does a suspect who works in a club running underage girls know you?" My words came out sharper than I'd intended, but I didn't backtrack.

Jackson's face froze for a second before he shook his head. "I don't know. I don't go to clubs like that, Loriah. I told you. The one I took you to, sure, but not *that* kind of place. I don't mess around with underage girls—I prefer my women well past drinking age." He laughed nervously but met my eyes.

"She was certain, Jackson. Respect me enough to tell the truth."

He pinched the bridge of his nose. "Listen, it's complicated."

"For fuck's sake, Christian," I snapped, nearly spilling coffee in my frustration.

"I was there for Woods," he admitted finally, his words settling between us.

"Woods?" My heart kicked up a notch.

"Yes. I overheard him having strange conversations, so I followed him to *Harmonies* one night. I saw him go into that club. Maybe that's how Angel saw me—I wasn't hiding, just waiting. And then I confronted him outside."

"What night?" I asked, narrowing my eyes.

"The night after the murder. A Saturday maybe? I don't remember."

"You realize that could put you on the Baldini's cameras, right? This won't look good for you if someone puts two and two together. What the *hell* were you thinking?"

"I know. I *know*," he said, exhaling hard and sitting back, his leg restlessly thumping up and down. "But I didn't do anything. I needed to see what he was into. He'd been acting off."

"And?"

"And nothing. He denied it. I didn't have proof, so I backed off. But I swear, Loriah, I didn't *do* anything wrong."

I stared at him, searching for cracks in his story. "You'd better hope to hell the cameras can verify that."

"They *will*."

Jackson shifted in his chair, leaning forward slightly, his usual confident demeanor softening, and his voice becoming quieter. "I don't want this to mess up—whatever this is that we've got going on."

"What do you mean?" I asked, taken aback by the vulnerability in his tone.

"I like spending time with you, Loriah. I mean, we've been good, right?" I watched as he opened himself to me as he continued, "I'd hate for this misunderstanding to make things weird. I didn't do anything wrong, Loriah, and I'd like to take you out again. *Properly* this time. No work stuff hanging over our heads." His gaze locked on mine, earnest and unwavering.

I hesitated. Jackson *had* been good to me—better than good with the kindness and attentiveness he'd shown over the weeks. And his presence brought a calm steadiness that I hadn't expected to want so much. Angel's reaction when she saw him, though, was undeniable and nagged at me.

"Christian, I–"

"Just think about it," he said quickly, cutting me off before I could decide. "I'll make it a great night. No case talk, no work. Just us. Saturday?"

I sighed, weighing his words. "Maybe. Let me see how the week goes. I feel like I'm drowning right now, trying to keep my head above water with all these follow-ups and paperwork."

He nodded, a small smile tugging at his lips. "Okay. But I'm holding you to that '*maybe*.'"

As he stood to leave, he paused in the doorway, glancing back at me with a mixture of hope and apprehension. "We're good together. I don't want to lose that."

He was right—we were. And I hated that even the tiniest bit of doubt scratched at the back of my mind as I grew even closer to him. I returned his tentative smile, unsure of what else to say, and watched him walk away.

CHAPTER 15
Loriah

Perez waltzed into the precinct around noon, appearing worse for wear but carrying himself with that self-assured stride—completely ready to tackle the day. His hand bore fresh scrapes, a split lip, and evidence of another fight. Despite the frustration bubbling, a twisted part of me felt some relief—at least he hadn't been out trying to erase the memory of me by slipping into just any willing body. Not that I had the right to judge.

As soon as he shut his office door behind him, I made my move by quickly creeping inside and closing it firmly behind me. No "good morning" or "hello".

"What the hell, Agustin?" I marched closer, trying to get a better look at his face.

"Don't call me that."

"Fine." I snorted. "Detective Perez, then. Why are you showing up late, looking like you took on a bear single-handedly?"

"It's none of your business, Fairsbane," he replied in a clipped tone, but his eyes betrayed a flicker of something. Regret, maybe?

"Actually, it is my business," I snapped. "We're partners, remember?"

He sighed and finally met my gaze. I caught a glimpse of shame there, fleeting but unmistakable. "I'm fine," he said. "Seriously. Just something I had to handle. How's *your* face?"

"It's *fine*," I said, echoing his own words. "I mean, compared to you, I got off easy. Just took an elbow from a giant ogre, cosplaying as a detective."

"That sounds about right." His lips quirked up in what could have been the barest hint of a smile, but it was gone in an instant, replaced with a sadness that reflected in his green eyes. "Have you gotten anything done today, or were you waiting around for me to show up?"

"Actually, yes." I narrowed my eyes, but I let his comment slide, knowing this was easier. My hand rose to skim my lips as a memory rose unbidden.

"So..." he said, snapping me back to attention.

"Right." I folded my hands behind me. "IT talked to Jackson this morning. She said she unlocked something on Woods's computer hard drive."

His brows lifted slightly. "Have you seen it yet?"

"No. Lana wanted to show it to *you* first. She's making copies for us, though. Did you ever get hold of Woods's phone? She didn't mention that."

"No. His phone wasn't at the scene."

"Maybe it was at his home," I suggested. "Want to check with her today, or put it off until tomorrow?"

"I'll handle it today. Let's go see what's on that hard drive first."

The IT room was chilly, as always, but I'd come prepared with a coat. Perez, of course, looked perfectly comfortable in a dark, fitted suit—his perpetual armor. I tried to focus on the case and not the way his presence lingered like a ghost in the corner of my mind, his cologne swirling and settling into my marrow.

Focus, Loriah.

A short, cheerful woman with blonde hair in a bouncing ponytail greeted us at the door. "Hi! I'm Lana. I don't think we've met yet. Come on in—I'll show you what we've got." Her energy was a surprising contrast to the usual solemnity of her department.

She led us to a desk where she pulled up a mountain of data: financial records in indecipherable codes, shipping manifests, emails, and photos. *So. Many. Photos.* And, of course, all in their own strangely labeled folders.

"This is a bit overwhelming," I murmured, glancing at Perez. "Was this all related to y'all's cases?"

He stared at the screen, a blank expression on his face. "That's years' worth of files," he said.

Lana closed the laptop and handed it to Perez. "I've narrowed it down to the last couple of years to try and make it easier. Some photos might match faces from the night of the murder's footage. However, you'll need to comb through everything carefully—it's going to take time. Let me know if you need more help."

"Thanks, Lana," I said, grateful for her thoroughness. "You've been fantastic. We owe you some bagels or something."

She grinned. "I'll never say no to that." She winked and turned back to her work as we left.

At 1:30 PM, I walked back to Perez's office and found him deep in concentration. His hair was slightly disheveled, his hands clearly having combed through it as he stared intently at his laptop.

"Anything interesting?" I asked, startling him out of his focus.

Frowning at me, he quickly caught himself, and tried to smooth his hair back down.

"These manifests," he said, sitting back and scratching at his unshaven chin. "They're clearly codes for something, mostly small quantities, but huge sums of money are attached. Whatever it was must have been incredibly valuable. I cross-referenced his financials, and Woods had an account worth $6.2 million."

My stomach dropped.

"Excuse me?"

"You heard correctly."

"A New York cop with that kind of money? That's not normal. You think it's tied to the missing girls?"

"I'd bet on it," he replied, rubbing his temple. "But I haven't connected all the dots yet."

I took a moment to absorb that before switching gears. "Do you know who the best forgers are in the city?"

His brow furrowed, but he continued to stare at the endless pages of accounting. "Why? Checks not cashing?"

"Funny," I deadpanned. "It's about Angel. She must have obtained a fake ID to fly here. It had to be pretty good to get past the TSA, and I keep thinking it's a lead."

He nodded, typing away on his computer. The printer whirred to life, and soon he was placing a warm sheet of paper into my hand, fingers carefully avoiding mine.

"We compiled this list a few months back. It's not exhaustive, but it *might* help." He hesitated, and I could feel him watching me as I scanned the list, gauging my reaction. "Do you want me to go with you?"

"No," I blurted. Though it perhaps came out too abruptly. The confined space of Perez's office already felt charged with things unsaid between us. Every nerve in my body was on alert to his proximity. I could imagine all the ways he'd try to explain how kissing me was a terrible lapse in judgment. Thus, Perez would effectively crush my self-esteem into oblivion.

Not a fucking chance.

"You stay here and keep working. I've got this." I turned to leave, eager to escape the confusing heat of his gaze that threatened to pull me back like gravity.

"Loriah," he said softly, stopping me in my tracks.

His voice was low and calm, holding none of the usual command. My hand froze on the doorknob. The seriousness of *my* name on his tongue had me waiting for what I knew was coming next. And I wanted to run from the regret, from the pity, that made up those two tiny words—*I'm sorry*.

"Perez," I cut him off, gripping the door handle, not daring to turn around or giving him a chance to say what I knew would confuse and potentially hurt me further. "Please, Perez. Just. Don't."

I stepped into the hallway, closing the door with deliberate softness behind me, releasing a breath I'd been holding for what felt like days.

Three steps later, the small crack that thumped in my heart mirrored the sound of a fist hitting a desk.

CHAPTER 16
Loriah

I picked the closest address on the list, hoping it would prove promising, and checked out a car from the precinct. It smelled faintly of cigarettes, greasy fast food, and cheap coffee—the holy trinity of long police shifts.

The third stop on my hunt was a laundromat nestled between brick buildings that had clearly been there for decades. Soap residue streaked the storefront windows, and the smell of chemicals and starch hung in the air like the whole place had its own caustic atmosphere. The fumes made my eyes water as I stepped inside, and the bell above the door announced my presence with a cheerful jingle that felt jarringly out of place. A small plastic cat sat on the counter, waving its little paw, while a radio crackled from the back.

I rang the bell and waited.

"Hello? Dropping off or picking up?" A small Asian woman in an apron appeared, her voice sweet and practiced.

"Actually, I'm here for something else. Maybe you can help me?" I stepped closer, watching her posture change. "If I wanted to get an ID made for, let's say, a friend. *Hypothetically* of course, do you know where I could do that?"

Her demeanor shifted instantly, smile thinning and eyes growing wary. "We only do laundry here."

"Angela Lu," I said, keeping my voice calm but firm as I pulled back my jacket to discreetly flash her my badge. "I know who you are. I know what your husband does—or *used* to do. And I *know* what happens here." My tone was honeyed, but from the look on her face, she caught my meaning.

"I don't want trouble," she whispered, stealing a glance at a patron patiently waiting in a seat near the door, then back to me. "We don't do *that* anymore. Just laundry now, that's the truth."

"Let's say, I believe you. Which I want to, but I need information about someone forging New York State IDs with the Real ID feature. Who would I talk to?"

Angela glanced toward the back of the shop, clearly worried. A washing machine thumped violently against the wall, throwing itself off-balance in its spin cycle. The sound made us both jump.

"I only know one person who can make something like that, but I don't want to get involved."

"You won't *be* involved, but I need to find them and ask a few questions."

Or twenty. With handcuffs. Same difference.

She hesitated, then said, "There's a man at the DMV in Greenwich. He's expensive, but he gets it done. People send him photos, and he makes the IDs at work. They're real, though, we could *never* match them."

"Do you have a name?"

"They call him *The Forge.*"

"Do you know what he looks like or which DMV he works at?"

"He's older, with gray hair, and always wears a bow tie."

Mrs. Lu continued to whisper and stole a glance at a camera in the corner of the room, no doubt where her husband was monitoring the whole interaction from a back room.

"A bow tie? Are you serious?" I narrowed my eyes, ready to call her bluff. If she were messing with me, I'd come back and personally feed her a damned bow tie.

"I swear!" she said, voice trembling with panic. "But you can't let him know I sent you. He works for powerful people. My family's only now getting back on track since my husband got out. Please!"

"You have my word," I said, softening my tone. "I won't say anything. But if you hear anything else, let me know."

I handed her my card. She hesitated, then tucked it discreetly into the folds of her apron before nodding and calling cheerfully, "So sorry it's not ready yet. It won't be much longer. Thank you!"

The man in the corner looked up and gave me a knowing smile as the tinkling door shut behind me.

I walked back to the car, the midday sun feeling too bright after the dim laundromat. *A bow tie?* This case kept getting weirder. If the "Forge" tapped directly into the DMV system to create legitimate IDs, that would explain why our victims' identities disappeared with such surgical precision.

I had an alias. It wasn't much, but it was a start.

Dialing Jackson, I slid into the driver's seat, the smell of cigarettes and fast food strangely comforting.

"What's up?" His deep voice answered on the second ring.

"I need you to check our system for someone using the alias 'The Forge.'"

"You got it. Do you need it now, or can I take a minute?"

"Sooner the better, but if you're busy, have someone else do it."

"I'll send it as soon as I find something," he said, the rustle of papers audible in the background.

"Thanks, Jackson." I slid the key into the ignition and started the car.

"Anytime." The call cut out, and I decided to drive to the Greenwich DMV to see if anyone matched Angela's description.

The DMV entrance was busy as people moved in and out at a consistent pace. I struggled to see all the faces that passed through the glass doors from where I sat, and my eyes ached with the strain of it.

Buzz-buzz.

"Hey, Dad!" I answered, spotting a woman with two children exiting the building, followed by a younger man.

Definitely not my guy.

"Hey, Lor. Got a minute?"

"Of course. Is everything okay?"

"Yeah, yeah," he chuckled warmly. "I was wondering, how do you feel about me coming out to visit?"

"I'd love that!" I said, distracted, just as a man in a brown bow tie with blue polka dots exited the building. He went to his car, pulled out a pack of cigarettes, and lit one. *Seriously? A bow tie like that?* Either this guy didn't care about being noticed, or he was hiding in plain sight. I couldn't tell whether he was a genius or an idiot.

"Maybe in a week or so?" Dad asked. "Or, if you're too busy, we could aim for Thanksgiving."

"November might be better," I said, still watching *Bow Tie Guy* puff on his cigarette. "But if this case wraps up, you'll be my first call."

"Sounds good. Just let me know, kid."

"Will do. Love you, Dad." We exchanged quick goodbyes, and I turned my attention back to my stakeout.

An hour later, Jackson called back. "Got him—Alexander Dolino. They wiped his files clean over twenty-five years ago, and he's stayed off the radar since. You think he's your guy?"

"I do. Angel said the girls are getting real or near-perfect New York IDs, and another reliable hit confirmed it. She claims he handles large jobs for influential clients. Dolino *has* to be it."

"Want me to assign a unit to him?"

"Yes. Keep it quiet. If he's connected to the wrong people, we can't risk tipping anyone off."

"Got it. I'll have a team ready in twenty."

"Perfect. Thanks, Jackson."

Back at the station, I briefed two plainclothes officers on the surveillance plan. Perez, unsurprisingly, was silent during the entire discussion, but his sharp gaze suggested he was filing details away for later. Jackson had busied himself gathering the rest of the information we needed, and the small team prepared to implement the plan to alternate surveillance between his apartment in Williamsburg, a trendy neighborhood in Brooklyn, and the DMV in Greenwich.

We were finally making progress. And for the first time in weeks, I felt like the pieces were falling into place.

Perez's eyes lingered on me a moment too long, then he nodded and turned away, but not before I caught a flicker of something—concern, frustration, or something else entirely, I couldn't be sure. Whatever storm was brewing between us would have to wait.

We had a forger to catch.

CHAPTER 17
Loriah

Thursday morning left me with one more day to prepare for my dinner meeting with Baldini Sr. I had been running possible strategies through my mind since the invitation, knowing I'd need to tread carefully. Something shady was going on at that club, but whether Baldini himself was involved was another matter entirely. Like Perez had mentioned, he struck me as a man who valued his business above all else, his shady dealings at a close second.

Fluorescent lights hummed overhead, casting a clinical glare on the tables and chairs in the briefing room. The boards we'd set up the night before loomed at the front of the room, their white surfaces cluttered with photos, dates, and connecting strings. There were too many gaps in our case, and I stared, willing something, anything, to jump out at me and make itself known.

Standing there, utterly absorbed in thought, I jolted back to reality at the sound of Perez's voice—nearly dropping the pen I'd been twirling in my fingers.

"Fairsbane?" he repeated, his tone cutting through the silence with impatience.

"Sorry, what?" I blinked, refocusing on him.

"Are we ready to go? Is there anything else we need?" he asked, moving to the ancient coffee pot in the back of the room and flipping the switch.

The smell of brewing coffee immediately filled the air, a minor comfort amid the anxiety in my stomach that was wrenching at me. I wasn't great at speaking in front of crowds, or in front of anyone for that matter, though I'd slowly gotten better at it due to the nature of the job. The thought had my heart dropping, remembering a time in seventh grade when my History class had taken to calling me *Leaky Loriah* because I lightly vomited in my hands during a Civil War presentation. God, kids were cruel.

"Fairsbane?"

"No, we're all set," I told him, tapping the pen absently against my thigh. "Do you have the files to hand out?"

"Yeah, right here," he said, holding up a stack of folders. "You think this forger's going to give us something useful?"

"I do," I said confidently, squaring my shoulders. "Even if it's only one piece, it could be *the* piece that makes all else fall into place. And we have to believe that."

He handed me the folders to double-check the contents. When his fingers brushed mine, the delicate hairs on my arms rose in response. Seeing me staring at the spot, he took a step back.

"I hope you're right. So far, we don't have what we need to bring Dolino in." He watched me in that analytical way of his, evaluating every emotion and sigh, and knowing just what was going through my mind.

"There will be," I said, my confidence unwavering.

"I don't know how you stay so damn optimistic," he muttered, shaking his head.

"It's simple. I think every person, alive or dead, has a story, no matter how big or insignificant it may seem. We only have to dig deep enough to find it. But I *know* it's there. They need us."

He surveyed me for a long moment, contemplating my little speech before nodding and letting out a huff like he was impressed, or maybe conceding the fact that I knew a thing or two. Or perhaps that I was full of shit and only trying to gaslight myself into believing it *was* the truth.

"Fair point. I'm heading to Woods's house later. His wife called, said she has a phone she doesn't recognize. Do you want to come?"

"Wow, you're willing to take me this time? Sure," I said, knowing, in his Perez way, he was offering what he could with his actions—an olive branch after the rigidity between us over the past few days. I absentmindedly reached for the sore spot on my cheek.

"Good. While I keep her busy, you can go sleuthing. See if there's anything in Woods' office or elsewhere that stands out."

"Wouldn't you have a better idea of where he might hide something? You two were friends."

"That's exactly why I *can't*. I need fresh eyes from someone who's not emotionally involved."

I studied him, noting his mournful expression that seemed to wage war with the juxtaposition of his often cold words and attitude.

Before I could press further, Jackson poked his head into the room. "You ready in here?" he asked, his energy as unflappable as ever.

"Yeah, we're ready. Can you gather everyone?" I asked, grabbing a cup of coffee from the pot.

"Gotcha," he said with a wink before heading off. The aroma of the cheap canned coffee had begun to lure people in, and the room soon filled up.

The briefing commenced with the usual hum of voices and shuffling chairs, before a slow, quiet wave rolled over the small room.

"Alright y'all," I said, gripping my fingers with my right hand. "Let's give it five more minutes for Chief Daniels to join us."

And five more minutes for me to get my shit together. Come on, Loriah, you got this. They're not strangers. Imagine them in their underwear.

Soon, the image of Perez's bare chest came to mind from the night before, my hands running over the black lines of ink, and I instantly regretted my decision.

As if on cue, Chief strode in, appearing harried but composed. "Sorry, I had a call from 'The Sentinel' for a quote from the dumpster murders," he explained. I peered over at Perez in time to see him rest his elbow on the table, close his eyes, and press his fingers to the crease between his brows.

When he opened them wide again, his demeanor made it clear—he wasn't amused.

"Thanks, Chief. We can address that after the brief," I replied, mentally filing that away to deal with later and cringing at his reference to our deceased girls.

"Alright," I said, pulling up the first slide. "Here's what we know so far. Jane Doe came in on September 22nd. She was in the early stages of her pregnancy, getting close to the second trimester, so between ten and twelve weeks." I stopped for a moment, taking a sip of water, and allowing the emotion that choked me before to wash over instead of embedding itself further. "No drugs were in her system, she was without any identification, and no one has claimed her."

I walked around to the corner of the board, trying not to focus on the staring faces, all eyes on me as if I were a bug pinned to the viewing table. Bile rose, causing me to cough, and I pushed it down.

You are not Leaky Loriah today, Fairsbane!

"We believe she may have worked at an exclusive club, and we're actively verifying that. Security footage from the Baldini's club captures an unidentified male strangling her and disposing of her body in a dumpster." The footage played, capturing the man's meticulous efforts to erase any trace of evidence. I watched for a moment, caught in the eerie detachment of witnessing someone's life slip away so easily—*too* easily.

I turned, scanning the room. No one was smiling. The air was weighted with a somber feeling. But beneath it all, a shared current of anger simmered, quiet but undeniable.

Good.

"We've traced the car used in the crime back to the impound lot, where Chief Daniels drove it to the auction house. From there, someone stole it. Unfortunately, the cameras at the lot weren't operational that night, so we have no leads on who took it. Blood samples from the victim are in the lab for testing to identify the baby's father, but results are pending."

I clicked to the next slide. "Now, onto our second victim, Addie. Her friend provided us with her name and basic info. We're waiting for confirmation from Oklahoma authorities to notify her family officially. Both victims worked at the same club. Her friend mentioned that when the girl stopped showing up, she took her job." I paused, my hand pointing to the face of Addie on the display screen. "It seems the club has a specific type: vulnerable young women, often Native American or Hispanic, lured to New York through social media and provided with false IDs. We have a lead on the forger making them, and are going to acquire a subpoena for that, hopefully this week."

A hand shot up. "Yes, Officer?"

"Has the girl's friend been able to identify her initial contact?"

"She's hesitant to share details given what she witnessed," I admitted. "But she's coming around. I expect more answers soon."

Perez shifted in his seat, giving me a barely noticeable nod when I glanced his way for a sense of solidarity. Personal matters aside, I knew we were aligned when it came to this case.

The briefing wrapped up, officers murmuring among themselves as they filed out. I caught snippets—some muttering about conspiracies, others brushing it off as bullshit, saying girls go missing all the time. It reminded me of army ants spilling out of a hive, each carrying their own version of the truth.

Perez stayed behind, leaning casually against the back wall, watching me the whole time. He didn't say anything—he didn't need to. When the last of the officers had cleared out and Chief stepped forward, Perez pushed off the wall and walked out without a word.

I was gathering the folders as Daniels approached.

"You're doing good work, Fairsbane," he said. "Let me know if there's anything I can do to help."

"Thanks, Chief. I appreciate that. I know you probably wouldn't guess it by the way my hands shake when I speak, but this case means a lot to me. If you can keep 'The Sentinel' off our backs, that'd be great. But if they need a statement, I can have one ready for Monday morning."

"Send it to me by tomorrow," he said. "I'll handle the rest."

With that pressure finally lifted, I headed back to my office, pulling out my phone to text Allie and see if she was free for lunch. I knew it was time to finally get it off my chest—everything that had happened with Perez and the way it left me with a confused, gnawing feeling sitting in my gut that distracted me from every bit of my day.

CHAPTER 18

Loriah

Me - *Lunch?*

Allie - *YES! I have things to tell you. Just drop me a pin so I know where to meet you. I only have 45 minutes.*

Me - *Will do. Give me 15 to get myself together.*

Allie - *Hurry up, woman!!*

B efore I could put my phone down, Jackson's voice cut through my focus. "Got a second?"

"Barely," I replied, shuffling papers into a haphazard pile and firing off an email. "But what's up?"

"That girl, Angel. She called. Do you want me to get back to her?"

I paused, glancing up. "No, that's alright. She probably won't say much to you anyway—no offense."

He held his hands up in mock surrender. "None taken," he said. "I figured you could use the help with—" He gestured at the avalanche of files spilling across my desk.

"It's fine. She's scared and young. I'll handle it later today. Anything else? I'm supposed to meet Allie for lunch."

"Well—" He drew my attention as he placed his hands on my desk and leaned in close, arms flexing. "I was hoping you'd thought more about letting me take you out this weekend?"

"Oh," I said, stalling as I went back to stacking a pile of folders. "I'm sorry, Jackson. I haven't had the mental capacity to think about it."

"How's Friday?" He smiled like he already knew I'd say yes. "I'll do the planning."

"Actually..." I hesitated, setting the papers down. "I have plans for Friday." There was no chance in hell I'd admit those plans involved Baldini Sr.

"Saturday, then?" he offered without missing a beat.

"That works. Got something in mind?"

"I do. But it's a surprise."

"Oh, Lord. I'm terrible with surprises."

"Trust me," he said with a grin. "You'll like it."

Before I could respond, the door swung open, and Perez strode in, his towering presence filling every inch of space. He didn't knock, of course, though he never did.

"Wow, okay," I quipped, narrowing my eyes. "Perez, do those primate-driven fists of yours know how to do anything besides punch things? Like, say, knocking?"

He glanced at the door as though noticing it for the first time. "Don't leave your door open if you don't want people walking through it." He slid a manila folder across my desk, cast a murderous glance at Jackson, and marched out like he owned the place. For good measure, he shut the door behind him, the click louder than it needed to be.

"What the hell is *his* problem?" I muttered, glaring at the folder.

"That was awkward," Jackson observed, rubbing a hand over his stubbled jaw and walking to the door to peer sideways out my small window to where Perez had entered his own office.

When I arrived at the café, Allie was already waiting, a drink in each hand. "Saved you a seat," she said with a grin.

As I scooted into the booth, she slid a second drink across the table, the aroma of Chai tea soothing my frazzled nerves. Though I wished it were something stronger, my muscles eased a little at her nearness, and I let out a wearisome sigh.

"Thanks," I replied, taking a long sip. "This is *exactly* what I needed."

Lunch with Allie felt like a lifeline. Between work and the chaos of recent days, I hadn't been as attentive to her beyond a few texts and the occasional meme. Despite living next door, our lives often felt worlds apart.

"I have something to tell you," she announced, grin widening. "And don't interrupt. I know I said I wasn't looking, but—"

I reached across the table, placing my hand on hers. "Allie. Just say it."

"Okay." She exhaled dramatically. "Do you remember Tory?"

I smiled, lifting my cup for a second sip. "Concert Tory?"

"That's the one." Her cheeks flushed as she toyed with her straw. "We're seeing each other. Seriously, I think."

My coffee cup paused midair as I processed her words. A flicker of unease passed through me, like how it might change things with Jackson. But as soon as the thought came, I realized I was also overthinking it.

"That's amazing, Allie!" I said, and to my astonishment, I meant it. The beautiful, bubbly creature in front of me deserved everything and anyone who would make her cheeks flush with excitement like that.

Her eyes searched mine for a hint of doubt. "You mean it? I don't want to make things awkward for you. You know, with *everything*."

"Don't be ridiculous." I squeezed her hand. "If you're happy, then I'm happy."

"I am," she admitted with a shy smile. "It's new, but it feels good. We'll all have to go out sometime."

"Funny you mention that," I said. "Jackson asked me out again. We're going out Saturday."

"Girl stop, that man is smitten."

"Yeah, well. I don't want things to get messy," I confessed, stirring my coffee. "The strain between Jackson and Perez is already a headache that I can't figure out. Jackson claims he doesn't know what it's about, and Perez—" I sighed, the burden of it settling. "He won't even talk to me. Especially since he—" I bit my lips, as if pulling the words back.

"Since *what*?" She was practically vibrating with anticipation.

"Well, since he kissed me."

"Holy shit, no. I mean, yes. I mean— Okay." She bounced her legs under the table like a kid and wove her fingers below her chin to stare at me with wide eyes. "Was it *amazing*?"

I didn't know what to say. Did I tell Allie that of course, it was amazing, and I had never had someone kiss me and convey so much through that one act without using a single word? Did I tell her how, when I was around him, my heart managed to skip beats and break all over again with the sheer want of having him hold me, while also being terrified he'd reject me for a *second* time?

"Earth to Loriah."

"Yes, sorry. I was—"

"Thinking of your exceptionally handsome and temperamental partner?"

"No. Allie, it isn't that easy. I can't. I mean, *we* can't. He even said that to me when he pulled away. To be honest, yeah, it was *absolutely* amazing. But now, he's distant again, and I think things are okay between us, but it's been difficult. Jackson is exactly what I need him to be right now. I think the best thing I can do for myself and my heart is focus on that."

Allie rolled her eyes. "If it comes to it, you'll at least have two hot guys fighting over you," she teased. "Could be worse."

I laughed despite myself. "Right. Because that's what I need—a testosterone-fueled showdown."

"Well, if Perez can't get his act together, screw him. You're amazing, and Jackson knows it. Also, where's he taking you?"

"No idea. Jackson said it's a surprise." I shot her a mock glare. "And thank you, by the way. I feel better getting it out there."

She grinned, raising her cup like a toast. "Always."

CHAPTER 19

Loriah

"**G**ood, you're back. Ready to head out?" Perez leaned against my doorframe. I brushed past him, balancing my coffee and bag, catching a whiff of his intoxicating cologne. *Damn him.*

"Sure, give me five. I'll meet you downstairs."

"I'll be in the car."

Ten minutes later, I settled into the passenger seat next to him, making an effort not to dwell on my conversation with Allie. The traffic moved at a snail's pace. The silence between us felt heavy and uncomfortable, but neither of us was willing to break it. When we parked outside a beautiful brownstone, I was momentarily taken aback. I had only seen homes like that in movies, and they seemed to belong to a forgotten era.

"This is Woods' place?" I asked, stepping out of the car and taking in the manicured perfection. Golden mums framed the black door, and vines spilled artfully from window boxes. The scene appeared plucked from a magazine cover, timeless and serene.

"It is," he confirmed, locking the car. "Don't let it distract you. Once we're in, focus on finding anything he might've hidden."

I shot him a mock salute. "Will do, buckaroo."

His glare could have frozen fire. "I should have left you."

"You'd miss me too much," I muttered as I followed him up the stone steps.

Before we could knock, the door opened, revealing an elegant middle-aged woman who radiated warmth.

"Agustin, I'm glad you could come," she greeted him, her hand brushing his arm in a friendly show of affection. "It's the strangest thing, though—I found this phone tucked away. I thought you'd want to see it before I threw it out. And, yes, I already asked the girls if it was theirs." She turned to me with a practiced smile. "I apologize, I was being rude, you must be Detective Fairsbane."

"Not at all, but yes, that's me. Thank you so much for having us, Mrs. Woods," I replied, shaking her outstretched hand.

"Please, call me Margaret, Loriah, though I wish it were under better circumstances that we were meeting," she said, her voice tinged with sadness. She turned then to start up the stairs.

We followed her inside, and I admired the artfully curated walls lined with photos of an idyllic life: children laughing, a younger Woods kissing Margaret's neck, the family on a sunlit beach. Each picture was another bittersweet reminder of what they'd lost.

My hands trailed along an intimate black and white shot of Woods and Margaret together, faces untouched by the passing of time, cradling a fuzzy-haired baby between them. My heart squeezed, and pins pricked behind my eyes and nose—the kind of ache that came with truly understanding the depth of someone else's loss.

Margaret led us into a pristine office and handed Perez a flip phone. "Here it is. I was afraid I'd lock out the phone if I tried the passcode too many times, but I'm sure you can figure it out, right?"

"We'll definitely try," Perez said, slipping the phone into his pocket. "Do you have time for tea? I want to ask you a few questions."

"Of course. I'll put the kettle on." Margaret's heels thudded with a quiet noise against the thin carpeting of the stairs as she headed down to the kitchen, Perez in tow.

"I'll join you in a moment," I called after her. "Mind if I use the restroom?"

"Second door on the right," she replied without glancing back.

Opening and closing each door carefully, I took inventory.

The first bedroom—likely the master—held a large, neatly made bed with carefully arranged pillows. More family photos lined the walls, and a cozy chair sat by the window with a perfect view of the street.

Another door opened to a room with two matching beds, twinkle lights strung around the perimeter, and pastel-colored clothes scattered across the bedspreads. The last door led to a bathroom, tastefully decorated in soft beiges with sleek bronze fixtures.

Backtracking to the office, I paused at Woods's desk—immaculate, yet unnaturally so. Not a single fingerprint smudged the surface, which gleamed under the light, polished to a near mirror finish.

I searched for what felt like an exorbitant amount of time, bordering on rude, and worry seeped into me that I wouldn't be able to find what we were searching for. I scanned the room once more, gripping the doorknob, about to leave, when the heavy oriental rug beneath the desk snagged my attention. I walked along the fringe when a floorboard creaked underfoot. I shifted my weight, feeling a slight give in the wood. Bending down, I peeled back the rug and ran my fingers along the seams. When my fingers met an obvious notch, I let out an excited squeal and immediately cursed myself, pausing to make sure no one heard.

Using my pocketknife, I pried the secret compartment open with minimal noise. Hidden in the hollow space beneath was a gleaming black thumb drive and a non-police-issued handgun wrapped in cloth.

Gotcha.

I replaced the boards and smoothed the rug back into place before retreating to the bathroom. After flushing the toilet and running the sink for good measure, I headed down the path to the kitchen. A thin sheen of nervous sweat coated my forehead. Margaret's laughter floated through the air, accompanied by the soft clinking of teacups and stirring of spoons.

I caught Perez's eye as I entered and joined them at the raised countertop. With Margaret's gaze drifting away, I seized the moment and deliberately let my eyes flicker down to my hands, exaggerating the gesture for effect. Taking the hint, he subtly shifted his gaze to see the thumb drive between two fingers before I tucked it into my coat pocket with a wink.

"Thank you for your hospitality, Margaret," I said as we prepared to leave. "If there's anything you need, please know you can reach out."

"You're too kind," she replied, her eyes lingering on Perez. "Let me know if you find anything useful, won't you?"

Perez assured her with a nod and said his farewells. Once outside, my excitement peaked as I needed to show him what I'd secured. I waited until we were a few blocks away before pulling out the thumb drive.

"That's it?" Perez asked, glancing from the road to the gleaming object in my hand.

"Eyes forward, Detective," I teased. "But yes. You'll never guess where it was."

"Enlighten me."

"Under a loose floorboard in his office," I said, watching his jaw work with interest.

"The floorboard," he repeated, his voice low. "Crafty."

"Do we log these into evidence?" I asked, holding up the gun and thumb drive.

"I'll handle it," he replied, his tone leaving little room for argument.

"How?"

He paused, the air between us thick. "Do you really want to know?"

I studied him for a moment, weighing the risks. So far, he'd earned my professional trust, but his enigmatic tendencies gnawed at me. Still, the idea of these items falling into the wrong hands pushed me to a decision.

I handed him the gun, wrapped neatly in the cloth I'd pulled from my pocket. "One condition," I said, fixing him with a firm stare. "Stop shutting me out. Trust goes *both* ways."

His hand closed around the weapon, his grip deliberate. "I know," he said, his voice soft. His thumb grazed mine, a fleeting but calculated move that sent warmth up my arm.

I dropped the thumb drive into his suit pocket, patting it once for emphasis. "Don't make me regret this."

"You won't," he murmured with quiet conviction.

As the car pulled into the station, I braced myself for whatever lay ahead and prayed that Perez would keep his word.

CHAPTER 20
Loriah

F riday morning greeted me with a sharp chill and a dense fog that clung to the city like a damp blanket. I tightened my ombré green scarf around my neck, the wool scratching my skin as I braced against the wind. Growing up in a place where October meant stifling 80-degree days, this kind of cold felt like a punishment. My Grammy's voice echoed in my head: "Cold as a well-digger's ass."

New Yorkers bustled along, unfazed, as if the biting air was an afterthought. As I approached the precinct, I spotted a man swinging off a sleek black motorcycle. His dark-washed jeans hugged his legs, and his leather jacket stretched perfectly over broad shoulders. When his helmet came off, he raked his fingers through the dark waves, and I knew exactly who it was.

For fuck's sake, Loriah. Don't look. Don't even think about looking.

I tugged my scarf higher, shielding most of my face, and sped up, my boots clicking on the wet pavement.

"Fairsbane." His voice cut through the morning din, beckoning.

Keep walking. You didn't hear him.

"Loriah! Dammit, Loriah, I know you can hear me."

"Nope, sorry."

"Stop!"

I groaned internally but obeyed, pausing on the steps and slowly turning to face him with exaggerated exasperation. "No, I couldn't hear you. My ears fell off a few blocks back. Mind helping me find them?"

Perez closed the gap between us in three long strides, his hand lightly gripping my padded elbow, and his face so close I could smell his minty breath. His green eyes pinned me in place. "You haven't talked to anyone about what we found, right?"

I tilted my head, feigning innocence. "Said anything about what? Do *you* have something to be worried about?" A shiver betrayed me, and I wrapped my arms tighter around myself.

His mouth twitched into a rare half-smile, flashing teeth that could sell toothpaste. "Good. Thank you."

The way those words rolled out of his mouth sent an entirely uncalled-for amount of heat through me. If he weren't so insufferable, and if I weren't clinging to normalcy between us like a lifeline, I might've tried to recapture the one moment we shared where things were more than *professional.*

But if he could stop touching me, that would be great.

Perez released me and strode ahead, holding the door open like it was second nature. "You owe me," I muttered, rubbing my hands together as the warmth of the building washed over me.

"Give me twenty," he called from behind.

True to his word, twenty minutes later, he appeared at my desk, placing a steaming cup of coffee in front of me. His tailored suit was a stark contrast to the riding leathers he previously wore.

"Vanilla was out," he announced, "so you get sweet cream."

When the hot liquid slipped past my lips, I grimaced theatrically. "How am I supposed to survive under these barbaric conditions? It's unacceptable."

"You're a pain in my ass," he replied, shaking his head.

"Yeah." I grinned. "I know."

I clicked open my email, the bright screen displaying a new message from Lieutenant Charles Moore in Oklahoma.

Perez craned over my shoulder as I opened the email. "I haven't been to my office yet. Can I read from yours?"

"Sure," I said, adjusting my chair, trying to put a little space between us. But even as I shifted, I could feel Perez's presence—his warmth brushing the air between us, the subtle scent of him curling around me. He was close—*too* close—mere millimeters between us where he wasn't technically touching me, but that small bit of distance felt more intimate than any physical contact.

To: Perez.AD@ny.pd.gov
Bcc: Loriah.Fairsbane@ny.pd.gov
From: Moore.Charles.K@Stillwellpd.gov
Detectives,

I apologize for the delay. We've had developments here that I wanted to include.

We've identified your Jane Doe. Her name was Kayleigh Hughes. Her parents are eager to fly to New York to confirm the ID and claim her body, likely this weekend or Monday. I'll confirm their plans and share their contact details soon.

Regarding the second victim, her name was Kasa Wells, eighteen, soon to be nineteen. She left home three months ago with a presumed boyfriend. Kasa kept regular contact with her family and sent money weekly—until this past Monday. That break in communication led her parents to file a missing persons report. They plan to come to New York to claim her remains.

Two more girls from our area are also missing. Both are underage and have a history of running away. Their parents recently came forward. I'm forwarding their information and photos for your records.

Please keep me updated. The family is willing to travel at their own expense to New York for an official meeting.

Regards,
Charles Moore, Badge #8157

I exhaled heavily, leaning back in my chair. Perez straightened, rubbing his hand through his hair—a gesture I'd come to identify as frustration or deep thought.

"What's on your mind?" I asked, glancing at the rain pelting the fogged-up window behind my desk.

Perez settled into the chair opposite me, running his hand through his hair. "We need to prepare for the families. Figure out who these so-called boyfriends were. Someone's targeting these girls, probably preying on younger ones as well."

He sat forward in the chair, his hands more animated than usual. "And why there? Why recruit from so far out?" He slapped his hands against the edge of my desk. "You need to push Angel harder. We *need* details: where she worked, who approached her, anything. Plus, why the name she gave us doesn't match Moore's."

He jotted notes in his pocket notebook while I typed up reminders on my computer. Paper and I had a tumultuous relationship—technology never let me down.

"I'm already waiting on Angel. And that name she knew was probably the one they had given her on her ID. I doubt whoever is taking these girls wanted them going around telling everyone who they were," I said, fingers flying over the keyboard. "If she doesn't return my calls today, I'll trace her phone and find her myself. I tried her several times after Jackson said she called, but she'd been silent."

"Good." He flipped the notebook shut. "I'll focus on Woods's phone and computer. Maybe financial crimes will find something in his accounts."

By midmorning, my phone buzzed with a call from an unfamiliar number. I answered after two rings, my heart sinking at the quiet, trembling voice on the other end.

"Detective Fairsbane? It's Angel," she whispered. Background noises—rustling fabric, blinds, scraping glass—revealed her tension.

"Angel? Where are you? Are you safe?"

"I'm at my friend's place, but I think someone's watching me." Her voice cracked. "Two guys in a car. I think they're from the club."

My grip tightened on the phone. "Stay put. Don't open the door. I'll send officers to watch the street and move you somewhere safe. Text me the address now."

"What if they—" Her voice broke. "What if they do to me what they did to Addie?"

"Angel, listen to me. You did the right thing by calling. We'll keep you safe. Just hold tight, okay? I'll have someone on the way."

After hanging up, I called Perez, skipping pleasantries. "Angel's in trouble. She thinks some of Baldini's men are watching her. I need plainclothes officers and approval for a safe house. Now."

"You'll have it. Send the forms."

Within thirty minutes, I received a message that two officers had successfully retrieved Angel. I slumped in relief, hoping this tiny victory would hold.

Lunch came with its own distraction when Christian stopped by my office, his smile fading the moment he caught sight of my face.

"Hey, I need to talk to you," I said, pushing aside my half-eaten sandwich and gesturing for him to sit. "Shut the door."

"Oh yeah? What is it?" Christian asked, stepping into my office with a curious expression and gently pushing the door closed with a satisfying click.

"Angel's at a safe house. You were originally on her rotation, but I took you off. I thought it might be better for her since she's in a vulnerable place right now and scared of everything. "

"Okayyy" He responded, his voice trailing off as confusion gave way to surprise.

"I'm sorry," I added quickly. "I didn't want to tell you to hurt you, but in case you see an old list, then you'll know why."

"Well, I can't say I don't understand. I'm sorry, Loriah. For putting you in this position." The remorse in his eyes was shocking. I knew I was doing right by Angel, but I couldn't help feeling like I'd been unfair to him.

The knock at my door came sharp and deliberate. Perez entered with a file under his arm and his jaw set.

"Look at you," I teased, smirking. "Learning to knock like a civilized human."

His sharp gaze flicked to the security rotation notes on my desk. "I manage."

Rising to go without acknowledging Perez, Jackson walked to the door, leaving the room with a final, "See you Saturday."

Perez's eyes narrowed—a slight flicker and a faint grimace I might've missed if I hadn't been learning to be attuned to his body as much as mine.

His gaze lingered on the closed door even after Jackson disappeared through it. Jealousy clung to him, quiet but unmistakable.

He had no right to it, especially after how he had pulled away. It was clear that what happened between us was a mistake—a fleeting moment, nothing more. So why did it feel like he was still holding on to something he pretended to let go of?

Not my problem.

He finally turned to me and dropped into the chair across from mine, that closed-off mask slipping back into place.

"So," he said, his voice cool. "Shall we get to work?"

CHAPTER 21
Loriah

"What's wrong?" I addressed him, leaning closer to hold Perez's indignant gaze. He didn't scare me. Not in the way he'd probably hoped to. I could see him working hard to carefully reconstruct the wall around his mind, which I was slowly burrowing under like a damned prairie dog.

"Don't worry about it."

"Don't do that." And a bit of hurt slipped into my voice before I could stop it.

When he didn't say a word, instead choosing to stare at me, I knew that it wasn't about the case.

Not this again.

"Loriah–"

"No," I cut him off, shaking my head as my voice grew colder. "I'm trying, Perez. I'm trying so *fucking* hard to act like nothing happened and that it didn't bother me when you stepped away, because we're partners, and that is what I'm *allowed* to have of us. Which is fine. It's better that way. But you don't get to make that choice for me and then get *mad* when someone else decides that they *do* want me."

He flinched like I had struck him. "You know I had to make that decision. For both of us."

"Why? Why, Perez? You can barely stand being in the same room with me, so you assume no one else can? It must kill you to think someone actually enjoys my company." My voice filled with the frustration I felt in response to his critiques, which simmered just below the surface.

"That's not the problem." His voice dropped to a growl, each word bitten off with precision. His jaw feathered in response to how hard he appeared to be clenching his teeth.

"Could've fooled me, *Agustin*." The name landed like a dart, hitting its mark. He flinched again, an infinitesimal movement, but noticeable, making me feel like I'd gained the upper hand in whatever this back-and-forth was between us.

"I don't think you'd believe me anyway," he said, his voice tight. "But I'll prove it. Or better yet, he'll do it himself."

"I guess we're at an impasse," I shot back, crossing my arms. "You don't have shit. Jackson's been nothing but kind, and he doesn't ask for anything in return. That's more than I can say about you."

"That's not the point. And I don't expect anything from you either, to be clear." He groaned in exasperation, his fingers tapping against his thigh. The restless movement betrayed the strain beneath his composed facade.

"What *is* the point then?" I leaned back, letting my fingers brush my bottom lip as I studied his face. His jaw clenched once more, and I feared he would lose a tooth. His hand rested over the armrest, twitching as it picked at the seam of his pants.

"Look at me, Perez."

His eyes snapped to mine, a storm brewing behind them. Anger? Hurt? I couldn't pin it down, but the intensity hit me like a wave.

"I'll trust you when you give me a reason to," I said, my tone softening. "But you can't expect me to act on *your* gut feelings. Show me something real, and I promise, I'll listen."

He didn't respond, his mouth set in a hard line as he stood. The folder in his hand remained closed and crumpled at the borders from where he'd gripped it so hard. He moved toward the door, shoulders set in a rigid line, the tension in his frame palpable.

The rollercoaster of emotions left me with nothing but a low simmering current of rage. I was so angry. And tired. Tired of Perez's lingering gazes, his small touches, his words of warning that held nothing but the ramblings of a clearly frustrated man.

I am finished.

He paused at my door, holding onto the handle but not looking back at me. "Be careful," he said, his voice low and measured, before he stepped out of my office.

I rolled my eyes, mumbling a polite, *screw you*, under my breath as the door clicked shut behind him.

CHAPTER 22
Perez

Can't stand being near her? Are you fucking kidding me?

Hell, maybe she did believe I hated her, that her presence grated on me. If only it were that simple. The truth was crueler—her presence didn't just unnerve me; it clawed at my insides, hollowing me out. Every glance, every slight, unintentional smile she tossed my way felt like a blade twisting in my chest. Was she doing it on purpose?

If she knew why I pushed her away, maybe she'd understand. But what then? What would I see in her eyes? Pity? Disgust? I couldn't stomach it. Letting her believe I didn't choose her was unfortunately easier.

Or at least, that's what I kept telling myself.

Woods's flip phone sat on my desk; its silence louder than a scream. It had been a dead end—no cracked codes, no revelations, nothing but wasted time and an ego bruised by my own impulsive mistakes. The coffee mug wobbled, and a pencil clattered to the floor as I slammed my hand against the desk, the dull ache a poor distraction from my frustration. *Idiot.* I shouldn't have left like that—her expression—confusion, hurt—burned in my mind like a brand.

I told myself I'd fix it when the time was right.

The afternoon dragged on. The wall clock's ticking a metronome of my self-loathing. Jackson left early, dropping a quick goodbye in Loriah's office on his way out. Good. At least I wouldn't have to see him hovering around her and endure the tightening knot in my chest when he'd lean too close. I buried myself in paperwork under my desk lamp's dim glow as the city came to life in the dark beyond my window.

Then I saw her.

Movement drew my attention, and there she was, stepping out of her office like a vision. My breath hitched. She wore a black wrap dress that clung to her curves with an effortless elegance, the high slit revealing the smooth expanse of her thigh. The neckline dipped low enough to accentuate the gentle swell of her breasts. Delicate straps crossed her usually covered back, revealing tiny hidden tattoos, before tying at the waist—one slight tug away from ruin. She pulled on her coat, oblivious to the way her movement had me transfixed, and slung a small handbag over her shoulder.

That woman is going to be the death of me.

I told myself to let her go, to let her slip into the night. But the sight of her walking away, of her leaving me behind again, tightened something deep and instinctive in my chest. Before I could stop myself, I grabbed my helmet, moved through the office like a man possessed, and stalked after her.

I jammed the helmet between the elevator doors, surprising her.

"Perez? What the *hell* are you doing?" she half-shrieked, her voice sharp with a mix of shock and irritation. The machine groaned in protest. Her wide blue eyes met mine, and a flush spread across her cheeks.

"That's a better question for you," I shot back, stepping inside. My voice came out rougher than I meant, laced with a desperation I couldn't hold back—the kind that came from wanting something I couldn't have. "Showing up looking like that."

Her eyes darted to my open collar, and a palpable charge crackled in the air between us, laden with unspoken tension. In that moment, I was transported backwards in time, her soft hands running along my body in question. She hesitated when she caught me looking at her and brushed a stray lock of hair from her face—my eyes tracking the movement.

"I have a dinner appointment," she said finally, her tone defensive.

"An appointment?" I repeated, my lips curling into a smirk. "Do you dress like that for all *appointments*, or is this one special?"

Her eyes narrowed, and she tugged at the slit in her dress as if to tame it. "It's not my dress," she snapped. "Plus, it's none of your business. Again. You ask a lot of questions that have nothing to do with you, Perez."

"Stop trying to hide yourself," I said, my voice slicing through her protest as I stepped closer, catching the faint trace of citrus on her skin. I wanted—badly—to have her, and before I knew it, my face hovered just an inch from hers. It was intoxicating, maddening. I was driving myself insane. "You look–" I faltered, the words catching in my throat. *Beautiful. Exquisite. Dangerous?*

She turned her face, blinked at me, our lips only inches apart, and suddenly she looked self-conscious. "I don't normally wear this kind of thing," she said, quieter, as if sharing a secret.

"Good," I murmured, standing back up, my ravenous gaze traveling over her. "It makes it all the more memorable."

The elevator seemed to shrink, the space between us electric. My hand moved along the railing near her hip, and I leaned in again, deliberate, my voice low. "I hope whoever this is for knows how lucky they are. That dress belongs somewhere far less boring than at a dinner table." My words brushed her skin like my lips longed to do near the junction of where her jaw met her neck.

Lips parting, a beautiful pink flush crept up her neck, and she moved her hip closer to my hand. Seeming to realize what she was doing, she moved away quickly, her steps sharp and indignant as the elevator doors opened. I watched her go, captivated by the sway of her hips, my fists clenching at my sides to keep myself from following. I knew I had already pushed more than I had a right to after our talk.

That was what I did, though—push her, tease her, drive her away. But the thought of Loriah walking into someone else's arms tonight made my stomach twist. Shoving my helmet on, I slid the visor down to hide my expression. The bitter taste of restraint lay thick on my tongue.

I rode hard that night, trying to drown her memory with the roar of the engine and the chilled wind tearing past me. I was itching for a fight and knew precisely where to find one.

CHAPTER 23
Loriah

I could kill him.

Who says that?

The worst part was that I could easily imagine the damn dress draped and bunched at my hips while I straddled him. I imagined he wouldn't be gentle either. Nothing about the man was.

The car ride to Baldini's restaurant stretched on, the city lights blurring past the windows. I pressed my earbuds in and scrolled aimlessly through songs to distract myself, though nothing worked. My thoughts churned, settling on the ache in my core that had no outlet. It had been so long since I'd been anything other than loneliness.

Not the time for this, Loriah, you have a job to do. People are dying.

The driver, a middle-aged man with an unremarkable face, kept silent for most of the trip. His stoic presence suited me fine. When we finally arrived, he stepped out and opened my door, offering his hand. I gratefully accepted the help as I struggled to maneuver out of the car in the impractical dress Allie had talked me into.

Chill October air bit at my legs, sharpening my senses. I turned to take in the restaurant: twinkling lights wrapped pillars, ivy climbed the walls, pergolas framed terraces. The place exuded an old-world Italian romance, a setting plucked straight from a dream. The scent of garlic, roasted tomatoes, and fresh bread wafted through the open doorway, teasing my stomach till it growled.

Inside, a woman in an elegant black dress greeted me. "Mr. Baldini is expecting you," she said, gesturing for me to follow.

Every step gave me time to think—what he might say first, how I'd counter, which questions to dodge, and which to press. I wasn't there to play nice; I was there to find an opening, an advantage, anything that would tilt the balance in my favor.

The place was empty, of course it was. Baldini didn't strike me as the type of man who would share his time—or his space—easily.

At the back, in a private alcove, Baldini stood as we approached. His tailored blue suit complemented his silver hair, and his presence radiated authority. "Allow me," he said smoothly, pulling out my chair.

"Thank you. This place is stunning," I said, glancing around.

"It pales in comparison to you tonight," he replied, his intimation clear.

"You're kind," I said, smiling politely. I couldn't imagine this man being easily impressed by anyone, let alone me. He had undoubtedly seen every type of beauty and appeal imaginable.

"I don't give false compliments, Miss Fairsbane."

"Loriah, please. I can't sit here dressed like this and have you call me 'Miss Fairsbane.' It feels wrong."

"Very well. *Loriah.*"

The low timbre of his voice sent a ripple of unease down my spine. This man wasn't just dangerous—he was lethal. The kind who could clear a room with nothing more than a glance, the kind whose rivals had a habit of disappearing, yet somehow, the police never had enough to make charges stick.

I'd done my homework before the meeting, digging into his past in hopes of understanding what I was walking into. But I wasn't here to marvel at the predator in his den—I was here for answers.

The waiter approached, and Francesco switched seamlessly to Italian, ordering for both of us. His command of the language sounded like poetry, fluid and effortless. Soon, wine appeared, a dark, rich red. Francesco tasted it first, swirling the glass and savoring it with practiced ease. He nodded, signaling the sommelier to pour mine.

"I hope you don't mind," he said, gesturing to the wine. "I have particular tastes."

"It's perfect, thank you," I said, taking a cautious sip. It was. Smooth, complex, and not too dry. "But one glass. I'm here on business, remember?"

"Of course. Let's get to it, then," Francesco said, his eyes sharpening. "I assume this is about the girl?"

"It is. But first, thank you for the video footage. It's been helpful."

"I'm glad to hear it," he replied, leaning back. "A terrible thing. And bad for business."

I set my glass down, lacing my fingers together. "Do you handle the hiring at your club?"

He tilted his head, considering me. "Sometimes. Often, my son Dante oversees that. Have you met him?"

"Not yet. Does Dante hire underage girls?"

Francesco's face tightened, a flicker of annoyance flashing in his eyes. "Loriah, I run a business. Illegal practices don't serve me well."

"For a legitimate business, yes. But we both know young girls are a high-demand commodity in, shall we say, certain circles?"

His gaze roamed over me, assessing, before he answered. "That's debatable."

"More subjective than debatable," I countered. "But it shouldn't be. Do you personally oversee or meet the new hires?"

"No. I review reports after the hiring process is complete. Dante handles the day-to-day goings on."

"Have you heard of a club called *Enchanted Sanctuary*?"

His smile didn't falter. "No. Is it new?"

"Not exactly. I believe it's a hidden operation running right under your nose—possibly inside *your* club."

Francesco's jaw tightened. "We have many VIP sections. Some are more exclusive than others."

"No. More like a speakeasy. Something hidden. Have you had any renovations recently?"

He nodded, slowly swirling his wine. "We expanded last year. Private rooms, office space. Dante managed it while I was away."

"For how long?"

"After three months visiting family in Italy, I returned to find everything had been completed. It would've been ready by"—he paused to think—"last September."

A whole year before Jane Doe was murdered, indicating the duration of events would be unknown. Kayleigh and Addie, or Kasa, were inevitably not the first, but if I could help it, they'd be the last.

"And you trust Dante?"

"I trust him as far as I can throw him," Francesco admitted, his voice laced with frustration. "He's always had too much to prove."

I leaned toward the edge of the table. "I need access."

His laugh was low and sharp. "To my son's secret club that I supposedly don't know exists? How do you propose I do that?"

"You're resourceful. You'll think of something."

Francesco's sharp eyes narrowed, and he studied me for a long moment. "Unless you can dance, Loriah, I don't see how this works."

I leaned back, draping a hand over the arm of my chair. "That's the thing, Francesco. I *can* dance, but I'm sure there are other positions available."

His face registered surprise, a rare crack in his composure. He chuckled softly. "This I have to see."

"Take my word for it," I said with a smile, scooting forward ever so slightly to let the statement hang in the air.

The conversation shifted as our food arrived. The aroma of the *Stracotto di Fassona Piemontese* pulled me back to the present. My first bite was glorious—and blistering hot. Francesco's laugh rumbled, low and amused.

"Careful, *Tesora*. It's hot," he said, shaking his head with a wry grin.

The rest of the meal flowed with a practiced ease that felt like anything but business. Francesco guided the conversation effortlessly, mixing charisma with a subtle authority that was impossible to ignore.

As the dessert arrived and the espresso was served, Francesco leaned in again. "Loriah, I believe I can help. However, I'll need something in return."

"If you find something on Dante, you come to me first. Family is precious."

I hesitated, feeling cornered. "I'll think about it."

"That's all I ask. My only terms. I hope you don't think too long." He sat back, clearly satisfied.

As we finished our meal and the servers deftly cleared our plates, Baldini strolled alongside me, guiding me toward the exit.

"Don't underestimate Dante," he whispered once we reached the front doors. "He's clever. *Dangerous* even."

"So am I," I replied, meeting his gaze.

He smiled, enigmatic as ever. "Until next time, *Tesora*."

The car's radiator filled the interior with a gentle heat, blending with the lingering scent of cherries and Diet Coke—but I couldn't shake the chill that settled deep in my bones. I knew this wouldn't be easy. There was no way in hell Perez or the station would ever agree to let me go undercover to get the information we needed.

No, they'd rather kick down the door, grab what they could, and treat the girls' lives as an afterthought. We'd never get past the surface like that. And I refused to settle for brute force indifference.

But if Baldini double-crossed me, I wasn't sure what I'd do. I couldn't kill him. But maybe—hopefully, I could dig up the kind of evidence that would let me take something from him.

CHAPTER 24

Loriah

At precisely 7:30 AM, the smell of brewing coffee woke me. Flipping onto my other side, I grabbed my phone to check the weather. The sunshine streaming through my window felt deceptive this far into the fall months, but the forecast showed a mild fifty-two degrees and sunny. *I can work with that.* Three notifications expectantly blinked at me, and I opened Allie's first.

> **Allie -** *Dance day! Get your ass over here when you're awake. I'll provide the goods.*

> **Me -** *Ugh!! So earlyyyy. I just woke up. Give me a minute to become human, and I'll be over. Also,*

> do you have creamer? I'm pretty sure I ran out and forgot to buy more.

The other messages were from Christian and Baldini. I hesitated, debating whether I wanted to begin my morning with Christian's romantic banter or Baldini's calculated plans. Deciding I'd rather blanket myself in the warmth of his words before diving headfirst into whatever treacherous waters awaited me with Baldini, I flipped to the thread.

> **Christian -** *I've got a couple of things planned for tonight. I'd say dress up, but you could wear anything and look incredible. Tory wants to make it a double date with Allie—she got us on the list for this dark fantasy-themed spot for Halloween. Let me know if it's not your thing.*

> **Me -** *Yeah, that sounds good. How dressed up are we talking?*

His reply came within seconds.

> **Christian -** *Suits, dresses. That type of thing. If it's too much, we can go somewhere else.*

I sighed, imagining Allie tearing apart her closet to dress her mannequin and planning for the perfect group photo.

Taking a breath and trying to convince myself I needed socialization, I messaged back on a sigh.

> **Me -** *No, if they're excited, let's join them. Maybe we can find our own quiet fun after? Also, I'll definitely need a nap before this.*

> **Christian -** *Ohh, I like the way that sounds. 9 PM then?*

Me - *Yes! See you then.*

Satisfied, I clicked on Baldini's message.

Francesco Baldini - *We're set for the 19th. Your interview is at 730pm before the club opens. I've told Dante I'm anticipating your arrival, knowing he can't resist stepping in. He won't suspect a thing.*

Me - *Perfect. I'll be ready.*

After pulling my hair into a sleek bun and throwing on a zip-up hoodie and sweats over my leggings, I grabbed my gym bag and coffee mug. Knocking on Allie's door minutes later, I braced myself for her inevitable excitement.

The door flew open to a squeal. "Tory just told me! We're doubling tonight!"

"Yeah, Christian said she got us on a list or something? Sounds fancy."

I tried my hardest to match her enthusiasm, but truth be told, I would have enjoyed a night to pick back up from where we left off the last time we were interrupted.

"Oh, *girl*, you have no idea. We *have* to find the perfect outfits," she continues, oblivious to my internal struggle.

Indeed, her bedroom was a battlefield of clothes, shoes, and accessories. The mannequin she kept for planning stood half-dressed.

"I was thinking of wearing this," I joked, gesturing to my sweats and giving a mock runway shimmy.

"I love you, but absolutely not." She burst out laughing.

"Okay, we'll plan later. For now, show me where your creamer is."

When class ended, I could hardly muster the energy to carry on a conversation with Allie. I didn't know where her stamina came from, but I envied it. After four flights of stairs, I was ready to pool at my front door.

"Hair and makeup at my place?" Allie asked once we reached our landing.

"Sounds good. But first, I'm taking a hot shower and a nap. Meet at eight with pizza?"

"You know me *too* well."

I groaned and rolled out of bed to the irritatingly chipper tune of the alarm I'd set before my evening nap.

I have got to change that damned thing.

A quick shower wiped away the day's sweat, leaving me refreshed and ready for round two.

"Open up, woman! I know you're in there," Allie shouted, pounding on my door.

Laughing, I opened it to find her holding pizza triumphantly. "Bacon and olives for you, veggie for me. Half and half, as always."

"You're the best."

"I know." She grinned, setting the box on my counter.

By the time we finished applying our makeup and fighting over which eyeshadow to use, I stood in front of the mirror, stunned. Allie had chosen a short black dress with a thigh-high slit, pairing it with a sheer, rhinestone-studded top, knee-high boots, and a leather moto jacket. She'd tightened my curls, weaving tiny braids on either side of my center part.

"Allie, you've outdone yourself."

"You gave me good bones to work with, babe."

We'd managed to arrive 20 minutes early and stood outside the club where the bass from the music thrummed through the pavement and flashes from paparazzi cameras lit up the entrance, desperate for a shot of someone special. Celebrities drifted in and out, laughter mixing with the hum of the crowd, giving us the perfect vantage point—front row for the show.

A growing sense of overwhelm was beginning its slow ascent up my body.

And then I saw him. For a moment, my heart was able to beat again.

Christian stepped out of a blacked-out sedan, the lights from passing cars catching on his sharp suit and that confident smile that made my legs a little weak. For a moment, plaguing thoughts of Perez slipped to the background—maybe not entirely, but all I wanted right then was to let myself get swept up in that feeling.

CHAPTER 25
Loriah

"Like what you see?"

"I had no idea this was part of your wardrobe," I teased, stepping back to give an exaggerated once-over. "Though I think I prefer you in jeans."

"Thanks. To say you look good would be the understatement of the year." His gaze swept over me, lingering like a sunburn, making my skin tingle. "Shall we go in? First rounds on me."

"Yes! Finally," Allie cheered, slipping her hand into Tory's and leading us toward the entrance. After a quick exchange with the bouncer, a beefy man ushered us to a private elevator.

"Enjoy," he said smoothly, pressing the button for the twentieth floor.

The doors opened to reveal a realm of pure, seductive luxury. Plush velvet seating dotted the space, each adorned with a private table occupied by striking women and bottles of expensive champagne. A raised walkway wound behind the booths, where half-dressed dancers moved fluidly to the rhythm. Floor-to-ceiling windows framed the DJ platform and dance floor, offering a dazzling view of the city lights. The opposite wall boasted another expanse of windows, leading to a wraparound patio. Above, the second-floor alcoves provided a shadowy, private ambiance complete with exclusive bars.

I took a moment to let it all sink in, thankful Allie had insisted on the outfit. The music pulsed through the space, its beat syncing with my heartbeat. My body swayed instinctively.

"Drinks?" Christian asked, already heading toward the bar.

Two shots later, I was feeling my muscles loosen and inhibitions lowering. Allie grabbed my hand, her excitement bubbling over. "Dance floor. *Now.*"

The packed floor throbbed with bodies moving to the rhythm, and I surrendered to it all, my hands exploring my body as my head bent back and absorbed the thrumming music like a sponge seeking water.

Two hands slid around my waist, spinning me effortlessly. I turned to meet Christian's blue eyes.

"God, I love watching you," he murmured into my ear, his voice low and warm, giving me goosebumps.

"I love to dance. Truth be told, I used to dance," I admitted, leaning closer so he could hear me. "Or did, before *life*, I guess."

More like before escaping a town I hated to move to an even bigger city with a fucked up murder case, and a partner who I can't keep his green eyes and scorching kisses to himself.

Before that.

"Well, don't stop on my account," he replied, brushing his lips along the curve of my neck, above the sheer fabric of my top, and pulling me from my downward spiral of thoughts.

I was slipping into a pool of need as his hands roved over my body. Everything felt overwhelming, a whirlwind of emotions that left me breathless, yet somehow never seemed to satisfy the deep yearning that I wrestled with. His hands skimmed down across my belly, splaying fingers to slide down my thighs and grip my bare thighs. Each squeeze of his fingers made me need more: more pressure, more closeness, more of *him*. I knew I was getting close to letting the pressure of the moment take control.

"I need to cool off. Will you be okay here?" I asked him, slipping off the dance floor with my jacket in hand.

He looked at me for a moment, a flicker of confusion passing over his face.

"I'll be fine. It's you I worry about. Need some backup?"

"No! I'll be right back!" I called over the music, our hands lingering a little too long.

Welcoming the solitude, I stepped onto the terrace and closed my eyes, enjoying the quiet moment. I relished the cool breeze from so many stories up, and I wandered to a quiet corner near a small warming station overlooking the city below. Taking a sip of my drink, I let the night wash over me.

I was watching people come and go, laughing, kissing, and dancing, when out of the corner of my eye, I saw a familiar silhouette slipping through the terrace doors. My heart skipped. The dim lighting and foggy glass obscured his features, but something about the way he moved sparked recognition, and the pull to follow tugged at my core.

I'm not that drunk, am I?

I downed the rest of my drink, practically slamming it onto a nearby table, and followed inside, curiosity gnawing at me. I reentered the club, my eyes scanning the crowd as I circled the floor.

And then I saw him.

Son of a bitch.

There he was, Agustin Perez, sitting comfortably in a darkened corner. The tailored black suit fit him like a glove, the unbuttoned collar exposing the edge of tattoos I'd only glimpsed before, and a new, freshly cropped fade accentuated his jawline.

Our eyes locked. His slow, deliberate gaze traveled the length of my body, setting my nerves on fire. I closed the distance between us with determined steps, my blood pounding so loud in my ears it threatened to drown out the music around me.

When I stopped in front of him, he leaned forward, a smirk playing at the corner of his mouth.

Good God, that mouth.

Before I could speak, his hand slid around the back of my knee, the warmth of his palm searing my skin, and he sat up a little straighter, letting his thumb carefully rub up and down the sensitive flesh.

"Excuse me. Can I help you?" I snapped, trying to keep my composure.

That fool dared to feel so entitled to touch me after leaving me when he had the opportunity to do more, and all after claiming it was *for my own good.*

"More like, can *I* help you?" His voice, rich and accented, curled around me like smoke and drew the word 'I' out. As he slid his hand higher, a slow burn followed. And damn my traitorous body, I didn't really *want* to pull away.

"What are you doing here? Couldn't resist stalking me?" I challenged, trying in vain to pull out of his reach, to give me space to think, but his grip only became stronger. "Is this some crusade you're on to make sure no one else can have me? Or some fucked up game that I don't understand?"

He chuckled, the sound low and infuriatingly smug. Turning to the man beside him, he shared a laugh like I'd confirmed some private joke.

"You've been enjoying yourself," he said smoothly, his emerald eyes glinting under the club's flashing lights. "I've seen you dancing."

"And?"

He stood, looming over me, his presence impossible to ignore. His hand slipped to my waist, drawing me in until his warm breath brushed the edge of my cheek. My body melted into his warmth, and the anticipation of him kissing me threatened to shatter my bravado.

"Keep your *fucking* hands off her before I break them," a growl interrupted from behind.

I turned, my pulse spiking like a kid caught with their hand in the cookie jar.

CHAPTER 26
Loriah

A voice cut through the haze, sharp and unmistakable. Anger laced every word, precisely like the nights he'd fought for me.

I spun around, and there he was—*the* Agustin Perez, the devil *I* knew.

His frame mirrored the man behind me, a familiar scowl etched onto the same sharp features I'd memorized after weeks of seeing it aimed at me. The two men wore almost identical black suits, like mirror images separated only by Agustin's longer hair and the cold fury in his eyes.

"But—what the hell?" I snapped, my confusion crystallizing into irritation. Without thinking, I turned back and slapped the man who had dared to mimic my partner. He barely flinched, though his grin widened—as maddening as Agustin's—and he reached up to press where my hand had struck. My body vibrated with anger. I felt like I was caught in a trap, although the joke was on me.

"A fan of yours, Agustin?" the impostor drawled, his tone teasing.

"Loriah, *this* is my brother, Ares. This is his club."

"Of course, it is." I laughed, the sound bitter even to my own ears. "Another thing no one knows about you?"

Agustin's jaw tightened. "I don't think my family life is relevant to how we work together. Do you?"

"No, I guess you wouldn't." The anger bubbled in my chest as I turned to leave. His hand shot out, catching my wrist. Before I could pull away, he twisted me toward him, his grip firm but not painful. I found myself off balance, my hand on his chest for support. His warmth was both frustrating and enticing! In that moment, I felt a spark of longing, even though I knew I shouldn't allow myself to feel anything for him.

"*Don't* touch me, Perez," I hissed, willing my voice to stay composed despite the alcohol coursing through me, transforming anxiety-riddled Loriah into Loriah that would punch him and ask questions later. Knuckles be damned.

Fuck, he's rubbing off on me.

His face flickered with something like hurt, maybe? But he swiftly buried it behind the professional façade he'd perfected.

"You didn't appear to mind when you thought I was him," he said, nodding toward Ares.

Ares eased back in his chair, utterly unbothered, and my face flushed with either anger or the embarrassment of him being right. I couldn't tell which, when the two emotions were so tightly intertwined.

"Fuuuck, brother. She definitely hates you. She can come back to me, though. I'll play nice." He patted his thigh, gaze sweeping over me with unrestrained amusement. The predator in him was as blatant as the smugness on his face.

"I won't waste my time with *either* of you—one Perez is bad enough," I snapped, jerking my wrist free from Agustin's grip. "I'm here with someone. Now, if you'll kindly fuck off, I need to find my friends. My *actual* friends."

Agustin's thumb had been tracing slow circles on my wrist, and the absence of his fingers left my skin buzzing. His silence followed me as I spun around, only to collide with someone else.

Strong, familiar hands steadied me.

"Loriah?" Christian's voice broke through the tension. Then, seeing Agustin, his tone shifted. "Perez?" Disbelief mingled with confusion. "Is everything okay here? You can't help yourself, can you?"

"Everything's fine," Ares interjected, standing to join his brother. His voice carried that same cool, assured bite. Gone was the teasing light-heartedness from moments before.

Agustin remained silent, jaw clenched so tightly I thought it might snap. His eyes burned as they flicked between Christian and I, the realization settling over him. He knew. He knew Christian was my "someone," and the realization seemed to set his already simmering anger ablaze. I had no doubt he was on the verge of snapping.

Allie and Tory appeared behind Christian, their arrival only adding to the chaos. Allie's eyes darted between the brothers. A broad grin betrayed her amusement, and she cast a wide-eyed glance between me and the brothers.

Tory's face, though, lit with recognition when spotting the duo.

"Ares! Do you know them?" she asked, giving him a side hug. His arm enveloped her with ease. "Your engagement online is *amazing* right now," Tory continued. "Do you want me to take your photos?"

Ares shook his head, a smile that didn't quite reach his eyes. "I don't think that's a good idea," he said, his tone calm but firm. "Drinks on me. Enjoy yourselves."

He dismissed us with an air of finality, and I grabbed Christian's hand, needing to put distance between myself and the Perez brothers.

Back at the bar, we took shots—one, then another—feeling the burn of tequila loosen the knot in my chest as Christian pulled me onto the dance floor.

The music thrummed, and soon it was just the two of us, lost in the rhythm. Christian's hands reverently traced the curve of my hips, sliding down to cup my ass under the hem of my dress. My skin gleamed with sweat, and the room blurred into a haze of lights and sound.

I knew Agustin was watching. I could feel his eyes like a brand searing into my body. When I spun myself and settled my backside against Christian's muscled body, I glanced at the private alcoves above.

There he was, standing at the railing. Even from where I swayed, I saw his white-knuckled grip on the edge. His intense gaze fixed on mine, tracking my movements as I reached up and tangled my fingers in Christian's hair. My hips pressed into Christian, eliciting a satisfying sound from him.

When his lips trailed hot kisses down to my collarbone, I closed my eyes. The feel of him on my skin sent a shiver down my spine, and I tilted my head, giving unfettered access. My hair fell over one shoulder, and I invited him closer with an arch of my back. Continuing his slow exploration, I fluttered my eyes open, catching sight of Agustin as he turned from our display and slammed a glass onto the table before stalking off into the shadows.

That small, petty part of me—that stung from his rejection—felt a certain satisfaction in knowing I'd gotten under his skin. He wasn't unaffected, no matter how hard he tried to pretend otherwise.

Christian leaned in, his lips brushing the shell of my ear as he growled low, "Finish this back at your place?"

"Yes," I whispered, meeting his gaze. His eyes burned with raw desire, that familiar smile curling on his lips. The same one that regularly made my knees feel a little less steady. "Take me home."

But as he slipped his arm around me, guiding me toward the exit, my mind betrayed me. I could feel the ghost of Perez's touch on my wrist—brief, electric, and far too present for something that was supposed to mean *nothing* to either of us.

CHAPTER 27
Loriah

C hristian's lips trailed along my jaw, fingers fisting in my hair as the city blurred past the windows in the back of the cab. We barely managed to get through my apartment door before he kicked it shut behind us, the sound echoing through the small space with a finality that made my pulse thunder harder with desire.

He didn't hesitate, shrugging out of his jacket till it hit the floor with a soft thud. Scooping me up with ease, my legs wrapped possessively around his waist. His hands gripped my ass firmly, the smooth fabric of my dress sliding up with the effort. I pressed kisses along his neck, unbuttoning his shirt with eager fingers to reveal the sculpted planes of his chest.

Before I knew it, he set me on the cool surface of the kitchen counter, hands already slipping beneath the lace waistband of my underwear. Eagerly, he tugged them aside and moaned into my kiss. "God, Loriah, you don't know how bad I have wanted this."

"Wait," I whispered desperately, suddenly aware of the lingering sweat and salt on my skin. "I've been dancing, and—"

"Loriah," he interrupted, his voice dropping to a rough whisper that sent shivers skittering across my bare skin. "I've been waiting *all night* to taste you." His eyes darkened with lust as he held my gaze. "Now, take this damn dress off."

Without another word, he lifted me back into his arms, his fingers rousing me as he carried me to the bedroom. Each stroke sent jolts of pleasure through me, making me quiver and gasp against his neck. He sat me down on the bed, and the absence of his touch left me wanting for more.

Christian knelt before me, movements deliberate as he undid the remaining buttons on his shirt. He studied me with awe—so different from the professional restraint he showed at work. My hands came up to smooth over his skin, feeling the controlled desire beneath my fingertips as I pushed the shirt from his broad frame. It slipped from his shoulders, and I mirrored him, sliding the straps of my dress off my own and letting the bodice fall to bare myself to him.

His blue eyes darkened as they roamed over me. The hunger in his gaze was evident. Tentatively, he pulled me closer, his hands wrapped behind my knees, until I could arch my hips for him to pull the dress off completely, leaving me in nothing but my knee-high boots.

"Loriah," he groaned, the sound vibrating deep in his throat.

"Your turn," I smirked, unbuckling his belt and pushing his pants down. He sprang free, thick and ready, and my pulse sped. He kicked off his shoes and gently pushed me back onto the bed, his body following to cover mine as he pushed my knees apart.

He kissed me deeply, the depth of it leaving me breathless. His mouth trailed downward, leaving a scorching path over my collarbone, my breasts, and finally to the sensitive spot between my thighs. His tongue traced over me, while his rough hands kept my hips steady as I writhed beneath him.

"Mmm," he moaned into my flesh.

A gasp escaped me, my fingers gripping the sheets as he worked me closer to the edge. Each stroke of his tongue, each press of his fingers, built a pressure that threatened to shatter me. He slid his fingers inside, curling and coaxing my climax closer. My breath quickened—my body tensing—as I felt myself teeter on the edge of release. Then he pulled back, leaving me begging and needy.

"Christian."

"Not yet," he whispered, his voice like gravel. He undid my boots with practiced efficiency till they hit the floor, punctuating the silence. His hands moved back up my legs, igniting every nerve.

"This is for you," he said as he positioned himself at my entrance, rubbing the head of his cock achingly slowly over my sensitive flesh, precum dripping with every deliberate pass till I was slick with my arousal and his.

"The next is *mine*," he said, his thumb circling my most sensitive spot. "Is that good?"

"Yes," I rasped, the word barely audible as I lifted my hips to meet him, begging.

With that, he thrust into me, filling me. The sensation was at once overwhelming, a perfect mix of pressure and pleasure. I cried out, fingers and nails digging into him as he moved inside me.

Each thrust was purposeful, his hips rolling with a rhythm that made my body hum in anticipation. His hand gripped the back of my thigh, then he placed my knee over his shoulder to deepen the angle. The stretch was delicious, my body alight.

"You need to see this, Loriah," he said, his voice tight with restraint. His gaze dropped to where our bodies joined, the sight spurring him on. "You're perfect."

I couldn't hold back as the tension built inside me. "Harder, Christian."

A growl tore from his throat as he obeyed, his thrusts becoming harder, faster, more desperate. I arched into him, my body trembling as I felt my orgasm building again.

"Please, Christian, harder!" I gasped, my voice raw.

His response came as a series of punishing thrusts. Each one sent shockwaves of pleasure through me. And when I finally tipped over the edge, my entire body convulsed with the intensity of it, my mind emptying of everything except sensation.

"That's it," he murmured, his voice laced with satisfaction.

Before I could fully recover, he flipped me effortlessly onto my stomach. His hands gripped my hips, pulling me up so he could enter me from behind. The shift in position brought a new, deeper depth, and I cried out as he drove into me.

"Don't scream," he commanded. "I told you, this is mine."

I could barely get out his name as he picked up the pace. His thighs slammed against my ass with unrelenting force.

I caught sight of us in the full-length mirror—his muscular frame moving with raw power, my body arching, breasts heavy and swaying to meet his thrusts. It was primal, untamed, and utterly consuming.

"Take it, Loriah," he growled.

My hand moved between my legs, desperate to advance my climax faster. The sensation built rapidly, overwhelmingly, until there was nothing but him, me, and the electricity coursing through us.

When I came, it was blinding, my cries echoing in the room. Christian followed moments later, pulling out to finish on my back, his release warm against my skin.

We collapsed onto the bed, chests heaving.

"Do you want me to stay?" he asked, his tone light with curiosity.

I hesitated. "Would you be offended if I said no?"

He appeared to think for a moment, but then shrugged. "No. But I'm smoking a cigarette before I go."

I pulled on a sweatshirt and joined him on my small balcony after cleaning up, the cool air a balm to my overheated skin. We smoked in silence, sipping the coffee I'd made on the way out.

"This doesn't have to change anything," he said finally.

I stopped him with a wave of dismissal. "We don't *need* to talk about it. We're two adults. It doesn't have to be complicated."

His grin was shy and disarming. "Well, if you ever want more uncomplicated time, let me know. I'm happy to oblige."

I clinked my mug against his, a smile tugging at the corners of my lips. "It's a plan."

After he'd left, I settled against the railing, letting the night's events wash over me. I was praying for calm, though all I felt was that same gnawing tug.

CHAPTER 28
Loriah

"S o," Allie said, arching her brow and leaning across the table while she swirled her mimosa with deliberate slowness.

"Sooo" I echoed, feigning innocence as I stared into my drink, the bubbling orange liquid a far safer focus than her knowing gaze.

"Come *onnn*!" she urged, finally frustrated. "You and Christian bailed early last night. By the way, I grabbed your jacket for you—remind me later." Her casual mention didn't mask the anticipation in her voice.

"Yeah, well–" I paused, debating how much to share. "It was great. Exactly what I needed to clear my head and, you know. Move on."

Allie's eyes sparkled with mischief. "Move on, huh? *That's* your story. You'd be shit at poker." She leaned back, sipping her drink as if she wasn't about to press me further.

"Stop it," I groaned. "I mean it. It's not a big deal."

"Not a big deal?" She practically choked on her mimosa. "Loriah, who was the insanely hot Spanish god looking like he was about to devour you whole?"

"Take a wild guess."

Her jaw dropped, and she gasped so loudly that heads at nearby tables turned. "Nooo. *Perez?*" she whispered, then added with a giggle. "Or do I call him *Agustin* now?"

I sighed in exasperation, sinking into my seat as the memory of his consuming gaze burned anew in my mind.

"No. *You* don't call him anything."

"Holy shit though, Lor. He's really intense. The way he was staring at you?" She fanned her face dramatically. "No wonder you dragged Christian home. All that built-up frustration had to go somewhere, right?"

"Stop it. You're gonna make me regret telling you." I laughed despite myself. "It was fun, not serious."

"Sure," she said with mock sincerity, idly rotating her glass. "But tell that to either of those men—from where I stood—they all had *decidedly* different ideas."

"Yeah, well. *They're* not me," I countered, nursing my drink with a sigh. "Plus, I don't owe Perez anything. He made his decision. And let's be honest, it's been two years. I needed this."

Allie choked, nearly dropping her glass. "Two years?!" Her voice carried to a dramatic pitch, making me wince. I reached across the table, clamping a hand over hers.

"For God's sake, Allie! Yes. I told you—long relationship, messy ending. It's not something you can bounce back from overnight."

She gave me a pitying look, though her mischievous grin was back in seconds. "We need to get you out more. Stat."

"No thanks." I laughed, shaking my head. "I'm good, honestly. Please don't *help* me."

"Whatever you say–" Her playful tone made it clear she wouldn't be listening.

When I got home, the quiet brought a flood of thoughts with it. My heart was a confused mess. The case, the club, the mounting evidence—it all spiraled in my mind. I had a lot to sort out: the blood sample, Woods's electronics, and the families arriving the following week. Somewhere in this mess was a thread that connected it all, I just hadn't found it yet.

As I typed up notes, my phone buzzed with an incoming message. The music playing in the background, Taylor Swift's *Delicate*, felt too fitting.

> **Christian -** *I had a great time last night.*

> **Me -** *Me too. Thank you.*

The moment I hit send, I cringed. Really? I thanked him like we'd closed a business deal?

> **Christian -** *It was a chore for sure, lol. Let's do it again sometime soon?*

> **Me** - *Possibly. Probably. Lol. I'm swamped with case notes right now.*

> **Christian** - *I could help you relax. Hungry?*

I hesitated, taking a moment to consider, knowing I should say no, but after weeks of emotional turmoil, the thought of his touch was just too captivating to willingly throw away.

> **Me** - *How soon can you be here?*

> **Christian** - *Open your door.*

My heart skipped a beat.

He's messing with me.

I set my laptop aside and tentatively crossed the room to the door. When I opened it, there he was—Christian, holding a bag of takeout, his backwards cap highlighting those playful blue eyes. My eyes took in his muscular chest peeking under his partially unbuttoned gray plaid shirt and the way his jeans hugged him in all the right ways. And his smirk—oh God, that smirk—it promised trouble.

I grabbed and yanked him inside. His mouth crushed mine in a kiss that stole my breath. He dropped the bag on the floor, threw off his jacket, and pushed me with his body toward the hallway. Clothes hit the floor in a trail leading to my bedroom, and soon his lips were everywhere, unraveling me in ways I hadn't realized I needed.

Hours later, we lay entwined in the sheets, my body deliciously sore and my mind blissfully blank. Christian propped himself on one elbow, tracing lazy patterns on my stomach with his finger.

"I could stay like this all day," he murmured, his voice low and promising more.

"I can't have you do that." I laughed, swatting his hand. "I need to call my dad, and I have so much work to go through."

He groaned, adjusting onto his back. "Fine. I *guess* I have things to do, too." He stood, stretching before pulling on his jeans. "But next time, I'm not letting you off so easily." He winked, leaning down to press a lingering kiss on my lips.

I watched him leave. My heart was lighter than it had been in weeks. As the door clicked shut, I let out a deep exhale, already feeling the quiet seep back in. This little slice of peaceful domesticity wouldn't last forever—I knew that. But for now, it had to be enough.

CHAPTER 29
Perez

The growl of my motorcycle's engine mirrored my shit mood when I'd made my way out to ride to my family's estate. The autumn chill cut through my open jacket and was barely able to soothe the fire smoldering inside during the hour-long ride to Scarsdale from SoHo. I gunned the throttle, the wind whipping at my clothing as the city disappeared behind me. 'Virus' by Elija blasted in my earbuds, but it couldn't drown out the torrent of thoughts and the memory of her in that dress.

Loriah's face haunted me like a stubborn shadow. What gnawed at me most, though, wasn't that she hadn't flinched when Ares had his hands on her, or even that she'd mistaken me for him. I was used to that mix-up. No. None burned deeper than when I watched her with Jackson. She'd let someone else get close. It pushed me to my breaking point. But I'd been the one to keep her at arm's length. That choice had been *mine*—not hers. Being angry was something I'd probably forfeited my rights to, but there it was—front and center. My hands gripped the handlebars, knuckles aching under the weight of my own bitterness.

I swerved to dodge a car edging too close, flipping the driver off without a second thought. Their honk barely registered as I twisted the throttle, pushing the bike faster.

Fuck you, dude.

No matter how fast I went, it did little to ease the way I seethed. Her beauty, so unapologetically raw, and the way she threw herself into life with a reckless kind of care—it was intoxicating. Loriah Fairsbane was undoing me.

The estate came into view, and I wound my way down the tree-lined drive. I killed the engine, swung off the bike, and stalked toward the house. My family's butler opened the door before I could even raise a hand to knock.

"I'll take those for you, sir," he said, reaching for my helmet and jacket.

"Thanks," I muttered, shrugging them off. "Where is everyone?"

"The library," he replied with his usual formality.

"Thank you."

I headed down the familiar hallway, where the scent of tobacco, lemon polish, and aged books greeted me like an old acquaintance as the door drew closer. The library had consistently been a place of reverence or fear—a room where we were typically only lectured or celebrated, depending on our father's mood. Today, it was another reminder of the expectations placed on me and how I'd been failing at many of them.

"Agustin! You've made it. Took the bike, I see." A disapproving tisk cut through the air from my immaculate mother. Not once had I ever seen a hair out of place. She gave me a quick hug, then stepped back to examine me.

"I did. You know I'm careful." I smoothed my hair back out of my eyes, offering a smile to ease her concern.

"It's not you I worry about—it's everyone else," she said, pressing a kiss to my cheek before moving to pour me a whiskey from a nearby cart. The ice clinked as she dropped it into the glass, her subtle way of bribing me to stay the night, knowing I'd decline any offer to do so.

"I'm glad to see you could join us," Ares called out, striding across the room with a smirk that was too much like my own. He clapped me on the back, his tone dripping with feigned camaraderie. "By the way, my guy isn't too happy about what you did to his face."

"Maybe he should keep his mouth shut about things that don't concern him," I said flatly, rubbing my knuckles.

"Things? Or *someone*?" Ares raised an eyebrow, amusement gleaming in his eyes.

"This isn't what I came to discuss." My tone was sharp. The memory of Loriah intertwined with his insinuations made my blood boil.

"Relax. We need to talk about logistics. One of our drivers is causing problems."

"And why does that involve me?" I asked, crossing my arms.

"Because shipments are disappearing once they hit New York. I need you to find out if there's been an influx from other dealers or if the DEA is making moves. You've got connections in the department."

"I'll look into it," I said reluctantly, already regretting being dragged into another one of Ares's schemes. "But you know I don't deal with that side of things."

Ares reclined in the leather chair, his smile growing. "Oh, forgive me. I didn't realize you'd turned saintly. Tell me, does that woman of yours realize you live so comfortably on drug money?"

"Don't you dare bring her into this." My voice dropped dangerously low.

"Calm down, *hermano*. No need to get defensive. However, you should be aware that there's a leak. Someone's feeding information to the wrong people."

"You think it's me?" I bent over the desk, my hands gripping the edges.

"I didn't say that. But..."

"¡*Basta*!" Our mother's voice sliced through the tension. "Do not shame this family by even attempting to throw that kind of accusation around."

She was right, as always. I straightened, stepping back from the desk. "Send me the details," I said curtly, already done with the conversation.

As I turned to leave, Ares's voice followed me. "You need to get laid, Agustin."

I heard my mother gasp in protest, and a flow of chastising in Spanish followed, but I didn't dignify him with a response.

Hidden away in the security of my old room, I plugged in the HDD containing Woods's hard drive. The events of the weekend had been too distracting for me to explore it fully, but one file, cryptically labeled *SWEETS*, caught my attention. It required a code to decrypt—luckily, I had one from forensics. My fingers flew over the keyboard, the screen coming to life with a treasure trove of information.

Jackpot.

Before heading back to the city, I stopped by my father's private suite. The door creaked open to reveal him dozing in bed, a book resting on his chest. He seemed so small, so fragile—a shadow of the man who had once commanded rooms with a single look.

"*Hola*, Papa," I whispered, stepping inside. His eyes fluttered open, a smile breaking across his lined face.

"Agustin," he said, his voice rasping but warm.

"Come outside with me," I offered. "It's a beautiful evening."

He hesitated, his gaze drifting to the wheelchair in the corner. "I don't know, *hijo*. I can't walk too far."

"Do you trust me?" I asked, switching to Spanish.

His smile grew. "Of course."

Lifting him gently, I carried him out into the garden, the cool air brushing against us. The stars shimmered overhead, and for a moment, the pressure of the world eased. We sat in silence, the kind only a father and son could share.

"How did you know Mama was the one?" I asked, my voice barely audible above the rustling of wind in the trees.

"She was my everything," he said, his voice quiet but steady. "Love doesn't ask for permission, *hijo*. It claims you, and every day, you have to decide if it's worth the risk. I know you haven't always had it the easiest."

"You know. I thought I had everything figured out for so long, and then. Well. I guess I was wrong."

"Sometimes we are the last to know what our plans are going to be in this world. Especially when those plans involve others."

His words settled deep in my chest. I didn't respond because there was nothing more to say. Instead, I stayed with him until the chill became too much, then carried him back inside.

"*Te amo*, Papa," I whispered as I tucked his covers back around him.

"*Te amo, hijo*," he murmured before drifting back to sleep.

As I walked away, the day's anger and frustration clung to me like a second skin. My father's words echoed in my mind, relentless and unshakable: *You have to decide if it's worth the risk.* But what if the risk wasn't as simple as losing her? What if the real danger was me?

After leaving so much pain in the wake of my stupid decisions, Loriah didn't deserve to be another casualty of my choices. And yet, every instinct I had screamed to hold on, to pull her closer. I didn't know how to protect her, not from the world. Or the case. And certainly not from myself.

The choice I had to make left me stranded between what *I* wanted and what I feared *she* needed most.

CHAPTER 30
Loriah

The sharp smell of brewing coffee coaxed me out of bed, enough to shuffle toward the bathroom, wishing it were any other day than Monday. The face staring back at me in the mirror reminded me too much of my mother—her features etched into mine, though the life I'd chosen couldn't be further from hers.

I shook my head, pushing the past away and refocusing on the day ahead.

Agustin Perez was sure to spend the day brooding after all that happened over the weekend. I'd been petty, using Christian as a way to get under his skin—trying to provoke something in him I wasn't even sure I wanted to see.

However, the truth was that I knew he had a temper. Not just irritation or cutting words—something darker, more profound. And part of me couldn't stop wondering if I'd pushed him too close to that thin edge.

What I'd done clung to me, twisting in my gut with a discomfort I couldn't shake. I needed that morning run—needed something to clear the noise before I fell into a spiral of anxiety from overthinking.

The city hummed with early risers as I hit the pavement. The air was cool and damp, mingling with the distant scent of hot baked goods and coffee from a nearby street vendor. I pulled my orange reflective vest tighter and adjusted the strap of the water pack. I had tucked my service pistol discreetly under my gilet, a habit I couldn't break even during something as mundane as a jog.

As I made my way toward Central Park, the sidewalks became increasingly congested with commuters, dog walkers, and tourists. I evaded a man walking three unruly terriers and cut through a cluster of joggers to reach my favorite spot. Stretching out beneath the changing leaves, I pressed my earbuds in and cranked up my playlist; the pounding beats would propel me into a harder pace as the sun was still rising, casting the park in a hazy blue glow.

The run felt cleansing, my muscles burning in the best way. But as my mind was clearing of lingering thoughts, a hand gripped my elbow. Instinct kicked in. I spun to the side, driving my elbow into my attacker's gut. The grunt of surprise was satisfying, but as I spun again and brought my fist up to land another hit, a firm hand caught it in midair, immobilizing and spinning me before I could get a look at the pervert.

I struggled against a hard chest when they ripped an earbud out, causing me to flinch from the sudden ambient noises, disorienting my senses.

A rich and all too familiar voice purred into my ear, "It's me. Relax, and I'll let you go."

My body betrayed me, yielding to the authority in his voice before my brain could catch up. When recognition hit me, I turned and extended my open palm. He placed the small black earbud in it, music still blaring from its tiny speaker. His fingers remained a beat too long, grazing my palm as he withdrew.

"I called your name." He offered by way of greeting, eyes gleaming with amusement. "Thought I'd be polite instead of tackling you."

"Well, you failed spectacularly," I snapped, trying to ignore how his sweat-damp shirt clung to his body. "What do you want? And don't tell me you just *happened* to be here."

"Crazy. A person running in Central Park. What *are* the odds?" His sarcasm dripped with feigned innocence.

I folded my arms, glaring at him like the intruder he was. "I've never *seen* you here before."

"Well, should I text you my schedule so we can avoid this awkwardness next time?"

"Take your sarcasm and your bullshit somewhere else, Perez. I'm busy."

"I didn't stop to fight with you." He held his hands up in surrender, though his tone suggested anything but peace. "I need to talk to you."

"Personal or professional?" I fired back, already preparing to jog away.

"Both," he admitted, his arms crossing in a way that blocked my escape route without moving a muscle.

"Well, pick one," I said. "Because I'm about three seconds away from running till I vomit."

"That's dramatic."

"Two seconds."

"Fine, personal." The words came out in a rush, frustration flashing in his eyes when I took a step back.

"Take a number, Perez. I'll see you at work."

Without giving him a chance to respond, I shoved my earbuds back in and took off, my strides lengthening as my muscles burned with the effort. I could feel his gaze on me as the distance became longer. His voice carried after me, but I didn't slow down, instead pumping my legs faster with the effort to outrun my growing anger and praying he'd take a hint and not follow.

By the time I arrived at the station to shower and change, my thighs throbbed with a welcome strain that couldn't quite mask my simmering irritation. The run had taken the edge off the nagging tension from earlier, settling into something manageable. Making my way from the women's locker rooms, I caught sight of Perez through his office window, mid-conversation with another officer. His gaze snapped to mine with a severity that proved our morning encounter wasn't over. I refused to acknowledge him, instead grabbing coffee and choosing to throw myself into reviewing voice-mails.

The first voicemail I listened to hit like a physical sucker punch. Cody Hughes, the father of our Jane Doe, wanted to retrieve his daughter's body. I jotted down the details mechanically, needing to replay the message three times to understand him through his tears. On the third attempt, my own tears spilled freely onto the notepad from the anguish I heard in his voice, blurring the details. I wiped at them with my sleeve, slowing with thought, and dreading the call to the medical examiner.

Arranging Kayleigh's transfer to the funeral director would be one of the hardest things I'd face all week, but it was part of the job—the part they never showed in police procedurals.

Lost in thought, I stared out the window. Couples parted ways with quick kisses, a woman struggled to wrangle her overenthusiastic dog, and a man spilled coffee as he dodged through traffic. The city had a way of continuing, no matter what darkness we uncovered within it.

The soft *thwack* of a manila envelope hitting my desk pulled me out of my reverie. I glanced up to find Agustin standing over my desk with a determined expression.

"What's this?" I asked.

"Open it." His tone left no room for argument. He crossed the room and closed the door with a soft click before turning expectantly towards me.

"You can't just say?" I tried, but he only shook his head. Haltingly, I opened the envelope and pulled out the first photo.

My stomach dropped like I'd missed a step on a dark staircase. The grainy black-and-white image showed a man seated in a chair with a young woman straddling him. Her face was jarringly young—*too* young—and his hands gripped the sides of the chair as if he were bracing himself against something inevitable.

"What the hell *is* this?" I whispered, the words scraping my suddenly dry throat. I flipped to the next photo before he could answer.

The next one punched harder. The man, now standing, had his hand on her hip as she leaned into him, her small breasts brushing his chest. My pulse pounded against my temples as I turned to the last image, dread pooling in my gut.

Christian?

The man I had spent the weekend with, tangled in each other's bodies, had his hand wrapped around the girl's waist as she pressed into him. Her face was unmistakable.

My throat tightened. "Why are you showing me this?"

"You tell *me* what's wrong with that situation, Fairsbane."

"I—" My voice cracked. "I don't understand."

"We need to question him." His voice was low, firm, like the barrel of a loaded gun pointed at my chest. Except I was the one forced to pull the trigger.

"And what is this supposed to mean? People go to clubs all the time." My protest sounded weak even to my own ears. Bile rose threateningly, but I shoved it down hard. "This"—I tossed the folder back at him—"is not proof of *anything*."

"*Except*, he assured you he doesn't go to clubs, remember?"

"You're so desperate for him to be the bad guy, aren't you?" I snapped, my voice shaking with equal parts anger and humiliation.

"And you're so desperate for him to be in your bed," he threw at me. And like any good archer, they found their mark. He narrowed the space between us, his eyes locking onto mine with an intensity that made my stomach churn. "Fifteen minutes. Interrogation Room Three. Either you go with me, or I do it alone."

He turned and strode out, leaving the door ajar. My anger threatened to choke me. I wanted to scream in response to his accusation, but damning photos stared back from my desk, their grainy details unraveling the tenuous threads of trust I'd woven.

I clenched my fists, trying to ward off the storm brewing, when I felt a sob scratching to escape.

How will I confront him?

How could I possibly meet his gaze, demanding answers to questions I wasn't even certain I wanted to ask?

Perez's words echoed in my mind, sharp and unrelenting: *Prove me wrong.*

But this wasn't about proving anyone wrong. It was about trust, about lies—about me willingly letting my guard down, only to have it exploited. My jaw clenched as the realization settled like a stone in my gut.

I glanced at the images one last time, their harsh truths impossible to deny. The fury that flared wasn't solely at Perez, though he made a convenient target. It wasn't even entirely at Christian. It was on me.

I'd slept with Jackson, partly to spite Perez, brushing off his cryptic warnings simply because they came wrapped in that maddening air of superiority he always had. But I'd been caught in the crossfire of their power struggle, with photographic evidence proving my impulsive choice might have been precisely the mistake Perez had tried to prevent.

I'd turned my body into a weapon to make a point—yet somehow, I was the one who ended up ambushed.

It struck me how ironic the situation was as I grabbed the folder, my resolve hardening like ice. The sting of betrayal was sharp, but the warmth of my determination burned brighter, pushing aside the hurt. I was eager to uncover the truth behind whatever Christian was hiding.

Clutching the folder tightly, I felt the crumple of the paper beneath my fingers, with the photos inside bearing witness to my silent rage.

CHAPTER 31
Loriah

I escorted Christian into Interview Room Three, feeling suddenly uneasy at the growing tension, as I struggled to smile easily or answer his questions. When we entered, Perez was seated at the metal table, the damning folder lying like a bomb in front of him. His expression was maddeningly neutral, but I could feel the undercurrent of anticipation radiating off him. He was dangerous because he never needed to say, *I told you so*—he made you *feel* it instead.

"What's this about?" Christian asked, gaze darting between me, Perez, and the folder. "Are we expecting someone?" He tried a weak smile, his usual assuredness dimmed by confusion that only pulled at my heart more.

"We need to have a discussion," I said, steadying my voice and looking him in the eye. The weight of what was in that folder threatened to crack my composure, but I couldn't let it show.

Perez pulled out a small recorder, the same type I'd used for Angel's interview, and set it on the table without pressing the button.

"Are you serious?" Christian asked, suspicion creeping into his tone.

"Have a seat, please," Perez told him coolly.

Reluctantly, Christian sat, eyes narrowing. I walked around the table and took the seat beside Perez. Perez's dominance filled the room, his attention locked on Christian with an intensity that made me uneasy.

Perez leaned forward, his fingers drumming a slow, deliberate rhythm on the table. "So, Jackson. About a week ago, a witness identified you as being the same man that she saw at the club where a recently murdered woman worked. You told Detective Fairsbane you didn't frequent that establishment, that it was a misunderstanding. So, tell me, why *were* you there?"

"I told Loriah—" Christian started, but Perez cut him off sharply.

"Fairsbane," Perez corrected, his tone like ice.

Christian paused, his confusion melting into something darker. He leaned back, slowly nodding in understanding. His voice was tinged with bitterness when he spoke. "I see what this is," he said, waving his finger between the folder and Perez.

"Please, let's just stay on track," I interjected, trying to steer the conversation back before it derailed altogether.

"Yes," Christian said, his jaw tightening. "I told *Detective Fairsbane* I hadn't frequented that club. And it wasn't a lie. I went there *once*. That's what's in the folder, isn't it?" His tone was cutting as he gestured dismissively at the folder and held up one finger to make his point.

"You'd be correct," he said. "But can you imagine *our* surprise at what else we found?"

"We? Or *you*?"

Perez didn't answer him. Instead, he grabbed the folder and opened it slowly, turning the pages one by one, dragging out the silence like a blade across a whetstone.

Christian's face darkened, shame and frustration warring for dominance. "Listen," he said, his voice low. "Someone was obviously taking those, but how was I supposed to know? It was a one-time thing."

I braced myself against the table, knuckles whitening as my fists clenched. "Then explain, Christian. Currently, it looks pretty bad." I hated the desperation that flooded my voice.

Christian rubbed his hand over his face, the weight of the situation dragging his shoulders down. "Woods invited me. Said it was a department party. I didn't *want* to go, but I thought refusing might make me look like an asshole. I truly had no idea what I was walking into."

"And the woman in the photos?" Perez pressed. "Do you know her?"

"No!" Christian snapped. "I didn't even talk to her. She approached me for a dance, and I'd already had a couple of drinks, so I didn't question. How was I supposed to know anything illegal was happening? I was there for maybe an hour before I left."

"And you didn't think to mention this?" I asked.

"Why would I? How could I? The fact that you've seen pictures of me like that is humiliating enough as it is!" His voice cracked, and for a moment, I saw the vulnerable man beneath the bravado.

"Perez, can you go get us some coffee?"

As soon as he walked out, I knew I had precious moments to reach Christian on a level that he wouldn't be comfortable with around Perez.

I pressed my palms against the table, trying to ground myself, and breathed through my nose, willing my pulse to calm.

"Did you confront Woods about this?"

"I did," Christian said, his voice softer now. "I told him I thought something shady was going on. He got nervous and stopped talking to me altogether after that. Then, a couple of days later, he's dead. What was I supposed to do, Loriah?"

I leaned closer, my voice quieter but no less firm. "Why didn't you go to Daniels? Or Perez? They could've helped you."

Christian laughed bitterly. "Perez? Seriously? He's been gunning for me since day one. And Daniels? I didn't know who to trust. Woods was on the force, which meant someone higher up might've been covering for him."

I stole a glance at the two-way mirror, knowing Perez was likely watching from the other side. The weight of Christian's words pressed down on me. If Woods was dirty, how much did Perez know—or not know?

"I'll talk to him," I said, my voice steady but my resolve crumbling.

"Yeah?" Christian shot back, his anger spilling to the surface. "Are you gonna put him in this chair too? Make him feel like a goddamned criminal?"

"Christian—" I reached for his hand, but he pulled back, shaking his head.

"I've been honest with you, Loriah. Can you say the same about your partner?" He turned to the mirror, his gaze like a challenge. "You can come in now, Perez. She'll probably want that coffee."

The door opened, and Perez walked in, coffee cups in hand. Christian stood, his chair scraping against the floor as he pushed it back.

"I've heard enough. If there's nothing else, I have work to do," Christian said and stood to walk to the door. He paused. "I hope you got what you needed, Loriah. You could've just asked me."

The door slammed shut behind him, leaving a suffocating silence in his wake.

Perez set a cup of coffee on the table, his movements measured and deliberate. "Well, that went well."

I glared at him, my chest tight with resentment. "Fuck off, Perez!" I yelled at him. "Maybe he's right. Maybe *you* should be in that chair too."

Perez didn't flinch. "If it gets us closer to the truth, I'd sit there willingly."

I stood, grabbing the coffee and turning away. "You don't get to play noble, Perez. You could've let me handle this my way. Like I *asked*."

"That wasn't my intention."

I didn't turn around to see if he meant it.

"No," I replied, my voice sharp. "You've made your intentions clear. I'm done being part of your witch hunts."

I shoved past, making for the door, leaving him—and the weight of his judgment—behind.

CHAPTER 32
Loriah

My desk phone rang, and seeing Christian's extension on the display sent my heart into an anxious somersault.

"Fairsbane," I answered, keeping my tone neutral and professional despite the knot forming in my stomach.

"The guys think they got a hit on that DMV forger," he said, voice clipped, all business.

"What is it?"

"They saw him meeting with a guy we know has cartel ties."

"OK, bring him in," I said, the possibility of a breakthrough lighting a spark of energy in me. "Christian, I—"

"I need to go," he cut me off, and the line went dead before I could offer the apology I'd been rehearsing since that morning, knowing that over the phone was a cowardly excuse.

Two officers flanked Alexander Dolino as they escorted him into the station an hour later. He didn't strike me as particularly remarkable: his nose was too small for his face, his eyes were too close together, and his mousy brown hair, streaked with gray, was neatly trimmed but utterly forgettable. His demeanor, however, made up for his mundane appearance. He walked with the unshakeable confidence of someone who'd dodged accusations so many times, they no longer fazed him.

Perez appeared at my side, his presence steadying and irritating in equal measure after the events of earlier.

"Do you want to take the lead?" he asked.

"Yes," I said, meeting his gaze. "Hop in if you think I've forgotten something. I know you won't be able to help yourself."

He smirked faintly, but it didn't reach his eyes.

Inside the interrogation room, Dolino sat with his hands folded neatly in front of him. He wore an obnoxious purple satin bow tie dotted with yellow hearts, a garish choice that practically begged for attention.

"Interesting choice," I remarked as I sat down, nodding toward the tie.

"Some people collect shoes or watches," he said, adjusting it with a quick flick of his fingers. "I collect bow ties. I see no difference."

His arrogance instantly grated on my nerves, and all I could think was *that smarmy lil' shit looks like he needs a good throat punch.*

"How many do you own?" Perez asked from his spot beside me, his tone conversational.

"Two hundred and thirty-seven."

"*Impressive,*" we both said in bland unison.

The small talk abruptly ended when I slid a photograph across the table. "Do you know José Gonzáles?"

Dolino barely glanced at the picture. "I interact with many individuals, Detective."

"Fairsbane," I told him, keeping my tone calm and even. "And this is my partner, Detective Perez. Do you specifically remember *this* man?" I asked again, jabbing a manicured finger at the picture.

Dolino leaned forward slightly, his eyes slowly following the grainy photo of him speaking with an older Hispanic man in the parking garage of a local apartment complex. "Ah, yes," he said after a moment. "He was inquiring about the car I'm selling."

"Is that right?" I feigned interest. "Why are you selling it?"

"Why does anyone sell a car? I don't need it anymore," he replied.

"So, to confirm," I continued, matching his posture, "your meeting with one of New York's most notorious drug lords was purely to what? Discuss selling a car? How perfectly suburban of you."

"Whatever that man does in his spare time is no concern of mine," Dolino said, a faint smile tugging at the corners of his mouth. "Is my lawyer here yet?"

"Interesting," Perez said, his tone deceptively casual. "Why would an innocent man need a lawyer over a simple conversation about a car?"

"Call it moral support," Dolino said, his confidence unwavering.

Time was ticking down to when Dolino's lawyer would arrive, so I pressed harder. "You expect us to believe that a man with Gonzáles's resources would waste his time shopping for cars on Craigslist?"

"I can send you the link if you'd like. I'm open to negotiations." Dolino offered a derisive smile as he sat back in his chair.

Perez's voice cut in, low and firm. "Traffickers are bringing young women into New York with IDs that look legitimate—IDs someone like you could easily make."

"The sex trade is a terrible thing." Dolino sighed. "But it has nothing to do with me."

Before I could respond, the door burst open, and a tall, sharp-featured man in a charcoal suit stormed in. His horn-rimmed glasses perched precariously on his nose, and a flustered officer trailed behind him.

"I'm Jericho Schwartz," he announced, his deep voice commanding attention. "Mr. Dolino's legal counsel. Do not answer another question."

"I'm sorry, Detectives, he rushed past me." A younger female officer, whom I hadn't seen before, breathed out while staring daggers at the emboldened lawyer.

"Don't worry about it. Thank you," I assured her as the door shut.

"Nice of you to join us, Mr. Schwartz," Perez said, standing and crossing his arms.

Schwartz turned to me, his tone clipped. "Do you have any evidence to hold my client, or is this little chat over?"

Perez pushed off the wall he'd been posted up on and took three long strides, placing himself closer to the table, his imposing frame filling the space between us and the lawyer. "We have photos of your client meeting with a known drug lord."

"A chance encounter in a parking garage," Schwartz shot back, unfazed. "Not exactly incriminating."

Perez leaned in, his voice dropping with an underlying promise. "We'll see about that."

Once Dolino and his weasely lawyer were gone, Perez and I regrouped outside the room.

"We need that search warrant *now*," I said, frustrated by how close we were, yet lacking the evidence to make anything stick.

"I submitted the request this morning," Perez replied. "I'll follow up when I get back to my desk."

"Good," I said, running a hand over my lips and tugging at a dry bit. "I'll make sure Angel's watch rotation is covered tonight, and if she can ID any suspects."

"I'll keep you updated," Perez said.

As he walked away, his broad shoulders disappearing down the hall, I was left wishing every interaction with him could be that straightforward, professional, and easy.

But nothing about this case—or Perez—was *ever* easy.

CHAPTER 33
Loriah

There was an urgent rap on my office door.

"We got it," Perez reported as he peered in. "Gear up. We roll in ten."

"I'll meet you downstairs," I said, adrenaline already surging through me.

I slipped my ballistic vest under my jacket; the bulk of it felt foreign after months of suits. The weight pressed down on my chest, a tactile reminder of what lay ahead. In the elevator, I caught sight of Christian's cubicle. He looked up as I passed, his gaze holding mine long enough for me to register his hurt before he returned to his work. The gulf between us felt impossible to bridge.

Perez was leaning against the squad car when I stepped outside, arms crossed, eyes fixed on the building above. His profile was sharp against the midday light, jaw set with that familiar determination. He didn't acknowledge me, lost in some private thought, but jerked upright when I opened the car door.

Unspoken currents of energy crackled through the half-hour ride, each minute stretching like a wire about to snap. I wanted to ask what had been on Perez's mind—if he had felt bad, if this was all a game to him—anything to understand why he did what he did. When we arrived, Perez's hand briefly landed on my shoulder, a rare gesture of camaraderie before exiting the car.

"Be careful."

"You too," I replied, trying to match his solemn tone.

The sounds of city life leaked through open windows of the nondescript apartment building: TV shows, pots clattering, children laughing. A young woman perched on the fire escape, a cigarette dangling from her lips, watched us with disinterest.

Our eyes met briefly. I brought a finger to my lips in a shushing gesture, and the woman responded with a dismissive turn of her head, exhaling a plume of smoke.

Perez led the team up the stairs, his voice low with authority.

"Let's get in, get what we need, and keep it clean. Dolino's thorough. He'll have hidden anything worth finding. And keep your eyes open."

The officers nodded, their focus sharpening.

On the third floor, Perez banged on the door to apartment 302. "Police! Open up! We've got a warrant!"

Silence.

He signaled for the door ram. One solid hit, and the door flew open, splintering at the frame. Perez's voice echoed through the sparse, sterile space. "Police! Warrant!"

Again, no response came.

The apartment was impeccable, almost resembling a clinical environment. It featured two bedrooms and had minimal furnishings: a pristine leather couch, end tables that seemed to have been taken straight from an art gallery, and expensive paintings hung with meticulous precision. The air carried a faint scent of lemon polish and nothing else.

"This guy's hiding something," I muttered to Perez as we moved through the space.

"If he's not, I'll start wearing a bow tie," he replied, earning him a sidelong glance from me and another officer.

The search stretched into an hour, then two. Every drawer and cabinet yielded nothing but pristine emptiness. Nothing out of place. Not even a speck of dust. It struck me as odd. This went beyond just OCD, or whatever else compelled someone to clean to such an extreme level. This was a sanitation job.

"This isn't where he does his work," I said, frustration creeping into my voice. "Too clean. Too calculating."

"Exactly," Perez agreed. "We need to hit the DMV."

"Agreed," I said, scanning the room one more time before noticing that the back of the couch had been pulled away from the wall. A section of stitching near the bottom appeared out of place, as if it had been hastily repaired. Dolino didn't seem like the type to tolerate such a poorly done mending job.

"Someone, grab a knife," I called out, pointing to the suspicious spot.

An officer stepped forward, slicing through the stitching. The fabric gave way, revealing loose fluff and a hidden compartment.

He reached inside before exclaiming, "I've got something!"

Removing his hand from the hole, he held up a small, milky-white cylinder.

Perez joined me as I tore off the top with a satisfying *pop*. Inside lay a roll of negatives, tightly coiled like a secret. When I held them to the light, my breath caught: images of young women, some in compromising positions, others with men whose faces hovered just beyond identification.

"Trophies?" Perez asked, his voice dropping to that dangerous register.

"Or leverage," I replied.

"Get these to the lab," I instructed. "Have them digitized and copied immediately. I want to know exactly what's on them."

The officer nodded and left, but not before dropping the small tube into a clear evidence bag and labeling it.

"That wasn't what I was expecting," I admitted to Perez as we headed back to the car.

"No," he agreed. "His home is his sanctuary. He wouldn't mix his personal life with his work. Everything we need is at that DMV."

I sighed with frustration. I knew what we had could be big, but it felt too much like we were pawns on someone else's chessboard.

Perez was suddenly serious and turned to me, hand on the steering wheel. "Look. Fairsbane." The steering wheel groaned under his white-knuckled grip. "You know I didn't mean to hurt you, right? That might have seemed like my intention. But it wasn't."

"Perez, I mean this in exactly the way it sounds right now. Fuck off." The words shot out like bullets. "You knew what you were doing, and you did it anyway."

The friction between us pulsed and strained, thick in the air, suffocating. I waited for his defensiveness, a justification, anything. He didn't reply for so long, I thought he wouldn't acknowledge what I had said. But there was nothing.

I leaned back in the seat, and the fight left me. As much as that man infuriated me, those pictures were damning. I realized then that I would have done the same thing if the roles were reversed.

"I'm sorry" was all he managed to say.

CHAPTER 34

Loriah

$\mathbf{A}$s I returned to the station, a sense of unease settled over me—Christian was nowhere to be found. His desk sat empty, and the usual bustle of the rec room offered no sign of him either.

"Has anyone seen Jackson?" I asked an officer who usually sat next to him.

"Yeah, Chief assigned him to that girl's detail at the ho-tel—Williams never showed up."

Assigned to watch over Angel at her hotel? My fingers pressed the knot forming at the base of my skull. I massaged it, willing the stress away. I hoped—prayed, even—that the night would pass uneventfully. With any luck, Angel wouldn't take notice of who was standing guard outside her door.

By late afternoon, there was no word from the photo lab, though that wasn't surprising so close to the end of the workday. The hours dragged as paperwork consumed the rest of my time. The hum of the office beyond my door provided background noise, punctuated by the soft music playing through weak speakers, as a feeble attempt to stave off the monotony.

My phone buzzed against the desk. *Once. Twice.* Then a flurry of vibrations sent it skittering across my paperwork. When I grabbed it, Angel's name filled the screen with escalating panic:

> **Angel -** *Why is he here?!*

> **Angel -** *Fairsbane?*

> **Angel -** *Please.*

> **Angel -** *I know people are after me.*

> **Angel -** *What if he's working with them?*

> **Angel -** *You said I'd be safe!*

> **Angel -** *Please, make him leave.*

Each message hit like a small detonation, the timestamps barely seconds apart. My stomach dropped. I immediately called Angel, and she answered before the first ring ended. Her voice was a whisper and trembling with fear.

"Loriah, please. What is he doing here?" Panic laced her voice as a door closed softly somewhere behind her.

"Angel," I said gently, trying to steady her. "He's there to protect you. We've taken every precaution. It was a misunderstanding."

"But he was there!" Her whisper climbed several octaves. "What if he's working with them?"

"It's okay, Angel." I slipped into the rhythm of controlled calm. "Let's take a few deep breaths. I do believe you, and we questioned him thoroughly. We're working hard to find out who's behind all this, and he was also there trying to do the same thing. He is not your enemy."

"It's the club! I can tell you who—it's the club!" Her voice was low but urgent, the words a hiss.

"I know," I soothed. "I'm building a case to stop these men from hurting anyone else, including you. But until then, I need you to trust me. Stay inside. Don't call anyone else. Watch some TV, relax, and stay put. Officer Jackson won't bother you. He's there to do his job."

"Okay. Okay," she said with more resignation. "I can do that. Will I see you soon?"

"I don't want to make promises, but I will try. Have you thought more about the rape test?"

She hesitated so long the line crackled with static.

"Angel?"

"I don't think I will."

"I'll be there, if that helps."

"I appreciate what you're trying to do, but I don't want to."

"Are you sure? If you change your mind you can always reach back out."

"I'm sure."

My stomach dropped, wishing I could have gotten even a fraction more evidence before the window of opportunity closed, but also feeling so much sadness for this girl who had an impossible choice to make.

"I understand," I finally resolved to say.

After a few more reassurances, we ended the call. I leaned back in my chair, feeling helpless to get more answers without sounding pushy and dispassionate.

Several hours later, I sat and looked around me. My desk was a complete mess---papers were piled haphazardly, and notes were scattered everywhere to the point that I couldn't find anything. I grabbed handfuls of papers and shoved them into a file, mentally promising myself that I would sort them out later.

When I finally stepped into my apartment, the familiar cozy space wrapped around me like a well-loved sweater. Then my eyes caught the couch, and the memory ambushed me—Christian pushing me down onto the sofa, his hands at my waist, the heat of his mouth on my neck, my back pressed against those cushions. So much had happened since then that it was already feeling like a distant memory, corroded by Perez's relentless crusade against him.

Desperation nudged me toward my phone. I needed to apologize. Selfishly, I also needed Christian to forgive me. A small, treacherous part of me hoped he'd let me show him how sorry I was in a way words couldn't manage, but that my body was desperate for.

> **Me -** *I know you're working, so you might not see this for a bit, but I should have come to you first. Please know that's the truth.*

Hours passed without a response. Each minute was a tiny dagger. I imagined him hurt, disappointed, and angry—and I deserved all of it. Perez had pushed me, and I'd folded, afraid of what he might think of me if I didn't comply.

Why did Perez have this power over me? How did he unfailingly manage to find the tiniest insecurity and crawl his way under my skin so efficiently? The frustration mounted, an invisible noose tightening around me.

My eyes burned, and I rubbed at them, trying to clear the haze of exhaustion. The muffled sounds of the city outside lulled me into a serene calm when my phone buzzed, scaring the shit out of me. I snatched it up, disappointed when I saw Baldini's name.

> **Francesco Baldini-** *You're on for Wednesday?*

> **Me -** *Of course.*

> **Francesco Baldini -** *Please ensure you have the proper attire.*

My stomach twisted into a painful knot of anticipation.

> **Me -** *This isn't the type of interview where I'll have to take my clothes off, right?*

Three dots appeared. Disappeared. Reappeared. My heart sped a little more with each passing second.

> **Francesco Baldini -** *No, your interview is…*

I waited, not looking away, as the dots populated for what felt like eternity.

> **Francesco Baldini -** *More "burlesque," let's say.*

> **Me -** *You're sure this will work?*

> **Francesco Baldini -** *Trust me. I know my son. He'll take the bait. Make sure your routine looks legitimate.*

> **Me -** *I'm counting on it.*

> **Francesco Baldini -** *The video will be enjoyable.*

I rolled my eyes. *This fucking guy.*

When sleep never came, I spent the next half an hour cobbling together something resembling a routine. My playlist blared upbeat tracks as I rifled through my closet, clothes flying onto the bed in heaps, but nothing seemed right.

I was excited to be moving closer to tangible results in the case, but I was scared at how far I had to go to achieve them. When realization dawned that I was no closer to finding a convincing outfit, I slammed the rest of the drink and shuffled across the hall to Allie's door.

She answered after three knocks, her hair a mess and her cheeks flushed. From the clinking of glasses in the background, it was clear she wasn't alone.

"I'll come back," I muttered, already retreating.

"Sorry," she said with a sheepish grin, miming a phone with her hand before closing the door.

Back in my apartment, I shoved the mountain of discarded clothes off my bed with one violent arc of my arm, watching it tumble to the floor, and collapsed onto the sheets, trying again for sweet oblivion.

The day's events were a weight I couldn't shake. Staring at the ceiling while passing cars cast long shadows, I pressed my palms into my eyes and watched the stars dance before finally allowing sleep to claim me.

CHAPTER 35
Loriah

"**A**re you going to the funeral home today?" Perez asked over the phone the next morning, his voice unusually subdued.

"I was planning on it. Why?" I replied, already reaching for my notepad to find Mr. Hughes's cell number.

"Just wondering if you'd like company."

"If you want to come, you're welcome to. Though I have a feeling that wasn't really a question." I sighed. "It's probably for the best, though. Showing up together to offer official condolences and ask them to come in for further questioning might go over better with us both there."

"You're probably right. What time?" I could hear the shuffle of papers on his end as well.

"Let me call Mr. Hughes first. They got in late yesterday, and I imagine they'll be exhausted. Then again, I don't know how anyone could sleep in their situation."

"I know I couldn't," he murmured, his voice low and honest.

"I'll let you know."

I hung up and called the funeral home to arrange a meeting time. By the time I called Perez back, the meeting was set: 10:15 AM at Wallace Funeral Home.

The drive was uneventful but tense, marked by the silence that had become our new normal. Perez parked outside the classically beautiful building, its dignified exterior belying the unending grief and pain it witnessed daily.

Walking inside, I crossed myself instinctively, sending up a silent prayer for Kayleigh Hughes, her unborn child, and all the souls who had passed through those doors. The modern interior surprised me—soft beige walls, gleaming wood floors, and lamps meticulously cared for, casting warm pools of light. Arrangements of well-meaning flowers did little to mask the faint chemical smells. The bright and cheery ambience only made the purpose of our visit feel more somber.

A young man greeted us, his pleasant demeanor disarming. His smile was the kind that immediately set people at ease—an invaluable asset in his line of work.

"I'm Chase Wallace. You must be Detective Fairsbane and—"

"Detective Perez," Agustin said, shaking his hand firmly.

Chase led us toward the family viewing room, explaining the care they had taken with Kayleigh's body despite its condition.

"We appreciate everything you've done, Mr. Wallace," I said, moved by his compassion.

"Please, Mr. Wallace is my father," he replied with a slight laugh before turning to Perez. His eyes narrowed in thought. "Detective, have we met before?"

Perez's face drained of color so quickly, I thought he might be ill.

"Possibly. I've been here for various cases," Perez said, his tone clipped and shoulders rigid.

"Hmm. No, I thought it was for more personal reasons." Chase tilted his head. Perez avoided it by glancing away. "I could be mistaken." We stopped at the entrance to a softly lit room. "I'll give you time alone. If you need anything, press the button on the wall and it'll buzz me."

"Handy," I said, tempted. Perez shot me a warning look, eyebrow raised.

"Do *not*," he hissed.

"Ok, *Dad.*"

Mr. and Mrs. Hughes stood close to Kayleigh's casket when we entered, their hands lightly resting on the edge of the polished wood. The floral scent from bouquets of sympathy flowers placed around the room couldn't staunch the smell of chemicals and death. Lilies, carnations, and roses wafted through the air; their arrangements sent by well-meaning friends or family when words were not enough.

"Mr. Hughes," I whispered, trying not to startle him. "I'm Detective Loriah Fairsbane, and this is my partner, Detective Perez," I said, offering my hand when he turned to me, eyes glistening with unshed tears.

We exchanged introductions, though Mrs. Hughes could barely look up, instead dabbing at her eyes with a crumpled tissue. Grief was etched into the lines of their faces, and I looked away to count the buds on a massive bouquet of white roses, trying to compose myself.

"She was our baby," Mrs. Hughes whispered as I approached the casket to stand near her.

Kayleigh's dark hair had been carefully arranged, and her face was painted with a soft blush, making her look as if she were sleeping. Nestled atop her maroon sweater, she cradled a tiny casket of what would've been Hughes' grandchild.

"She never told us she was pregnant," Mr. Hughes said, his voice breaking on the last word.

Tears spilled freely down my face, and I made no attempt to stop them. Beside me, Perez crossed himself, then turned away as if to shield his own emotions. It was a scene neither of us could have prepared for. There was no amount of training or books I could read that would convey how to manage my emotions when faced with the ending of a life. Yet there we were, with two innocents that weren't given the chance even to begin.

Hours later, the four of us sat in the sterile confines of the interview room. A room that only earlier bore witness to my own grief, now absorbed another's.

"No, she was happy. She had friends," Mr. Hughes tried, then choked on his words, stifling a sob. "Was. She *was* happy. Or so I thought. She was constantly on her phone, but what teenager isn't?"

"Did she ever mention dating?" I asked gently.

"Do you have teenagers, detectives?" He sighed heavily. "You'll understand if you ever have a daughter. There's only so much you can push before they shut you out."

"I can only imagine," I said, my heart aching for him.

"She never said much about boys," Mrs. Hughes added. "But she was close to her best friend. If she told anyone, it'd be her."

"Do you have her contact information?"

Mrs. Hughes nodded, pulling out her phone to jot down the number. She hesitated before reaching into her purse and producing another.

"This is Kayleigh's old one. It's tied to her account. She'd use it as a backup sometimes."

"Is it a direct copy?" Perez asked, leaning forward.

"I think so. Kayleigh would switch seamlessly between them."

I slid the phone into an evidence bag. "Thank you. This could be invaluable."

As they left with heartfelt gratitude, their sorrow followed them like a shadow.

Perez and I stood inside the room for a moment, blanketed by the transference of anguish, a cloak that felt like an oily residue clinging to every crevice.

"Loriah—"

"I don't know what I was thinking," I said, cutting him off. "Hoping this place would be any different than what I'd left behind."

"Nowhere is immune to evil. I'm sorry."

I dashed at the moisture gathering on my lashes, not wanting his comfort.

"I'll write up the warrant for Apple today. We should have access within the week."

"Good. I'll follow up on the DNA, should I confirm it's in process?"

"Not a bad idea," Perez agreed, already turning toward Daniels's office.

On my way back to my desk, I caught Christian's eye. He gave me a small, imperceptible smile, which made me recall the unanswered text, and the pang of guilt returned.

CHAPTER 36
Loriah

No sooner had I dropped my bag in the entryway than the door swung open again, catching me off guard. Allie breezed in, holding two beers and dressed in comfy clothes, signaling she'd likely been home for at least an hour.

"Hey. I'm sorry about last night," she said, handing me a cold can.

"Don't be, it could wait."

I sank into the couch, the weight of the day settling over me. I was starting to think I was doing a poor job of managing my expectations. This place was no different than anywhere else.

"Do you want to talk about it?"

"What?" I asked, being pulled back to the moment by her question.

"Lor. I can see you're not okay. Do you want to talk about it?"

"No. I'm sorry. That is not what you or I need right now. I'll be fine."

"Okay, then what *do* you need?"

"Clothes, actually. Something you'd wear to a strip club," I said, watching Allie's eyebrows shoot up.

"What the hell, Loriah? Getting a second job? I can't say that I blame you."

She wasn't entirely wrong. "I can't tell you much, but I need help to find something perfect."

"Lucky for you, I have a shocking amount of clothing for any occasion. Come, step into my office."

We grabbed our beers and walked the short distance to her apartment. Within minutes, we were standing in the center of her room, which now looked like a mini boutique. She had every imaginable color and texture laid out carefully for my perusal.

An hour later, my head throbbed from sifting through sequins, leather, and lace.

It all felt surreal—the lengths I had to go to for answers, the secrecy that now defined my every move. I was hiding the truth from everyone who was supposed to be close to me, from the very people I should trust. But none of that mattered. Because at the end of the day, I knew I couldn't live with myself if I didn't do everything in my power to bring those other girls home. Alive.

"Okay, so, see anything that catches your eye?" Allie asked, flopping onto the couch and watching me with mild amusement.

"I think I'll go with the green dress." I reached for the sleek, form-fitting number that immediately caught my eye.

"Need shoes?"

"No, I've got that covered."

We enjoyed the rest of the evening eating pizza and discussing the complexities of my work life. She listened closely while also attempting to set me up with a coworker she described as a "safe bet." Somehow, coming from Allie, that phrase felt more like a warning than a compliment.

Wednesday came, bringing nothing but silence from Christian.

I was standing at the coffee pot, reaching for a refill, when he walked up, mug in hand. His shift was about to start, and I wanted to say something—anything to close the rift between us that seemed to grow larger every day.

"Getting ready for your shift?" I offered lamely, as he drew closer, knowing my words were pathetic in their attempt.

He didn't ignore me. Not exactly. No, it was worse. He just stared. Not a glance, not a flicker of acknowledgment—just a cold, piercing gaze that cut straight through me. I knew he'd heard me. There was no way he hadn't. But without uttering a single word, he left me feeling smaller than a speck of dirt on his boot.

And honestly, I didn't know how much more my heart could take.

Later in the day, Perez and I received an invitation to Kayleigh Hughes's celebration of life and burial in Stilwell, scheduled for Saturday. With such short notice, there wasn't much time to plan. After visiting multiple websites, I finally printed off ticket prices to bring to Chief Daniels.

"Hey, Chief," I began, holding up the papers. "I'd like to take some time to attend the funeral for Kayleigh Hughes this weekend. I know it's short notice, but I think it'd be an excellent opportunity to observe who's in attendance and speak with her friends without making them come here."

"Of course, Fairsbane. That's probably for the best. Keep the receipts. Is Perez going with you?"

"I haven't asked him yet," I admitted sheepishly, hoping that I wouldn't have to spend an entire weekend with one of the people I was desperate to avoid.

"Ask him, then. I'll approve of his absence as well. Just make sure you're both back on Monday to file your reports."

Fuck.

"Will do. Thank you, Sir."

As I turned to leave, Chief Daniels called out. "Oh, Loriah, how's our witness doing?"

"She's a little rattled, Chief, but I genuinely believe her life is in danger. I think we've made the right call by protecting her."

"It was a wise decision. She'll be monumental if this comes to trial."

"Thank you. That means a lot." I hesitated before adding, "One more thing, Chief. The DNA sample for our Jane Doe went missing, presumably misplaced. We retrieved another, but the current wait time is another two weeks. Is there any way you can get someone to expedite it?"

"I'll see what I can do. Forward me the info."

"Will do. Thanks again."

Ten minutes later, I was standing in Perez's office, dreading the conversation I was about to have and feeling the damp gather at my hairline. Things had been cordial between us since that last interaction. I could still feel the way I'd wanted so badly to lean into his comfort as a friend, a partner, but I didn't allow myself. I couldn't. If he could sense my unease, he made no show of it when I stopped before his desk to address the funerary request.

"I think we should attend Kayleigh's funeral," I said, laying out the details as quickly as possible, hoping he'd say he couldn't go. "It'll be a significant chance to observe and maybe speak to her friends while we're there. But I don't think we *both* need to show up since we greeted the parents together already."

"You're right," he replied without hesitation, cutting off my little speech.

"Okay. I'll uh—start my request now, then."

"Good, me too."

"Well, great," I said, forcing a tight smile.

"I'll get the tickets," he called as I turned to leave.

"Two rooms!" I shot back over my shoulder.

The door closed behind me, and I exhaled slowly.

CHAPTER 37
Loriah

T he whiskey burned going down, and music echoed
through the small bathroom as I prepped and perfected every inch of myself, ticking off everything I knew about
Dante and coming up decidedly short. By the end, I didn't
feel like Loriah anymore. I was Serena. I was someone bold
enough to walk into a club and convince them she belonged.

The music was pounding through the doors of the club
when the taxi dropped me off, reverberating in my chest
like a second heartbeat. I walked to the front of the building,
taking a deep breath and giving my blonde wig a few discreet
tugs—praying the thing wouldn't fly off. The same little man
from the last visit answered the door, no less dismissive as
his eyes swept over me, lingering far too long.

"You, Serena?" he asked, voice gruff and chin tipping.

"That's me. I'm here to see Mr. Baldini for an interview." I pulled my coat tighter around me.

"Sure, honey. Follow me." He opened the door and ushered me inside.

We ascended to the lavish office I remembered all too well. This time, though, *Dante* Baldini sat behind the desk as if it were a place he felt most comfortable, and smiled at me, pleased with what he saw. I looked around the space, feeling nervous, as if a spotlight was shining on my nerves, making them sparkle like the brass pole before me.

"You're not Baldini," I said, trying to sound confident.

"I am, actually. *Dante* Baldini," he said, standing to greet me. "You'll be dealing with me. Your name again?"

"Petrov. Serena Petrov, sir," I replied, adding a hint of a Russian accent as I met his eyes.

"Petrov. Russian, then? My father mentioned you. Said you had real potential."

"Yes, sir. I hope to prove him right." I forced a small coquettish smile, earning a slight nod of approval.

"We're waiting on one more," Dante said, his tone casual but firm. "He's a business partner, and I value his opinion. But if my father's interested, I doubt it'll take much persuasion."

"Understandable," I said, trying to keep my voice steady, though the mention of another person made my pulse quicken. That *wasn't* part of the plan.

"You're early. I like that." Dante moved to the bar and gestured to a decanter. "Drink?"

"Thank you," I replied, accepting the glass he handed me. I scanned the room again over the rim of my glass, but nothing was amiss from my last visit. "To new possibilities," I added, raising it before downing the amber liquid in one gulp.

Dante chuckled as he poured me another drink. "There's no need to rush. The best things in life should be savored." His words echoed the same sentiment his father had voiced mere days earlier.

The apple doesn't fall too far.

Ten minutes passed as Dante grilled me with questions. Where was I from? How had I ended up in New York? Why did I want to dance at the club? I stuck to the script, weaving in details borrowed from my childhood caretaker, Yelena, whose Russian phrases and cultural habits helped add real weight to my storytelling.

When his partner arrived, the air shifted. He lingered in the shadows, his presence pressing against me from afar, unsettling. The hairs on my arms began to stand on end. Then he moved forward, the darkness seeming to solidify as he stepped into the light.

The room shrank, the air charging with a dangerous current as he moved with predatory ease, settling into a chair near the private seating area. The carefully constructed façade of Serena Petrov fractured as recognition dawned.

Ares Perez.

My pulse skyrocketed as his eyes locked on mine, sharp and assessing, as though he could see through the artfully constructed layers of my disguise. Would he give me away? My heart pounded, but I forced myself to keep steady.

"Let's see what you've got," Dante said, motioning toward the dance floor. "We'll start with a song of your choice, then something a bit more interactive?"

I nodded, setting my glass down and stepping onto the floor as a new song spilled into the room—slow, dark, and pulsing with sensual rhythm. I let it wrap around me, guiding the sway of my hips, the arch of my spine, every movement curated to capture the attention of a dangerous man.

I felt Dante's gaze rake over my body.

"Now, let's see how you would handle a client," he said, taking a slow sip of his drink, his tone laced with amusement that turned my stomach. I wasn't expecting the physical response I would have at performing in front of this man. And the drink that was previously fueling my reckless show was beginning to ebb from my body, leaving me with sheer adrenaline.

I moved toward him, each step deliberate, a performance layered over unease. I placed a hand on his shoulder and leaned in close, my lips near his clean-shaven cheek, hoping he wouldn't catch on to my nervous tremor. His cologne was expensive but cloying to my senses.

I was aware of everything underneath the surface. Dante's wealth. His reputation. What I suspected he did for a living—the kind of darkness that didn't leave only bruises on unknown girls, but bodies in dumpsters.

My gut twisted at the thought of being near him longer than I had to.

"Not me, sweetheart," he said with a slow smile. "I just like to watch."

I forced a polite nod and turned away, dragging out the roll of my body as I crossed the room toward Ares.

He watched me with a look that was impossible to read—intense and too familiar. He looked like his brother; the realization unsettled me more than I cared to admit.

Still, I kept moving, letting the music lead me. Ares' tattooed hands gripped my waist when I got close enough to grab onto, drawing me in closer without hesitation. A small gasp of excitement and nerves left my lips before I straddled his lap, tossing my hair over one shoulder with a practiced flip, the thin fabric of my dress sliding higher with each slow movement, each artful sway choreographed to distract.

His hands didn't wander. Not yet. But they held on. Firm, possessive, lingering on the edge of something that made the air between us feel too thick.

"Impressive." His voice was low and rough—but his eyes burned as he dragged out the word. His fingers flexed against my bare skin, a subtle response to the tension now humming beneath the surface, and the stubble of his face tickled my neck when he spoke again. "Is murder not paying the bills?"

I didn't answer. I just kept dancing.

I tilted my head back, letting my hair cascade down my back as I rolled my breasts and belly into him. The movement earned a soft exhale from Ares, his eyes darkening as they roamed to my lips.

"Say anything, and I'll murder *you*," I casually whispered in his ear, followed by, "touching costs more, hun."

Ares let out a groan, peeling a hundred from his wallet. His fingers traveled slowly up the curve of my thigh, bared by the slit of my dress, before sliding the bill against the narrow strap of my black thong.

From the corner of my eye, I saw Dante shift in his seat, his posture tense, his gaze burning into us. I ignored him, focusing on Ares, who was more than happy to soak up the attention.

"Serena," Ares said, his voice a velvet command. "Look at me."

I hesitated, unwilling to face the need in his eyes that reminded me too much of his brother. But his fingers tightened on my chin, guiding me until I met his gaze, and I found myself leaning closer despite myself. The nearness sparked, electric, until I forgot why I was there at all. His lips parted, his breath brushing mine as the song slipped to an end.

"Well," Ares said, his smirk returning as he leaned back, releasing me from a trance. "You've got *my* attention."

I slid off his lap, smoothing my dress as I stood. My heart raced so hard and fast, I didn't know how Ares couldn't feel it. But I kept my expression unremarkable, reluctant to let either man see how deeply they'd rattled me.

"I think I've seen enough," Dante announced, standing and extending his hand. "Welcome to the club, Serena."

"Thank you, sir." I shook his hand, acutely aware of Ares watching my every move.

"She can't work a pole for shit," Ares said with a laugh, standing to rearrange his jacket. "But if you don't hire her, I *will*."

"Not happening," Dante shot back, his tone firm, though amusement flitted across his face when he looked at his friend.

"I'll escort her out," Ares offered, his grin widening when he stood to walk toward me with my coat.

"What the—"

Ares leaned in close, cutting me off as the elevator doors slid shut. His cologne and warmth overwhelmed my personal space.

"Not here," he murmured into my ear, nodding toward the camera in the corner. The elevator felt like the slowest descent on the planet, with all the things I wanted to say to him burning pits in my stomach.

Once outside, I spun to face him. "This isn't a joke, Ares. If you interfere—"

"I won't," he interrupted, raising his hands in mock surrender. "But don't tempt me to tell Agustin. It'd be worth it to see his reaction."

My chest tightened at the thought, but I pushed it aside. "Stay out of my way." As if being in one tug-of-war wasn't enough, now I was beginning to think I'd entangled myself in yet another one.

"Relax," he said with a soft laugh. "I'll keep your secret. *For now*. I think we might be able to help each other." His eyes lingered, studying me with his sideways glance, allowing me a moment to observe the wheels turning in his head.

A cab he hailed came to a stop in front of us, and Ares held the door open, his playful grin slipping to reveal something more profound.

"Is Agustin aware of your involvement with the Baldinis?" I asked him as I slid into the rear seat.

"Goodnight, Detective," he replied with a shut of the door.

Settling back, I was immediately overwhelmed by a feeling that I'd gotten myself into something far more dangerous than I'd imagined.

CHAPTER 38
Ares

L *oriah Fairsbane.*

The moment I saw her, I knew she wasn't *any* Russian woman off the street. First off, I wasn't a fucking moron. And secondly, she was too controlled, although reckless enough to let her eyes betray her in a mix of desperation and danger. I closed the cab door behind her, resisting the urge to follow. Those big blue eyes burned into my memory.

Say anything, and I'll murder you.

A spark of laughter escaped me, honest and unguarded, something absent from my life for longer than I cared to admit. The reality of her was something refreshingly intriguing. If she had any idea who I was, she might think twice about throwing threats my way. But the fact that she didn't? Wellll. That only made her even more fascinating.

My thoughts circled her like a wasp to honey as I made my way back into *Harmonies* to find Dante. That dress—if you could even call it that—had been a distraction all on its own, clinging to her like a second skin. My fist flexed at the memory of her body against mine, the way her heartbeat thundered under my fingers when my lips brushed her ear. If I'd sensed that pull, that raw connection, there was no way Agustin was handling her any better. And if he knew what she was truly up to-- The thought alone brought a crooked smile to my face. My brother's fury would be a beautiful sight, although I wasn't willing to share. *Yet.*

Agustin. Always the twin who did as he was told—until he didn't. If our father had said, "Jump," Agustin would've asked, "How high?" He did—at least, until his conscience finally caught up with him, and he decided he was done following the Perez Family way. Not that he'd lost his taste for violence. That part of him would never change. I'd heard whispers about him returning to our old stomping grounds, earning his money through less savory means—just not the kind that involved beating people to a pulp anymore on behalf of our father.

And then came she.

Sweet, feeling, sarcastic Loriah—turning everything on its head for both of us without even meaning to.

But tonight, there'd been something in her eyes. Something haunted. And I couldn't stop wondering why.

"So, what did you think?" Dante asked, leaning back in his chair as I stepped into his private office.

"She was okay," I said, keeping my tone flat.

"Really? Just *okay*? My, my, Ares Perez—I didn't take you for the lying type."

But I had to lie. If I were to help Loriah, I would use her for my own purposes. She wasn't the only one with a game at play.

"No, she was good," I admitted after a beat, my voice softer, reluctant in my admission.

Dante leered, but I didn't give him a chance to dig further. I made some excuse and left, my thoughts already drifting back to her.

The quiet of my high-rise apartment was usually something I welcomed, but in that moment, it was oppressive. I poured a drink, the burn of the aged scotch doing nothing to dull the memory of her. The way she moved, the fire in her eyes, the vulnerability that was hidden so close to the surface that it would only take one—little—tug to unravel her. It was all knotted up in my mind, refusing to let go of my senses.

I leaned back on the couch, my jacket discarded and shirt undone, the city buzzing outside the windows that overlooked the world below. Helping her meant putting myself in the middle of whatever game she was playing, but I couldn't deny the pull she had on me. She was trouble, and I had no business getting involved. But damnit if I wasn't ready to see where she would lead us.

CHAPTER 39

Loriah

"**G**ood night?" Perez asked as he strolled into my office the next morning with an irritatingly casual demeanor.

"Not especially?" I replied, refusing to look up from my screen.

"Oh, I thought you'd be in more of a chipper mood."

"What's your problem today, Perez?" I asked, finally glancing at him, praying my anxiety wasn't scrawled across my face for all to see. The memory of his twin brother's hands on me the night before still lingered—far too intimate, far too vivid. Just weeks ago, I wanted that from Agustin, not Ares. The thought alone sent heat rushing to my cheeks.

Was he testing the waters between us? Had Ares betrayed my trust—told him, to get a reaction or drive a wedge between us? I had no way of knowing, as he owed me nothing, no matter what he'd said about helping each other.

Perez smirked and sank into the chair across from me, as if he had nowhere else in the world he'd rather be.

"I have a surprise," he said. "Want to know what it is?"

I didn't answer right away, still tangled in my own thoughts. Perez waited anyway, eyes fixed on mine with quiet persistence until I finally met his gaze.

"If you insist," I shot back, tilting back in my chair and staring at him blankly.

He leaned in with exaggerated importance. "We're getting the DNA sample earlier than expected."

"How early?" The excitement in my voice gave me away.

"Monday. Chief pulled some strings."

"That's great," I said, relief washing over me. Then, with a jolt, I remembered. "Oh, shit. I forgot to get tickets!"

Perez gave me a smug look. "Already handled. Told you I'd take care of it."

I avoided his gaze, feeling the weight of relying on him more than I wanted to admit. "Thanks," I mumbled. "I'll check on Dolino's search warrant. Can you follow up with the financial crimes about Woods? I think I saw an email about it yesterday."

"Most likely," he said, standing to leave. "We'll chat later, though. Lunch?"

"Sure. Mexican this time," I called out.

If he was going to play nice, then it could be at the detriment of *his* wallet.

By the time lunch rolled around, my eyes were blurry from combing through reports and endless amounts of surveillance. I had taken a moment to close my eyes, though the only thing I could see was the office in vivid detail. I tried removing the layers—men and music—to focus. Was there something I was missing?

Perez didn't bother knocking, unceremoniously walking in with bags of spicy-smelling food and a stack of files, startling me from my reverie.

We ate in silence at first, too consumed with inhaling the food to talk, but gradually, the quiet settled into something comfortable. Perez had rolled up the sleeves of his white shirt, revealing tattoos winding up his forearms. He ate without hesitation, unconcerned about the mess, and caught me staring when I gestured to my face.

"You've got something," I said, trying not to smile.

He gave me a skeptical look but grabbed a napkin anyway, wiping at the wrong spot.

"Other side," I said, having fun with him despite myself.

He sighed, finally cleaning it off. "Happy?"

"Yes, actually. I didn't want to stare at you with food on your face for the next half hour," I replied, sliding a folder across the desk.

Perez opened it and scanned the pages. The momentary amusement evaporated, his expression darkening with every line.

"Fuuuck."

"Exactly," I said.

"They don't know where this is coming from?" he asked, pointing to the five- and six-figure deposits scattered across the pages.

"Not yet. The accounts are offshore, probably hidden behind layers of shell corporations. I've already filed subpoenas, but it's going to take time."

He nodded, closing the folder. "Good. I assume you're on top of that?"

"Obviously," I said. "But whoever set this up knew what they were doing."

Perez didn't respond immediately; his brow furrowed in thought. Finally, he pulled a laptop from his bag and opened it, turning the screen toward me. "You're probably right. Take a look at these. Months' worth of messages from Kayleigh's social media. She was talking to someone named Will."

I scrolled through three months of exchanges, beginning innocently enough—small talk about family and dreams of escaping her small town. Then it escalated into flirtation and photo exchanges. Kayleigh begged him for pictures of his face, but Will only sent carefully cropped body shots—no tattoos, no jewelry, nothing identifiable. Each of those girls was selected with great care.

"I bet these aren't even of him," I muttered, smoothing the ever-deepening furrow in my brow with my fingers.

This case is going to have me needing Botox before I turn 30.

Perez nodded grimly. "He lured her here, and we need to figure out why."

"Do we have anything on the phone he used?"

"Burner. He's most likely using different phones for every victim."

"Well, shit," I said, sitting up a little more to think. "We'll have to dig through these messages for clues. Where this guy told her to meet him, how she got here, anything."

"I'll keep working on her movements," Perez said, closing the laptop. "But we need to talk to her friends this weekend. They probably know more than her parents did."

"Agreed, teenagers can go either way with loyalty or gossip, and I'm hoping for the latter."

As Perez stood to leave, a knock at the door interrupted us. Jackson poked his head in, clipboard in hand. His eyes took in the scene—the mess of food boxes, notes scattered around my desk, Perez's rolled up sleeves—and I felt my cheeks heat, knowing it looked far too informal.

"Detective," he said pointedly, looking at Perez and then back at me. "We got word. The DMV warrants will be ready first thing in the morning."

"Perfect. Thanks for letting me know," I said.

"Anything else?" His voice was flat and curt.

"Yes," I said too quickly. "Call everyone who was with us last time to meeting room 3. Could you keep it on a need-to-know basis? Please."

"Got it," Jackson said, jotting notes in his book. Efficient as always, even if he hadn't yet forgiven me.

Perez raised an eyebrow as Jackson left. "You trust him with this one?"

"I do," I replied, watching the door close behind him. "He's methodical. Exactly what we need right now."

Perez nodded, gathering his things with the look of a man who didn't quite believe my assurances, but decided to follow my choice anyway. "See you at the briefing."

I felt a flicker of hope as he strode away. We were finally pulling the threads together. Whether it was enough to untangle the mess in front of us was another question entirely.

CHAPTER 40
Loriah

The warrant arrived early, as promised. Our team, fully geared up and tense with anticipation, assembled near the DMV before dawn. Frost clung to the grass around the building, the chill biting at the delicate skin on my face.

Anxiety coiled tight in my stomach, a familiar sensation on operations like this. Dolino was a cunning bastard, and whoever he worked for would have to be as meticulous. There wouldn't be much time before the dominoes began falling. Across the lot, Perez stood near the rear entrance, his presence unyielding and ready to pounce as soon as we got the signal. He hadn't said much to me before leaving the station, but I could feel the agitation emanating from him with every articulated movement.

At 7:17 AM, we moved.

We caught Dolino the moment he stepped inside, blind-sided by officers who emerged from their waiting positions like bloodhounds given a scent. Employees arriving for their shifts watched in shock as we locked down the building and shuffled them away. Within minutes, the DMV became a crime scene. Uniformed officers worked methodically to comb through the building.

The first hour dragged, the seconds stretching like an eternity. Dolino, ever the smug bastard, sat with his arms crossed as if we were nothing more than a minor inconve-nience to his perfect day. His obnoxious, gleaming gold bow tie had me imagining he was about to attend a costumed dinner party, not a professional office job. His gaze swept the room, a flicker of defiance flashing in his eyes, causing my annoyance to rise while we searched.

Then, the breakthrough came.

"I think I've got something!" an officer called out from the far end of the room. My pulse quickened as I pushed myself up from the folders I'd been sifting through.

"What is it?" I asked, stopping beside a blonde officer sporting a severe hair bun.

She pointed to a file, her face a mix of pride and urgency. "Take a look. This is your girl. The Jane Doe."

I leaned in, a small gasp escaping. "It is. Perez, look at this!" My voice carried across the room, turning heads. Kayleigh's face stared back at us, a half-smile on her lips.

Perez joined us, his hand clapping on the officer's shoul-der, sending a twinge of jealousy through me at the contact. "Good job," he said with admiration. The officer's cheeks reddened, and I couldn't blame her—it wasn't every day you got praise from *The* Agustin Perez. "And you as well, Fairsbane. Your instincts were correct."

I straightened, mumbling a half-hearted thanks before turning to another officer stationed near Dolino. "Read him his rights and cuff him," I ordered.

As the officer stepped forward, Dolino didn't so much as flinch. His expression remained detached and indifferent. The audacity of his composure fueled my determination to take him and the whole operation down. This man wasn't untouchable—not anymore.

For the next several hours, the team worked relentlessly, collecting computers, files, and any other items that could be considered evidence. By noon, the DMV had been stripped of anything relevant; the painstaking search provided more than enough to keep us busy for weeks.

"Alright, everyone, bag and tag the last of things, and let's get out of here," Perez announced, his voice cutting through the hum of activity.

I nodded in agreement, ready to get back and regroup. As I made my way outside, the rain had started, its steady patter a fitting backdrop to the grim nature of our work.

The blonde officer approached Perez with a grin, her posture casual but her eagerness evident. Their exchange was brief, and I couldn't make out what she said. But when Perez approached me with a "Good work, Fairsbane, I'll see you back at the station," then climbed into a squad car, something tightened in my chest as her smile lingered.

"Where's your partner?" Horus asked, his grin infectious, when I walked up to the little food cart.

"He's off betraying you for another falafel stand," I joked, though my heart wasn't entirely in it.

Horus laughed, piling extra onto my tray with an almost pitying look. "This one's on me. Make him jealous, kid. We know you're my true favorite anyway."

I smiled and thanked him, trying hard not to spill my food as I made my way back to the car and struggled to find the keys in my pocket. The drizzle from moments before had turned into a steady rain by the time I climbed into the driver's seat.

Sitting in the car, the soft patter of rain against the glass eased the edge off my nerves. The adrenaline I'd been running on for hours was finally fading, giving way to a quiet, heavy sadness. When we'd finished bagging the evidence, there had been more photos than I'd emotionally prepared for. And yet, Dolino had just sat there, watching it all unfold with that same self-satisfied expression etched across his face.

It had been a long, brutal week—one I was more than ready to leave behind.

But we'd found our missing link.

Once I placed the food in the passenger seat, my phone buzzed with a new message. I pulled out my phone, expecting it to be from Perez.

> **Unknown -** *I watch as you move, every step, every breath,*

> *Your heart beats so loud, it's a song of sweet death.*

> *In shadows, I linger, so quiet, so true—*

> *No escape from my eyes, I'll always see you.*

My chest tightened, the cryptic poetry sinking into my skin like a cold blade. My fingers moved quickly, typing a reply.

> **Me -** *Who is this?*

The response came immediately.

> **Unknown -** *Enjoy your lunch, Loriah.*

I froze, the chill in the air seeping into my bones. Outside, Horus was busy packing up his stand, oblivious to the real storm brewing inside my head. With my heart pounding, I scanned the busy street, looking for anything—anyone—out of place. This person had obtained my personal number, and not just that, but they also knew what I was doing.

Was it someone from the club? Was Ares trying to send a message? My thoughts spiraled, falling faster than I could catch them. Nothing made sense. I couldn't breathe around the flood of dread crashing through me.

The rain blurred the edges of my vision as the words repeated in my mind. Whoever this was, they weren't only watching.

They had been waiting.

CHAPTER 41
Loriah

A looming figure appeared over my desk as I was shoving another forkful of food into my mouth.

"Horus?" Perez asked, his tone casual.

I nearly choked on a bite, nodding as I swallowed. "Horus says I'm the favorite," I teased, aiming for smugness around a mouthful of food.

"What?"

"I said"—I swallowed dramatically for effect—"*I'm* the favorite!"

"Ahhh. That traitor." His voice dripped mock disdain, though his easy, lopsided smile softened the jab.

I wanted to laugh, but the unease from earlier—after receiving that eerie poem—lingered in my psyche. I needed to know if Perez could have been playing a cruel trick on me.

"You didn't send me some creepy anonymous poem earlier, did you?" I asked, trying to sound as natural as possible.

His amusement shifted to curiosity as he took a seat across from me, folding his arms. "No. Why? What did it say?"

I began reciting it, and when I finished, I observed his reaction, not knowing what I was expecting to see. Shock had rippled across his face, quickly replaced by something darker.

"Well, that's fuckin' weird." He ran a hand through his dark hair, mussing it further.

"I know."

"You think it's Jackson? Maybe he's pissed and trying to rattle you after what went down."

I shook my head, skeptical. "I doubt it, but I'll reach out to him, see where his head's at. Still, this feels off."

"I don't know. It is right after we get one of the top guys providing info for whatever ring of exploitation we're getting closer to. However, it could also have been someone messing with you. Whoever or whatever this is, I promise, it's not me."

Perez placed his head in his hands, scratching at his facial hair in contemplation, his eyes narrowing, before he spoke up again. "You need to be careful. This investigation's heating up, and somewhere, someone's going to get desperate."

He wasn't wrong. The significance of the investigation felt more substantial by the day.

"Speaking of desperate people,"—I stood, brushing crumbs from my lap and slipping my shoes back on—"we need to pay Dolino a visit."

In the elevator on our way down to the interview rooms, my watch buzzed. Glancing at the screen, I saw a message from Christian:

> *Are you free tonight? I want to talk.*

A rope coiled in my chest, wrapping its way around my heart. The idea of smoothing things over with him sent a mix of relief and apprehension rushing through me.

"Important?" Perez asked, his eyes flicking to my watch.

I tucked my wrist close, shielding it instinctively. "No, it's nothing."

His raised brow said he didn't entirely believe me, but he let it go. I'd told him I was going to message Christian—but this wasn't about him, or us. This was for me. After everything we'd put Christian through, I owed him the space to come to me on his own terms. I could discuss the message with him later, when it mattered.

The interview room was as uninviting as ever—harsh lighting, cold metal furniture, and an overpowering chemical scent.

As we entered, my thoughts returned to Christian. How had *he* felt being questioned like a criminal in this room? I imagined it would be like a person who had been flayed open and left bare for others to pick at his raw shame. With a nudge to my elbow, Perez pulled me back to the present.

Alexander Dolino sat with a stiff back on the opposite side of the table. Beside him, the same wiry lawyer from days earlier was seated with a practiced calm, his fingers tented and a briefcase resting neatly in front of him.

I pulled the recording device from my pocket and set it on the table, pressing the button with a deliberate click. Perez introduced us all again, and I jotted down Schwartz's name in my notebook for later research.

Perez opened the file, sliding photos across the table: images of young girls, their faces filled with hope, hurt, or fear. Among them were crime scene photos of the murdered women we'd been working to identify.

"These were on your work computer," Perez began, his tone clipped. "Girls as young as fourteen. Would you care to explain how they ended up there, Alex? And don't worry, we're comparing them to the undeveloped film we have from your couch. Clever hiding spot by the way. We almost missed it."

Dolino's lip curled slightly, his first real show of emotion. "My name is Alexander. Not *Alex*."

Perez leaned in, undeterred. "*Alexander*, then. I'm sure someone in your position wouldn't risk their entire career for this alone. So. Who's pulling the strings?"

Dolino's lawyer jumped in, his voice smooth. "Mr. Dolino isn't obligated to explain himself. Anyone could have accessed that computer."

"Right," I said, shifting closer to spread the photos out further. "But you knew. You had to know something bigger was at play when you were making fake IDs for these girls. Who paid you? What did you get out of it?"

Dolino kept his eyes on the table, his fingers twitching toward his bow tie—a nervous tick I hadn't noticed until then.

"You're baiting my client, Detective," Schwartz interjected.

Perez ignored him, laying out more photos. One by one. Slow and calculated. "What do you think happened to these girls, Alexander? They didn't show up in New York for cocoa and a bedtime story. No, they were greeted by monsters that forced them into horrors you can't even imagine. Or, maybe you can."

"I never touched them!" Dolino's voice rose sharply, his composure cracking.

I tried to suppress an inappropriate, yet timely, laugh. All I could picture was Dolino—*not* Angela Lu—choking on his own tie collection, one by one, until he either begged for mercy or suffocated. And I'd make damn sure the last thing he saw was the faces of all the girls he'd helped move like cargo across the country.

Perez leaned closer, voice low and menacing. "You're sure about that? Not even a little? Maybe after you took their photos, someone paid you more than cash?"

Dolino's hands clenched into fists, but he remained mute.

Perez stood abruptly. "We'll give you some time to think about it, *Alex*. In the meantime, we'll review those photos from your couch. Maybe they'll tell us more about what you've been up to."

The door clicked shut behind us, and Perez ran his hands through his hair and let out a frustrated sigh.

"He knows more than he's saying," I said, my mind already spinning through the possibilities.

"No doubt," Perez agreed. "But we'll get him to crack."

As we headed for the break room, I poured us both coffee while Perez pulled up his phone. "Get a load of this," he said, passing the screen to me.

It was a photo from *The Sentinel* of Schwartz, standing with Dante Baldini and various suited men at *Harmonies Night Club* two months before Kayleigh was found dead in the club's dumpster. My stomach twisted.

"Guess we're getting closer," I muttered, handing the phone back. I drained my coffee and was already heading for the door. "I feel like ruining Dolino's day, Detective Perez."

He smirked, holding the door open. "After you, Detective Fairsbane. Vengeful looks good on you."

CHAPTER 42
Loriah

Perez entered with refilled coffee cups as I pushed open the door, photos clutched in hand. Dolino's gaze flicked up sharply, his eyes darting from me to his lawyer, Schwartz. Their tight expressions betrayed a quiet, simmering frustration, giving the impression that our arrival from the impromptu coffee break had somehow inconvenienced their discussion.

The room's atmosphere shifted as Perez sat back, his arms folded and gaze unyielding. He didn't need to say anything—his predatory presence alone filled the sterile space, applying a silent pressure that made even me uneasy at times. It was a pressing weight that would have made hardened criminals falter.

Dolino felt it too. You could see it in his posture and the way perspiration broke out along his pasty brow.

I placed the photos down, fanning them out like cards in a losing hand; *his* losing hand. The images—a combination of ones taken from the roll found in his couch and work computer—exposed a haunting reality: teenage girls, some barely out of childhood, staring into the camera with a mix of terror and resignation. Each face told a story, one that Dolino couldn't deny being a part of. But there was one, one that we had left out for just the right moment.

"This is your work, Alex." His voice commanded the room, and Dolino couldn't look away.

"I-I don't know those girls." Dolino's hand moved involuntarily again to his ridiculous tie. He quickly masked his unease, retreating behind a facade of disinterest.

"Reach for that *fucking* tie again, and I'll make you eat it. What are you—a goddamn child? Pay attention, Dolino. These girls' blood is on *your* hands, just as much as on the hands of the people you work for." I leaned in, fists clenched, fury boiling over. "And—surprise, surprise—men like you don't last long in prison."

Schwartz finally snapped forward in his seat, spine so rigid it was a wonder he hadn't cracked in half. "Is this how you conduct all your investigations? I will have your badge, miss."

"It's *detective* to you. And good luck with that."

Out of the corner of my eye, I saw Perez glance my way—his expression unreadable at first, but then it became almost proud, accompanied by a sideways smirk. Like, despite the chaos, some part of him respected the fire I wasn't trying to hide anymore.

He rested a warm, steadying hand on my shoulder—subtle and grounding.

"My partner's right, Dolino." His voice was low and deliberate. "Prisoners don't take kindly to men who hurt innocent little girls." He pushed a photo across the table—one of a girl, bare-shouldered, her eyes swimming with tears as she looked directly into the camera. "Did you get something extra out of this? Control? A thrill?"

Dolino stammered, his voice cracking beneath the weight of the accusation.

I inhaled slowly, then exhaled—*one, two*—counting all the way to fifteen before I trusted myself to look at Dolino again. Or his lawyer. Who I was starting to feel—in my bones—was tied to all of this, too.

Perez's smile was sharp, cutting in its accusatory tone. "*You don't know them?* That's interesting because these photos didn't magically walk onto your computer. And they certainly didn't hide themselves in *your* couch. Did they? *Alex.*"

Schwartz interjected, his voice slick and calculated. "Detectives, you've presented no concrete evidence. You're harassing my client, plain and simple."

Perez barely spared him a glance. "You think *we're* bluffing?" He reached for the final photo, one we'd deliberately held back: a close-up of Dolino's signature on a forged ID document. The face on the ID was Angel's.

Dolino's eyes widened, panic flickering through the cracks of his composure. Perez leaned forward, his voice low and lethal. "This is your name. Please don't lie to me, Alex. It's insulting. You think the people paying you will protect you when this hits the fan?"

Dolino's gaze flicked to Schwartz, doubt etched across his face. The lawyer leaned in, whispering something in his ear, but the damage was done. Fear began to settle in, spreading like a virus.

"You think your lawyer cares about you?" I asked, my tone calm, almost flippant. "He's here to make sure you don't implicate his other clients so he can collect a massive check. You're expendable." I blew against the palm of my hand to watch imaginary dust blow into the ether as I added, "You're nothing but a means to an end."

Schwartz's veneer of control slipped as he barked, "This is speculative at best. My client is under no obligation to answer these baseless accusations."

"Baseless?" Perez countered, his voice brimming with faux incredulity. "We have evidence linking him to underage trafficking and now *murder*. If he wants to save himself, now is the time to talk."

Dolino's previous smugness evaporated, his gaze fixed on a photo of a girl with dark, wavy hair. A single tear slipped down his cheek, landing on the glossy surface of her image.

"Alexander, one name. That's all we need. Who's behind this?" I coaxed.

His lips trembled as he whispered, "Chimera."

"Don't," Schwartz warned through gritted teeth, looking like he was one word away from ripping his hideous hairpiece off and running through the door.

Perez straightened, his brow furrowing. "The mythical creature? What does *that* mean?"

"It's a code name," Dolino rasped, his voice barely audible. "That's *all* I know."

"Do not say *another* word!" Schwartz shouted, his voice shrill, his calm demeanor finally breaking.

"How do we contact him?" Perez pressed, ignoring the lawyer.

"I can't. I mean—he, Chimera, contacted me. It was always through an unknown number," Dolino stammered, tears streaming down his face in rivulets.

Perez exchanged a glance with me, the unspoken understanding passing between us: *we had something*.

Schwartz tried to regain control. "Are you arresting my client or continuing this farce?"

Perez didn't hesitate. "Alexander Dolino, you're under arrest for conspiracy to traffic minors and conspiracy to murder." The satisfying clicks of handcuffs followed his words, crisp and final.

Dolino jerked back, panic setting in. "Murder? I—I didn't kill anyone! I gave you a name!"

Perez tightened his grip, his voice icy. "Two of the girls in your photos are dead, Alexander Dolino. If *you* didn't kill them, then you'd better start helping us find who did."

"I gave you a name!" He shouted more desperately, his eyes wide and frightened.

The lawyer slammed his hand on the table, his voice rising in anger. "This is outrageous! My client has said nothing to implicate himself in any crime!"

Perez stepped closer, his presence towering over the walking skeleton of a man. "Then maybe you should let him talk before he ends up taking the fall for *all* involved. Or maybe, that's the plan?"

As we escorted Dolino out, tension and fear coated the air. Perez's eyes met mine briefly, a flicker of satisfaction in his gaze.

*C*himera.

I was relishing the tiny win when my phone buzzed on the corner of my desk, nearly falling to the floor when I jerked a hand out to catch it.

Christian - *Today's been terrible. Can I see you? I need to talk and don't want to deal with this alone.*

Me - *Of course! What time? I'm at the office.*

Christian - *I'll be done with this shift at 7.*

> **Me -** *That sounds perfect. Do you need to talk about it now? I have a moment.*

> **Christian -** *No, I'd rather do it in person. And I want to see your face and not think about things for 5 minutes.*

I sat back in my chair, chewing my lip as I re-read his texts. What had him so rattled? Was he ready to push our relationship forward—a step I wasn't sure I could take? Physically, sure. Emotionally? That was murkier, primarily due to Perez's kiss lingering in the back of my mind every time I was near him. Still, Christian was everything anyone could ask for in a partner. My hesitation was clearly a reflection of my own issues rather than anything related to him.

> **Me -** *Do you want me to help you not think about it?*

> **Christian -** *Yes, ma'am.*

My pulse quickened, knowing I was playing with fire, especially after our last misunderstanding, but the thought of Christian holding me, keeping me safe after the messages I'd received, was too tempting to resist.

Just after 7:30, a sharp knock rattled my door. My heart leapt in my chest, anticipation mingling with the remnants of nerves from the cryptic poem from earlier. Christian stood in the doorway, his hair mussed, scruff framing his jaw like he was struggling to keep himself together as much as I was. But it was his blue eyes—intense and turbulent—that pinned me in place.

The words died on my lips as he took a deliberate step forward, his hands reaching for me and curling into my hair. The air sizzled with unspoken words and feelings that were heavy between us. He rested his forehead against mine.

"Do you have any idea what you put me through?" he asked, voice low, edged with frustration and need. He moved his hands to my waist, fingers pressing sharply into my skin, making me moan into his chest.

"I thought about you constantly." He continued. "Without even wanting to. Do you know how frustrating that is?"

My breath hitched. I couldn't respond. Not with the way he was holding me in place and looking at me so hungrily. Seeing he'd left the door open, he kicked it closed with his boot, then leaned in again, grabbing me by the back of my neck once more. A gasp escaped me at the fierceness of it.

"Christian, I didn't mean to—"

"Didn't mean to? Then show me. Show me *how* sorry you are. Show me you believe me." He kissed me hard then, nipping at my neck and pulling me by my hair so I had nowhere to go and nothing to do but obey his commands.

"On your knees, Loriah."

I did as he asked. The need and want to give myself to him was overpowering any sense I had left in my body at that point. This version of him was a stranger.

"Unzip me."

I did again as I was told, unzipping him and sliding his jeans down to bunch at his calves. His cock was already stiff and throbbing, an inch from my face. I took it in both hands and ran his tip along my bottom lip. A slow groan escaped his mouth.

"Look at me," he said through gritted teeth, his thighs tightening.

I looked up at him, and he grabbed the back of my hair, pushing himself so deep into my mouth that my eyes watered. He consumed me in every sense.

"That's good. I was hoping you could show me how much you missed this, Loriah. Missed *me.*"

Another moan escaped my mouth, humming around his dick and sliding my lips with the motion. His head tilted back, and he let me rhythmically suck him and slowly work my hands up and down his shaft for a few minutes before he was fucking into my face with abandon.

"Chris—" I tried to say around him, but he cut me off, driving hard into my throat until I was streaming tears down my face. He called out my name and said, "Swallow me. All of it. Oh God, Loriah. Don't let a single drop out of those perfect lips."

My name was a plea. I had wanted him inside me to ease the tension building, but I knew this was also something he needed from me, so I did as he asked.

"You are so beautiful like this," he got out before a low, throaty sound overtook him, and he pumped so far into my throat I could hardly breathe. My eyes burned, tears rolling down when the warmth of him hit the back of my throat, and I struggled to swallow every drop.

I continued to look up into his eyes and sat back on my haunches with a smile, wiping my mouth.

He pulled me to my feet and kissed me, pouring all the words he hadn't been able to say before into those few moments. The tension I'd been carrying in my shoulders began to melt away as he held me close, guiding me effortlessly into his lap. And there, under his hold, with his lips still brushing mine and his hands coaxing every inch of tension from my body, I unraveled—reduced to a writhing, endorphin-drenched mess in his arms.

We sat at my small table, the remains of our meal scattered between us, and my emotions in a strange knot. The tension from earlier had softened, replaced with a languid quiet. I hesitated, then asked, "Did you send me a message from a different phone? A poem?" I observed him, measuring every bit of his face for even the smallest reaction, my detective brain not able to shut down.

He frowned, his fork pausing midair. "A poem? No. If I did, you'd know it was from me."

I felt silly for even bringing it up when his face betrayed no understanding, but I pressed on. "It was from an unknown number. It felt like. Like someone was watching me."

His brow furrowed, the playful light in his eyes replaced by a skeptical expression. "You didn't trace it?"

"I couldn't. They blocked the number. I thought maybe it was nothing, but I—"

"It's not *nothing*, Loriah," he cut in, his tone firm. "Not with everything going on. You need to let someone look into it."

"Maybe," I conceded, though the idea made me uneasy. "I feel paranoid."

"Paranoia keeps people alive." His gaze softened. "I'm serious. Let Al check it out. "

I nodded, grateful for his concern but reluctant to involve anyone else.

"What happened to you today?" I asked, hoping to change the subject.

He sighed, the tension returning to his posture. "My dad. He's getting out of the hospital, and my mom wants me home to help out. He's been sick for a while with dementia. He fell and broke his leg this time. I'm just mad because I should have been there. Or my brothers, but one is away on business, and the other just moved. So, now there's no one."

"Oh, Christian." I reached for his hand and squeezed it gently.

"It's fine. It's only—I've been avoiding going home, and now, I don't really have a choice."

"It's not fine. It's your family, and you love them."

I hugged him, letting him relax against me. But the peace didn't last. His phone buzzed, and he muttered an apology before stepping into the hallway to take the call.

When he returned, his face was somber. "I have to go," he said, slipping his shirt back on.

"Is everything okay?"

"It will be." He kissed me, a soft, lingering goodbye that left me aching. "We're okay, Loriah. I've missed you."

"I missed you, too," I whispered, watching as he walked out.

Once the door clicked shut, I was left with a confusing tangle of warmth and chaos, both vying for emotional superiority.

My gaze drifted to the phone on the coffee table, a knot tightening in my chest as I remembered what still sat there, unread.

CHAPTER 44
Loriah

M y mind was groggy when the alarm blared, the sun not fully risen. I wiped the remnants of sleep from my eyes and reached for my phone, glowing faintly with a missed message.

> **Christian** - *Last night was incredible. Heading in early, so I might end up missing you. But I'll see you soon.*

> **Me** - *I'm glad we worked things out. Let me know when you're back. I hope your dad's okay.*

I arrived at the station just shy of 8 AM, cutting it close, as usual. My only mission was to slip into my office unnoticed—anything to avoid Agustin and his questions about last night. The mere thought of it caused my insides to twist. I couldn't lie to save my life, and Agustin had a knack for seeing through people, especially me.

As I passed through the central area, a familiar figure caught my eye. Christian, with his sandy-blonde hair and plaid shirt, sat at a desk hunched over a leave form. He looked up as I approached, a grin spreading wide and easy, disarming as always.

"Howdy, stranger," I drawled, leaning casually against the desk.

"You know," he said, his voice warm, "I never appreciated that accent until I moved away. You make it sound so sexy."

He leaned over, grabbed my hand, and pressed a kiss to the palm. Shivers ran down my spine, and I knew my cheeks had turned pink, warmth creeping into my face. I sensed a shift in the air. The unmistakable presence of someone behind me made my stomach drop. Christian's gaze hardened, locking onto the new arrival.

"Morning, Detective," Agustin greeted, his voice shrewd. His posture was relaxed, though the way his jaw clenched betrayed him. He ran a hand through his hair, a tell I knew all too well.

"I was helping Christian with a leave request," I said quickly, fumbling for some semblance of professionalism.

"Of course. Don't forget, we need to fill out our own leave forms for tomorrow. I'll be picking you up."

Excuse me?

"No, you won't." My protest came faster than I intended. "I'll meet you there."

"Your place is on the way," he countered, his tone firm but devoid of argument.

"We'll discuss it later," I said, desperate to defuse the tension brewing between the two men. Christian's eyes narrowed, his hand curling into a fist around the pen he was holding. If Agustin said another word about the trip, I was sure Christian would lose it. Rank be damned.

"Briefing in forty-five," Agustin said, stepping back, but not before delivering a pointed look to Christian. "Safe travels, Officer."

As he walked away, Christian muttered, "That man makes me want to hit something." Before leaving, fingers brushing against mine, his voice was low and meant only for me when he said, "I'll see you in two days, three max, and we'll pick up where we left off."

The morning briefing was efficient, with updates rapidly shared around the room through folders and brief explanations. Timelines were adjusted, financial records were reviewed, and the new locations of interest were added to an ever-expanding list. Everything appeared to be falling into place—or so it seemed.

By the time lunch rolled around, my phone buzzed.

> **Unknown** - *Walk away before you end up like the others.*

"Oh, *for fuck's sake*," I shouted in as hushed a tone as I could muster, slamming the phone down harder than necessary. Rage filled me all at once at the intrusion and implications.

The sound must have carried because Agustin's head appeared in the doorway, one eyebrow arched.

"Sorry!" I said, forcing a smile. "Just my bank being stupid and locking me out of my account again."

He studied me, his sharp eyes lingering a moment too long. "Oh yeah?"

"Yup, no worries." I waved him off, hoping he'd let it go.

With a slight nod, he left—though he didn't look convinced. My hands trembled as I picked up the phone again, rereading the text. Whoever this was, they were watching—and they weren't subtle about it.

I knew, deep down, I shouldn't be lying to Perez. It was the third time now, and each time, it chipped away at me a little more. I wasn't that kind of person. Not usually. But if he was entitled to his secrets—and to the company of that pretty little blonde officer—then I could have my own life too.

I'd only seen her with him once before, so maybe nothing was really happening between them. Or maybe my unfounded jealousy was distorting my perception and making my hidden fears seem more real.

Perez stood in the doorway, his motorcycle helmet in hand.

"Six tomorrow?" he asked, a smirk tugging at his lips when I groaned in protest.

"That's brutal, Agustin. I thought you said you *don't* hate me."

"You'll survive. Check your email, I forwarded the tickets."

"Thanks." I waved him off, returning to the last bit of paperwork on my desk.

Instead of printing the ticket like a responsible adult, I rushed home, tossing clothes into an old bag with barely a second thought, and prayed like hell I wouldn't be late for my first night at *Harmonies*. A shift ending at 1 AM, followed by a flight at 6 AM, had my brain short-circuiting.

Nerves were still buzzing under my skin as I stepped out into the night, ready to face whatever lay ahead.

CHAPTER 45
Loriah

The neon lights pulsed in time with the bass, casting the street outside in a hazy glow. As I approached the entrance, I noticed a different man guarding the door, not the usual gatekeeper I'd dealt with before. My heart jumped, but I squared my shoulders, adjusted the plunging neckline of my cream dress, and forced a pleasant smile.

The bouncer stopped me before I reached him.

"Hey," I drawled, softening my tone. "I'm the new girl, Serena. Dante told me to be here tonight." I added a tinge of flirtation, leaning into the Russian-American accent I'd been practicing, and pulling out the burner phone with his texts to confirm.

"Is that right?" he asked, giving nothing away as his eyes roamed over me and only briefly glanced at the message. He spoke into a small mic near his ear and paused to listen.

"Look," I said, injecting a hint of urgency, "I *really* need this job, and I can't afford to be late when the boss says to show up."

After a pause that felt like an eternity, he nodded toward the door. "Go in. Find Nadine at the bar. She'll get you set up."

"Thank you!" Relief flooded through me as I slipped inside before I could second-guess myself.

The club enveloped me in its energy. A cocoon of vibrant colors and the low thrum of music felt transformative. The disorienting lights and pounding music made it hard to get my bearings.

It wasn't busy yet, but I could sense the promise of a wild night ahead. The mingling scents of alcohol, expensive perfume, and something faintly sweet filled the space, making me wonder if my nerves were playing tricks on me.

This club wasn't the sticky, seedy type of club you'd see in late-night reality TV dramas. No, this was Baldini's domain—slick, polished, and dripping with carefully crafted allure.

I scanned the room, curling my fingers in so my nails could bite into the palms, attempting to ground myself while I took it all in. When I spotted her, a tall, striking woman with impossibly long legs and sleek black hair, standing by the bar, I felt a surge of recognition. Her purple miniskirt shimmered under the lights as she moved with effortless grace.

"Nadine?" I called out, raising my voice above the din of the music.

She turned, her bright smile radiating unbridled warmth. "That's me! You must be the new girl."

"Serena," I introduced myself, sticking out my hand. Before she could respond, a voice interrupted.

"Ah, *there* you are. I've got a special spot for you," he said smoothly, placing a hand on Nadine's shoulder before giving her a disarming smile. "I'll take her from here, Nadine."

I barely had time to process the words before Dante turned and headed to the opposite end of the club. His long strides forced me to jog slightly in my heels.

"We don't bring just anyone here," Dante said, glancing over his shoulder. "But I think you'll fit in."

"What exactly do you have planned for me?" I asked, masking my nerves with a hint of curiosity.

He led me through a door labeled *Employees Only*, gesturing for me to go ahead. I stepped into an empty hallway, the sounds of the central club fading behind us. Then two dancers appeared from the other end. Their skin shimmered with gold powder. They moved across the space in fluid steps, otherworldly looking. Dante's musk wafted, and they both languidly looked to our side of the hall, offering Dante polite nods with a synchronized "Good evening, Sir" as they passed, without sparing a glance at me.

The hallway grew quieter with each step, the noise fading into silence until we reached a door with a keypad. A brass plate beside it read *ES* in elegant calligraphy—*Enchanted Sanctuary*. Dante shifted his body between me and the keypad as he entered a code. The lock clicked open, revealing a staircase that led to what felt like another world.

There was no security guard in sight, but a sleek black camera was fixed above the door, its glass lens watching like an unblinking eye. From here, I could hear faint music drifting down the corridor, and the scents, much like those above, grew stronger, curling around us with every step we took.

Dante gestured toward the chandeliers. "Acquired from an old speakeasy. Rare pieces."

I nodded, feigning admiration as I took in the room. Plush couches circled low tables, and private poles showcased dancers moving with practiced sensuality. The ratio of men to women was staggering—just as I'd expected—and it immediately put me on edge. The kind of men invited to a place like this weren't only wealthy. They were dangerous.

Only one other exit sign was visible from where we stood, a detail I silently clocked.

The polished bar gleamed beneath the soft lighting, where men in tailored suits lounged with beautiful women draped on their arms. This place was a playground for the city's privileged class.

The *Enchanted Sanctuary* was a world apart from the main floor. The lavish chandeliers cast a warm, golden glow, while the plush seating arrangements whispered of indulgence and exclusivity. The music here was different too—soft, seductive, more intimate than the pounding bass above. Everything about this space felt intentional, yet it was also disgusting in its opulence. Controlled. Tailored for secrecy and for people with something to hide.

"This," Dante began, turning to me, "is where you'll be working. The clients here expect the best. You'll be serving drinks, keeping their glasses full, and making sure everyone is comfortable. Occasionally, you'll check the private rooms to see if they need *refreshing*." His eyes lingered on me as if waiting for a reaction.

I gave him a bright smile, pretending the job was exactly what I'd been hoping for. "Sounds perfect. This is spectacular."

He nodded, satisfied. "I'll leave you with Tony. He'll show you the ropes."

Tony, the curly-haired bartender with a sharp jawline, embodied everything I expected from a place like this—prepossessing yet edged with a warning not to mess with him. Over the next hour, he walked me through the basics, his movements efficient as he set up the bar.

The night picked up quickly. A group of young men settled into a booth, their easy camaraderie filling the air as they flagged me down. The ringleader—a man with his tie half-loosened and a shit-eating grin—ordered shots of Patrón for the table and asked for a private room.

"I'll see what I can do," I told him with a polished smile, heading toward the back to check availability.

As I approached one room, the door stood slightly ajar. Someone had pulled the velvet curtain aside, revealing a young woman standing over a seated man, her hands bound behind her back, breasts on display. My stomach turned as I instinctively leaned closer to get a better look.

"Hey there. You're new," a slurred voice said behind me.

I startled, spinning to face the source. A sweaty, clammy hand gripped my wrist, the sour stench of alcohol escaping from the man's mouth like a sewer hit in a nauseating wave.

"Where are *you* off to, hun?" he slurred, his grin lecherous.

"Just doing my job, sir," I said, forcing sweetness into my voice while suppressing the urge to recoil.

"I've got something you can help me with." His grip tightened, and he tugged my hand toward his waistband.

Before I could react, a deep, menacing voice cut through the tension. "She said, *No.*"

The drunk man turned, blinking up at Ares Perez's towering form. The amusement I'd seen in Ares's face during our last encounter was gone, replaced by cold authority.

His hand clamped down on the man's shoulder. "The lady has work to do." His voice was relaxed, but the warning was unmistakable.

The man slurred something before releasing me, shrinking under Ares's firm grip, but he didn't let go until he'd steered the man back toward the lounge.

"You okay?" Ares asked, his eyes locking onto mine as he placed a steadying hand on my elbow.

"Yeah," I replied, a little shaken, but grateful.

Ares didn't release me as he guided us into an empty room, closing the door softly behind us. In the quiet, his presence was overwhelming, his closeness sending my already on-edge nerves into overdrive.

"Didn't expect to see you here, Dante must like you," he mused.

"*Or* he doesn't trust me," I shot back.

Ares's lips curved into a knowing smile. "Careful, Loriah. You don't want to play this game alone."

"I'm not playing," I whispered.

"Good," he murmured, his hand clasping mine. "Because neither am I when I say I need your help."

T he club had transformed by the time I stepped back into the lounge. The music pulsing with a sultry rhythm, its beat threading through the growing crowd like an invisible thread. Women of every type strutted through the speakeasy, mingling with the patrons. The mix of perfume, alcohol, and the salty sweat of close bodies carried across the expanse. Despite its exclusivity, the club thrived.

"Ah, there you are, Serena," Dante's voice purred from the bar as I waited for a drink order. His smooth, calculated tone sent a ripple of unease down my spine. "I trust you remember my partner? He certainly remembers you."

I turned, catching Ares's mischievous gaze as he leaned casually against the end of the bar, a faint smile playing at the corner of his lips, his eyes never leaving mine. In that moment, I could see just how much he resembled his brother.

It made me wonder—how did one end up in law enforcement while the other got tangled up with a human trafficker?

"Yes, of course," I replied, giving Ares a playful grin. "How could I forget?"

"How's your evening going?" Dante's eyes scanned the room, his demeanor a mix of authority and aloofness, before returning to me with a cocked brow. "Well, I hope."

"It's been wonderful," I said, my voice light. "Everyone's been helpful to settle in."

Dante's expression shifted slightly. "Ares mentioned there was an incident earlier?"

"It was nothing to worry about," I said smoothly. "A minor issue, but Ares was gracious for stepping in."

"Good. Glad to hear you handled it." Dante nodded, his attention already drifting elsewhere. "I have some matters to attend to upstairs. Let me know if there's anything you need to make your transition easier."

"Thanks, I appreciate it," I replied, shocked by how much I meant it. Little did Dante know that he had given me access to a world that might hold the answers I needed.

Between tending to patrons and indulging their every whim, I searched anywhere (rooms, alcoves, drawers) I could without drawing attention. However, every attempt fell short, and the lack of progress gnawed at me. A few of the girls looked too young to be there, and it unsettled me when I thought about it, but without proof—and no time to speak with them—I was at a loss. I hated feeling useless as the hours ticked by. I was there to find something, *do* something, but all I'd actually found was a growing sense of unease.

"It's 11:30. Time for your break," Ares whispered as he leaned close. "Meet me at the stairs." He straightened and more loudly added, "I'll see you later," likely for the benefit of Tony, who glanced up briefly before resuming his polishing of glasses.

"Not a chance," I shot back, but Ares smirked and disappeared into the crowd.

Tony wandered over, his sharp eyes tracking Ares's retreat. "Persistent, isn't he?"

"They all are. Must be the money."

Tony snorted. "Probably. But be careful. Decide for yourself how harmless a well-dressed wolf can be."

I laughed, low and real. "I'll keep that in mind. Where can I grab some air?"

Tony handed me a sleek metallic card, its weight solid in my hand. "Up the stairs, through the door. Use this to get back in."

"Thanks, Tony. You're a lifesaver."

"Yeah, yeah," he muttered. "Just watch yourself."

Minutes later, I was standing in a dim stairwell with Ares. He didn't waste time, taking my hand and leading me down the corridor toward what I assumed was Dante's office. At the coded door, he swiped his own card, and the lock clicked open.

"Don't worry," Ares said, pushing the door open. "As his partner, I have full access. No cameras here either—Dante likes his secrets."

"And you trust him not to lie about that?" I asked, stepping into the space and pulling my hand free of his.

The room's understated elegance contrasted with his father's lavish office above. Dark orange walls framed black wood furniture, and the subtle scent of cigars and sandalwood floated in the air. It was a masculine room, efficient yet inviting—well designed for whispered deals and unspoken truths.

"I don't trust him," Ares admitted, "but I know him. For better or worse."

"How does someone like you even get involved with someone like him?" I questioned, keeping my voice low.

Ares's lips curved into a faint smile. "What kind of person do you think he is, Loriah?"

"Someone who traffics women."

His smile faltered. "Is he?"

"How can you not know?" Frustration seeped into my tone. His detachment was vexing, as if he were playing both sides of a game I was the one desperate to win.

"I don't have proof. I think Dante's cooking the books—fraud, Loriah, not trafficking. But if I can confirm it, I'll dismantle his operation and take over. A legit business with no loose ends."

"Legit?" My skepticism earned a sharp laugh from him.

"You don't want to know," he said cryptically. "And no, Agustin isn't involved."

The mention of his twin made my stomach tighten. "Fine," I snapped, turning to the drawers. "Just help me find something about the girls. Names, photos, addresses."

We worked in tense silence. Minutes dragged as the faint ticking of a wall clock counted down my precious break time. I rifled through folders, frustration mounting as file after file revealed nothing useful. Then I found it—a locked drawer.

"Do you have a key to this?" I asked, glancing at my phone—11:57 PM. If I weren't back soon, I'd have to grovel for forgiveness on my first night.

"Check the desk," Ares said, moving to scan the shelves.

I felt around, my fingers brushing over pens, paperclips, and a cigar cutter, but I couldn't find the key.

"Damn it." I snarled. It took all my willpower not to slam the last drawer shut. "Do you have a lock pick?"

Ares's laugh was soft but exasperated. "What do you think I am, a walking movie cliché?"

I shot him a glare. "Could've fooled me."

"Let's get out of here," he said, snapping the drawer shut and carefully placing the contents back the way they were.

We stepped into the hallway, and my pulse spiked at the sound of deliberate, steady steps. Someone was coming.

"Shit," I muttered, spinning to Ares.

Ares looked at me, eyes widening. But before he could argue, I shoved him against the wall, winding my fingers up into his hair as I pulled his mouth to mine.

"What are y—"

My lips cut him off, but not before sending up a silent prayer that Agustin wouldn't find out about this.

I felt his rigid body relax, melting into our kiss. His hand came up and cupped my cheek while the other pressed against the small of my back, bringing me closer into him. His lips were warm, commanding. And for a dizzy moment,

I forgot the reason for our charade. The heat of his kiss drew me in along with the intensity in his movements.

The footsteps stopped.

"What the fuck are you two doing?" Dante's voice cut through the haze like a knife.

We broke apart, breathless and flushed. Ares kept a protective hand on my waist as he turned to face Dante, shielding me from the moment's awkwardness while I pressed my face against his back, trying to hide my embarrassment.

"What does it look like?" Ares's voice came out low, gravelly, and utterly unapologetic. I didn't need to see him to know he wore that maddeningly carefree smile.

Dante's silhouette cast a shadow in the deserted hall, his posture hinting at skepticism. "It's been *one* night, Ares."

Ares shrugged before straightening, keeping me close. "Lost track of time. My bad."

For a moment, I thought Dante might call us out, seeing through the ruse. But then he huffed a humorless laugh. "Keep her out of the restricted areas," he said, his tone framed more as a warning than a directive.

As his footsteps retreated, I exhaled, long and slow. My heart pounded, adrenaline coursing through me as I turned back to Ares.

CHAPTER 47
Loriah

"What was that?" Ares asked, stepping back and rubbing lightly at the bottom of his lip. It had become swollen with our kissing, and I didn't miss the way he touched it.

"You're welcome," I said, adjusting my clothing and hoping my wig was still in place. "We'd be screwed if one of us hadn't thought fast."

He shook his head, wiped at his mouth with the pad of his thumb, and flashed that damned sideways smile that seemed to know too much.

"Oh, you thought fast, alright," he said, taking a step closer and leaning in, his voice dipping low as his lips brushed against my ear, sending shivers down my spine. "Are you *sure* that was *just* for show?"

Heat rushed to my face, but I refused to let him see how flustered I was. "I did what I had to. You're the one who didn't pull away."

"Was I supposed to pretend as well?" he shot back, a smug smile growing at my exasperation.

"Let's get out of here before Dante changes his mind." I turned on my heel and headed down the hallway, desperate to put space between us. "And don't follow me too closely."

"Don't worry," he whispered. "I like the view better from back here."

The night passed in a blur. I stayed busy attending to customers, but I managed to make a few connections with the dancers. More than a handful of women waited like disposable flesh until a customer requested something particular.

The club would be closing in half an hour, and the thought of catching even a few hours of sleep before my early flight with Agustin felt laughable. Sneaking away to a quiet alcove, a series of missed calls and frantic messages from Angel awaited, immediately putting me on edge when the screen's face came to life.

> **Angel** - *Loriah, I need to talk to you.*

> **Angel** - *Please, I think they know about me.*

> **Angel** - *Does anyone know I'm here? Please answer. I think they know.*

Angel - *I'm serious. If you're asleep, call me as soon as you get this. Something is wrong! I don't know how, but someone knows what I've told. They know!*

By the time my shift ended, those messages had etched a knot of worry in my stomach. I couldn't shake them as I made one last sweep of the back rooms. That's when I found her.

A girl, with the face of a teenage child, was bound by her wrists and left hanging from an ornate brass hook placed in the ceiling. Her toes barely reached the floor, the weight forcing her to strain against the restraints, long hair moving side to side with her movements. The room reeked of discarded drinks and stale cigars. I rushed to her side, frantically searching for something to cut her down with and only coming up with a plush chair to shove under her. She was so weak she could barely lift her feet to hold herself up.

"I'll be right back," I said in a rush. When she didn't answer, I smoothed the sweat-dampened hair from her face, trying to gauge if she was alright for me to leave, but her vacant eyes didn't register my words. "I'll be back," I reiterated, guilt ricocheting through my chest as I left her.

With clipped strides, I walked to the bar, taking deep breaths to steady myself as I spotted Tony. "Do you have scissors I could borrow?" I counted to four, breathing through my nose. Ares appeared beside me, his timing unnervingly perfect, but not unwelcome.

"Are you alright?" he murmured as Tony searched behind the bar.

"Fine," I lied. "But I need your help." His eyes darted between mine, seeing the seriousness, and he nodded.

Tony handed me a pair of shears, and Ares, ever the opportunist, quipped. "Of course, I'll help you cut yourself out of that dress," he teased, with what I could only picture was a playful wink at Tony before following me down the hallway.

We reached the room in record time, given that I was speedwalking in heels. I knocked tentatively. Silence. I pushed the door open, scanning the room to make sure we were alone.

"Grab her by the waist," I instructed, stepping onto the chair to grasp the rope.

"Well, shit," Ares muttered, but moved to comply.

The girl's skin was ghostly pale, her wrists red and raw where the ropes bit into the flesh. Bruises darkened her face and body, evidence of someone's brutal indifference.

I hacked at the rope, the sound of snipping loud in the silence. Finally, the last strand gave way with a satisfying dry pop, and Ares caught her. She shied away, trying to turn her face, but managing little else. He placed her drooping form on the couch and draped his jacket over her. I took the opportunity to scan the room and its discarded debris.

Drinks littered the table, and cash of various denominations was crumpled on the ground nearby. I carefully ran my hands along the cushions, wishing I had a pair of gloves with me. When the search turned up nothing more, I knelt in front of the girl.

She slowly sat upright, clutching the fabric tightly around her. Distrust burned in her eyes, but it was dulled by what looked like exhaustion.

"Do you work here?" I asked gently. "My name is Serena. I work here too."

"Yeah, sometimes," she whispered, her voice small.

"What's your name?"

"Sapphire," she said.

"Sapphire, can you tell me your *real* name?"

"No." She practically screeched out, fear flitting across her eyes.

"Sapphire, I want to help you. I can't tell you much because it's not safe for you. But if you can give me your real name, I might be able to do more."

"I can't."

"I know you're scared. I am too. But I want to help you."

She hesitated before murmuring, "Livvy. Olivia. But don't tell anyone—Please!" She began to cry, the tears plopping onto Ares' jacket and dotting it with small dark spots.

"Who told you not to give your real name?"

"A man. I don't know his name." Her speech was becoming more slurred, exhaustion appearing to be taking root.

"Does he look like this?" Ares asked, showing her a photo of Dante.

Her eyes rolled back, but her body jolted as if she was fighting to stay focused. "No, he's the one who gave me this job."

Her answers came slowly, weighted by suspicion or perhaps drugs, and I could feel the familiar weight of time working against us.

The door creaked open, and a woman's voice interrupted. "Sapphire, love, it's Daniella, are you—" The woman froze, her sharp eyes taking in Ares and me, before hardening into a honeyed politeness laced with venom.

CHAPTER 48

Loriah

I dragged myself out of bed in a flurry of twisted sheets and disheveled hair when the alarm blared unnervingly loud at 5:40 AM. Groans escaped with every movement, and the creaking of my joints made it clear my body wasn't ready for the day ahead. I was sounding much less twenty-six and more sixty-six. I managed to pull on a pair of clean dark-wash jeans, my one nice emerald-green cashmere sweater, and white slip-on travel sneakers.

I sank onto the couch, coffee in hand, and tried to review what I knew about the case. Last night's conversation with Livvy consumed my thoughts as I sipped the coffee I'd prepared ahead of time.

"Shit!" I exclaimed, nearly dropping the mug when my phone rang at full volume, jolting me out of my daze. I glanced at the caller ID and sighed.

Do all the Perez men come with impeccable timing?

"Are you on your way?" Agustin's voice came through the line before I could even greet him.

"Surprisingly, I am," I fibbed while crossing my fingers.

"You're lying. Get in a cab."

"Fuck off, Perez. I'm up, and I'm about to leave."

He chuckled, clearly amused, and I hung up before grabbing my weekend bag and coat.

Organized chaos primarily characterized the city on a typical day. The city, when you were already stressed and running late? Pure, unfiltered chaos on *crack*.

I rushed to hail a cab, confident I could flag one down quickly. *Wrong.* I spent five agonizing minutes watching speeding cabs go by, already occupied—their passengers giving me sympathetic but smug looks. When one finally stopped, I practically leapt inside and shouted, "LaGuardia, please!"

I nodded politely as the cabbie made small talk that was preferably one-sided while I feigned interest and jotted notes about what to ask at the funeral. My heart pounded, and my neck stiffened from the driver's constant weaving through traffic. But he knew his business, and we made it to the terminal in exceptional time, earning him a large tip.

Slightly sweating and legs burning, I spotted Agustin near the gate, looking far too composed. He stood in the rush of people like a beacon in a crisp button-down, tailored gray trousers, and a long black wool coat slung over his arm. My heart stopped for a moment at the sight, almost exactly like Ares. Agustin had a way of looking like he was heading to a swanky destination wedding and not a funeral in the middle of nowhere, Oklahoma.

"Cutting it close, aren't you? I offered to pick you up," he said, his tone somewhere between amusement and reproach.

"Yeah, well, you know what they say," I muttered, fussing with my hair to squeeze it into a loose bun before giving up.

"No, what do they say?"

"Better late than never?"

"Right. Someone obviously invented that quote for people like you, habitually teetering on the edge of inexcusable tardiness."

"Wow. Rude. I'm here, so chill out."

He smartly said nothing else. Choosing to stand in companionable silence till the attendant started announcing boarding by sections.

"Flight 6082 to Tulsa is now boarding for groups one through three," a cheerful voice announced over the loudspeaker.

"That's us," Agustin said.

"Are you sure?" I squinted at him, skeptical. I'd never boarded anything earlier than group six in my life.

"Yes. Come on."

Too tired to argue, I followed him to the gate and handed over my ticket. To my surprise, the attendant smiled and waved me through.

Inside the plane, I trailed after Agustin until we reached a pair of plush seats in first class. My eyebrows shot up.

"I hope you don't mind. I upgraded our tickets," he said, placing my bag in the overhead bin.

"What's wrong with steerage?"

"Nothing, but I don't fit in those seats." He wasn't exaggerating. At his height, economy seating probably felt like being wedged into a sardine can.

"I guess, I'll make do," I told him and rolled my eyes in a dramatic show before settling into my seat and ordering orange juice when the stewardess came by. I wiped crumbs from my sweater, fallout from nibbling on a complimentary pastry while Agustin stared at me, unflinching with judgment.

"Seriously? It's been five minutes," he teased.

The plane taxied down the runway, and as we took off, a gripping anxiety began creeping up my neck. Heights had never been my thing. Agustin handed me a bottle of water.

"You look like you could use this."

"Thanks," I murmured, grateful for the distraction, and took it to press to my temples before opening and drinking deeply.

I leaned back in my seat, staring out the window as the city shrank beneath us. Guilt gnawed at me. I was supposed to be focusing on the funeral, on helping Agustin interview Kayleigh's friends and family for leads. But my thoughts kept straying to the club—to Ares, Livvy, that demon woman Daniella, and that damned locked drawer.

Agustin broke the silence with a quiet cough. "You're awfully quiet."

His words caught me off guard, and I turned to look at him as though seeing him for the first time that morning. I wished, irrationally, that he were Ares so I could discuss the previous night.

"Just tired," I replied after staring far too long at his face before brushing him off.

He studied me back. "You sure that's all? Nothing you want to talk about?"

I hesitated. There was plenty I wanted to say, but none of it that I could share with Perez—not without risking everything, he'd never allow me to continue with my plans, and I wasn't in the mood to listen to all his reasons why.

"Yeah, I'm sure. I didn't sleep well."

He nodded, seemingly accepting my answer, though none of it was a lie.

"It doesn't get easier. Death, I mean," he said after a moment. "But people expect that we act like it doesn't bother us. You're good at it, though, giving them the face they need."

His sincerity caught me off guard. For a moment, I felt a sense of solidarity. We weren't the best of friends, but at that moment, we were on the same side.

"I'll be ready. Don't worry about me, kid," I said with a wink, then closed my eyes and drifted off.

I woke up to a stewardess gently shaking my arm. "Would you like some coffee, miss?"

"Yes, please," I croaked, sitting up and wiping at the corner of my mouth, where drool betrayed how deeply I'd been sleeping. I muttered an apology to Agustin, who stifled a grin with his cup of coffee.

"Late nights don't suit you," he said, though not unkindly.

"Judging me doesn't suit *you*," I shot back, eagerly sipping the coffee—only to burn my tongue.

"Careful, it's—"

"Hot," I spluttered, fanning my mouth as he handed me a napkin.

I stole a glance at Agustin while he reviewed the autopsy photos, his face a mask of professional detachment that gave nothing away. Last night, Ares had worn that same expression when finding the girl—yet something in their eyes was fundamentally different. Agustin held righteous determination; Ares had a calculated assessment. Twin faces with opposing souls. And here I was, caught between their worlds, lying to one about the other.

"Trying to gaze into my soul, Fairsbane?" Agustin asked, catching me staring.

"No, just wondering how two people can look identical but be nothing alike," I muttered.

His brow furrowed slightly. "What are you talking about?"

"Nothing. Just thinking out loud," I said, focusing back on my coffee.

We used the rest of the flight to review case files and brainstorm strategies. Agustin jotted notes in his notebook while I continued to sip my milky coffee, my thoughts left drifting back to the club. I couldn't shake the feeling that the answers we needed were there, hiding in the lies and shadows I'd partially uncovered.

The pilot came over the speaker to announce that we would be landing in forty-five minutes. Stealing a glance at my phone, I saw a missed message waiting.

> **Unknown** - *Sapphire sends her thanks. What will she do without you here to help her?*

I looked at Perez, but he buried himself in the file notes and missed the terror and sickness consuming me.

Three things I felt. Three second breaths.

CHAPTER 49

Loriah

T he plane made its slow descent, little by turbulent little, the dusty outlying fields becoming closer, while my stomach protested the coffee and orange juice from earlier. My fingers gripped Agustin's arm like he was my lifeline to reality in the tiny plane, and his large hand came to rest on mine, his fingers warm.

"It's alright, Loriah. We're almost down," he said calmly while rubbing assuring strokes over my fingers.

"I know," I replied, gulping and tilting my chin toward the cabin's ceiling. But as the plane shuddered again, I couldn't help thinking that this feeling was too close to how everything in my life had felt recently—never knowing when the next drop would come. I focused on taking long, steady breaths, inhaling through my nose and exhaling through my mouth. "I *really* dislike heights."

"The great Detective Fairsbane has a weakness?"

I turned my head to glare at him, momentarily distracted by my impending doom. "Everyone has a weakness. Mine happens to be heights and ducks."

"Well, lucky for you, we're not visiting any ponds. Just a simple descent. No big deal."

A hard thump and the squeal of brakes signaled our arrival.

"See?" he said with an amiable smile. "Not *so* bad."

His hand was still holding mine, and when I looked down to where Perez and I were connected and then back at him, he quickly snatched it away as if I had burned him.

Neither of us had packed more than hand luggage, so we headed straight for the car rental counter. Minutes later, we were on the road in an SUV large enough to accommodate Agustin's frame, likely at the cost of his own wallet again.

The drive stretched ahead of us, long and uncomfortable. Conversation was sparse. The silence grew so deafening that I counted anything that passed by—farmhouses, cows, mile markers—desperate to distract myself from thoughts of Ares, the man sitting beside me, and Christian waiting for me back home. Was it home? I wasn't sure, but it was getting close to feeling that way.

Needing an escape from the awkwardness, I pulled out my phone and texted Christian a quick message to let him know I was thinking about him and his father. The moment I hit send, a knot of guilt tightened in my stomach. Memories of kissing Ares the night before flickered through my mind and made the heat of shame creep up my neck. It was a complication I hoped wouldn't grow into a bigger problem with him and jeopardize everything I was working toward.

Eleven long miles of farmland passed before my phone pinged.

> **Christian -** *Hey, I'm glad to hear from you. Dad's okay. I think they missed me, but I'm doing as much as I can before heading back.*

I was typing a reply when another notification interrupted me.

"Shit!" I spouted, surprising myself as much as Agustin.

I'd completely forgotten to check in with Angel last night. She was safe; I reminded myself—police were waiting near-by, and someone on-site would've reassured her. But I was supposed to be the one offering her comfort, even from hundreds of miles away, and I'd let the girl down by getting wrapped up in the drama of the previous night.

Agustin's jaw tightened, but he kept his eyes on the road. "Are you okay?" he asked after a few minutes of watching me frantically type.

"It's Angel," I admitted. "She thinks someone from the club tried to scare her last night."

He glanced at me, concerned. "What did they say?"

"I don't know yet. Angel's sending me screenshots."

We drove in tense silence until the following message came through. Agustin glanced at the clock. "Twenty-seven minutes until we reach the church," he said as I opened the first picture.

"Here's what they sent," I said, reading aloud. "'Do you think the police care about you? They're not protecting you; they're protecting their image.' And another: 'I can't protect you if you don't tell me what's going on, Angel. Think of your family. We're friends, remember?'"

"He's threatening her family to keep her quiet. He knows we're close." Agustin said, stealing glances at the phone. "Do we have anyone watching her family?"

"*Eyes on the road*," I snapped. "No, I didn't think it was necessary since they're in Oklahoma. It would be ridiculous for someone to go that far to gain leverage over one girl."

"You might be right," he conceded. "But we need to reach out to them after the funeral."

I nodded, knowing he was right, and sent a message to Angel.

> **Me** - *When was the last time you spoke to your family? Do they know where you are or how you're doing?*

Her response was quick:

> **Angel** - *Detective! I've been waiting for you. Where have you been?! I called my mom yesterday. They're fine.*

The next rapid reply confirmed how anxious she'd been.

> **Me** - *Good. Stay where you are. Don't reply to those messages. I'll have an officer pick up your phone and give you a temporary one tomorrow.*

> **Angel** - *What do I do if I need you?*

> **Me** - *I'll be back on Monday. Until then, use the officer's phone or the temporary one to contact me.*

> Don't answer your current cellphone for anyone else.

Angel - *I'm scared.*

> **Me -** *I know. We'll protect you, though. I promise.*

I placed the phone down and turned my gaze back to the road. My thoughts lingered on Angel, scared and alone in that hotel room. Limbo was a terrible place to be. The implications of not keeping my promise weighed heavily on me every hour, shifting sometimes from confidence to a false identity that I had worn and sold to protect people like Angel, as much as I tried to defend myself.

"Have you ever seen *Groundhog Day*?" I asked, breaking the silence.

"A long time ago," Agustin replied.

"I imagine that's what it feels like for her."

"Possibly." He flexed his hands on the steering wheel, agitated.

"Yeah," I murmured, lapsing back into silence.

The church came into view, its large white cross looming over the small town and casting a harsh shadow. The overly bright sky beat down on the paint, making it appear to glow everywhere else. Dust and the smell of an impending rainstorm lingered, coating my senses with ozone. Cars filled the parking lot as families hugged and clasped hands, mourning together. It wasn't just a funeral—it was a cruel reminder of how Kayleigh's and her unborn baby's lives were cut too short.

A girl her age should've been at college parties, planning spring break trips, or celebrating a friend's wedding—not lying cold in a casket, her future stolen by some sick predator walking free. The thought made my heart skip a beat, and tears came to my eyes, so I dashed away quickly.

"Are you okay?" Agustin asked gently, his hand resting on the door handle.

"Sure. I will be. Do I look okay?" I glanced down, brushing invisible crumbs from my sweater.

"You always look good."

I paused for a moment, not knowing what to say or how to take his words.

"You'll be fine," he followed up.

"Let's go," I said abruptly, cutting him off before his gentleness cracked my composure.

CHAPTER 50
Loriah

The church was small, the compaction of bodies raising the temperature, and making me wish I had chosen to wear something other than a sweater. The service was a testament to the love that the community had for this girl and her family. I could only think that maybe if she had felt that while she was alive, then perhaps she wouldn't have been so eager to leave it all behind.

One by one, the last of the guests slowly said their good-byes while Agustin and I excused ourselves to the tea-cake table near a group of young people. None of them was eating much; instead, they were standing around and picking at their food.

"Were you all friends with Kayleigh?" I asked, popping a bite of a pimento cheese sandwich into my mouth.

One girl stepped up, the small crowd moving to stand behind or to the side of her. I assumed she must be their appointed leader (every group had one).

"Yeah, well, I guess. Kayleigh left without even saying goodbye. Not very friendly."

"She didn't?" I asked, feigning curiosity. "I thought maybe she left to meet a boyfriend?"

"Maybe. Why do you say that?" the girl asked, narrowing her eyes at me. Her gaze flicked to Agustin, standing behind me. His tall, imposing, but handsome figure didn't go unnoticed. Straightening her posture, she asked, "Is he your boyfriend?"

Agustin smirked into his drink, clearly amused.

"Uh—no," I stammered like a rookie. "No, he's not." I added, trying to recover, "He's my partner. And I said that because we thought maybe she had met someone online."

"Oh, that's cool, I don't like labels either. But I never heard any mention of a boyfriend. Kayleigh didn't date. Like, at all," she said dramatically, giving me the sense this was a strange occurrence amongst her and her friends.

"No, not like that," I corrected hastily, having a hard time keeping up with the side-by-side conversations this girl was trying to keep. I looked to Agustin for help, only to find him enjoying the spectacle, waving his hand as if to silently say, *'Go ahead, you've got this.'* I glared at him and then turned my attention back to the group. "We're detectives. We work together—not *together*, romantically."

"Ohhh, I get it now," she said in an exaggerated verbal fry that didn't quite fit the region. "Why are you here?"

Agustin decided to join the conversation, his voice professional yet warm, and his accent blending in with the conversations happening around us in hushed tones. "We were hoping to talk to some of you. Learn more about Kayleigh—her life here, why she might've left, and who she might've gone with."

"We think she was talking to a man in New York through social media," I added, scanning their faces. "Did she ever mention anything to you? Or to anyone here?" I met each person's gaze, noting the way they shuffled uncomfortably and looked to each other for answers.

Their presumed leader gestured toward a dark-haired girl in the group, who had big, sad eyes and was clutching a plastic cup as if her life depended on it. "Sam probably talked to her the most. They were always together."

"Sam? I'm Loriah," I said gently, offering my hand. She shook it, her grip barely there.

"She was talking to someone," Sam admitted, her voice quiet. "She said she was going to New York for school, though."

"Did she say a name or which school?"

"No, some community college, that's all I remember. Kayleigh said she'd have a job and be living with him. She was excited to get out of this tiny-ass town, you know?"

I nodded. "All too well."

"I slept over one night, and we stayed up talking, and then a couple of days later, she was *gone*." Tears welled in her eyes, and I grabbed a nearby tissue box, handing it to her.

"Did she ever mention his name or show you a picture?"

"Not much. Just typical guy stuff—pictures of his body that he'd send, or him in bed saying he couldn't wait to see her." She rolled her eyes, casting a glance at the boys in the group as though they were guilty of similar behavior.

"Sounds about right," Agustin muttered behind me, unimpressed.

"When she left, do you know how she was planning to get there?" I pressed.

"She said she'd take the bus because it was cheaper, but he was supposed to fly out to meet her. I don't know what happened."

"Okay. If you think of anything else," I said, handing the girl my card. Agustin did the same.

"Oh, one thing," Sam added, glancing at the card before biting her lip in thought. "Chim– Chim-something."

"Chimera?" Agustin guessed.

"Yeah, that's it. How'd you know? That was his username on Instagram."

"Do you remember his handle?"

"It had that word in it, but I'm not sure of the rest. Sorry."

"That's great. Thank you," I said sincerely.

I was still processing what Sam had shared when we walked back to the car. The heavens finally opened, pelting the vehicle with heavy raindrops that mingled and swirled the dirt, creating little muddy rivulets that ran down the glass. I pulled out my phone to call Angel's parents once seated inside. My stomach tightened with anxiety as the phone rang, unsure of what I might hear.

"Hello?" a woman's voice answered warily.

"Hi, Mrs. Navarro? I'm Detective Loriah Fairsbane from the NYPD. I'm calling to check in—wanting to make sure everything's okay."

There was a pause, then, "Why would something not be okay? Is Angel alright?"

"Yes, she's safe," I reassured her quickly. "This is only a precaution. We're taking some extra steps to ensure everyone's safety."

"Well, we're fine, too," she said, her tone tinged with confusion. "But, Detective, we're about to head out the door. Is there anything else you need?"

"No, that's all. Thank you for your time," I said, forcing a calm tone.

"Alright, then. Goodbye."

The call ended abruptly, leaving me with more questions than answers. If Angel's family was fine, why was someone trying so hard to scare her? And what did they hope to gain? If someone called me from the police about my daughter, I think I'd have more to ask.

The hotel we checked into after the funeral was nicer than anything I would've booked for myself. Agustin had a taste for comfort—first-class tickets, an SUV, and now this.

"Bougie," I muttered, whistling as I looked around the open lobby with its chandeliers, velvet couches, and gold accents.

"It'll do," Agustin replied, stopping in front of my room. "That's yours."

Relieved, I took the keycard he offered and slipped inside without a second glance. I tossed my bag on the floor and threw myself onto the plush bed, savoring the luxurious comfort. I wasn't about to let him know how impressed I was. Left to my own devices, I probably would have ended up in a roadside motel stuck in the last century with yellow walls from tobacco buildup.

Lounging in the oversized garden tub, letting the warm foam envelop me while scrolling through Kayleigh's old Instagram posts, my heart picked up its pace when I stumbled across a detail that made me sit bolt upright in the water.

CHAPTER 51
Perez

I stripped off my shirt and headed to the bathroom, needing to scrub away the day. The silence felt unnerving, and my mind kept replaying the last few weeks—especially Loriah's behavior. She'd clung to me during the flight but barely spoke to me during the drive. Now, she was probably already tracking down the *Chimera* lead instead of waiting on the subpoena.

Loriah.

Always pushing boundaries. Always out of reach.

I'd tried to give her space, knowing I'd rattled her by bringing Christian into the interrogation room. It had been difficult for me to do what needed to be done. Then, that cowboy-wannabe son of a bitch had slithered his way back into her life, making things more complicated.

I sat for what felt like an hour on the edge of the bed, staring at my phone, at her name glowing on the screen. I wanted to text her—or better yet, go over and knock on her door until she looked me in the eye and told me what she was thinking. But I didn't.

Stepping into the shower, I allowed the water to stream over my head, creating a waterfall as I pressed my forehead into the cool tile and fought not to think of her and this case.

When I finished showering, I did the one thing I knew she wouldn't refuse: pizza.

"Thanks, keep the change," I told the delivery boy, slipping him a fifty before I knocked on her door.

"Agustin?" Her voice was soft, surprised even. The sound made me feel ridiculous for showing up unannounced, even with pizza as my shitty excuse.

She stood in the entryway, clutching the hotel's complimentary white robe to her chest, while damp hair curled against her face and neck. Her skin glistened, fresh from the bath, as if she'd just gotten out of the tub to answer the door.

"Sorry," I said, taking a step back and holding up the pizza as a peace offering. "I can come back."

"Oh, well, why didn't you say? Come in."

She opened the door wider, and as I walked past her, the faint scent of lavender and mint from her bath lingered in the air. Her phone was on the table, open to the Instagram app.

"Find anything?" I asked, nodding toward it as I set the pizza on the table by the couch.

"I think so, yeah. Just give me a minute to get dressed."

"Don't get dressed up on my account."

"Don't worry. I brought my best pajamas."

She reappeared a few minutes later in threadbare pajama bottoms and a faded high-school debate team T-shirt. She didn't seem to care, and honestly, it suited her.

"So, did you come here about the case?" she asked, grabbing a slice of pizza. "Or did you just want to bring me dinner?"

The sound she made as she took a bite—half a moan, half a sigh—derailed my train of thought.

"Uh, both." I coughed. "The case. *And* us."

She froze mid-bite, her eyes narrowing. "What do you mean: *us*?"

"This case, Loriah. You've been off lately—quiet, keeping things to yourself. *And* then there's Jackson."

She huffed a bitter laugh, set her pizza down, and stood. "*There it is*. This isn't about the case at all, is it?"

"Yes, it is." I bit out and stood to come closer to her. I knew I'd approached this all wrong, instantly regretting my decision to use this *one* night alone to talk about Jackson.

"What's the issue then? That he forgave me after what *you* put him through? Or is it that I'm seeing someone else? Or is it that I've been working my ass off and haven't had time to update you on every move I make?"

"Wait, what?" I frowned. "What moves have you been making?"

"About the case, Agustin. Don't twist it."

"Okay, fine. But Christian's not–" The words tumbled out before I could stop them.

"Not what? *You?* You think I don't know that?" She half yelled the words at me, hurling them like a bomb.

The hurt in her eyes was too much. I fisted my hand into my hair, knowing I was losing ground mentally and physically.

"Loriah, but you just... *believed* him."

She stared at me, her face flushed with frustration, and tears threatened to spill over. "*Believed* Christian? Yes, I did. And let me tell you something, Agustin Perez." Her chest was heaving as she stepped closer to look up at me with those piercing blue eyes. "He forgave *me.*"

Her words fell over me like a bucket of ice water. I stepped back, jaw tight, heart pounding against my ribs with anger.

"I know it's hard for you to understand, me wanting to be with someone who's kind to me, who treats me well, and who didn't lie to me, even when the truth was pretty damn ugly. Can you say the same, Agustin? What lies are *you* hiding from me?"

"This isn't about *me*," I shot back, but even I knew how insincere my words sounded, and it was becoming harder to look her in the eye as she stared me down.

She took one step back, crossing her arms, and I immediately felt the chill of her distance like a chasm. "Bullshit. You can't even be honest with yourself, can you?"

I opened my mouth to argue, but my phone rang. Looking down, I saw my mother's name flash across the screen, and I silenced it.

"Agustin—" she started again.

"I'm sorry," I muttered, answering the call after the fourth tremor from my phone in my pocket and holding up a finger to ask for a second.

"Convenient," she whispered, getting up to pour herself a drink from the minibar. I ended the call and turned back to her, but I couldn't undo the damage.

"Ready to share a single truth yet, Agustin?" she asked, her voice quiet but laced with disappointment.

I wanted to. I tried to tell Loriah everything: how much I cared, how much I hated seeing her with Christian, and how much I hated myself for feeling that way. I knew my life was a mess. She didn't deserve me dragging her into it, and I didn't know how to express that to her without coming off as an overbearing jerk. So I always stopped myself before I could begin.

God dammit.

In one swift movement, I was towering over her, wanting so badly to reach out to her. Frustration was seeping from me in waves, causing my muscles to strain from the effort of keeping my hands to myself.

"I want to tell you everything, every dark, ugly thing. But I can't. I can't do that to you."

"What the fuck does *that* mean?"

"It means I can't go through this again. I'm sorry. But Jackson's not good enough for you. That is just the truth of it."

She stepped closer to me, tentative like she was approaching a wild animal. Her hand came up to rest against my chest, and I looked down at it, then back up to her silently pleading face. Taking it in my hand, I moved her fingers to my mouth and kissed them, then let her place them against my face, savoring the moment, knowing this was only making everything so much worse.

"Agustin..." My name hung like a prayer in the ether, waiting for me to answer, but I wouldn't be the one to give her what she needed.

My voice was hoarse when I finally spoke, "I have to leave tonight."

Her face froze, then pinched with anger. "*Leave?*"

"Something's come up in New York. I have to head back without you."

Her head shook slowly, and she retreated behind those mental walls she was building to shut me out. "Right. And let me guess—you can't tell me why?"

"It's not like that, Loriah."

"Isn't it?" she shot back. "You demand honesty from me constantly, yet you give me none!" She was so close I could see every fleck of gold in her blazing eyes. "You expect that I keep pretending it's okay because we're *partners*, right? You don't get to decide who or what I deserve when you can't figure out what the hell *you* want."

I clenched my fists, knowing precisely what I wanted, and it came in the form of an angry redhead.

Trying to keep my voice steady, I told her, "I'm *trying* to protect you."

She laughed bitterly. "Protect me? Agustin, you're the one I need protection from."

Of all the things she could have chosen to come back with, I wasn't expecting that. It demolished me in a way that solidified my resolve to keep her away, knowing whatever I had to do was worth it if it kept her out of my bullshit.

She turned away, and I knew I should have left. But I whispered, "I'm sorry."

"For what?" she asked, sharp and furious.

"For a lot of things," I admitted, walking to the door.

I turned, trying to catch another glimpse of her, but she'd already shut me out by the time I whispered, "Goodbye, Loriah."

CHAPTER 52
Loriah

As the door clicked shut, I stared at it, the silence pressing in like a suffocating fog. I clutched my glass of Prosecco, its fruity taste now sour on my tongue, but drained it in one long gulp. The calming scents from my bath and the excitement at what I'd found dissipated, leaving me raw and restless.

I wanted to hate Agustin—hate how he made me second-guess myself, how he evaded all my questions, how he refused to trust me with his truth, how he mistrusts my own instincts. But more than anything, I wanted to despise myself for wishing he had stayed. That was Agustin, consistently running the moment I got close to uncovering who he was under that hard exterior. Agustin stood there with that damned hopeful look, clutching a pizza as if it were a peace offering. That was part of the real him.

Pulling the blanket tighter around me, I stared at the ceiling, dissecting every word and glance between us. There was nothing hidden, no subtext to uncover. I knew that. Agustin never said anything he didn't mean, but he never revealed what he truly felt either. That was the problem. I was left to drown in silence, tangled in unanswered questions, while my overactive imagination filled in the blanks.

When tears pricked the corners of my eyes, I wiped them away—I refused to cry. But the room felt cavernous without Perez there, too quiet, too cold. He was my partner, but something had to change. My phone buzzed suddenly, cutting through the stillness. I grabbed it in a rush.

> **Christian -** *Hey! I wanted to call, but if you're busy, this might be easier for you.*

Relief hit me like a balm. I needed Christian's voice, steady and grounding, a tether in the emotional storm.

> **Me -** *I can talk.*

The phone barely rang twice before he picked up.

"Hey, how're you holding up?" His voice lifted the weight from my chest.

"It's going. We might have a lead. Mostly, though, I'm glad to hear from you."

"That's progress, right?"

"Sure. But can we not talk about work?"

"Of course. Want me to tell you about the lasagna I'm making?"

For the rest of the conversation, I listened. Christian lovingly described the steps of his grandmother's recipe in fine detail so vividly that I could almost taste it if I closed my eyes and thought hard enough. His words melted the tension away, lulling me into a deep sleep.

I woke to a dark screen and a damp pillow.

"I'm checking out of room 272," I told the receptionist the next morning.

"Ms. Fairsbane? Your partner settled the bill but left this for you." She handed me a small envelope containing rental car keys and a folded letter, its frayed edges indicating that Perez had opened and refolded it many times.

I glanced up. "Did he say anything else?"

"I wasn't here last night, ma'am. Sorry. I was only told to pass this along."

"Lucky I didn't leave the key at the desk," I muttered with a nervous laugh. The receptionist smiled politely, turning back to her work as I left. Still feeling the burn of last night's interaction, I couldn't bear to look at a note written in his distinct handwriting without wanting to chuck it in the nearest bin.

By the time I landed in New York, exhaustion clung to me like a leech. I was frustrated—not only with how the weekend had unfolded, but with the fact that I hadn't had the chance to share my findings with Agustin. Now, it was just one more thing waiting for me in the week ahead, and the burden of it clouded my thoughts.

I spotted Christian leaning against his truck, dressed in jeans and a worn brown ranch coat. His warm smile pulled one out of me as he hauled me into a hug. For all his faults, Christian had always been my steady place—my calm in the chaos. And as much as I knew that was exactly what I needed, I couldn't help but ache for the reckless thrill of stolen touches, and the magnetic pull that only Agustin ever seemed to offer.

But that's all it would ever be: fleeting, chaotic moments.

My stupid, stubborn, beating heart. Falling for a coworker—worse, a *partner*—was probably the most recklessly clichéd thing I'd ever let myself do.

"Hey," he said, lifting me up. The kiss that followed was soft, sweet, and grounding. "Long flight?"

"Something like that. Thanks for coming."

"Always," he said, tossing my bag into the back seat.

"I think I might doze a little on the way, if that's ok."

He squeezed my hand before navigating us into the flow of airport traffic.

As we drove, my phone buzzed in my pocket. The vibration cut through the quiet hum of the truck and any attempts to catnap.

"Give me a second," I told him, answering quickly. "Detective Fairsbane."

"Detective, it's Chief Daniels. Sorry for using a different number—I'm shorthanded today. But I needed to tell you: Angel's missing."

CHAPTER 53
Loriah

C hief's words sunk into me like stones. I tightened my grip, forcing my mind to focus.

"Chief," I said slowly, anger simmering beneath my words. "What do you mean Angel is missing? How long has she been gone? And *what* happened?"

"There was a fire at the hotel in the early hours of this morning," he said, his voice heavy. "Smoke filled the hallways, and in the commotion, she disappeared. The officers thought she might've gotten lost, but then they found a note along with her phone that was left behind."

Christian kept stealing worried glances at me, but I couldn't meet his eyes. I had failed her. We had failed her.

"I'm on my way," I said. "Have the note and the scene locked down, including anything related to the fire. Is the fire chief on site yet?"

"He is. They want to speak with you and Agustin. Be careful, Fairsbane. This guy must have been watching."

The call ended with a click, leaving me staring at the blank screen. That familiar, suffocating pressure gripped my chest, the air around me thick. Christian reached over, his hand covering mine. "Loriah?"

"Take me to the hotel where Angel was staying."

"Was?" His brow furrowed, his concern etched deeply into his features. "What's going on?"

"She's gone, Christian. He took her. Right under our fucking noses."

His grip on the steering wheel tightened, the muscle in his jaw ticking as he processed what I said. "Shit."

"Yeah. *Shit*." I echoed barely audible over the throbbing pulse in my head.

Half an hour later, I stepped out of the truck in a black pantsuit, my holstered gun a grounding weight against my hip. The hotel was a scene of pure chaos—flashing lights painting the evening sky, smoke curling from the building, and a crowd of guests and onlookers buzzing with speculation.

Firefighters milled about, some combing through the debris, while others stood in tense clusters. The acrid stench of charred wood and melted plastic burned my throat as

I pushed through the throng toward the crime scene tape. Christian followed close behind.

"Detective Fairsbane," I said to the officer standing next to the yellow crime scene tape, and flashed her my badge. She nodded and stepped aside. Ducking under the tape, I scanned the scene, searching for a familiar face. Somewhere in this mess of lights and noise, Angel's trail was growing colder by the second.

She wasn't just a witness. She was a kid. A scared, vulnerable kid who'd already been through too much. And then she was gone.

"Fairsbane," Chief Daniels's gravelly voice cut through the din. I turned to see him approaching, his face grim and lined with fatigue.

"What's the situation?" I asked, not bothering with pleasantries.

"We're piecing it together. The fire took quite a while to contain." His eyes darted toward the smoldering building. "Witnesses claim they saw a man enter the room where the explosion originated. The rooms have small kitchens, but this wasn't an accident. We're waiting on the fire chief to confirm."

"What about the officers assigned to watch her?" My gaze flicked toward the paramedics working nearby.

"They're over there. They took in a lot of smoke trying to find her." He paused, his voice dropping. "It's not good, Detective. Whoever we're dealing with knows what they're doing."

I clenched my jaw, teeth grating against each other in protest. "What the *fuck* were they doing that they let someone walk right in?" I asked, gesturing at the damage surrounding us.

"I don't know," Daniels admitted, his tone frustrated. "Wait for them to be cleared first, then you can talk to them."

"Where's Agustin?" I asked, looking around for him. He should have been here already—this was our case, our witness.

As if summoned by his name, Perez appeared through the crowd, his face tight with an uncomfortable look I recognized immediately—guilt. He strode toward us, phone in hand.

"Where the hell have you been?" I demanded, my voice cutting through the chaos.

"I was following a lead," he said quickly, avoiding my glare.

"Your phone was off," I shot back, my anger rising. "Angel's gone, Agustin. I needed you, and you weren't there."

His jaw tightened, but he didn't argue. "I'm here now."

"That's not good enough," I snapped. "Angel was your responsibility as well."

Christian stepped up and cleared his throat. "Is there anything I can help with?"

Daniels, who had been watching our exchange with growing impatience, seemed to notice Christian for the first time. He gave him a quick once-over. "Start taking statements, assuming you have your badge, and make sure no one's hurt."

Christian gave my arm a quick, reassuring squeeze before moving off toward a woman clutching a bag to her chest.

Daniels turned his fiery eyes back to Agustin and me. "Get it together—both of you," he barked, stepping between us. "This isn't the time."

I nodded once and turned to walk away before I could say anything else, acutely aware of Agustin's eyes following me as I headed toward the smoking building.

I followed a firefighter who gestured to what remained of our safe house. Inside, the fire chief crouched beside a blackened countertop, his experienced eyes already identifying what I couldn't see.

"Detective Fairsbane?" he asked, glancing up. Soot streaked his face, and his helmet sat slightly askew.

"That's me. What are we dealing with?"

He tapped an indistinguishable object with his pen. "The fire started here. Looks like a small incendiary device. Fast, hot, and controlled. Not meant to destroy the structure, but to create panic and burn for a long time."

My stomach twisted as I traced the scorched pattern he pointed to. "This wasn't an accident?"

"Not a chance. Someone knew exactly what they were doing. The device was likely a simple bomb, rigged to ignite accelerants for a quick blaze, but with these old buildings, it kept burning hotter and trying to spread."

"They wanted confusion," I murmured, my mind racing. It was the same way they confused Kayleigh and the others. Create chaos and exploit vulnerability once our girls are alone.

The Chief nodded grimly. "Well, they got it. The fire gave them the perfect cover to take her."

I glanced at the shattered window across the room, the jagged remnants of glass glinting in the dim light, and pointed. "Did they go out that way?"

"Most likely. People would have packed every other route trying to escape, making it nearly impossible to get through."

I stared out at the city's fading light, the weight of the situation pressing down on me. Whoever took Angel wasn't wholly a criminal—they were a strategist—a predator who thrived on mayhem.

"We'll find her," Agustin said quietly, stepping beside me.

"We don't have a choice. Without Angel—Agustin, without her, we don't have a witness; we don't have a testimony. She was more than just a victim," I replied, my voice on the verge of breaking. "We're not losing her—we can't. Dammit! He knew how much we needed her."

CHAPTER 54
Loriah

The station had been buzzing since the day before, as everyone scrambled to find even the smallest piece of information to track down our man. Agustin had spoken with Dolino the night before, trying to work that angle, but it turned out to be a dead end. Chimera was too competent for that—he'd be monitoring all the right avenues, getting anything from Dolino would be a setup.

I sat in my darkened office, hands wrapped around a hot mug, though it did little to warm me. It had been far too long since I'd honestly let my body rest—my eyes stung, and the thoughts I struggled to keep in order were beginning to scatter. The coffee tasted like ash, but I needed the caffeine to stay upright.

After leaving the crime scene, I finished my paperwork at the station and headed home, while Christian went home to try and get some sleep as well. But as I had no sooner crawled into bed, my phone buzzed with a text. This one was disturbingly direct.

Unknown - *Did you like my surprise?*

Five words. Five little words that could mean the end of a young girl's life. Five words that kept me up all night. My nerves were threadbare, barely concealing my fury, sharper than it had been in days. The messages weren't entirely a game—this had become personal.

When I slept—those brief, tortured moments—I dreamed of Angel. A man had her in his grip, his long, shadowed fingers tightening around her throat until his knuckles turned white. I reached for my gun, but my hand patted fruitlessly at my side. A low, throaty chuckle echoed through the darkness, wrapping around me like a nightmarish cocoon.

Her mouth opened in a silent scream, smoke spilling from hollow sockets where amber eyes should have been. I tried to move, tried to scream—but my feet were bound, and a gag appeared in my mouth, muffling every desperate sound.

Tears streamed down my face as shadows emerged, girls I'd seen in other cases, in other crimes. One by one, they stepped into the dim light, their voices rising in a haunting, rhythmic chant.

Help me.
Help me.
Help me.

"Knock, knock."

"You can't say 'knock, knock,'" I snapped, not bothering to look up. I wasn't in the mood for Perez's antics.

"Well, I did." He shut the door behind him, glancing back to make sure no one was listening. "I need to go over something on Woods's computer. It might be a lead, but I don't want anyone else seeing it until I get your take."

"Surprise, surprise." My tone was flat as I took a sip of lukewarm coffee, willing myself not to reach across the desk and throttle him. The delirium was beginning to set in.

"Loriah, stop. I need you for this. And there aren't many people I can trust right now. Are you paying attention?"

He came around to my side of the desk. I jumped when he slammed a folder in front of my face. My coffee nearly toppled as he crouched next to my chair, far too close for comfort.

"What the hell, Perez?"

"Look at this." He pointed to the documents. "These financials don't make sense. Transactions are tying my family's business to this mess. But my brother doesn't even know Woods."

"Have you considered that Ares might be involved? " I asked, studying his face for any flicker of doubt.

"My brother wouldn't—" Agustin's jaw tightened, the muscle pulsing beneath his skin.

"Wouldn't what? Lie to you? " I tapped the folder. "These transactions suggest otherwise. "

"Family is complicated, Loriah. " His voice dropped.

I leaned forward, frowning. "Family loyalty is admirable, Perez, but I've seen it blind better cops than you. Do you want *me* to ask him?" I offered.

"You don't even know him," Agustin said, though his voice held more doubt than conviction.

"Sure, but if you're scared to..."

"No." He rocked back, running a hand through his hair. "I need more time to figure this out. There's another account tied to these transactions—small cash flows. Could it be Chimera?"

"Anything's possible at this point," I muttered, rubbing my temples. "I don't even know which way is up anymore."

"Loriah, I'm trying." His voice softened as he leaned in, and the faint trace of his cologne stirred something in me I didn't want to acknowledge. My body, tired and traitorous, ached to close the distance, to lean into the very person I was trying so hard to keep at arm's length.

Hope had a cruel way of blurring everything—pulling my heart one way, while my head fought to hold the line.

"Sorry. I can't do this right now." I pushed my chair back, needing the space. "Talk to Ares, or don't. But if it comes down to it, we'll bring him in. And what does your family even do that would connect them to this shady bullshit?"

He looked at me then, really seemed to see me, and his expression shifted.

"You don't look so good."

"No shit," I shot back. "Now, if you don't mind, I'd like a moment to go over my reports."

"Sure." He hesitated at the door. "But, Loriah?"

"What?"

"Please don't say anything about this until I figure it out."

"You've got a short window, Perez," I said, my tone cold. "I'm not risking this girl's life for anyone's secrets."

After he left, my phone rang.

"Al, what's up?"

"Fairsbane! Can you come down with Perez? We've got footage—might be a hit on your guy."

"I'll be there in fifteen."

I hung up, went and splashed cold water on my face, and refilled my coffee. Minutes later, I was leaning into Perez's office.

"Al wants us," I said, already walking to the elevator.

He followed, muttering complaints in Spanish as the elevator doors slowly closed. The polished metal gave back a distorted reflection of me: haggard with dark circles under my eyes and skin far too pale. I looked worn out. And yet Agustin stood beside me, composed and polished as ever, looking completely unbothered by the heavy burden of the case.

How could it be affecting us so differently? It didn't seem fair.

I couldn't bring myself to meet Perez's eyes when he glanced over. I didn't want him to see me like this—not just exhausted, but unraveling at the seams, desperate for answers if only to quiet the ghosts long enough to rest.

The grainy footage filled the screen, showing the hallway outside Angel's hotel room. Al fast-forwarded through the mundane parade—housekeeping carts, the same drunk couple arguing their way to their room, a uniformed officer making his rounds.

"Wait," I said, leaning forward. "Go back."

Al rewound. The officer paused at Angel's door, checked his watch, then entered. The timestamp read 2:46 AM.

"Who authorized that?" Perez asked, voicing my exact thought.

"Nobody," I murmured, a chill crawling up my spine as the hall emptied.

For twenty-three seconds, nothing moved. Then a shadow stretched across the wall before its owner appeared—a hooded figure gliding into the frame as if materializing from the darkness itself.

The camera feed glitched and cut to static. When it resumed, smoke filled the frame. The hooded figure emerged again, a smaller one trailing behind. Angel and Chimera reentered the room, chaos erupting in the hall around them.

"Pause it," I said.

Al froze the frame, zooming in. The resolution was terrible, allowing us only to make out vague details. But that face. It seemed *so* familiar.

"Can you clean this up?"

"I'll try," he said, typing furiously. "But this isn't Hollywood."

"I know. Thanks." I clapped him on the shoulder. As the slightly enhanced picture filled the screen, I nodded, my throat tight. The figure's silhouette burned into my retinas, matching the shadow from my nightmare perfectly. My hands trembled, not from exhaustion, but from a primal recognition that made no logical sense at all.

"Fairsbane?" Perez's voice sounded distant.

"I've seen him before," I whispered, not just meaning the dream.

CHAPTER 55
Loriah

To say I wasn't excited about working a night at the club after no sleep would be a disgusting understatement. Luckily, I was able to get a brief nap at Allie's apartment when I got off work. I remembered mumbling something about needing to be out of my own space for a bit, and she gave me her bed while she worked in the living room.

"You sure you don't want to stay here tonight?" She asked me when I got up to make my way back to my own apartment and get ready for the night.

"No," I said with what I hoped was a reassuring smile. "I'll be fine—just in my head with this case."

"Okayyy" she dragged out in an *I don't believe you* way. "Just know if you need to, you can knock any time."

"I do know, I love you."

"You better." And she laughed that silly laugh she had that brought a smile to my face.

The entire ride to the club that night, my mind kept circling back to Agustin—how adamant he'd been that his brother had nothing to do with Dante's trafficking operation. I wanted to believe he was right. I prayed he was right. But I refused to stop digging until I knew for sure—Agustin's family loyalty be damned.

The bass pulsed through the floor as I made my way to the private basement-level entrance. I'd nearly forgotten I didn't have a key yet—right up until I heard a voice behind me.

"I was hoping to see you tonight."

"Were you?" I mused, turning to find Ares stepping closer to me. "I need to talk to you."

He rested his hand at the small of my back, his heat seeped through the skintight red dress I was wearing. He held his key up, and the door unlocked with a green light. "Oh? I'm enjoying this night already."

"Get serious, Ares. Meet me in a private room in fifteen. I'll go 'check' in on them." I told him with a little air quote around 'check'.

"Fine." And he strode off toward Dante's office.

Seventeen minutes later, he walked into room number four and found me running my hands along the cushions, imagining what young girls were forced to do there.

"You're late."

"Couldn't be helped. We don't have long," Ares replied, stepping in and closing the door with a glance down the hall. It shut behind him with only the briefest of clicks.

"I *know we don't*. Agustin discovered something today, and it ties back to you."

"Okay. Well, what is it?"

"It's financial records tying you to Woods." There was no recognition on his face of what I was telling him, only confusion, and he ran a hand through his hair before leaning over the back of a seat and gripping at the plush cushion reflexively. For a moment, I had a sense of déjà vu, both Perez brothers sharing the same tell.

"Like his partner, Woods?"

"Exactly!"

"I never even met the guy. He had been to the club a couple of times, but not to talk to me."

"Then who?" I was pacing in front of him, my hand under my chin in contemplation.

"I don't know, some guy. He was in a couple of times. Maybe he had tried to get down here, but I don't think he had an invitation. I can't remember. Dante keeps records of all that. If we can get into his office again, I can look. Plus, I doubt a cop makes enough for this place. No offense."

"Unless they're your brother?"

"What do you mean?"

"What does your family do, Ares?"

"You don't want the answer to that, Loriah. Just leave it. I can tell you it's not fuckin' trafficking girls, though."

"Then what is it, if it's not that bad?" I stepped closer, circling him like a predator stalking its prey, rounding the chair to face him fully. I wanted to see his eyes—read him—cut through whatever he was trying to keep buried.

Only inches separated us now as I trailed a finger down his chest, slow and deliberate. His green eyes locked on mine, studying me just as intently. I hoped his more relaxed demeanor would give me something—anything—that Agustin's stonewalling never had.

"Why is it," I murmured, making him lean closer to hear me, "that all you Perez men insist on hiding things from me?"

"Loriah, it's not safe for you. You're already in over your head being here. For fuck's sake, look where you're at." His voice was low, but I didn't miss the command in it or the way he could see through my thin veneer of strength.

"I can handle myself. What I can't figure out, though, is why your brother, my partner, is so set on keeping me in the dark."

"What do you mean?" He was trying to remain in control. I swiped my hand away and took a step back.

"When we were at the funeral in Oklahoma, he had gotten a call and said he had to leave that night. Did you have anything to do with that?"

"No. I didn't even know Agustin was out of town, to be honest. We aren't exactly close if you couldn't tell." Annoyance at the line of questioning edged his words.

"I see." But I didn't see. If anything, things were becoming muddled; the list of questions in my mental Rolodex lengthening by the day.

"Back to your first question, though, I don't know why it says we're linked. I'm not. I don't know him, and that's the truth."

"I hope for your sake it is, Ares, because I thoroughly hate liars." I punctuated the last two words with a tap to his chest, right above his heart. And all the while, I was a complete hypocrite.

At that, I left the room and went to the bar where Tony was serving drinks and watching the patronage with the eye of a man who missed nothing.

The night was relatively quiet compared to my first one there, and I'd seen neither hide nor hair of Dante. I thought he must have been either not in the club or handling business elsewhere. I waited patiently for the right moment, when a group of men came in insisting on being at the bar, doing shots, and using Tony's time. I retreated to a darkened alcove to pull out my phone.

> **Me** - *I need to get into Dante's office again. Can you distract him in your office?*

I stood, waiting anxiously, not knowing if he was in the building when my phone pinged back.

> **Francesco Baldini** - *Give me 10 minutes.*

> **Me** - *Thank you!*

There was one more person I needed; otherwise, this would be for nothing.

> **Me** - *Meet me at the stairwell in 10 minutes?*

> **Ares** - *It's a date.*

Stepping from the alcove, I slipped my phone into a discreet pocket in my dress and grabbed an empty glass haphazardly discarded on a nearby high top.

"I'm taking a break, Tony," I told him, placing the glass down on the bar.

"I gotcha. Elise will cover." And he returned to pouring drinks, only looking up to nod at me.

I leaned against the wall, trying to pull down my dress and watching the seconds tick by on my phone. My nerves felt painfully taut. The last thing I needed was for anyone passing by to catch even a hint of what I was about to do and then report it back to Dante. The club's music continued to thump in the background, a rhythm that made the silence of the deserted stairwell even more ominous.

Ares arrived right on time, his stride confident, a little leer of a smile playing at his lips. "You're lucky I like you," he whispered, slipping his hands into his pockets as he joined me. "Breaking into Dante's office again isn't exactly at the top of my good ideas list."

"Yeah, well, neither is letting him run a trafficking ring out of this place," I shot back, keeping my voice low. "You said you wanted answers, Ares. This is how we get them. We finish this tonight. I don't want to come back if I don't have to."

He gave me a slight shrug, his smile fading as he scanned the hallway.

"I concede that's not a brilliant plan. But if we get caught, you're explaining it to Dante, if only for my amusement."

"I'll take my chances," I said, moving for the door to his office.

My shoulders tensed as I crossed the hallway leading to Dante's office, even if it appeared to be as deserted as the other one. There was no relaxing in a place like this. Ares trailed behind me, his quiet footfalls a testament to how often he must navigate the place unseen. When we reached the door, I caught Ares slipping his key card back in place as the lock clicked open.

Stealthy bastard.

I moved straight to the secured file cabinet, only to find it locked. I pulled out a small set of picks I'd hidden in a pouch strapped to my thigh and knelt to get a steadier position.

"God, Loriah, you always carry those?" he asked, watching me as I worked.

"Occupational hazard. Last time I forgot, and look, we needed them," I muttered. The lock was more sophisticated than I'd anticipated, only adding to the satisfaction of opening it and getting all the dirt I needed to put that sleazy bastard and his whole operation away.

After a few tense moments, there was a faint click, and the drawer moved open the slightest fraction.

"I don't know how long Francesco can keep Dante occupied."

The office was dark, and the air was heavy with the same smells as before, only making it more noxious in the rush to get what we needed.

Inside the cabinet were rows of neatly labeled folders, most of them financial records. But it was the smaller drawer at the bottom that caught my attention most. When I opened it, my stomach dropped.

"Holy shit," I whispered, pulling out the first file. The file contained photos of young girls. Many resembled the faces I'd seen on Dolino's computer. Each one had a clipped sheet of paper with their name on it. Their real names. And origins. Many were under the age of seventeen, some as young as thirteen.

Ares leaned over my shoulder as he scanned the pages, his upper lip lifting into a slight sneer.

"This is revolting," he muttered. "He's keeping records like it's a business."

"It is a business," I said, my voice tight. I flipped through the files until I landed on the one labeled 'RECRUITMENT.' Inside were lists of names, dates, and locations, along with payment records. I scanned across the pages, then stopped, my index finger hovering over the name: CHIMERA.

I froze, staring at the names scrawled on several of the following pages, along with the amounts of money paid to someone named J. Morales.

"Hold on," Ares said and reached for the file. "That's my shipment guy." His jaw clenched as he dropped the edge of the folder back into my hand. "If this is true," he fumed. "He's dead."

"Not if I get there first," I said, tucking the files to my side.

"Let me take those."

"No way, I need these. If we can track Morales, he might know where Angel is or how to get to Chimera."

"I'll give them back, but where the hell are you going to hide them? Up your dress? As arousing as that would be to watch, I'm guessing they won't fit."

His words were said in jest, though his eyes held the truth. He was just as desperate as I was. And in that moment, I could see that, whether either Perez would admit it, they were more alike than they knew.

"Okay, *fine*. But you'd better give them back. We share the info."

"Deal. Let's get out of here before someone notices you've been gone too long."

Leaving the office was more daunting than getting in. Ares stayed close to me, his presence steady but tense. We made it back to the main entrance in the stairwell without incident, but my nerves were on alert. I excused myself to the bar, needing a moment to compose myself while Ares did what he did best and disappeared into the crowd. Though I was sure Tony was studying me with more interest than when I'd left.

"Can I get water, Tony?"

"Sure, Serena. Want something stronger?"

"No. I'm good. It's been a long day."

"I can understand that. Is he trying it on with you?"

"Who?" I asked and looked around the lounge, expecting to see the same man who tried to come onto me in the hall the last time I'd worked, when I caught his head nod toward a prominent, dark figure talking to another group of women in a booth. Ares.

"Oh, yeah, a bit. But it's okay. I can handle him, and I'm not for sale." My pocket buzzed with a message, and I told him, "I'm going to go check the back rooms."

Tony gave me a noncommittal "mhm," which could have been an agreement.

I stopped in an empty room, pulling the cell phone out and seeing Francesco's name light up the screen.

Francesco Baldini - *He's on his way back.*

Me - Thank you!

The text came just as fast.

Francesco Baldini - *You owe me your company for dinner when this is over.*

I was about to type a reply when a message came as instantaneously as the last.

Unknown - *How does your partner feel about you snuggling up with his brother?*

CHAPTER 56
Loriah

My heart had been pounding against my ribs for the final two hours of my shift. I kept scanning for the girl from last time, or a shadowy, unnamed figure that I knew had to be watching me. Instead, I encountered the same disagreeable woman from that night when I'd found a trussed-up, half-conscious Livvy. This time, she seemed to take extreme delight in giving me an earful when I didn't have the right girl ready in room seven for a group of red-faced, pompous business types.

"Are you stupid on purpose?" she asked me, tapping her manicured nails against her crossed arms.

I curled my fingers into my palm. It took all my strength not to punch Daniella in the face, which was as clownishly frozen as it could be.

"Is there a problem here?" Ares materialized beside us, his voice deceptively casual.

"None." I flashed a tight smile at the woman, trying to murder her with my eyes. I wouldn't be working here much longer, if at all.

"Let's take a walk this way, Ms. Petrov."

I followed, grabbing my purse when we reached the bar, and paid a goodbye to Tony before weaving my way to the exit. Ares had stopped following, but soon he caught up to me on the sidewalk outside the club. His footsteps came quickly.

"I think our friend the bartender has the hots for you."

"Doubt it. Tony's watchful of everyone."

"Is he?"

"I need to get home, Ares. Can you give me the files?" The night air raised goosebumps on my exposed skin.

"I'll do you one better." He glanced at the street, then back at me. "I'll drive you home, and we can go over them together."

"I'd rather not. Please. I can make you copies."

"No." His tone softened but remained firm. "You're not safe, and I need to see that file too. Sooner, rather than later. Preferably."

A sleek black Audi glided to a stop at the curb. A young valet boy got out, and Ares pressed a folded bill in his palm before opening my door. I looked from the open door to him and back.

"Ares."

"Don't fight me on this. Get in."

"Where to?" he asked once we were sealed inside the car's leather interior, the outside world reduced to muffled street noise.

I gave him my address and let my body sink into the supple leather. The warmth of the seat eased into my muscles, and I practically melted, feeling like I hadn't slept in years. The soft glow of streetlights and the city's ambient lighting washed over us in a slow, rhythmic succession.

I took advantage of the quiet moment, lifting my dress just enough to undo the velcro around my thigh. The relief was immediate, a sigh slipping from my lips as the satisfying thud of the holster hitting the seat filled the space. I leaned my head back, exhaling deeply—only to glance over and catch Ares' eyes lingering on my thigh.

"Eyes on the road, mister."

He smirked without missing a beat. "I'm just making sure you're not hiding another surprise."

The door clicked shut behind us, and I sagged against the wall in relief. My apartment wasn't much—a small one-bedroom with mismatched furniture and the faint smell of old books and coffee lingering in the air. It was my sanctuary, though, a place where I could usually shut out the worst. But tonight, the world had decided to follow me home in the form of a large, annoyingly handsome, dark-haired Hispanic man, making the place feel all at once too small.

"Make yourself comfortable," I said over my shoulder, dropping my purse on the counter and heading to my bedroom. "I'm going to change real quick. There's coffee if you press the button."

"Water's fine," Ares replied, already taking off his jacket and tossing it over the back of my reading chair. His presence filled the small space, making me self-conscious in an unnerving way.

When I came back in an old college shirt and a pair of sweatpants, I poured two cups of coffee, adding too much creamer to mine and a little to his. He was flipping through the files with the same intensity he'd had at the club, his eyes scanning every line, every name. His focus on interpreting the given file reminded me of Agustin.

"These girls," he said, shaking his head. "You were right. This is worse than I thought. And somehow this Chimera fucker is trying to tie me to it?"

"Yeah," I said, sitting down beside him and handing him his mug. "It's not entirely trafficking either. Look at this." I pulled out a sheet I'd flagged from the moment I saw it, pointing to the repeated mention of Chimera. "The cases all tie back to him. Payments, recruitment, even transportation routes. It's all him."

Ares leaned closer, his leg pressing into mine, causing me to move away slightly so I wasn't giving the wrong impression of what we were doing. "Then there's Morales," he muttered, tracing the name on the ledger. "I trusted him. He's worked for my family for years, and I've trusted him."

"People are good at hiding who they are," I said, my voice preoccupied. "Especially when money's involved."

The room fell silent for a moment; the significance of our discovery hung over us like a dense fog. I reached for another sheet, but my phone buzzed on the table. My head snapped to its location. I had no idea who would be messaging me this late.

Ares noticed instantly, his eyes flicking to the phone. "What is it?"

I snatched the phone and unlocked it.

> **Unknown** - *Where was your partner when I took your sweet Angel? Do you know how much girls of her age bleed? Drop the case, or you'll find out.*

My stomach dropped, and I felt the blood drain from my face. The phone trembled in my hand as I reread the words, the threat sharp, and it played right into my insecurities.

"Loriah?" Ares's voice was softer, his tone careful. "What does it say?"

I hesitated, my instinct to hide the message warred with the realization that I couldn't keep this to myself anymore. Slowly, I handed him the phone, watching as his eyes darkened while he read the text.

I glanced past him toward the kitchen—where just a few weeks ago, I'd stood with Agustin and let him kiss me. It felt like another lifetime. Every time I reached for something real with him, he pulled away, leaving me grasping at shadows. And maybe that was why I hadn't told him about the messages yet.

The thought unsettled me more than I wanted to admit.

Why was it easier with Ares? Why had I shared this with *him* instead?

He offered a kind of quiet steadiness that felt like it belonged to an old friend, even though we barely knew each other. It made me feel seen in a way Agustin never allowed himself to. And that realization gnawed at me, even as I tried to push it aside.

"Fuck," he muttered, setting the phone down with more force than necessary. "How long has this been going on?" He sounded mad and incredulous.

"Just a little while," I admitted, my voice barely above a whisper. "It started with cryptic messages, but now, they're getting more specific."

"You should've told me, or someone," he said, his voice sharp, but not unkind. "Or Agustin. This isn't something you deal with alone."

I shook my head, leaning back against the couch. "I didn't want to drag anyone else into this bullshit. I thought maybe it would help me understand him better or get closer to finding him."

"It's not your burden to bear alone," he said, shifting closer. "This is fucking serious, Loriah. Don't be foolish."

"I know." I let out a shaky breath and felt better after lifting this secret off my shoulders and sharing it with him.

"You're no good to anyone if something happens to you." His voice softened. "You're scared?"

I hated how rational he sounded—hated even more that he could see through me. "Of course I'm scared," I said, my voice cracking. "But I can't stop. If I stop, he wins. *They* win." I gesture to the photos spread across the table. "And those girls—they don't have anyone else looking out for them. Some of them have absolutely no one, Ares."

"You're not doing this alone. You have Agustin, you have me."

"Do I have Agustin? Come on."

"I'm serious."

The mention of Agustin stung, but I didn't want to argue. Ares reached out for the files again and spread them out on the coffee table. Let's focus on what we can do right now," he said. "This name, Chimera—it's all over these documents. Some tracks lead to a Dolino. If we can figure out who he is, we might bring this down."

I nodded, grateful for the diversion. "Morales," I said, pointing to one of the ledgers. "He's a direct connection. If we can track him down, he may lead us to Chimera also."

"I'll handle Morales," Ares said, his tone leaving no room for argument. "But you—" He hesitated, his gaze steady on mine. "You need to be careful. Whoever sent you that message, they're watching you."

"I know," I said quietly. "But I'm not going to give up. And now I've dragged you into it. They sent me a message earlier tonight. They know, Ares. I can't hide."

He gave a slight nod with a look of resignation. "I didn't think you would. And don't worry about me, chica." Turning back to the file, he laughed and patted me on the knee.

For a moment, neither of us said anything. The faint hum of the fridge mingled with the sounds of traffic from the street below. Papers rustled as Ares gathered them into neater piles. Then he reached over, resting a hand lightly on mine. "We'll figure this out," he said. "I promise."

I wanted to believe him. I wanted so badly to believe that we could unravel the mess of lies, threats, and secrets surrounding this man, Chimera. But as I looked at the files spread before us, at the young faces staring back, the text message pulsed in my mind like a warning.

We were running out of time.

A res had fallen asleep on my couch but vanished before dawn. Only the smell of a fresh pot of brewing coffee greeted me. I inhaled the aroma, oddly moved by the simple gesture—a small kindness amid the mental torment from a lurking psychotic stranger.

Sipping the steaming mug and sitting down cross-legged, I grabbed for the file that we'd been combing over. Not much else became apparent beyond what we had already deduced. Whoever was behind this had to be setting up Ares and his family. This meant that anything else on Woods's computer was also suspect.

The precinct buzzed with ringing phones and clacking keyboards as I stepped off the elevator. I navigated between desks, nodding at familiar faces, clutching my briefcase as if it were something precious. Inside lay the folder—evidence worth killing for.

Reaching my office, I slipped into my desk chair and exhaled. Scooting forward, I focused on the computer screen and opened the missing persons database.

One by one, the faces of the girls in the folder flashed through my mind, committing them to memory as I typed in their names and approximate ages. The sound of my heart crescendoed between my ears with each name, resulting in some hits, including missing file reports from desperate families across the country.

But many showed nothing, and that felt even worse. These girls weren't just missing; someone had erased them.

"Fairsbane?"

My hand jerked at Perez's voice, mouse clicking as I minimized the screen. I shoved the folder beneath a stack of reports, heart hammering against my ribs.

"What?" I snapped, fingers drumming a panicked rhythm on my desk.

Perez perched on the edge of my desk like we were somehow on speaking terms again. His eyes narrowed as he scanned my space, gazing a beat too long on the half-hidden papers.

"What are you working on?" The question sounded casual, but I knew better.

"Nothing that is concerning you." I shuffled forms uselessly while nonchalantly pushing the file under them.

"Uh-huh," he said, dragging out the sound, clearly unconvinced. "I know things are tense. I know I've been off, I let you down, and I want it to change. It has to."

I glared at him, my defenses going up like grenade-proof barricades. "You know how to change this dynamic, Perez. Where were you when you came back early?"

"Loriah." He said my name like an apology, and I knew at once he wouldn't be sharing anything with me.

"I didn't think so," I told him coldly, my voice dropping. "You've been keeping secrets from me since day one, Perez. Why would I trust you now when all you've done is keep me in the dark, attack someone I care for, and blatantly avoid answering what should be a straightforward question?"

"I don't know if it's such a *simple* question. It was personal. I don't have to share everything with you outside of work."

"No, you don't. I don't share everything with you. But this week has been fucked. Maybe if things had been different, then Angel would be here."

"Thinking like that is going to drive you crazy."

I stared at him, unblinking, and the silence stretched taut between us. His shoulders tensed, then he straightened, running a hand through his dark hair as he stood.

"Bien. *Fine*." His voice flattened, emotion draining from his words. "Keep me in the dark if you must. You're not any better than me, Fairsbane. But don't come crying to me when it blows up in your face."

He stalked away, his back stiff with anger. I watched as frustration and guilt simmered in my stomach like oil and water. When I heard him go into his office, I turned back to my computer and reopened the database.

The words blurred before my eyes. Trust. It inevitably came back to trust.

By the time I got home that evening, exhaustion had wrung my nerves dry. The hairs on the back of my neck had been standing on end the whole walk. I couldn't shake the feeling someone was watching me. The air in my apartment felt thick, almost suffocating, as I locked the door. I had initially gone to Allie's door and knocked, but she hadn't been home and wasn't answering her phone, only adding to my unease.

My phone buzzed, and I froze, squeezing my eyes shut, not wanting to acknowledge the alert.

> **Unknown** - *You were so focused today, Detective. Shame you're wasting your time. You can't save them, you know. You couldn't even save Angel.*

The words hit me like a freight train. My heart lurched, and I dropped my bag. My fingers hovered over the call button for Agustin, but I couldn't bring myself to press it.

Instead, I dialed the only person I knew would comfort me without question.

"Christian?" I asked when I heard the phone pick up.

"Loriah?" His tone was instantly concerned, and I hated how comforting it was. "What's wrong?"

"I think–" I didn't want to say the words and give them life. "I think someone is watching me."

"I'm on my way," he said without hesitation.

I barely had time to argue before he hung up. Twenty minutes later, there was a knock at my door, and I opened it to find him standing there in that coat I liked too much, looking grim.

I handed him my phone, letting him read the message. His jaw tightened as he scanned the text.

"This is serious, Loriah," he said, setting the phone down on the coffee table and guiding me to take a seat next to him. "Have you told anyone?"

"No, I thought I could handle this ridiculous new stalker reality when Al's trace didn't give any results. And I didn't want to drag you into this." My voice was as shaky as my hands. "But I—"

"You were afraid," he finished for me, his eyes softening and running a rough hand along my cheek when a tear began to slip free.

I nodded, hating how vulnerable I felt as his words echoed what Ares had also surmised. Christian moved closer, taking my face between his hands, and kissed me. Soft and reassuring, his smell and taste enveloped me in comfort.

"I'll stay with you. You're not alone, you know that, right?"

I wanted to argue, to prove I was strong enough to handle it on my own. But in reality, I didn't want to be Detective Fairsbane. I wanted him—needed him. For the night, I wanted only to be Loriah, a girl who was shaken and afraid, and who could allow someone to actually care for her.

Christian kissed me again and carried me to my bedroom, helping me undress. His touches were tentative but hungry, two people seeking something that only the other could provide. His nips and kisses down my neck and to my breasts pulled my thoughts away from the horrible messages swirling in my head, Agustin's accusations, Ares's too-long looks, and this ridiculous triangle of push-pull that I'd gotten myself into. I closed my eyes and let his body drown out the roar in my ears and pull all thoughts but him from my mind.

"Christian, I need you," I admitted and drew him closer, but he hesitated.

"Loriah. I don't know if that's a good idea."

"It is. Please—be with me." I didn't want to hear all the reasons why I was too fragile. "I won't break."

"It's not you I worry about." He pushed me down into the bed, pinning me with his body, the smell of him enveloping me. When he was finally inside me, a desperate kind of need took over. I wanted him to erase every bad thing that had taken place as if they'd never occurred. His thrusts grounded me in reality. He wasn't gentle, but he took his time, and when we finally came together in a chorus of moans and sudden gasps, it was perfect oblivion.

I rested my head on the hard planes of his chest, feeling his heart race, and ran my hands along his arms, tracing the grooves and scars. My fingers found a rough spot behind his forearm. "Christian, what is that?" I asked him and grabbed his arm to turn it over for a closer inspection.

"Oh, it's nothing. I hurt myself the night I called you when getting lasagna out of the oven. You fell asleep, or you would have heard me yell."

"You? Mister meticulous had a cooking accident?" I laughed at him.

He joined in, but it didn't quite reach his eyes. His fingers rubbed the mark self-consciously. "Looks worse than it is, I promise. It'll be ok," he said, getting up from the bed.

The bathroom door closed behind him with a decisive click. When he came back to bed, we savored the feeling of being in each other's arms and let the night pass by outside, cocooned in our own bubble of quiet safety.

At some point, I fell asleep, lulled by the steady rhythm of his voice and the reassuring presence of someone else in my bed. But even in sleep, the words of the message haunted me like a lover's caress to my senses.

You couldn't even save Angel.

CHAPTER 58
Loriah

The morning hustle felt strangely comforting after the disturbing message I received the night before. Christian walked beside me, our steps in sync as we entered the elevator. His hand reached for mine—a brief squeeze that sent a warmth through me when they reopened. It was such a small thing that I didn't think anyone had seen it, but it felt like a spotlight had been turned on us.

Though one person *had* noticed.

I spotted him near the coffee station, posture relaxed as he stirred his cup. The moment we stepped outside the elevator, his sharp gaze cut to us like a blade. He didn't say anything, didn't even shift his stance—but I caught the subtle narrowing of his eyes before he turned his attention back to his coffee, dismissing us as swiftly as he'd noticed us.

Christian and I made our way to my office, and he leaned in close, voice low, so that only I could hear. "You good?"

I forced a smile, even though my mind was swirling. "Yeah. I will be."

Giving nothing away with his expression, Christian stood by my desk a few hours later, holding a small folder in his hand. When I finally looked up from combing through financials, he placed it in front of me and opened it to the front page.

"Thought you'd want to see this."

The header immediately drew my eyes to the bold print:

Forensic DNA Analysis Report
Case Number: 2817-0429
10-11-2022

As I flipped through the few pages, my pulse sped, each line of data confirming what I'd initially feared. The report listed Woods as a DNA match for the unborn child.

Christian leaned uneasily against my desk, watching me absorb the information. "I wonder how Perez is going to take this, considering..." He trailed off, but I knew what he meant.

Considering he was a trusted friend and partner.

"Yeah," I murmured, my fingers lingering on the paper. Something about it didn't sit right with me. Woods, being the father, explained part of the puzzle. Still, it didn't account for everything else, like the trafficking or Chimera's involvement, unless Woods had been more deeply involved than we realized, another casualty in this whole mess.

"You okay?" Christian asked, moving to my side.

Before I could answer, another figure darkened my doorway, making us both look up.

"What's that?" Agustin's gaze zeroed in on the folder in front of me.

Christian straightened, shoulders squaring in defense. "I'll leave you to it." He squeezed my shoulder and added, "Let me know if you need anything else."

"Thanks, Jackson," I said, keeping my voice steady despite the sudden shift in the room.

Agustin waited until Christian was gone. When he was no longer in earshot, Perez turned back to me, leaning forward with hands braced on my desk. "What's in the folder?"

"Sit down," I said. "You're going to want to."

He hesitated but did as I asked, eyes not leaving mine as I slid the report across the desk. "Tell me what you think of this."

His brows furrowed, eyes scanning the words again as if they might change. He flipped the paper over, then back again, as if rereading it would somehow change the words.

"No—I knew Woods." He said with a disbelieving finality.

"I know," I said softly. "I'm sorry, Perez."

"Have you shown this to the chief yet? Or anyone else?"

"No. Jackson picked it up from the lab on his way back and brought it to me."

Agustin scoffed. "Always so helpful, isn't he?"

"What is your problem?" I snapped. "Jackson's just doing his job."

"You expect me to believe that's all he's doing for his service to the city?" His tone was sharp, his words like a dagger aimed directly at me.

I flushed, the heat rising to my cheeks as I struggled to meet his eyes. "You know that's not fair."

He stood abruptly, his fist clenching at his side before he raked a hand through his hair. "Call me when you have something more."

"Perez!" I tried to shout without causing a scene.

His misplaced anger rolled off him in waves as he walked out, leaving me staring at the folder sitting on my desk.

Around lunchtime, my phone pinged with a message:

Ares - *We need to talk. Can't wait.*

I told Agustin I'd be out handling some business and left without saying goodbye to anyone else.

When I arrived at the restaurant, Ares was already waiting, one leg tucked under him as he leaned against the brick wall, checking his phone absent-mindedly. When he saw me, his lips curved into a sideways smile, inviting and maddeningly confident. Making his way to greet me, Ares's eyes danced with mischief as though he knew precisely the effect it had on people.

"I'm glad you could come," he said in his usual teasing tone, but then his face turned serious, letting me know that he wasn't wholly about games.

"Did I have a choice?" I asked, stepping past him as the cab I'd arrived in melted back into the lunchtime traffic frenzy. "You didn't exactly make it sound optional."

"It wasn't. But I'm still glad to see you."

"Do you always just say what you want?"

"Usually."

I gave him an unamused sideways glare that elicited a laugh. He led us to a booth tucked in the corner. Even though it was away from prying eyes, I felt exposed and anxious, nonetheless.

You couldn't even save Angel.

"We questioned Morales this morning," Ares began. "He swears he didn't know what was happening, but there were documents in his apartment: bank records, phone logs. Looks like someone's been using him as a middleman—and moving big money through his accounts."

"Who's behind it all?" I said, voicing my thoughts aloud. I played with the edge of the tablecloth, absentmindedly running my fingers nimbly along the hem to feel the rough sewn edges, trying to ground myself in the present.

"We're piecing it together because he wasn't in a position to say." He picked up the menu, flipping through it like we weren't discussing human trafficking, but instead the weather. "The pies here are great, by the way."

His cavalier attitude to everything going on was, well– It just was. I couldn't decide between comfort and irritation, because, internally, *I* was screaming.

Ares tilted his head, reading the menu, continuing, "He did say, the goods have made their way into New York, though, he's being paid not to be there while someone else comes to retrieve them."

He stopped talking for so long that I began to grow uneasy.

"Ares." I swallowed the bile that threatened to spew. "Goods as in?"

"*Girls*, Loriah," he said, exasperated. "And drugs. Counterfeit cash. Guns. It's a full operation." He sat back, looking around to make sure no one had heard his outburst.

My stomach turned. I placed my hands between my thighs, squeezing them together and mentally naming three things I saw in an attempt to ground myself: a red and white checked cloth, Ares's white pocket square, and a Parmesan shaker.

"Do you have an address?" I was finally able to muster.

"Not yet." His eyes narrowed. "And don't even think about recording this."

I laughed despite myself, the first time in what felt like a while. "Relax, Al Capone. I left my wire back at the office."

A flicker of warmth replaced the guarded look in his eyes. "Good. Because this thing? It's bigger than we thought. And you're already a target, Loriah. That asshole knows who you are, and I'm going to kill him."

For as calm and at ease as Ares seemed, a shiver ran through me at the thought. Somewhere deep down, I had no doubt that he would do terrible things to Chimera before I ever got a chance to serve up justice.

"I can handle it."

"I know you can, or at least I know you *think* you can," he said, his voice gentler now. "But you're not alone in this. I've already told you that."

Lunch ended after a too-long discussion about Morales and his involvement, making me glance nervously at my watch.

Ares insisted on driving me, his black Audi sliding to a smooth stop three blocks from the station—far enough that no one would spot me, most of all Perez. The man in question, though, was waiting at my desk, his countenance a stark contrast from the identical half I'd spent lunch with.

"Everything okay?" he asked, his tone casual, but his eyes sharp.

"Why wouldn't I be?" I replied. After his mild outburst earlier, I didn't think he was entitled to ask me anything other than professional pleasantries.

He didn't answer, but the tension in his jaw spoke volumes. He knew I was keeping secrets. However, there would be no sharing on my part until he was willing to reciprocate.

My phone buzzed again as I sat down, causing my hand to tremble slightly. Perez was watching me, as he regularly did, and I knew not looking at it would only be suspicious.

Unknown - *You can't trust the Perezes, Detective. I'm the only one who keeps their word.*

My pulse spiked as I fumbled to lock the screen, but not before he caught the flicker of unease on my face. A cold sweat pricked across my back, heart hammering until I was out of breath.

White letters on a keyboard, Perez's green eyes, and a ballpoint pen.

"You good?" Agustin asked again, but that time his voice was edged with suspicion.

"Sure. It's nothing." I slid the phone face down onto my desk.

He leaned close, voice dropping. "Your face says otherwise, Fairsbane."

"What do you want, Agustin? If you don't have anything, I'm busy."

His lips pressed into a line, but he didn't rise to the bait. "I'm taking tomorrow off. I'll check in, but I have things to handle."

I plastered a fake smile across my face, and my fingers were already returning to the keyboard. "Fine. See you in a day, partner."

As he walked away, the words on my phone burned in my mind.

I'm the only one who keeps their word.

CHAPTER 59

Perez

My phone's glow flickered against the bedroom walls, an island of light in the darkness. The unread report from the new PI I'd hired sat like a lead weight in my inbox.

I had appointed him to keep an eye on her, to make sure she was safe—at least that's what I told myself. She was too good for this bullshit, and her heart *too* trusting. But each time his name popped up, the guilt festered deeper inside my chest. This wasn't protection; it was surveillance. Invasion. Betrayal.

I couldn't even look at her without shame threatening to tear me apart. Loriah would never forgive me. But what choice did I have? I'd been backed into a corner.

She wasn't *simply* my partner.

She had unknowingly given me a sense of purpose—the one thing I couldn't lose, no matter what lines I had to cross.

I finally opened the report, dread coiling in my gut.

Subject observed at Dante's underground club. Could not gain access. Evidence indicates the subject is working undercover with Ares Perez.

The words blurred on the screen as my chest tightened, anger and disbelief fighting for territory.

I.

Will.

Kill him.

Undercover? She hadn't said a word. Not *one* fucking word. And with my brother—the same damned brother who lived to stick it to me every chance he got?

Jesucristo!

I sat up, slamming my fist into the nightstand.

The late nights. Loriah's secrecy. The tension between us.

My hand clenched the phone, its beveled edges pressing into my palm as I tried to tamp down the surge of fury that had me wanting to snap the phone in two. Something boiled deeper than anger.

I wasn't just lied to. I was... *replaced.*

The phone buzzed against my grip, pulling me from my spiraling thoughts, but the follow-up report only twisted the knife deeper.

DNA analysis tampered with. Recommend a deeper investigation into lab processes or contact directly.

My stomach churned. If the DNA report had been altered, someone inside was working to misdirect us. Everything I was holding onto was crumbling—Loriah's trust, this investigation, the lines I'd crossed to protect her. What would it all end up being for?

By the afternoon, I was parked outside Ares's club, my pulse pounding in my ears.

When he finally stepped out, he looked like he always did—polished, confident, and so overly sure of himself it made my blood boil. He moved with an air of superiority, the kind that said he had the upper hand, and today, I wasn't in the mood for his shit.

"Ares," I called, stepping out of the car.

He turned, shoulders still loose until his eyes met mine. The smile slipped. His posture straightened, jaw tightened, and his hands stilled, tension creeping in where ease had just been. His eyes—so like mine—scanned me with predatory instincts, sharp and calculating.

"*Agustin*. To what do I owe the pleasure, brother?" Every word dripped with mock civility.

"We need to talk." My voice was low, roughened by the rage I'd been nursing all morning.

He glanced at the passersby, then gestured toward the building with exaggerated courtesy. "Come inside. No need to make a scene."

"I'm not going inside," I snapped. "This won't take long."

His brow arched, but he didn't argue. Instead, he crossed his arms, leaning back slightly in a way that only made me angrier. "Alright. Talk."

"You've been working with Loriah."

He stared at me with his stern gaze for a long moment. Not confirming or denying my accusation. Whatever else my brother was, he wasn't a liar, and he wouldn't say whatever it took to spare my feelings, nor soothe them.

"She's undercover?" I continued with the accusation, my voice low and dangerous. "Did you think I wouldn't find out?"

"And what if she is?" Ares's tone was maddeningly flippant, like he was daring me to explode. "She's a damn good cop, Agustin. You don't get to control her."

"She's *my* partner. This isn't about control. It's about trust." My fists clenched at my sides. Ares eyed them, the shadow of a grin pulling at his mouth that only pushed me closer to the brink of absolute wrath.

"Trust? That's rich coming from you." He laughed, a sharp, mocking sound that scraped at my already frayed nerves. "You've been keeping secrets from her since day one, telling her half-truths. She knows. Ever think that's why she doesn't tell *you* things like this?"

The words hit harder than I expected, but I pushed past the sting. "And what about you? You're using her!" My voice rose despite my efforts. "It's a game for you to get what you want."

His smirk faltered, the practiced calm slipping away. Something darker, more predatory flashed across his features—a predatory understanding.

"You think I'm *using* her?" He stepped closer, invading my space. "Brother, she came to *me*. She wanted answers, someone to have her back, and *I* gave her that." His voice dropped. "I see her for who she *truly* is, not the version that you've built in your head." His lips curled. "She's not Corinne."

"Do. Not. Act like you know her better than I do," I growled, stepping closer, itching for a fight. And don't you *dare use* that name with me."

"Don't I know her better than you?" His voice dropped, eyes boring into mine. "I see the way you look at her. You can't hide from me, brother. You're in love with her, but you're too much of a coward to admit it. That's why you're so fucking pissed. Mad that she's undercover? *Bullshit*, Agustin. You're mad because she didn't choose *you*." To send his last word home, he poked one finger into my chest.

My punch connected with his face before I realized I'd thrown it. The hit to his jaw reverberated up my arm. I was sure I'd cracked a bone in my hand.

Ares staggered back, wiping the corner of his mouth where blood stained his smug face.

"Cheap shot, dickhead," he muttered, his voice low and deadly.

He charged at me like a linebacker. This wasn't like when we were kids, brawling over stupid shit; this was a perfect storm carefully made from years of tension, resentment, and something more profound that had grown into a smoldering bitterness.

"You don't deserve her," I spat, landing another punch.

"And you think you do?" Ares shoved me hard, forcing me to take a couple of steps back. "You've spent so much time keeping her in the dark, and you think she's going to stick around for that? She doesn't need your saving, Agustin. What she *needs* is someone who sees her and trusts her to make her own damn decisions."

The words cut deeper than any hit he could have thrown.

"I know I don't deserve her." The admission tore from my throat, raw and painful. "But you? You don't even know her."

"I know her better than you think," he shot back, his voice cold and laced with vulnerability. His voice dropped to a dangerous whisper, "I know the way her lips taste." My stomach lurched. "And the little way she gasps when she's kissed *just* right."

Rage pulsed through me, and the tight feeling in my chest grew stronger as the tunnel vision set in.

"You're so busy trying to play her savior," he continued, his relentless blows, "that you can't see *you're* the one breaking her heart."

"Fuck. You!" I bellowed with all the rage I'd been storing.

We went at it again, fists flying and words sharper than our punches. It wasn't until a passerby shouted at us to knock it off, or they'd call the cops, that we finally pulled apart, both of us bloody and panting.

Ares straightened his jacket, his hands trembling as he glared at me. "You don't want her getting hurt? Then stop suffocating her. You're the one pushing her away, Agustin. Not me. But when you've destroyed it all, I'll be here."

He turned and walked away, still heavily breathing when he answered his phone.

I stood there, flaking blood cooling on my knuckles, while my insides continued to burn in my own anger and self-loathing. Ares's words about kissing Loriah echoed in my mind in an unforgiving, torturous loop. The thought of his lips claiming what I'd only allowed myself to imagine in an unguarded moment twisted in my gut like a serrated blade.

The fire of my indignation was easier to feed than to face the truth lurking beneath it.

No matter how much I wanted to dismiss every word as another one of his manipulations, I couldn't silence the voice whispering that he might not be wrong. That in my desperate need to protect her, I'd never trusted Loriah enough to let her in.

Funny how it was going to take the one thing I was scared of—losing her to someone else—to make me realize she was only giving me back the same distance I'd handed her.

CHAPTER 60
Loriah

The sharp notification tinging of my phone jolted me from my thoughts. One glance at the notification, my heart plummeted.

My fingers trembled as I unlocked the screen.

> **Unknown -** *I have a special surprise for you tomorrow. Meet me for the big Halloween event at the Sanctuary. And I wrote you another poem. I hope you like it. Also, come alone, or I have contingencies in place to make sure you'll never see Angel again.*

> 6592 Wilder Way

> Her name was Angel, so soft, so sweet,

> A fragile flame on a broken street.

> But my shadows whispered, pulled her near,

> I'll bleed her light, no cries to hear.

Attached was a picture of Angel, tied up and bloody.
My father's address!

My stomach churned, bile clawing up, stinging my throat.
I grabbed desperately for the trash bin near my desk and
dropped to my knees, releasing the contents of my stomach.
Sitting on my haunches, I snatched a tissue from my desk,
then cleaned myself up.

Agustin's absence was a small mercy. One look at me and
he'd start with his digging questions I couldn't answer, con-
cerns I couldn't address, and exasperated Spanish sayings. I
needed to keep my head down, stay composed, and wait for
the moment to be right.

A cold shroud of realization settled over me: I couldn't
trust Agustin to understand. I couldn't risk dragging Christian into it. I had no one but myself to rely on.

I was alone.

But I'd be damned if I let anyone stop me from finding
Angel.

I knew one thing for sure—I needed Ares.

The moment I was back in my office, I yanked my phone out of my bag and scrolled until I landed on Ares's name. My finger hovered for only a second before I pressed the Call button.

He picked up after three rings, his voice light but breathless, like he'd been running.

"Loriah! I was just talking about you. ¿Qué pasa?"

I didn't bother with pleasantries. "It's urgent. Can we meet when I get off work?"

The playfulness vanished from his voice. "Of course. Your place or mine?"

"Yours," I said firmly. "I think mine's compromised."

"Understood. I'll send you the address."

Only a few seconds later, my phone buzzed with an incoming message.

"Ares?"

"Yeah?"

I closed my eyes, swallowing the knot in my throat. "Thank you."

The line went so quiet, I thought he had hung up. Right when I thought he hadn't heard me, his voice returned, softer than I'd ever heard it. "Always."

I ended the call and stared at the address on the screen, unable to read the words.

A res's apartment building was an imposing high-rise that screamed wealth and power. But inside, the space transformed. The design leaned toward a modern take on a bygone era: plush white couches, hand-crafted wood tables, and soft lighting that cast intimate pools of warmth rather than ostentatious brightness. The faint scent of whiskey and leather lingered in the air, mingling with something warmer, possibly vanilla.

When he opened the door, his green eyes locked on mine, sharp with curiosity and worry. Gone was the Ares I was used to, with his tailored suits and curated accessories that projected dominance. Here stood a man at home in sweats and a half-buttoned Henley, inviting a guest into his house.

He stepped aside, allowing me to enter. I was immediately thankful he wasn't being his over-the-top, beguiling self and instead was giving me the space I needed to be in the one place I hadn't foreseen for myself.

After a few aimless moments of wandering, I found myself sitting at his kitchen island, staring into a steaming mug of cocoa. Everything about the day felt like a blur, with too many choices I wasn't sure I was ready to make.

"So," he said, his voice gentle and warm, that familiar Spanish lilt softening the edge and making me melt into the comfort of it.

"I need your help," I told him, gripping the mug tightly.

"With?"

"Catching, Chimera." My words came out steadier than I felt. "Tomorrow night."

He nearly choked on his drink, setting the mug down with a sharp clink. His brows furrowed, and he pursed his lips as he stepped back and crossed his arms over his chest.

"He's coming to see me," I explained hurriedly, setting my cocoa aside and pacing the smooth wood floor. "He knows I'm undercover and sent me this cryptic poem along with a picture of Angel and my father's address. I can't protect them, Ares. I don't have another choice."

The tears came then. I hadn't wanted to, and the simple act made me angry.

His brows drew low, the sharp crease between them deepening. His jaw tightened, and he turned his back to me, gripping the countertop like it might ground him. My tears must've made him uncomfortable.

I circled the island—placed my hand on his arm—urging him to turn and meet my eyes.

"I don't have a choice," I repeated softly, my voice thickly coated in anguish at the powerlessness I felt. "If I don't show up, we lose the one lead we've been chasing for weeks. And if Chimera's coming to me, that's his mistake. Ares—" I reached up and cupped his face between my hands, the stubble tickling my fingers, forcing him to look at me, needing him to see the seriousness in my vulnerability. He brought his hands up to my face in turn, wiping away the tears. "He will make a mistake. And we'll be ready."

Not taking his eyes off mine, he gently pulled my hands away, kissing one in the process. He held them for a moment before letting go, shaking his head with the barest trace of a smile tugging at his lips. "You're insane, Loriah Fairsbane. Do you realize the danger of this? He's shown he can get to you whenever he wants."

"I know," I admitted. "But I can't back down. We're close, Ares. I am *so* close. If I don't do this, it will all be for nothing. Angel, these girls—they're counting on me. If I don't act now, their lives will mean nothing."

At first, he was silent, making me think I'd made a huge mistake by coming to him. But then, slowly, his eyes softened and crinkled at the edges, and a conspiratorial smile grew on his handsome face. "What's the plan, chica?"

We spent the next hour at his dining table, the warm light casting long shadows over the scattered papers and photos I'd pulled from my bag. Files from Dante's office, Chimera's messages, and financial statements sprawled across the surface in a chaotic, but intentional pattern.

"First," I said, tapping the crudely drawn map of the club I'd sketched, "we need eyes on the building. If Chimera's coming, we need to know when he arrives and where he's heading. Can you set that up?"

Ares nodded. "I'll have someone at all entrances and VIP areas, so he won't make a move without us knowing." He rubbed his beard. "Tomorrow is the biggest party of the year. It's a masked Halloween event where anonymity and debauchery will be the highlight; that's the *only* reason why he's picked it, I bet."

I stared at the map, frustration bubbling up in my chest at the thought of being played this close to our goal. "You're telling me, we're supposed to pick a stranger out of a room full of masked people?"

"Unfortunately, yes," Ares said, leaning forward, his green eyes glinting in the dim light. "It's exactly why he would have planned it that way. He knows we'll struggle with security."

I exhaled sharply, running a hand through my wild curls. "Fine. Then I'll have to make sure Chimera can't miss me."

"It's not him finding you that I'm afraid of, Loriah. "

"Then we have to be ahead of him and fill in any holes before he does. "

"Near the exclusive dancing areas," Ares suggested, tracing a path on the map. "The private lounges are just beyond there. Maybe that could be the setup point."

"Perfect," I said, circling the spot with a red pen. "What about Dante? If he figures out I'm trying to trap Chimera in his own club, this could all blow up."

Ares gave a crooked, knowing smile. "I'll handle Dante. He trusts me to keep things running smoothly, and he'll be too busy schmoozing partygoers to notice anything out of the ordinary."

I nodded, mentally checking off one more variable. "That's two pieces in place," I said, tapping the map again, "but we'll need people ready to move when we give the signal. No mistakes."

He frowned, his hand running over his lightly shadowed jaw. "I can get my people on it, but if Chimera gets even a whiff of being set up, we won't get another chance. We don't know that he doesn't have his own people there, either."

"Then we make sure the signal doesn't go out until we're ready," I said firmly. "No missteps. No screw-ups. I'll wear something he won't be able to ignore."

Ares shot me a hard look. "You're walking straight into a trap, Loriah. Chimera isn't dangerous—he's unpredictable. If anything feels off, you save yourself. Do you hear me?"

I swallowed, his words sinking in. "I understand."

"Good." He leaned back, his jaw ticking. "Because if anything happens to you, I won't forgive myself. And, you'd be giving Agustin another reason to kill me."

His mention of Agustin sent a fresh wave of regret through me. I hadn't told him what I knew. I couldn't. If I did, he'd step in, try to control the whole operation, and ruin the *one* shot we had at Chimera.

Later, as I sat on Ares's balcony, the cool night air bit at my skin. The city sprawled below in a grid of lights and sounds. I tried to let its constant hum calm my nerves.

But the longer I sat, the weight of the day settled on my shoulders, bringing a deep resentment toward Perez and myself for failing Angel, whom I promised to keep safe.

"You looked like you needed this," Ares said, handing me a glass of wine and lighting the heaters scattered across the balcony before sitting down across from me. "Stay," he said.

"I can't, Ares," I replied, though my voice lacked conviction. "I need to prepare for tomorrow."

"Loriah," he said, his tone steady, "I'm not asking."

Part of me wanted to give in, to stay in this safe, luxurious haven and pretend—for one night—that I wasn't carrying the burden of Angel, Chimera, and all the voiceless girls on my shoulders.

"Fine," I said finally. "But only if I can have a bath."

He laughed. "Say no more. If I knew it was that easy, I would have lured you here with the promise of bathing a long time ago. " He held out a large hand, and I took it, allowing him to pull me gracefully from the seat and lead me inside to a guest suite that could have belonged in a five-star hotel.

My foot paused, about to step into the steaming bath, when my phone pinged with a new message, my muscles instantly bunching in anticipation despite the wine loosening my thoughts.

> **Agustin** - *We need to talk.*

I paused, not wanting to deal with him.

> **Me** - *Not tonight.*

I knew his whole focus was on this conversation that I wasn't ready for when the phone buzzed five seconds later with a reply.

Agustin - *Tomorrow then?*

Me - *I'm taking a personal day.*

Agustin - *This is personal.*

I tossed the phone onto the bed and returned to my only priority—sinking into the water and washing away my nervous energy.

Whatever scheme he was planning could wait. Tonight was mine. Tomorrow belonged to Chimera.

CHAPTER 62

Loriah

The sunlight streaming through Ares's floor-to-ceiling windows felt mockingly bright—warm, and welcoming, a stark contrast to the cold knot tightening around my raw heart. It felt like the world was moving on without me, and I was stuck behind glass, watching it all pass by.

I'd taken the day off. I couldn't face the precinct, couldn't face Agustin. Not with Chimera's taunting message still weighing heavily on me. And I was avoiding whatever *personal* talk he was so eager to have.

As for Christian, he didn't deserve to be pulled into this mess. Not like this.

Ares and I had a mutual understanding—he had the resources to help make this possible, without all the red tape,

without the weight of official reports and interfering proto-
col—just action and progress. And right now, that was all I
could bring myself to focus on.

The thick blue robe from the guest closet that I'd wrapped
around myself smelled like his home, embracing me in a su-
perficial comfort that only went so deep. I hugged it tighter
as I wandered into the living area.

Ares was in the kitchen, chopping fruit with the kind of
precision that suggested cooking was more than a casual
hobby for him, allowing me yet another glimpse of the man
behind the tough exterior. He had the same focus and intensity as the previous night. It amazed me how he could be
so at ease in so many different scenarios.

"You should eat," he said, breaking the silence, but he
didn't bother to look up.

"I'm not hungry," I muttered, flipping through the notes
I'd spread across the dining table, more for something to do
than any real purpose.

Ares appeared a moment later, sliding a plate of fruit
and toast in front of me on the coffee table. He perched
himself on the couch's armrest, holding a steaming mug of
coffee. "You'll need it," he said, his voice firm. "Can't have
you passing out on me at midnight because you were too
stubborn to eat some fruit now, can I?"

I picked up a piece of toast, shooting him a sideways
look, but mostly trying to avoid arguing. I bit into it with a
comically large bite, the crunch loud in the otherwise quiet
room.

"Never mind," he said dryly, smirking. "You're going to
choke yourself before we even get there."

"Very funny," I said, glaring at him over the rim of my mug. "I was thinking about tonight. I'll need something that stands out, yet practical to conceal a weapon."

Ares leaned back, his smirk softening into a more thoughtful expression. "I've got a few ideas. There's a boutique downtown—discreet, expensive. And they owe me a favor."

"Of course they do," I muttered, finishing the toast before going to change.

The boutique was precisely what I expected: chic, exclusive, and absurdly overpriced. It smelled like what I thought a fancy Parisian hotel would smell like. The space was artfully decorated with curated pieces by local artists and photographs showcasing texture and movement, each one highlighted by individual museum lighting.

Ares greeted the sharply dressed owner by name, and I couldn't help but notice how the man's eyes flicked over me, assessing.

"She needs something striking," Ares explained, gesturing to me. "Elegant, bold, but functional."

"Ah," the man said, his French accent thick as he studied me. "I see. Follow me."

He led us to a private fitting area, and racks of gowns and jumpsuits lined the walls. As I sifted through never-ending hangers, the owner pulled a few options, holding them up for Ares's approval.

I stood in the multi-mirrored dressing room, surrounded by no one but myself. I saw my mother when I looked in the mirror, with the dark circles hanging below my eyes. The faces of Kayleigh, Addie, and now Angel all swam behind me. I felt so alone and so useless. Why couldn't I see that one missing piece? Why couldn't I be a little bit stronger?

"Loriah?" Ares said in a concerned voice from the other side of the heavy damask curtain.

I took a moment to compose myself before whispering, "Yeah?"

I could tell he'd moved closer. His voice came as a whisper, and his hand went through an open slit, tattooed fingers outstretched for mine.

"It's just you and me."

I straightened my spine and ran my hands over my face to pull myself together, and took his hand and gave it a squeeze of reassurance—for both of us.

I wanted to cry. I wanted to cry at the kindness and pity in Ares' voice. I wanted to scream at myself for being so fucking stupid. And most of all, I wanted vengeance. To punish the people who had hurt all those innocent girls. The optimism I usually carried was being bled out of me, and that hurt most of all.

Stepping out, I nearly collided with Ares's chest. He threw out his hands to catch me, but I steadied myself and spun once. "What do you think about this one?"

It was a red dress with a plunging neckline and a high slit along the leg. It reminded me of a modern *Queen of Hearts.*

Ares shook his head lightly, his mouth pursing to one side, one long finger tapping his lips. "Too flashy. He needs to focus on you, not the dress. But damn if that's not a nice dress."

I rolled my eyes but kept looking. Eventually, we settled on a tailored black jumpsuit with a satin-lined top that mimicked the lapels of a man's suit along the bust. The back dipped low, leaving my shoulders and spine exposed, all my little bits of artwork on display, but the fit was snug and practical.

"Where am I supposed to hide my gun?" I asked, frowning as I examined myself and smoothed the lines of the outfit.

Ares stepped closer, inspecting me with a critical eye. His hand came to rest near the highest part of my thigh. "Here. I'll have them tailor a pocket for you to reach through discreetly. And you can carry a smaller Sig—I've got one you can use."

"I can't take your gun."

"You can, and you will," he said firmly. "You're not sneaking that monster you normally carry under this thing."

I sighed, conceding that I'd never be able to get through the front door with my service pistol, and stepped back into the dressing room.

The rest of the afternoon passed in a haze of preparation. Ares coordinated with his people, double-checking the club's security and ensuring all eyes would be on the entrances and exits. I practiced in my room, moving with the holster strapped to my thigh, adjusting to the weight of the smaller weapon. The atelier had sent over the garment only two hours after we'd left. The efficiency was staggering, and I figured that must be standard when you had as much wealth and influence as the Perez family seemed to wield.

> **Ares -** *Are you going to hide in your room all night or come out to eat before we go?*

The grim line marring my forehead eased at reading his message.

> **Me -** *I don't feel like eating. And, I'm not hiding.*

Less than a heartbeat had passed when Ares swung my door open. I jumped, dropping my phone.

"Is walking in other people's doors unannounced a common trait in your whole family? Or is that only a twin quirk?"

"Wow," Ares said, ignoring my snark as I improved the fit of the jumpsuit in front of the mirror.

"Yeah?" I asked him self-consciously. "I've been practicing with your gun, and I think I've got it."

"You look almost ready."

"Almost?"

He came up behind me, holding a delicate black mask.

"Close your eyes."

I did as he asked, and he fit the mask to my face. The intricate metal design felt cool against my skin, but when I opened my eyes, the reflection staring back at me looked every bit the part. Gone was the weariness of earlier, replaced by a single-minded wave of confidence to capture Chimera, and I would see to it that he couldn't hurt anyone else.

"There," he said, stepping back. "*Now* you're ready."

By the time the car arrived, my nerves were beginning to fray like a pair of worn-out jeans. I paced back and forth, my slightly elevated heels tapping against the concrete, my heart struggling to keep rhythm, pounding out of my chest.

A shadow approached, pausing just in front of me, backlit by the soft glow of the street lamps. I was looking down, lost in my thoughts, silently counting the steps each concrete square demanded—until Ares's fingers reached up to lift my chin, gently coaxing me to meet his eyes.

"Remember," he said softly, "You're not alone."

Ares bent to kiss my forehead, his lips warm, firm, lingering a beat longer than necessary. Goosebumps skittered down my exposed arms, and I found myself closing my eyes and leaning into it. The gesture steadied me when nothing else could. When he pulled away, I felt the ghost of his touch like an invisible mark, one that would remain long after we left for the party.

I didn't know if I fully believed his words, but I knew in my heart that he would make them as true as he was able.

The club was alive with energy, the pulsing music and flickering lights making the air feel electric. Masks obscured every face, each one more intricate and elaborate than the last. It set me on edge the moment I stepped through the doors. The meaning of the night was anonymity, and I felt the furthest thing from hidden.

I adjusted the fine black mask covering half my face, the mocking words echoing in my mind.

You couldn't even save Angel.

"Looking good, Tony," I said to the bartender, forcing a lightness I didn't feel. "We kinda match."

He laughed, oblivious to the storm swirling inside me. "It's going to be a busy night."

I hoped not. Busy meant a potentially chaotic night—one that could spiral out of control as quickly as a grass fire. And something told me, the night was already shaping up to be one I'd never forget.

Hours passed in a blur of music and movement, my senses on high alert. I stayed near the low-lit hallway, strung with elegant decor, visible but strategic. I kept checking over my shoulder, scanning the crowd for any sign of Chimera.

When it happened, it wasn't how I'd expected.

A hand slipped around my waist while something hard pressed into my spine, chilling the exposed skin. My heart slammed against my ribs, dread coursed through me, and anger filled my chest when my body wanted to move closer to the warmth of his body instinctively.

Lips brushed the shell of my ear, warm and familiar. "Miss me?"

I didn't flinch, didn't turn, didn't let him see the terror clawing its way up my spine. "Why?" I asked, my voice breaking on the word.

"Revenge, Loriah. Glory. Money. Because I can. Take your pick, babe." His hand slid against my skin like a lover's caress, his rough face rubbing against my neck.

"Is she dead?" I asked, my voice barely above a whisper.

"Let's talk somewhere private." He gripped my wrist and stepped around me in an immaculately tailored blue suit, tucking his gun behind him, while a white mask covered the top half of his face.

I followed him, every nerve strung tight, and my muscles ached with tension. I needed answers—but more than that, I needed to stay alive long enough to get them. The solid weight of my gun pressed against my leg, the only thing anchoring me to the moment. Whatever was coming, I had to be ready. I was struggling to keep up with the grip of his hand around my wrist, pulling me forcefully through the crowd.

Then I saw Ares.

His eyes found mine, and in that split second, a woman staggered into him, spilling her drink and laughing through what appeared to be an apology. He struggled to keep me in his line of sight, shifting to move her aside, tension etched across every line of his face. I felt it too—deep in my chest—that sharp, cold jolt of realization. Someone had sabotaged us, compromising our carefully laid plan.

CHAPTER 63
Loriah

The next few minutes passed in a blur. From a distance, it probably looked like two lovers sneaking off for a private, intimate moment. No one stopped us. No one questioned the way he had a grip on me.

We slowed when he casually lifted his arm to check the time on his watch.

"Your surprise is here," he said.

"Wha—"

I turned my head, instinctively glancing back toward Ares. And the last thing I heard was the sound of my name, ripped from his throat in a guttural cry of rage.

A deafening boom filled the air. Dust and smoke choked everything. Christian pulled a mask from a bag, slipped it on, and pressed forward. I was left to squint into the haze, not wanting to take in the acrid smoke, still too stunned to get my bearings.

People scattered in all directions. Debris coated the building in a heavy wash. And Ares was nowhere to be seen.

"Ares!" I called out, only to feel metal digging into my back.

"I wouldn't do that," Christian warned.

I tried to yank my arm away, but his grip tightened, bruising my skin.

Amid the wreckage, I saw him—Ares, eyes closed, slumped to the ground, his head smeared with blood, and a woman's body covering his. I froze at the sight. A small sob broke past my lips before I could stop it. I forced the emotion back down, not wanting to let the monster see me cry.

Looking for some of Ares's men, I couldn't make anyone out, much less the few steps in front of me. We moved with purpose, weaving through the frantic crowd until we reached a service corridor. The door opened, and cool air rushed in, making me gasp like a drowned woman given life again.

"You won't get away with this. They'll come for me." My words sounded hollow, even to my ears.

A sick, yet satisfied smile stretched across his face. "Oh, babe. It looks like at least one Perez won't be coming for anyone. And the other one doesn't even know you're gone."

"You're wrong."

"Walk," he ordered, pushing me while maintaining a grip on my arm, forcing us deeper down the alley.

"Agustin *will* come for me," I spat at him, hoping against hope that my words would prove true.

As we approached his truck, I noticed Christian's hand moving inside his jacket. I barely registered the syringe before it suddenly plunged into my neck. A sharp sting shot through me, and warmth spread through my limbs, making them feel heavy. My body betrayed me as the world around me began to blur, and darkness closed in.

The last thing I heard before consciousness slipped away was his low, bitter voice murmuring against my ear, "I'm counting on it."

CHAPTER 64
Loriah

When I woke, the room was dim, softened only by muted light leaking through gauzy curtains. I gradually recognized the room at Ares's penthouse. Agustin sat beside me, fingers wrapped around mine. Behind him, Ares stood watchful. A dark gash ran along his forehead, stark against his sun-kissed skin, but it did nothing to detract from how undeniably handsome he was. That they both were. If anything, it added a rugged edge.

Overshadowing everything was the knowledge that he was alive. *Whole.* The sight of him hit me like a jolt, and the tears came before I could stop them, hot and heavy, streaming down my cheeks.

"Shhh," Ares murmured, stepping forward. He crouched at the edge of the bed, his face leveled with mine, those intense green eyes holding me. His rough fingers brushed my cheek, wiping tears away with a tenderness that unraveled me. I turned my face into his palm, allowing myself the comfort he offered.

Agustin rose to stand at my other side. His presence, somehow more consuming, was weighted with things left unsaid. "Loriah—"

"I'm sorry," I managed around the lump of emotion. My voice cracked with all the things I wanted to say. "I should have told you. I should have—"

"No." His voice was low, thick with a kind of anguish I hadn't expected. Agustin leaned closer, his hand brushing reverently over my hair. He looked at me like he was seeing me for the first time. Then, slowly, he bent and kissed me.

It wasn't like before—not like the heated, impulsive moment in my kitchen. It was slower, deeper, as if he were trying to hold on to something precious. He kissed me like I was the air to his lungs, and when he ended it, his forehead rested against mine before he pulled back.

"I should've never let you go like that," he whispered. "I should've told you everything."

The ache in his voice pressed against my chest, but I wasn't ready to respond. Not yet. My gaze shifted past him, searching for Ares, needing his presence. He'd moved imperceptibly, having put space between us, but his hand hadn't left my leg—a reminder of the promise he'd made earlier.

I wasn't alone.

The silence stretched on, verging on uncomfortable, until Agustin straightened. He turned to his brother, and for a fleeting moment, something unspoken passed between them, something I couldn't quite decipher.

"Thank you," Agustin said, his voice raw.

Ares's mouth twitched. "Yeah, well. Someone had to look after her, right?" The words were light, distracted, but I heard what he didn't say and felt it in my heart—the way his jaw tightened, how his gaze darted away, as though being this close was its own punishment.

I wanted to say something, to cut through that invisible wall he'd placed between us, but the words lodged in my throat. I reached for his hand. He let me take it without hesitation, his warm fingers curling around mine, slow and deliberate.

"Thank you," I whispered, barely more than a whisper.

Ares's eyes softened a fraction, but he said nothing. His thumb traced the faintest line over my knuckles—a touch that said everything.

"How long was I out?" My voice came out hoarse, breaking through the deafening silence.

Agustin squeezed my other hand. "Two days. You scared the shit out of us."

Two days. My mind reeled. My pulse thudded hard against my temples as flashes of the explosion—blinding light, the ear-splitting roar, Ares—returned in a disjointed swirl. My eyes darted back to Ares, drinking in every detail like I could will him to stay solid in front of me.

"You're alive." The words were a whisper, and the tears returned, unstoppable once more.

Ares met my gaze then, his expression softening in a way that felt like a secret. "I'm not that easy to get rid of, Fairsbane."

I choked out a shaky laugh, my fingers flexing against both men's grasps.

"The blast—" I started, my voice breaking.

"—knocked me clear across the club," Ares said evenly. "I'm fine. Just got a little too close to the fireworks." His mouth lifted in a faint smirk, but I saw the shadows behind his eyes.

"Don't let him downplay it," Agustin cut in, his voice taut. "He was one lucky son of a bitch not to be blown to pieces."

"Yeah, well, some guys get luckier than others." Ares's gaze flickered briefly toward his brother before coming back to me. "What matters is you're safe. And that we rescued Angel."

"What?" I breathed.

Agustin nodded, his shoulders loosening, and he gave me a sympathetic half smile. "Angel's alive. We got her out."

"How?"

Agustin leaned against the bed frame, his arms crossed. "Chimera talked. After the explosion, we got him, and seeing that he had no other choice, he sang like a canary."

I swallowed hard, relief flooding me. "And Angel?"

"She's safe, Loriah," Ares said quietly, his voice the gentlest I'd ever heard. "She's in the hospital, but she's going to be okay. You did it."

I sagged against the pillow, tears slipping silently down my temples to wet my hair.

Angel was alive.

Ares wasn't dead.

For once, my broken heart gave the first pangs of mending. The world hadn't stolen everything from me.

Agustin pressed a kiss to my temple. "We'll get Chimera put away for good. You don't have to worry about him anymore."

I nodded, but my attention was already drifting back to Ares. He hadn't moved, much less let go of my hand. There was a stillness to him, as though he were holding back. His thumb brushed absentmindedly across my knuckles.

I looked up at him, my voice soft. "You saved me."

He blinked once, his jaw muscles feathering. "I made a promise."

Something in his tone cracked my heart open. I squeezed his hand, ignoring the way Agustin watched us, like he noticed something shifting and wasn't sure whether to fight it or let it be.

"Thank you," I whispered. I would never stop saying those words until they both knew how much I meant them.

Ares opened his mouth but closed it again. He nodded, his thumb stuttering slightly over my skin before he let go. The loss of his touch left me colder. He turned toward the door, tension visible in the set of his shoulders.

"I'll let you two talk," he said, voice tight.

He was gone before I could stop him, footsteps echoing down the hall, my chest aching in ways I couldn't name.

Agustin leaned over, brushing his fingers against my cheek to turn my gaze back to him. "Loriah." His voice was warm and steady, full of a promise.

CHAPTER 65
Loriah

"Loriahhh."

A voice called out to me from somewhere in my dreams. "Loriah, it's time to wake up."

My head was swimming when I finally came to on a threadbare cot, sharp springs pressed into my sides. I tried to move, but a scratchy rope bound my feet and hands, chafing my skin raw. The bottom half of my outfit clung damp and heavy against me.

"Bath time, Loriah. You pissed yourself. But don't worry, I took the liberty of picking up clothes from your apartment for our *vacation*. Allie let me in and said to tell you, *'Hi.'* I like her, you know."

"Fuck you," I said, facing the wall. Rolling over to see Christian's handsome face would make everything real. So I clung to the hope it was just a bad dream.

A decidedly fucked up, *terrible* dream.

"Come on, I don't want to hurt you." He was so good at lying that it sounded genuine. It *felt* like he meant it when he reached to run a hand over my hair, caressing the side of my cheek. "But I will. *If* I have to."

"You already have," I spat.

"You don't know half of what I can do. Now. Sit up." He roughly grabbed my bindings, pulling me upright. My bare feet landed on the painfully cold concrete, but I made myself stand despite the dizziness filling my head.

A thin, piercing scream echoed through the air, faint and ragged as it sliced into the silence. Distance muffled it, but the terror in the sound was unmistakable, freezing my blood.

"What was that?"

"*That*, Loriah, is the sound of our friend, Angel. She's paying off some of her *debts*." Sarcasm dripped like sour honey from his lips, and I felt a wave of nausea come over me.

Muffling a cry, I struggled against my bindings. "Let Angel go, or I *will* kill you."

"I always enjoyed how optimistically feisty you could be. But not this time. She is going to pay me back for all the time wasted getting her here to New York."

"What the fuck is wrong with you?"

"So *many* things, I'm sure."

When my legs buckled beneath me, he reached behind me, grabbed hold of my bindings, and got me into a standing position.

"Here's your first test. Where is that asshole partner of yours?"

"How should I know?"

"Ah, well. No biggie. I have something in mind to make Agustin pay attention."

He carried himself with such ease that I found myself wondering why I hadn't noticed it before. But how could I? Christian's emotions seemed so carefully contained in a box of cold calculation that I couldn't tell which parts of him were authentic.

I shuffled along, the bindings around my feet left me with the slightest bit of slack to amble at a snail's pace. The warehouse was cold, the November air chilling my body. The screams from Angel had subsided, replaced by an occasional echo of whimpers—more akin to an injured animal than a young woman. Rage and helplessness threatened to swallow me if I dwelled on it.

"Stop," he commanded at an open door. A large industrial hook hung from the middle of the room. It looked ominous in the dim light where harsh shadows spiderwebbed across the walls. The iron tang of blood permeated the air, invading my senses. A lone camera pointed to the spot where he would string me up like an animal.

"Step over to it, and place your hands above your head, please."

I hesitated.

He gave me a hard shove. "I said, Please. You're being rude."

He placed my bound wrists in the hook and stepped back.

"Did you care about me at all, Christian?" I asked, a sob threatening to break free.

The question seemed to surprise him. He dropped the remote and looked at me. The look was confusing, as if it had never occurred to him.

"I think—under remarkably different circumstances—I could have loved you once. But it was never me that you really wanted, was it? If we're choosing now to be honest."

I can't recall if my heart audibly broke, or if it was the sound of my own cry escaping my lips.

"I'll take your silence as admission," he said calmly when I couldn't speak.

Christian turned and grabbed a remote hanging on the wall, with one long wire running to the pulley that held my hook. He pressed a button that made a whirring sound, and a chain began to rattle. It slowly moved, inch by torturous inch, until I was stretched and standing on the balls of my feet.

"Much better," he cooed like a lover. "But I am sorry for this, Loriah. You were only ever collateral."

Moving to the camera, he pressed a button; a red light came on. My tears dripped in rhythm to its pulsing light.

"Say hello for the camera, Loriah. Agustin has wanted desperately to get to you for so long. I figured I'd do what any good friend would and put him out of his misery by curbing those inward thoughts about what you might look like under all those clothes."

"You don't have to do this."

"Yes—I do. It's the only way this will work. And if Agustin doesn't want to watch, I'll make sure he has no. Other. Choice," he sneered through clenched teeth. So much hate filled his voice that spittle flew into my face. His eyes had turned so dark that his pupils consumed most of his eyes.

This man was not the one I spent nights with. Not the one I bared my heart to. Christian was a monster in human form.

"I'll take my time, though, I know how much you enjoyed that." He pulled a knife from his pants and flicked it open, watching me with curiosity. He grabbed my hair and yanked my head back, running the knife from my chin to my navel. Then I felt it catch my skin as he jammed it through the fabric in an upward motion, cutting to the top, exposing my bare flesh. Shame swept over me, hot and tingling. My tight arms on either side of my face kept me from turning away from the camera.

"Don't watch, Agustin," I yelled in desperation. "Don't give him what he wants."

"Oh, but darling." The cruel smile returned to Christian's face, and the calm tenor of his voice that I had loved settled in the room like a natural conversation between friends. "I have a surprise for him, and he *has* to watch, or he'll never know what it is! How fun for both of you. It's a bonding moment, Loriah."

He continued cutting my top until it hung in rags around my waist, held up only by the snug waistband at my hips.

Christian ran the knife along my skin, smiling as he did so. Adrenaline had my heart slamming against my chest in a desperate attempt to free itself. A fresh wave of dizziness hit me, and I felt the familiar sensation of limbs growing cold before the darkness took me.

"Oh no, you don't," he said roughly, throwing a bucket of water over my head. I jerked against my bindings and gasped, breath coming sharply. My skin drew taut, pimpling with gooseflesh. My head swam before the vision cleared. "You can't go passing out yet. We have to have words."

"Then speak, Christian!" I yelled.

"Not those kinds of words, babe, I was thinking of more *permanent* ones?"

He placed the tip of his knife under my right breast. The sharp metal bit in, causing me to grit my teeth. Slowly, he dragged it through my skin. I felt blood—warm and thick—running down my stomach, mixing with the droplets of water cooling on my skin.

"Stop! Please, Christian! Stop!" The pain was so intense that the room seemed to tilt around me, and my head lolled forward.

He drenched me again after refilling the bucket. The warehouse was unforgiving—my skin burned from the shock. Christian ran the blade along one nipple and looked back at the camera. "Is this what you wanted, Agustin?"

Christian returned to his carving, adding six more letters and taking his time on each, until tears streamed down my face and stung the fresh wounds they landed in.

After what felt like hours, my body finally gave up. Exhausted from a lack of food or water, I slumped against the bindings, rattling the chain above me.

"I'm finished with you," he said as he lowered the chains, and I collapsed onto the ground. He squatted in front of me, tipping my chin so I looked into those cold blue eyes before he cut my bindings. "Now, get yourself cleaned up. I'll be back in five minutes after I check on our girl." He threw a bundle of clothing at me—my clothing.

I crawled toward the bucket he'd been filling from a spigot in the wall. My eyes flicked to the camera, but he caught my gaze. He snatched the camera and its stand, heading for the door. Yet, just before stepping out, he turned back to me.

"Don't think about escaping, Loriah. Don't make this harder than it has to be. This door locks from the outside." True to his word, a lock clicked into place, and deep male voices rumbled outside.

The water was freezing, but I needed to clean myself. The stench of the wet jumpsuit had me gagging when I pulled it off with trembling fingers. My hair was a hopelessly tangled mess, smelling of sweat, blood, and fear. I barely had time to button my flannel before he was grabbing me under the arm, carefully rebinding my hands and feet with a tiny bit more slack than he'd allowed me to have before.

"You know they'll look for me."

"Who? The police? The Perezes? From the sounds of it, a well-placed bomb at Baldini's nightclub claimed a lot of lives. Including a certain brother, so they say," he said with a dismissive shrug.

"I hate you."

He grabbed my hair and turned my head to face him, the pain curling into my scalp, forcing me to comply. He smiled, slowly, confidently, the dimple in his right cheek making an appearance and adding another nail to my already ailing heart.

"You can lie to yourself to make this easier, but you and I both know that's not true."

I was nearly hysterical. "Why are you doing this?"

"You've asked enough questions for today. You're going to need to eat so that we can play again tomorrow."

At the mention of food, my stomach growled, betraying me. If I had any hope of finding my way out, I needed strength.

He'd set a tray down on a small plastic table near the door—a child's tray with cutouts to hold portions of food. It resembled rice and a type of stew. A large plastic cup of water sat on the tray as well.

"No spoon?"

"I'm sorry, Loriah, but I don't want you getting any ideas."

"Really? What am I going to do with bound hands and feet?" I shook my hands at him.

"You're a clever girl. If you're very good, they can come off tomorrow."

Tomorrow? Before I could even ask how I was supposed to use the bathroom, I spotted a bright orange painter's bucket in the corner with a half roll of toilet paper beside it. *Ah, the "bathroom" in question.*

"How long have I been out?"

"Almost two days. But I'll leave you for now. Don't be stubborn, and eat your food. I'll be watching you," he told me with a snap of his fingers and pointed toward a small CCTV in the corner. He left without waiting for my response and relocked the door, telling the person standing outside not to listen to anything I said.

I shuffled my way to the bucket and positioned it as far under the camera as possible, hoping to obscure the view as I hovered over it like an animal. When I finished, I went back to my cot and used the small pump of hand sanitizer he'd left next to my bed.

How considerate.

I tried my best to scoop food into my mouth. The stew was surprisingly good—leftovers from his own plate, probably. The thought only made my heart ache more, remembering all the times we'd shared meals together. And not once did I imagine this would be the way I'd end up tasting something he'd made.

I lay on the cold cot with a thin blanket, staring into the darkness once the light had cut out.

Agustin was trying to help me at every turn, and I stubbornly refused to see it. Ares promised me that he would have my back, but it was all a setup—the night, the girl stopping him, the explosion, everything. And I wouldn't have the chance to tell him it was okay. Because of me, Agustin had lost the only brother he had.

As soon as the thought crossed my mind, tears began to slip down my cheeks. I rolled over to face the wall, refusing to give Christian the satisfaction of seeing my despair.

And then, I did the only thing I could think of—I prayed.

Each tear held a sorrow of its own: for the other girls, for my shattered heart, for my father. And for Ares.

For Agustin.

And in that consuming darkness, I made a silent promise that this would not be for nothing.

T wice a day, Christian or someone working for him brought me food. I suspected he was drugging me in my meals. My mind would fog, my vision would become muddled, and my consciousness would fade quickly after I ate.

There were no windows or natural light of any kind to tell the time of day by. I relied solely on the sounds of the timer on the wall outside my room, building equipment clanging, trucks rumbling in and out, and voices shouting, usually in Spanish. I heard Christian speaking too. His voice was unmistakable, although I'd never heard him speak the language before, and it surprised me.

I was dirty and in pain. My cuts were becoming raw and inflamed. Although they were deep, they had started to scab over in some areas, while other places actively oozed. The ropes were biting into my wrists when I moved, serving as a constant reminder of my last *mistake*.

When Christian had tried to untie me the first time, I bit his shoulder. He struck me so hard I saw stars. Then he stormed out and slammed the door behind him, locking me in again. I didn't see him for four meal rotations. The bucket in the corner began to fill until the stench became overwhelmingly putrid, and holding my breath was no longer an option. When he finally returned, I didn't resist as he cut the bindings from my wrists, letting him believe I was defeated.

On what I assumed was the fifth day, he came again to sit on my cot without a word. For a long while, he just stared at me, his presence filling the small, suffocating space with a closeness I could barely stomach.

"What is it?" I rasped when he didn't say anything for many long minutes. My voice cracked from disuse—a pitiful sound.

"I haven't heard from Perez."

"So?"

Christian smirked, his once beautiful blue eyes taking on a sinister edge. "Wellll, I'll have to encourage him, yet again. And if we're being honest, I really didn't want to."

My insides twisted, my body recoiling with remembrance of how he'd *encouraged* him before.

"NO!" I begged, scrambling back against the wall. My skin tore from the scabs at the sudden movement, making me wince. "Please, Christian. He doesn't care enough for me to come. Please!"

He grabbed my arm, trying to pull me to him. I struggled to find my footing and kicked his chest. He barely staggered. My resistance only spurred him. He pulled harder until my skin met the cold concrete littered with bits of debris.

The silence that filled the warehouse was unsettling. Deep within my soul, I knew that if I called for help, no one would hear me.

I trudged along reluctantly at his instruction, stopping at a metal door bound with a chain and padlock. I recognized it immediately. It was the same door he had dragged me through days before.

"No, I don't want to go in there. Please, Christian!"

"I'm sorry, Loriah," he said, pausing to stroke a tear from my cheek. "Sometimes, we have to do things we don't want to, right?"

When it swung open, my knees nearly gave out.

"Angel!" I cried, the sob tearing through the oppressive silence and bouncing against the walls in a mockery of my agony.

She hung limp from the same hook he'd used on me. Her body was battered and broken, her once-beautiful head tilted to one side, dark hair spilling over her face. Her skin—normally warm with a natural glow—was now ghostly pale beneath streaks of dirt and blood.

"Go on," Christian teased, his voice light, almost playful. "Go be with her. I want to give Agustin a display of what will happen to you if he doesn't do exactly as I say."

"She's just a girl, little more than a child," I pleaded, stumbling forward. "What has she done to you?"

When I reached Angel, my hands trembled as I felt for her pulse, then moved to run them over her face. In my desperate attempts and fumbling hands, I finally felt her precious life between my fingers, sparking a hope inside me. I pressed my ear to her chest and heard the weak flutter of her heart, confirming. It was the sweetest sound I'd ever heard.

Alive!

"Angel," I said, brushing her hair back, trying to keep my words calm while my hands shook. "It's me. Loriah. I'm here. Please, wake up." My tears fell freely as I begged her to open her eyes.

Her eyelids fluttered, eyes struggling to focus as they opened. "Loriah?" she rasped, voice barely audible.

"It's me, I'm here," I choked out, forcing a smile through my tears. "I told you I'd come for you."

Rough hands tore me away.

"No!" I cried out, reaching for her. "What have you done to her?"

Stumbling, I barely caught myself before hitting the ground.

"Angel has been a bad girl," Christian said, his tone dripping with mockery. "And when girls are bad, we have to teach them a lesson. Just as when boys misbehave, they receive lessons. Like this one. You'll love this, Loriah. If Agustin doesn't leave the force, transfer forty million dollars to my offshore account, and sign over all his property to me, I'll have to teach *him* a particularly harsh lesson." His eyes locked onto me, his gaze predatory. "By sending you to him in bits. Don't worry, though, you won't die. Right away."

I shook my head, glaring at him in disbelief, then a slow chuckle burst from my mouth before turning into peals of laughter. "That's ridiculous," I said, hysteria creeping into my voice. "No one—least of all him—is going to pay that for me.

You're planning to bargain with someone who doesn't even give a damn about me? Brilliant plan!"

Christian looked nonplussed with my outburst, then grinned. I swallowed.

"You are truly dumber than I thought if you believe that. You don't know, do you?"

"Know *what*?" I screamed. "There's nothing to know!" The words reverberated off the walls.

I could see it in his eyes—there was no reasoning with him, and slowly my laughter slowed till I was back to feeling numb. The version of Christian standing before me was too far gone for logic to reach. But there was no way out.

Angel. She was innocent. And Perez didn't deserve to lose everything. His family, his life. Not because of me. I was nothing. Nobody.

But Christian wanted a show, and he'd make damn sure he got one. He kicked at a piece of dirt, then paced in circles around us.

"He's been watching you like some vigilante guardian angel this whole time, you know," he sneered. "Hired some private detective to make sure you were okay. Don't feel too special—he hired one for me too. But they had a little *accident* on the job."

My face must've betrayed the shock tightening in my chest, because he laughed—a cold, hollow sound—and kept going.

"This *whole* time, that pathetic man has been trying to keep you safe, completely clueless that his worst fucking nightmare was twenty feet away. Every day! And then you show up and shit *all* over him!" He laughed then, a rich, throaty sound. "This is better than any telenovela!"

"You're lying," I snapped, but my voice felt thin, brittle against his words.

"Look, Loriah," he said, his voice changing to match the lover I once knew. "This isn't a choice. You know that, right? You're going to help me. I need you, one last time," he said against the hollow of my ear.

I glared forward, and a chill ran down my body.

He offered his knife to me.

"Look at her. She's ready. She's broken. You can choose to do her a kindness and make it quick. Or I'll drag out every moment and pin your eyelids open so you watch the whole thing."

Bile rose in my throat, but I didn't reach for it.

He grabbed my wrist and forced my fingers around the hilt when I fought him. The metal was cold, heavier than I expected. I hated the way my hand fit around it. I hated even more thinking that it might be an act of kindness to do what he asked. Spare her from the cruelty he'd inflict.

"Do I have to guide you?" Christian asked, his voice softening to a gentler tone. He brought my hand up, guiding the blade toward Angel's chest. I dug my heels into the ground, trembling under his grip.

Angel's eyes fluttered before opening to slits. Bloodshot and desperate. She didn't speak—I didn't know if she could—but her eyes said it all in that one slow blink.

"I can't, I'm sorry," I whispered to her, tears trailing their hot descent down my cheeks.

I felt the moment that Christian's patience snapped. He jerked my hand forward, angling the knife toward Angel's ribs, but I resisted. I felt the cold tip press against her supple skin, and something inside me broke.

Before I could think, a scream came from the depths of my soul and bellowed from my mouth as I twisted my hand. The blade sliced through the air, then met resistance as it tore through cloth and flesh.

Christian grunted, releasing me as he staggered back, palm clamping over his side. Blood seeped between his fingers, dark and glistening.

I didn't hesitate. I mustered whatever strength remained and came at Christian again.

"No!" Christian roared.

He lunged. I tried sidestepping but tripped. He reclaimed his grip on the knife, and then I felt it—the pain. It blossomed in my gut. Not the raw heat from the carvings. This was different. Colder.

Christian ripped the knife from my hand, cursing. "You *stupid* bitch."

I blinked up at him, dizzy and fading. He swatted my hand away as I tried to stop him. But he got to Angel. His eyes never left mine as the knife moved in slow motion across her throat, clean and decisive.

Angel had no time to scream. Only a wet, final moan left her body as her head fell forward. Blood gushed from her throat in small, pulsing torrents, splattering my legs, the floor, and her clothing. Beneath her, it trailed toward the drain like tainted water.

"See what you made me do?" Christian said, holding his stomach, looking utterly imposed upon.

My hands grew slick with my blood as I pressed weakly at my wound, gasping for air. But I couldn't look away. Even in death, I couldn't let her be alone.

I'd made a promise...

"Patch her up. We need her," Christian snapped at someone behind me. The world spun as hands dragged me away. The last thing I saw was Angel's face—eyes staring unblinking, color draining, one tear streaking through the grime on her cheek.

CHAPTER 67
Loriah

I woke with a jolt, fingers instinctively finding the wound on my side, brushing against the crude stitches that pulled my skin tight. I had no idea when or by whom they'd been done, but infection had already set in. The area was hot, swollen, throbbing with every shallow intake of breath that rattled its way through me.

The room reeked of damp concrete and despair.

Fall's cold settled around the bottom of the room, clinging to my bones. The stench of unwashed skin and filth tickled my nose, but my movements were stiff and difficult. My torn, stained flannel caught on the wounds every time I moved. Though it hung open most of the time, I didn't bother closing it.

Modesty had no place in what I knew would surely be the place I'd die.

The night Christian carved me up, he stole the last shred of dignity I'd carried in with me.

Fatigue washed over me, all-consuming, making the most basic of tasks insurmountable. Christian had been gone for what felt like days, maybe weeks—time had become relative. At first, I welcomed the silence. No mocking remarks. No cruel games. No icy fingers trailing over my skin. But soon, the quiet became oppressive, suffocating. The only sound at night was the slow thrumming of my heart.

A man delivered my meals without much thought. I spoke to him at first, pleading for help, but he ignored me as if I didn't exist.

My stomach growled in vain, hunger pangs fading into a dull ache when I'd stopped counting how many days since my last full meal. The scraps grew gradually more sparse, but I was too weak to care. I leaned my head against the wall and let my eyes close.

My labored breaths dragged against bruised ribs, a parting gift from my last meeting with Christian. He had come in one night, stroking my hair and whispering how much he missed me in the gentlest of whispers. The kind he'd use when we were alone and life seemed so easy. I bucked my hips, kicked, and even spat at him, but it had been useless. He flipped me to my mangled stomach and pinned me to the mattress, my face biting into the springs as tears and blood soaked the fabric beneath. I begged and screamed until my words came in hoarse gasps, but it meant nothing. He took what he wanted like a thief, leaving me with a hollow pit of growing hate.

He smiled as he struck me afterward, payment for fighting him. *It wasn't personal,* he said—it never was. But when he turned to wink at the camera, I knew it was another sick message to Agustin. Another warning.

No one was coming.

The memories replayed in my mind, sharp and jagged like glass. I hated how his voice slithered into my ears like poisonous gas. Hated how he loomed over me, gaze cold and cruel. Most of all, I hated myself for crying in front of him. For giving him that satisfaction and letting him take the pleasure he wanted from my body, when I had nothing left of myself to hold onto.

I slumped against the wall, hollow and drained. Even the anger had burned out, leaving only soul-deep weariness. My hands trembled beyond my control.

I slept little. The fevered dreams of infection haunted me, vivid and relentless. Angel's face loomed, the moment Christian slit her throat, playing on loop. Her lifeless eyes had that one tear falling silently. The way her blood pooled at my feet and drained away like she was nothing. In some dreams, I tried uselessly to staunch the flow until I could no longer tell where I ended and she began.

I would jerk awake, gasping, her face lingering in my vision. My chest heaved, sending fresh pain coursing through my infected wound, the sum of it causing me to vomit. I pressed against the filthy dressing, wincing as tears escaped despite my efforts.

The room was silent, but my mind screamed. So many faces haunting my thoughts. Ares. Angel. Kayleigh. Addie. I wouldn't forget them.

When inexplicable fatigue threatened to overtake my body, I'd run their names through my head and dig my fingers into torn skin until sleep retreated. I wasn't afraid to die. I was afraid to leave my father behind with no answers. But no matter how much I fought the hold of sleep, I always lost in the end.

The smell of salt air invaded my senses. My toes curled in the sand, hands tracing lazy circles on book pages. Behind me, I heard my name. Christian walked toward me with that beautiful smile that once made my stomach flutter. His tanned chest was visible beneath a half-unbuttoned Hawaiian shirt, two red drinks sloshing over the rim, tiny umbrellas balanced precariously.

"Noo," I laughed, already feeling woozy. "I can't."

"Who says one's for you?"

"Oh, well, now I have to take it." The laugh that came was so easy, as most things with him were.

He clutched them with mock horror before handing me one. The cold on my lips felt extraordinary. The insatiable need to drink consumed me, but as I drank, the taste turned foul and sour. Christian didn't seem to mind, continuing to drink and smile encouragingly between sips.

"Don't you like it?" He asked, setting his down to run his hands up my thighs and across my belly.

"It's– I– What's in this?" I managed, fighting the urge to spit it out.

"I call it *Angel.*"

Whatever humor I'd felt vanished as an icy tendril wound around my insides.

"Angel?"

"Well, she was the main ingredient."

I woke, scrambling to the bucket, losing what little remained in my stomach. Acid burned my throat, precious hydration lost.

Hours continued that way—in and out of nightmare-fueled deliriums until reality became a construct of my imagination.

CHAPTER 68
Loriah

I n the distance, I heard what I thought was gunfire, but my mind had been such a kaleidoscope of dreams—imagined and real—that I could no longer know what constituted *my* reality.

Heavy boots pounded from all directions. I opened my eyes, trying to orient myself and sit up, but the pain in my side radiated down into my hips and back, an unrelenting weakness settling through me. Lying still, I prayed Christian hadn't decided to wash the entire operation and finish me after Agustin refused to pay. I'd end up as an unknown in an unmarked grave somewhere, I was sure.

I couldn't blame Agustin, though—he owed me nothing. If nothing else, I owed him a life for the one his brother had wasted on me. Ares had believed I could catch Christian, had believed *in* me. And Agustin? I never even gave him a chance to try.

More shots rang out, growing closer, followed by grunts of wounded men. I tried again and slowly dragged myself into a sitting position. The effort made my limbs tremble and my head throb; my heart was already pounding from all the small movements.

What I assumed was a body slammed into the other side of the door, slid down, then all went silent. A muffled curse and the sound of movement grew closer. The chains of the door rattled, yet the door remained closed. I leaned my head against the cool wall and exhaled, waiting for death to claim me.

But death never came.

What came was a gunshot to the door, the sound of metal being blown open, and a prominent figure bathed in a dim light. Blinking against the haze, I rubbed my eyes, unable to focus on the stranger.

"If you have come here to kill me, I'm sorry to say, some-one's beat you to it," I told the person, slumping further down on the cot. "And I don't want any more red drinks."

"If you die on me, Loriah, I swear to God I will *never* forgive you."

My eyes fluttered open, not trusting my ears.

"It appears I *am* dead." I surrendered to the heaviness of my eyelids, letting darkness reclaim me.

"Loriah, wake up."

Large hands clasped the sides of my face, lightly jostling me. I reopened my eyes to find eyes the color of ferns in a summer garden staring back at me. I gasped, tears stinging from disuse—the movement pulling at my side. My shirt was hanging in pieces. I groped for the cloth, trying desperately to hide my nakedness. His eyes roved over my body. The horror mirrored there let me know it *was* as bad as I'd feared.

"I will kill him," Agustin growled, more to himself than me. He gently rubbed at my hair, his hands settling on my shoulders before lifting my arms to place them around his neck. "We have to go now, Loriah."

"Promise me I can help with killing him."

Agustin's low chuckle against my body washed me with the warmth and comfort I had longed for in the depths of my despair. He scooped me up, cradling me to him as we moved along the open bays—slow and careful. Even with his cautious pace, the strain tore at the poorly done stitches, and my cuts rubbed along his chest.

"Do you need me to stop?"

"No," I moaned, desperate to be rid of this place and all its horrors. "I told Christian you *wouldn't* come."

At that, he did stop and sighed deeply. The pain etched on his face was so agonizing, I felt forced to look away. I had seen too much. *Felt* too much. My mind wandered to that long-ago dream when I thought Agustin had come for me, and Ares was alive.

It was too much, reliving a kiss in my head that wasn't mine to hold onto.

But he *had* come.

CHAPTER 69

Loriah

A gustin carried me effortlessly, remaining quiet and stopping occasionally to check for danger. He didn't respond to what I had said, but as the November winds whipped through the bay doors and blew my hair, he held me tighter. As we neared the entrance, the sharp smell of saltwater pierced the stale, metallic air, mingling with the faint odors of algae and diesel. It felt gritty and alive—a reminder that freedom lay just beyond these walls.

Men shouted outside as Agustin paused, clearly making a decision. He then sat me on the cold ground next to a stack of pallets and slid his wool coat off his shoulders. "Stay here and wear this," he said, wrapping the coat around me and helping me pull my arms through the sleeves, making me grimace. "I'll be back. I promise."

"Agustin."

"Don't argue, please. For *once*, do what you're told." His gaze held sadness I'd never seen before.

"Thank you, Agustin."

He paused, gripping my hand and kissing my forehead, his lips lingering for mere heartbeats before he took a breath, leaned back, exhaled deeply, then stood. Gun out, he cautiously approached the door, opening it a fraction to peer outside and giving me one last look.

I heard mocking voices, each laced with venom, but I couldn't make out the words. My heart pounded a painful rhythm that echoed the ache in my body. Agustin slipped through the crack like a wraith ready to deal death, leaving me alone with his scent—gun smoke, leather, and something faintly woodsy—drowning me in nostalgia.

I should've stayed put. I knew I should have.

But I didn't.

Every instinct screamed at me to stay hidden, to wait like he told me, but something pulled me toward him. The sound of boots scraping against gravel and the low growl of anger, cut off by a sharp retort, had me gripping the pallets to steady myself as I inched toward the door. I needed the closure of seeing. I was so tired of being left with only half-deranged thoughts to fill in the gaps.

My knees threatened to buckle, and the air in my lungs left in a stunned rush.

Ares.

Alive and fiercely beautiful, precisely as I remembered. Blood streaked his face, emerald eyes darker and burning with defiance even as his body swayed. He was trying to hold off Christian, a gun barrel trained on him, but I could see his hand falter.

Christian sneered, his words too low to hear, but the malice in his face was unmistakable. The same look that he wore when he'd tortured me.

"I'm so glad you can join us, Agustin. She didn't believe that you'd come for her. But I knew you couldn't resist, *could you?*" Christian leered, gun trained on Ares.

"Of course I would come for her. I will *always* come for her. There is no place you could run or hide that I wouldn't find you." Agustin stepped toward Christian. Ares threw out a hand to stop him.

"Ah, Agustin. Always the hero. Always cleaning up the mess, like you're not part of the filth yourself." He grinned, teeth bared like a wolf, his gun eerily still compared to the quaver in his voice. "Tell me, do you see her face when you close your eyes?"

"Shut up," Agustin spat. His voice was barely more than a growl, a tremor edging in. His gun remained unwavering, but his eyes—his eyes were dangerous, practically glowing in the harsh sodium lights. "You don't get to say *her* name. Not after what you've done."

"What *I've* done?" He laughed, bitter and hollow. "What about what *you've* done? You brought her into this! You promised to protect her, and look where that got her. Corinne is dead because of *you.*" Christian jabbed his gun in Agustin's direction, but Agustin didn't even so much as flinch from the gesture.

"She's dead because *you* couldn't let go." Agustin roared, "Because *you* turned her into a pawn in your sick little game to move up in the world." He stepped forward, jaw tight, knuckles white around the grip of his gun. "You want to blame *me*? Fine. But carving her name into Loriah? Dragging her into this? That's all on you. You think that's what she would have wanted?"

"Oh, Loriah." His grin widened, his voice dripping with mockery. "She's tougher than she looks, isn't she? But I wonder, what *would* she think if she knew the truth? Does she remind you of Corinne, Agustin? Is that why you can't let her go? I've already been over every inch of her—marked her—she'll never wash me away."

My hands flew to grasp my stomach. *Corinne?*

"You don't know anything. And you sure as hell don't know what Corinne would have wanted."

"Oh, but I do. She told me, you know. Before she died, she was begging for you." Something feral and broken flashed in his eyes. "She begged for you, and you weren't there. Just like you weren't there when Loriah needed you."

"What do you expect to gain from all this?" Agustin's voice was steady, cold fury settling over him. "This ends tonight, Christian."

"Go ahead, pull the trigger. But you'll never get my sister out of your head. She'll haunt you just like she haunts me. You took from me, and now I've taken from you."

From the corner of my eye, I saw movement. Ares was attempting to get closer, his gun trained on Christian.

The sound of the shot echoed off every surface in the quiet night.

I didn't have time to think.

I pushed the door open as Christian fired. The crack of the gunshot shattered the air, and Ares jerked backward. My scream was raw and instinctive, ripping out of me like a living thing, but drowned by the sound of another shot—Agustin's. Christian's body convulsed, the impact sending him staggering toward the edge of the dock.

My eyes fixed on Ares as he collapsed. My legs buckled, but I crawled forward, ignoring the slick wetness on my hands and knees—blood, maybe mine, maybe his. Everything ran together.

Not again. God no, not again!

"Ares!" I choked out his name, a broken plea. I reached him as Agustin approached, his face unreadable, torn between fury and something softer, more fragile.

"He's alive," Agustin said, his tone clinical, as if convincing himself. He knelt and pressed his hands against Ares's chest, blood pooling beneath his fingers. "Stay with me, *hermano*. Don't you dare—"

The words dissolved: gentle waves slapped against the dock, distant sirens wailed, my own sobs, wild and uncontained, drowned out all else. I pressed my hands against Ares's face, his skin cool and damp beneath my trembling, bloody fingers.

"You're okay," I whispered into his hair, as if saying it would make it accurate. "You're okay."

Agustin didn't stop working; his movements were efficient but desperate. "Loriah, you have to move back. Let me—"

"I'm not leaving him," I rasped. My eyes locked on Ares's, and for the briefest moment, I saw recognition there. The faintest smile curved his lips before they parted, his breath rattling as if snagged on something final.

"No," I sobbed, clutching him tighter, tears flowing uncontrollably. "Stay with me. Please. Please, Ares, I can't do this again."

The sirens grew louder.

"But—"

"No arguments." Agustin scooped Ares up and nodded toward the distant approaching lights. "We'll save him. But he has to go."

I staggered to my feet, my body screaming in protest, but I didn't hesitate. With one last look at the bloodstained dock, I followed Agustin as he carried Ares into the dark toward a waiting SUV, my heart splintering with every agonizing step.

EPILOGUE
Loriah

"I 'm here. You're not alone. I've got you. It was just a dream."

His platitudes slowly eased the ache plaguing my subconscious. When I relaxed, Ares leaned back—staying near, a calming fixture in my space—but not so close that I would feel crowded.

"I'm sorry," I whispered.

"What was it this time?"

"Angel. I didn't mean to fall asleep."

"You need it, though, Loriah. You're barely sleeping."

"I'm not sure if this is doing me any good, though. I'm terrified of meeting their faces, or worse, his. It's always worse when he's there. I can never save them, or myself."

"You did, though. Because of you, forty-three other girls will get to see their children grow up, attend college, and experience their first love. All because of you."

Authorities found forty-three women and girls in a shipping container, waiting to be trafficked to Eastern Europe. I hadn't known about the others. After Christian's death, Agustin quietly ushered his brother into a waiting car with a bodyguard I vaguely recognized.

He stayed behind, cradling me in a heap on the ground like a child, buying Ares time to disappear and avoid any connection to what had happened.

The ambulance arrived soon after and took me to the hospital, where I remained for four days before Ares offered to let me recover at his private residence in Maine.

It felt like a lifetime ago, though only two weeks had passed. Each day blurred into the next—like some twisted version of Groundhog Day—nightmares and heartache lingering beneath every gentle kindness Ares tried to offer.

"Loriah?" he said. "I know you don't feel like you've made a difference, but you have. And one day, you'll see it too."

"That does nothing for the others, though."

"Since when are you a pessimist?"

I looked at him as tears once again filled my eyes and spilled down my cheeks, making dark spots on the blanket wrapped around me. Ares's warm hand came up, pausing.

My heart broke anew to see the hesitation. When I showed up in New York, I was ready to take charge and make a difference. But now, every close interaction was something I struggled with. He let only a heartbeat pass before he pressed his palm to my cheek, thumbing the tear away, turning my face to him with such tenderness.

"I'm sorry. You are strong, but that wasn't fair. Christian can't take away who you are is all I meant."

"Hasn't he, though?"

I turned into his touch, trying not to pull away but instead to take comfort from his nearness. Somewhere in the darkest recesses of my soul, the slightest glimmer of hope flickered that he might be right.

"No. Not as long as I'm alive, he hasn't."

Tires crunched on the gravel drive, making me stiffen. Ares stood, grabbing his gun from the mantle.

"Stay here," he said before stepping onto the porch, his broad shoulders tensed for confrontation.

Harsh, muffled words cut through the air like an argument, sending chills down my spine and locking my muscles in fear. I attempted to stand and reach for my own gun when the door swung open—Ares holding the handle, ushering a tired-looking Agustin inside.

"Loriah," Agustin said, standing in the doorway as if he didn't know what to do with himself. The broken look from the night he rescued me returned to his eyes. It was so at odds with the way he normally carried himself.

"Agustin." My voice was soft, relief sweeping through me at the sight of him. I had missed his constant presence. Since leaving the hospital, we hadn't had the opportunity to talk about that night or what led up to it.

"Can we have a moment?" he asked Ares, who stood like a sentry, ready to attack at the first sign of my distress.

Ares had told me about their fight over my undercover work. I knew I had hurt Agustin by not telling him the truth. But I had so many questions for him. My memories weren't the same since they rescued me. I had vague recollections of the standoff on the docks, prompting my fingers to trace absently over the red scarring under my shirt.

Corinne.

Ares nodded once, giving me a departing wink before going to the porch to watch the sunset. When I had fallen asleep, the sun was high on the horizon, but as I looked past him into the growing darkness I realized I'd slept longer than I initially thought.

As soon as the door shut, Agustin strode toward me, more confident now that we were alone. I raised a hand to stop him.

"Agustin," I whispered, dipping my head before beginning what I knew would be difficult. "I need you to help me."

"Anything," he said, reaching for my hand. I pulled away at the last moment, placing it on my lap, knowing his touch would rob me of courage.

"Who is Corinne?"

"Loriah—" He exhaled, sinking into the cushions and rubbing his face.

"Oh. I see. Anything but that? We're back to secrets?"

"I— Please. I promise I will. It's just that. I can't right now."

"Can't what, Agustin?" Anger built in my voice. I was thankful for any emotional outlet that wasn't shame, fear, or sadness. "My memories are hazy, at best. I can barely remember that night, but I keep having these... dreams. Without fail, they're always of you and Christian arguing, with that name slipping in every time."

He said nothing, eyes trained on his knee. There was no way he could deny it. I had a name etched into my skin like a stone tablet, a daily reminder of how real it all was.

"I know I'm not crazy, Agustin, and Ares won't tell me anything." Angry tears fell as I pushed his chest. I hit him with my fists, pounding relentlessly. He let me cry and pound until the fight left me, and I collapsed against him, allowing his arms to encircle me, his hand finding my head to pull me closer. His smell reminded me of the first time he'd danced with me so long ago, holding me tight, with that smile that never crossed his face anymore.

"Loriah," he said mournfully, taking my face in his hands.

"Please, Agustin. Please! I feel crazy. Broken. Like I can't trust myself." The admission surprised me. In that moment, we broke apart together, our hearts shattering, until the rubble melded and we had nothing but shared sadness.

"You're not crazy. But I can't right now. I will share everything with you when this isn't so fresh." He rubbed his thumbs in small motions along my cheeks, holding my gaze.

Agustin had bent to place a kiss on my forehead, but stopped when the front door opened. Ares stood there with his arms crossed, looking between us.

"Everything okay, Loriah?"

"Of course. I'm fine."

I didn't feel fine. I was only half a person, cursed to remember a woman I didn't know—another name to add to the list of those I recited like a poem each night before sleep took me. Arya Stark would be proud.

Angel Navarro.

Kayleigh Hughes and her baby.

Kasa Adairis Wells.

... Corinne Jackson.

Ares was standing when my phone pinged, breaking the tension. I expected another Pinterest baking fail picture from Allie, or my dad's photos from his yearly fall hunting trip.

Unknown - *You'll never be rid of me.*

The End?